P9-DOB-484

PRAISE FOR KATHERINE KINGSLEY

Winner of a *Romantic Times* Career Achievement Award for Historical Adventure

"One of the romance genre's best and brightest. Ms. Kingsley is a writer of infinite grace and exquisite perception." —*Romantic Times*

"If you haven't discovered Katherine Kingsley, you don't know what you're missing. She's a writer who never disappoints." —Lindsay Chase

"Unique . . . elegant . . . sensitive." —Connie Rinehold

"Irresistible." —Mary Jo Putney

THEIR LIPS LOCKED IN A PASSIONATE EMBRACE

"You're enough to tempt even a saint, and that I'm surely not."

Serafina wriggled out of his grasp, her cheeks on fire, appalled with herself. "I—I don't know what happened," she whispered. I didn't mean to do that. . . ."

Aiden laughed lazily, slanting a look down at her. "I don't know why not. You did it very nicely." He rubbed his hands over his face, then gazed up at the ceiling. "Well, that should answer two questions," he said.

"What questions?" she asked shakily, gripping her hands in her lap.

"That your feminine instincts are entirely operational." He stood abruptly and turned his back to her, one hand digging into his hair, his breathing still rough. "And that I'm a bloody gentleman. No self-respecting rogue would have stopped things there. I think I'd better leave you before I change my mind and move on to the next lesson."

Serafina longed to ask him what the next lesson was, but quickly decided it was a question best left unasked. . . ."

KATHERINE KINGSLEY

In the Wake of the Wind

A DELL BOOK

Published by
Dell Publishing
a division of
Bantam Doubleday Dell Publishing Group, Inc.
1540 Broadway
New York, New York 10036

The trademark Dell® is registered in the U.S. Patent and Trademark Office.

ISBN: 0-440-22075-0

Printed in the United States of America

Published simultaneously in Canada

March 1996

10   9   8   7   6   5   4   3   2   1
RAD

To Joel May,
Friend, Visionary, Journeyer

Acknowledgments

I'd like to thank Jan Hiland, as always, for her unerring eye to the first draft of manuscript, not to mention her brilliant administrative skills. Lisa Hamilton gave me not only a generous ear but much research advice concerning Wicca, and Jan Jouflas was a staunch friend and supporter. I thank them both.

Vangelis Socratous of Paphos was very generous with his time and friendship, introducing me to the "inner" spirit of Cyprus. It was also a pleasure to see my friends Ron and Margaret Evans, residents of Cyprus, who supplied invaluable help.

Most especially I thank my editor, Marjorie Braman, who had the faith to take this book on nothing more than a wing and a prayer and allowed me to fly. Her patience and enthusiasm for the project kept me going during many long, trying months.

To the readers: I love to hear your comments, so please feel free to write me at P.O. Box 37, Wolcott, Colorado 81655. If you include an SASE, I promise to answer each letter. You are the reason I write, and your letters are treasured.

I am certain of nothing but the holiness of the Heart's affections and the truth of the Imagination.

—John Keats

Prologue

February 6, 1808
Bowhill House, Leicestershire

Serafina pressed back against the wall, her small, thin body huddled into itself as she watched the doctor leave her father's bedroom. The fall of the draperies at the window created a safe haven where he couldn't see her, but she could see him well enough, and she instantly knew by his grim expression that all of her prayers were for naught. Her father would not last the night.

She numbly turned her face against the windowpane, the glass cool and hard beneath her cheek. Aunt Elspeth stood in the courtyard below, speaking with an older gentleman who had arrived in a carriage not ten minutes before. Her aunt was crying into a handkerchief.

She could imagine why. Aunt Elspeth, whom she hardly knew at all, was going to be forced to take her away to a place called Wales, and she wasn't to be allowed to live at beautiful Bowhill anymore. Horrible Cousin Edmund and his equally horrible mother were to live here now. That much Aunt Elspeth had told her, even though no one was telling her much of anything else, which was why she'd taken to skulking behind curtains and listening through keyholes.

Serafina despised Edmund. He'd arrived with his mother two days before, the two of them circling around Bowhill like a pair of hawks, just waiting for her papa to die, only pretending grief. Serafina knew. She'd heard them talking after dinner in the library that first night.

"Don't worry, darling, it will all soon be ours," Mrs. Se-grave had said, her voice only slightly muffled by the priest's hole in which Serafina hid. "That nasty little girl will be out of here the moment her father's body is laid to rest, and by the look of things, it won't be long now."

"I can't bear her, Mama," Edmund said petulantly, his voice strung with the jarring, uneven notes of adolescence. "She looks at us as if we have no right to be here, and we have far more right than she. *I'm* to be the baron now, and she's nothing more than a piece of riffraff. Anyway, she's ugly."

Inside the priest's hole, Serafina had colored hotly, even though she knew it was true. And she probably was a piece of riffraff too, now that she was being orphaned and turned out of house and home. Edmund put her in mind of a weasel and his mother a jackal. They both shared the same long, narrow face, the same sharp, beady eyes. The idea that they would live in her beloved house made her sick.

"Exactly, my darling, exactly," Mrs. Segrave said. "Just you wait; along with your Uncle John's title comes his fortune, his house, and all the social position I ever dreamed of. This is everything we've been waiting for."

"You're sure it's not a false alarm?" Edmund asked anxiously. "I don't think I could bear to go back to our horrid little house in Reading if Uncle John recovers."

"No, dearest," his mother cooed. "Those days are gone forever. Your Uncle John is on his last legs, that's a certainty—he won't last much longer. We will live in grand style, and you shall have everything you ever wanted. It's only what you deserve, my pet."

Serafina's fists knotted into tight balls and she wanted to smash them into the wall, but she knew that would be ill-advised. Her stomach twisted with loathing. How could two people be so callous, so uncaring of her poor papa's suffering?

But at least her papa would be out of pain, she thought, and she could only be thankful for that, for she knew how difficult it had been for him to be brave these last three months as the sickness in his lungs had taken its toll. And she knew how deeply he had missed her mama these last four years, so all in all he'd be happier in heaven.

She, on the other hand, faced nothing but emptiness. Her Aunt Elspeth was kind enough, but she knew her father was worried that her aunt would not be "a suitable influence." Serafina wasn't entirely sure what that was supposed to mean, but she knew her father wasn't happy about Serafina going to live with her in her crumbling castle, as he'd called it. She'd heard part of that conversation as well through the half-open door soon after her aunt had arrived.

"I realize that my wife loved you dearly, Elspeth," he'd said in his weak voice. "And although she tolerated your unorthodox behavior and beliefs, I don't think she ever thought you would be in a position to bring up her only child."

"I don't see what other choice you have but to hand your daughter over to me," Elspeth said. "There's no one else, and you can't *possibly* send her to a convent. She's not even Catholic, and the nuns would be a far worse influence on her than I could ever be. Give her to me, John, and I will look after her with great care and honor your wishes as to her religious upbringing, regardless of what I think of it. By the time Serafina is eighteen she'll be perfectly prepared for the future we discussed. All you have to do now is bring Delaware into agreement. . . ."

To Serafina's chagrin, Aunt Elspeth had closed the door at that point, almost as if she knew Serafina was listening outside, and Serafina heard no more. She'd been wondering ever since who or what Delaware was.

The man who had been down in the courtyard now appeared in the hallway, her aunt at his side, and Serafina watched him curiously, taking in the graying hair at the temples, the ruddy cheeks, the bright blue eyes. Together they went into her father's bedroom, and Serafina slipped out from her hiding place. But although she pressed her ear hard against the heavy door, she could only hear the faint murmur of voices coming from behind the wood. She anxiously wondered if the stranger inside was the mysterious Delaware, and if so, what sort of agreement her papa was making with him.

A minute later Serafina had her answer as the door suddenly opened and she stumbled back, her hands pressed to her mouth, her eyes wide with fear at the consequences of being caught eavesdropping.

But surprisingly her aunt didn't seem the least perturbed. "Oh, good, here you are, dearest. How timely. Do make your curtsy to Lord Delaware," she said, nodding her head vigorously in encouragement, her hairpins threatening to go flying at any moment.

The man standing behind her aunt stepped forward, his beaver hat held loosely in one hand as he looked down at her, regarding her with an odd expression. Serafina met his gaze evenly and silently, wondering what this Lord Delaware had to do with her future.

Lord Delaware reached out a hand and touched her cheek. "She's an odd-looking thing, isn't she?" he said. "Nothing at all like her mother, God rest her soul. An angel, a pure angel, that one. The heavens must be celebrating to have her among their own."

"She's more like my sister than you realize," Elspeth said tartly. "And as the only person to whom Serafina's looks are going to matter is your son, I suggest you keep your opinion to yourself."

"Indeed I will," Lord Delaware said fervently. "Indeed I will. Well. At least I can feel that John's mind has been put at ease."

Elspeth regarded him sharply. "You gave your word, Delaware. I trust you will keep it."

"Naturally. Naturally," he repeated, shifting his hat to his other hand. "Of course, one can never tell what the future holds."

"Perhaps not," Elspeth replied, her mouth pursing. "But one thing is certain, and that is that the future very often imitates the past. I, for one, have no intention of seeing that come to pass."

"I can't think what you mean," Lord Delaware said, looking as baffled as Serafina felt.

"Never you mind that now. You just see that you keep to your end of the agreement. My niece is only nine, which gives you another nine years to put everything in place, plenty of time to my way of thinking." Elspeth suddenly seemed to remember Serafina's presence. "Oh, my dear child," she said, patting her back, "forgive me. Your father wishes to see you. He has something to tell you, and you must be strong, dearest, for I believe his time is near. Try not to let him tax his strength overmuch, and listen to what he has to say in good faith that all will be well."

Serafina nodded bravely, choking back tears. She squared her small shoulders and went to receive her father's final words, for his sake trying not to let her heartbreak show.

1

January 12, 1819
Clwydd Castle, Wales

Serafina closed her eyes as the world spun before her, her head thrown back, her hair falling down her back, her arms raised to the sky in invocation as she sang her song. It was set to the melody of "Joyful, joyful, we adore Thee, God of glory, Lord of love."

Serafina had changed the lyrics to suit herself, which she knew would make the vicar's eyes roll up in his head and induce a slow faint behind the pulpit, but she hardly cared about that. And anyway, since God *was* the Lord of love, she didn't think He'd mind.

"Bring him to me, bring him to me, I've been waiting for so long. Blessed be the god and goddess, and I pray that they hear my song. . . ."

Her voice rang high and pure as she swept the last of the circles, her feet dancing so swiftly they felt as if they might lift her from the ground altogether and catapult her into flight. Serafina would have liked nothing better, but as all her childhood attempts at discovering the secret of flight had left her bruised and sore for days, she had given up that particular pursuit.

She laughed aloud in pleasure as a sudden gust of wind picked up the fragments of her song and swept it over the edge of the cliff, lifting it up to heaven like a bird on the wing. It would be heard, she was sure of that, but it never hurt to offer a daily reminder that she was patiently waiting. *Very* patiently waiting.

She lowered her arms and dropped to the frozen ground,

pulling her worn cloak more tightly about her and tucking her legs up under it, suppressing a shiver as the cold wind cut across her back.

When it came down to it, she thought, she'd been waiting most of her life. First she'd waited nearly three months for her mother to return from London, a promise made as she'd left for the season in a swirl of skirts and perfume. But instead of her mother, a carriage had arrived swathed in black, carrying a coffin and her distraught father. His grief-stricken explanations of a runaway horse and a terrible fall had been hard for a child of five to understand, as hard as trying to grasp why her mother was locked away in a box and couldn't ever come out again.

And she had waited four years later as the doctors came and went for weeks from her father's room, until one day they didn't come at all and her beloved father was laid in the ground next to her mother. By then Serafina was old enough to understand the grim finality of death. She knew that no matter how many tears she cried, they wouldn't bring her father back.

But her father had left her with a promise before he'd gone, and it was the fulfillment of that promise that Serafina waited for now.

Aiden will be your husband when the time comes, Serafina, and he will love you with all his heart and look after you just as I would do. You won't be alone, child, I swear it to you. And his father has sworn the same to me this very day.

Serafina knew her father would never lie to her. And she knew that the man who had come that last day of her father's life, kindly Lord Delaware who had bent down and touched her face, pinched with misery and grief, would keep his word too. So now it was just a matter of time before Aiden arrived to sweep her off on the shining wings of love.

The only comfort she had while she waited was what she'd come to think of as the Dream. It had started in the summer of her fourteenth year and reoccurred with reassuring frequency. It was always the same: she rode on horseback toward a small city, a company of people with her, their richly colored costumes different from anything she'd seen in England and yet somehow perfectly familiar to her, as familiar as the man who stood on the hill, his golden hair blowing in the wind, his hand shading his eyes as he scanned the distance.

He too wore one of those costumes—his a white tunic with a blue embroidered cloak clasped by a brooch at his right shoulder. A calm, azure sea glittered far off to the south and the city climbed up the lushly vegetated hillside behind him, crowned by a castle that made her think of the Crusades.

Her heart burst with joy at the sight of him, and she couldn't wait another minute to be in his arms. She kicked her horse into a gallop and moved ahead of the company, calling and waving, and he suddenly saw her and called back to her, his voice filled with glad welcome. Only instead of calling her Serafina, he called her Sarah. And she called him Adam.

"Sarah, my love—praise God you're finally home!" He started down the hill at a run, and Sarah slipped off her horse and tore toward him, her arms outstretched.

"Adam! Oh, Adam, I can't believe it—it seemed like forever!"

He caught her up and spun her around in a wide circle before he pulled her close and kissed her hard.

"Don't ever leave me again, beloved," he whispered. "I can't live without you for more than a day, as these last four weeks have proved—I've wasted away from longing."

"That's odd; you look exactly like the magnificent husband I left," she teased him, running her fingers through his hair, gazing into his dark eyes, eyes that were filled with love for her. "Dear God in heaven, how I missed you." She buried her head in the crook of his shoulder and held him tightly to her, drinking in his warm, beloved scent.

"Swear you'll love me forever?" he said in a litany that had been repeated between them time and again.

"I swear it," she answered fervently, wrapping her arms even more tightly around his strong back. "I swear it. Forever and beyond."

"I'll hold you to your vow," he said, kissing her again until her senses swam and her knees turned to water. "And I'll renew my own pledge in the flesh the minute I have you to myself. Unfortunately my parents insist on seeing you immediately. I think I really might expire with longing." He nipped her ear with his teeth, his soft laugh filled with intimate promise as she shivered and raised her mouth to his again.

Sadly, Serafina always woke up at that point. It was terribly frustrating, since she longed to know just how one pledged one's vow in the flesh. Every sense told her it was a magnificent process, but she couldn't exactly ask her aunt. Aunt Elspeth had very firm ideas about propriety, to the point of forbidding Serafina any contact with men of her own age, citing the deep dark impulses to which they were prone.

Serafina suspected she might like those impulses, which was why she kept her dream to herself. Aunt Elspeth would never approve.

She couldn't explain it, or even how she knew without a doubt the two people were herself and Aiden in another time and place. But she knew. Oh, she knew it with every fiber of her being. And she knew that their vow had been truly made, that they belonged together through time and beyond.

" 'Ere, Miss Serafina, have you been out there freezing yourself to pieces again?" Tinkerby turned from the stove and surveyed her with concern. "I was just making a nice hot pot of tea, and you look to me as if you're needing a cup. I don't know what foolishness it is that takes you out to that cliff every single day to go singing to the wind about some daydream yer auntie's put in your head." He reached stiffly for another cup and saucer and put them on the tray.

"It's not foolishness," Serafina said, rubbing her frozen hands together over the blazing kitchen fire. "It's simple practicality, Tinkerby. If you don't ask, how are you supposed to receive?"

Tinkerby shook his balding head as he filled the pot with water just off the boil. "If I didn't know better, I'd think you'd learned that pretty sentiment in church. But you can't fool an old dog like me, missie. I know all about the heathen notions Miss Elspeth's brought you up with, and your poor father would be rolling in his grave if he had any idea." He placed the tray down on the kitchen table and pulled out a chair, gingerly settling himself into it.

Serafina turned from the fire with a smile. Tinkerby had been in the family for as long as she could remember, loyally accompanying her to Clwydd after her father had died. And although he expressed intolerance for her Aunt Elspeth's notions, she knew he was as fond of Elspeth as she was.

"Oh, I don't know, Tinkerby. I think Papa knew all about Auntie's ways, and he still let me come to live with her. And you know yourself that there's no harm in what she does."

Tinkerby snorted. "Not unless you count blowing up the cow shed. Then there was that little problem with the west wing, which I've spent most of this cold day trying to patch up. Then there was the time—"

"I know, I do know," Serafina said, cutting him off. She joined him at the table and poured tea for them both. "But what I mean is that she doesn't *intend* any harm, even if her spells sometimes go amiss. You have to admit, she can do quite a lot of good as well, especially when it comes to using her herbs for healing. Look at how much better your rheumatism is."

"Aye, it's a mite better," he admitted grudgingly. "But what I'm talking about is putting ideas into your head about gods and goddesses and divine plans for husbands. And you know just what I mean, so don't you try to deny it. It just don't seem right, Miss Serafina."

"But, Tinkerby, it's not as if Papa didn't make the arrangements himself."

"That's not what I mean, not that young Lord Aubrey shouldn't have showed up on your eighteenth birthday when he was supposed to, instead of leaving you hanging for these nearly three years. I'm talking about this nonsense about living lives before, and all the rest of the claptrap I hear Miss Elspeth pouring into your ear."

Serafina absently stirred a teaspoon of sugar into her tea,

trying to think of yet another approach to explain to Tinkerby why Elspeth's theory made all the sense in the world. "Look, Tinkerby," she said after a long pause, "do you know the sea gulls that you like to watch off the cliff when the weather's fine?"

He made a grudging little noise of assent in his throat. "It's only because we didn't have sea gulls in Leicestershire," he said, as if embarrassed by this suggestion of sentimentality. "I like to observe the way they work the wind currents. It's a scientific interest, you understand."

"Yes, I know," Serafina said, suppressing a smile. "But my point is that a sea gull doesn't dive just once into the sea, does it, and then fly up into the sky and disappear forever? It dives over and over again."

"And how else do you think it's going to fill its belly?" Tinkerby asked sourly.

"That's what I mean," Serafina said, leaning forward to press her point. "Think of the sea as life, and the fish the sea gull feeds on as experience, and the sea gull itself as your soul. The only way your soul can fill itself with experience is to dive time and time again into life."

Tinkerby stared at her, his cup frozen in midair. "You've lost your bloomin' marbles, miss, begging your pardon. Yer auntie's made even more of a mess of your noggin than I realized."

Serafina laughed. "Don't blame Aunt Elspeth. This is my own analogy."

"Analogy, phooey," Tinkerby added with a scowl. "No good God-fearing girl should be spouting nonsense about sea gulls and souls in the sea. You die, and if you've behaved yourself, you go to heaven to receive Our Lord's reward, and that's that."

"But I'm not saying that you don't go to heaven," Serafina persisted. "I'm only saying that after a while you leave it to try again. Honestly, Tinkerby, how do you expect *not* to make a hash of life the first few times you try it? That would be like expecting a babe to learn how to run after taking only one step. Life takes a lot of practice to get right, just like walking."

Tinkerby put his head in his hands. "Stark, raving mad," he muttered.

"I think it's a very sensible proposition," Serafina said. "I don't believe anything is a random accident, any more than the moon randomly completes its monthly cycle in the sky, or the earth randomly moves around the sun once a year, or the seasons randomly change. So why should my marriage to Aiden be random, either—why shouldn't there be a divine plan for us too?"

He lifted his head slowly and gazed at her with weary eyes. "I knew it," he said. "I knew you'd get around to him sooner or later. You always do."

"It's because I still believe he's coming for me, even if you don't," she said, twisting her cup around in the saucer. "I don't see why you have such a hard time trusting that he will."

"Because the world don't work like that," he said with exasperation. "Aye, the sun might rise and set because God put it in the sky and wanted it that way, but people aren't nearly so ordered. You haven't heard a word from that family since the day your dear father died, and I say you're not going to be hearing." He reached for the pot and refilled his cup. "Just because Miss Elspeth insists on filling your head with foolish dreams doesn't mean they're going to come true any more than I'm going to sprout wings and fly."

"You'll see, Tinkerby," Serafina said. She squeezed her eyes shut for a brief moment. *Believe it, Serafina. You have to believe it with all of your heart and hold tight to your love for him. He'll come. He has to come.*

April 26, 1819
Townsend Hall, Rutland

"You did *what*?"

Aiden, staggered by his father's announcement, took a furious step toward his father's chair, and the marquess's face, already pale, turned even whiter, two flaming spots of red the only color left in his cheeks.

"I did the only thing left to be done," Lord Delaware stammered, recoiling against his son's rage, his hands tightening on the arms of the chair. "The banks wouldn't give me another loan—I'm already in debt up to my eyebrows." He took a large swallow of wine from the ever-present glass at his side.

"So you now bother to inform me, although I had an inkling we might be in trouble when I was refused credit for the last load of goods I was supposed to ship home from Barbados. That only came as a bad shock. But now you tell me you've arranged my marriage to someone I've never even heard of—what in the name of God has gotten into you?"

"I—I realized that you might be angry, but there was not time to consult you," Lord Delaware said, wiping away the thin film of perspiration that had sprung to his brow. "You were halfway across the Atlantic Ocean, unreachable in a time of crisis, and the marriage was the only way to secure enough money to save us from ruin. Serafina Segrave has a fortune, a very large fortune, and it is yours the day you marry. The contracts are already signed between her aunt and myself."

"I see," Aiden said, his voice sounding amazingly controlled to him, considering the acute shock he was laboring under. He'd been home only ten minutes and his father had wasted no time in informing Aiden of his latest and most profound idiocy in a lifetime of idiotic mistakes. But this one really took the prize. And it appeared that from this one there was to be no salvation.

"So to save the shipping company and your own skin, you bartered me," he said coldly, his mouth tightening into a hard line. "You *bartered* me, damn you, sold me off like some prize piece of cattle!"

"Now Aiden, be reasonable," his father said nervously, the tips of his fingers working fretfully on the threadbare tapestry of the armchair. "If I hadn't acted quickly, what would have become of us? Just think of your poor sister. . . ."

Aiden glared at him with disgust. The man never missed an opportunity to drive Aiden's obligations home, as if Aiden hadn't always taken responsibility for Charlotte. But his father was right. Charlotte didn't deserve to live in poverty, not on top of everything else she had suffered. Still, he wasn't about to let his father off the hook so easily.

"Be reasonable?" Aiden said dangerously, leaning slightly forward, his fists clenched by his sides. "Tell me, why should I be reasonable? In one fell swoop you've taken away my freedom, not to mention making a travesty of my free will. And I'm supposed to get down on my knees and be thankful, I suppose?"

"It's no good losing your temper now," his father said, not meeting his eyes. "The bargain is sealed, and unless we want to face a breach-of-promise suit on top of everything else, you'll have to go through with the marriage. The situation can't be unmade at this late date."

Aiden bowed his head, staring at the floor, at the tip of his boot, at anything that might distract him and keep him from putting his hands around his father's neck and wringing it. "Maybe you'd like to explain how you got us into this financial mess to begin with?"

"I—I made some bad investments," he said. "I thought I could recoup them by taking some risks on the 'Change, but I was wrong. Eventually I had to take a loan out against the company, and then I found I couldn't repay it, and I'd already mortgaged everything else. . . ." He trailed off into silence.

Aiden looked up. "I suppose if Townsend and its lands weren't entailed, we'd be on the verge of losing this as well. And now you want me to tell you that you're brilliant for having come up with a solution to keep us from bankruptcy?"

"I couldn't think of anything else," Lord Delaware said, hanging his head.

Aiden ground the sole of his boot into the carpet as if he could somehow smother his frustration, his outrage, his sense of helplessness. All of his life he'd done his best to compensate for his father's mistakes, his inadequacies. But he'd never once imagined that he'd end up being the sacrificial lamb. "And how did you manage to secure a fabulously rich heiress at a moment's notice—a woman, I might add, who has never laid eyes on me? I find that singularly unsettling in itself."

"It was a promise, Aiden." His father reached out an imploring hand. "A promise made eleven years ago to my dearest friend."

Aiden's gaze snapped back to his father, his eyes narrowed. "A *promise*? What kind of promise?"

"Well, you see, John was dying, and I wished to put his mind at ease about his daughter, who had only her aunt left to look after her. John was naturally concerned about Serafina's future. So I agreed that when the time was right, you would, er . . . marry her."

Aiden stared at his father in disbelief. "You took it upon yourself to engage me to be married eleven years ago, when I was what—the tender age of seventeen?" He plunged his hands through his hair. "What the bloody hell were you thinking?" he said, his voice rising to a shout. "It can't have been about money—we had plenty of our own back then!"

"As I said, I was trying to provide comfort to a dying man," Lord Delaware mumbled. "I didn't want to upset him in his last hours by refusing his request to join our two families."

"I find it most interesting that you've never mentioned Segrave's name before, or this pact with the devil you made with him on his daughter's behalf," Aiden said frigidly. "I also find it interesting that you never bothered to inform me of it. I think that my forthcoming marriage would have been of some slight interest to me."

"I was only waiting until I thought you were ready for marriage," Lord Delaware said defensively. "I hoped you would court her, see if she suited you. I planned to give you a gentle push in the right direction."

"Rubbish," Aiden spat out, glaring at him. "I know you too well to believe that story for an instant. If that's what you'd had in mind, Serafina Segrave's name would have come up on every occasion you could find to mention it over the last eleven years."

Lord Delaware shifted uncomfortably under Aiden's unrelenting gaze. "Oh, very well. The girl disappeared with her aunt, and I confess I forgot about her. Out of sight, out of mind." He attempted a weak laugh, instantly suppressed by the daggers in Aiden's eyes.

"Let's see if I have this right," Aiden said, pressing his fingers against his temples as if that could stifle the pounding headache that had taken up residence there. "You conveniently forgot all about a promise you made a dying man, just as you forgot all about his daughter until the need for a substantial amount of money drove them both back into your mind?"

"Well, yes. I was going through some old papers in the hope of finding a way out of our difficulties, and there it was," he continued, looking acutely embarrassed now that the full truth was finally coming out. "Segrave had drawn up a suggested marital contract before he died, along with a list of his daughter's assets. I hadn't bothered to read it at the time, but as I told you, her assets are more than enough to get us out of our present difficulties. We should be thankful that she hasn't been snapped up by someone else before this."

"I wonder why," Aiden said tightly. "Or did you also forget to mention that she has two heads?"

"Well . . ." his father said, avoiding Aiden's eyes.

"Oh, God," Aiden groaned, his chest tightening with severe alarm. "What else haven't you told me, Father?"

Lord Delaware scratched his cheek. "I suppose I might as well prepare you, since you'll see for yourself soon enough."

Aiden closed his eyes.

"She isn't the most—well, the most *attractive* girl," Lord Delaware said. "I only met her that once, mind you, but I had quite a shock as both her parents were so handsome, and she was, er—not so fortunate in her looks."

"You're saying she's ugly." Aiden pinched the bridge of his nose, thinking he surely was having a bad dream. Nothing he'd done in his twenty-eight years, no matter how terrible, warranted this horrific fate.

"Um, yes, yes I'm afraid I am. She's rather sallow and

pinched looking with bulging eyes and bad teeth and an awkward, knobby body. But you needn't look at her very often, Aiden. I'm sure you can put her in the east wing or some such thing."

"*That's* your remedy for this preposterous marriage?" Aiden choked out. "You throw an ugly heiress at me and you suggest I lock her away in the east wing for the rest of her days?"

"I don't know what else you're going to do with her," Lord Delaware said helplessly. "I don't think you'll want to parade her around London. On top of being ugly, she's not very personable—rather sullen and taken to listening at keyholes, actually."

Aiden covered his face with his hands. "Oh, my God," he moaned. "Oh, my God."

"I can understand why her aunt is so anxious to see her married, and I gather the girl is just as anxious. Apparently there have been no other suitors, despite her inheritance," Lord Delaware said, shaking his head sadly. "I expect you see now why I didn't intend to honor the agreement. But trust me, my boy, there is no other solution. Serafina Segrave is our only hope."

Aiden scrubbed his hands over his head. *Serafina?* What kind of absurd name was Serafina, anyway? A hideous vision danced before him of the girl—a bag of bones crowned by a pinched face with sharp, feral little teeth and protruding eyes. A girl desperate for marriage and willing to take what she could.

He could just see Miss Serafina Segrave now, congratulating herself over her booty: Aiden Delaware, Earl of Aubrey, heir to an ancient marquessate—impoverished perhaps, but only for the moment, since apparently Miss Segrave was prepared to pay well for a husband with title and position.

She obviously cared nothing about any other aspect of marriage if she hadn't even bothered to ask for an introduction to him before committing to the arrangement. Too bad—maybe he could have somehow contrived to give her a thorough disgust of him, although he doubted there was much he could have done to accomplish that, short of confessing himself to be an ax-murderer. Which he wasn't. Yet.

Aiden swallowed hard against the knot of despair that had formed in his throat. Sunk. Condemned. Honor bound by an agreement he hadn't even been consulted about. Engaged to be married to a woman no one else wanted despite her vast fortune, which told him a very great deal.

He wearily raised his head, feeling cold as death on the inside. "Very well, Father," he said, knowing there was no way out, not if he was to save his family from penury and disgrace. "I'll marry your hideous heiress, since I can't see what else to do. But know I damn you to hell for the bumbling fool that you are. And thanks very much for ruining my life."

His father exhaled on a long breath of relief, Aiden's plight clearly the least of his concerns. "Thank you," he said in a low voice. "I'll send for Miss Segrave immediately. You'll have to apply for a special license, as the marriage must take place as soon as humanly possible. There's no time to waste."

Aiden nodded, then turned on his heel and walked out without a backward look. He'd never felt so sick in all his life.

April 30, 1819
Clwydd Castle, Wales

"Did you have a nice time tonight, Auntie?" Serafina glanced up from her tedious paperwork as Elspeth flew in the door, tossing her cape on one chair and her bag of odds and ends on another.

"Divine, my child, simply divine," Elspeth trilled. "I do so love celebrating Beltane with all its lovely fertility rites. We made *such* a nice circle, and we even had an initiation tonight—I can't think how long it's been since one of those. People are so . . . skittish about covens."

"And for good reason," Serafina said, putting her pen

down. "I realize there's no harm in what you do, but you really must be a little more careful, don't you think?"

"Careful of what?" Elspeth said disdainfully. "If I wish to be a Wiccan, I shall be a Wiccan, and I don't give two snaps if the vicar finds out. What is he going to do—burn me at the stake?"

Serafina smiled fondly at her dear, eccentric little aunt, who embraced all the ancient Celtic practices of Wales with unbridled enthusiasm, although her techniques generally left something to be desired. "I think he'd already like to do that, given the way you sit in the back of the church every Sunday and scowl and snort at most of what he says."

"Well, if he said anything useful I wouldn't feel so agitated," Elspeth said. "But he has a particular fondness for carrying on about guilt and hellfire and original sin, and really, Serafina, all his foolish jabbering puts my poor back out, as if the damp isn't bad enough."

She tossed her head and one of her bone hairpins went flying in a ninety-degree arc and landed in the cauldron simmering on the stove. "I wouldn't be there at all if it wasn't for having to cart you back and forth, and all because of a silly promise I made to your father."

She tried to fish her hairpin out of the cauldron with a ladle, but gave up after a moment. "Can't hurt, can't hurt, nice clean bone after all," she muttered. Throwing on a stained apron, she bent over the cauldron again and sniffed the brew. "Hmm. A little more mugwort, I think," she said, poking in a canister. "Oh, and Serafina, dearest, I need some strands of your hair."

Serafina rolled her eyes. "What for now?" she asked with exasperation. "I'll be bald if you keep plucking me. Can't you use your own?"

"Certainly not. My entire head is gray and the hair has to be dark or the spell won't work. Just fetch a few from your hairbrush, won't you, dearie? Have you had your supper?"

"Tinkerby and I ate ages ago. We had the last of the stew."

"And did you feed my dear Basil?" Elspeth asked, shooting a stern look over her shoulder.

"Yes," Serafina said absently, looking down at her books again. "He threw most of his food on the floor, made rude comments, and tried to bite Tinkerby—nothing out of the ordinary. I put him back on his perch upstairs. Auntie," she said cautiously, knowing exactly what reaction she was going to get, "I've been going over the household books, and I think we need to make a few adjustments in our budget. There are some receipts here from an order you recently made. . . ."

"If you're going to start in again about how much I spend on my special ingredients, I shall become very cross, Serafina. You can be a big Miss Bossy-Boots, you know. And answer me this—without my spells, where would we be?"

"Well . . ." Serafina said, "we'd still be living in the west wing, for one."

"Oh, that," Elspeth said, waving her hand in dismissal. "A little too much sulfur in the mixture, that was all. I couldn't help it that the wind was up and the draperies caught on fire, now could I?"

Serafina put her forehead in her hands and sighed. "But deer antler tips? And red jujube dates? And really, Auntie, precious eye of newt? These things are awfully expensive, and you know there's no money to spare. Are they really that useful?"

"Well, won't *you* just find out, Miss Know-Everything?" Elspeth said smugly. "Especially now that *he's* come back." She wiped her hands down her front, leaving a dirty wet streak.

"Who's come back?" Serafina said as patiently as she could manage, wondering whether her aunt was referring to an actual person or one of the earth deities. Elspeth might have tried to conjure anything up tonight, and given her suddenly superior expression, she probably thought she had, and wanted Serafina to serve tea to it. As much as Serafina loved her aunt, the woman really could be trying.

"Aubrey's back," her aunt said, setting her hands on her bony hips. "You didn't know that, now did you? Ha!"

"Aubrey?" Serafina said, her heart nearly stopping in her chest. "Do—do you mean *Aiden?*"

"I don't know what other Aubrey there is." She scratched her head with one finger. "Now where did I put Delaware's letter? Let's see . . . maybe under the salt cellar." She pulled out a grimy piece of paper, curling at the edges. "No, that's my recipe. Oh, silly me, it's right here in the pocket of my apron." She reached in and produced something crumpled that Serafina thought might be a letter, although it had some greasy splotches on it.

Serafina eyed her aunt suspiciously, hoping against hope that this wasn't another one of her aunt's vivid flights of fancy. She didn't think she could bear it if it was. "Auntie—you're absolutely sure you have it right? Do you think perhaps I could see Lord Delaware's letter?"

"See it? Certainly not—it's far too complicated, and in any case, young girls should not be involved in legal matters. He just says that it's all been arranged and Aubrey is waiting at Townsend for you. So appropriate to receive the news on Beltane, the day that honors the wedding of the god and goddess." She shoved her glasses up on her nose and peered more closely at the paper, smoothing out the creases.

Serafina blinked. "But—but how? Why? I mean, why so suddenly after so much time and no word?" She was so dazed by her aunt's announcement that she could hardly think coherently.

"I can hardly help it that Aubrey was out of the country these last three years, Serafina, or at least that's what his father says. But now that he's home, he wants to get on with the wedding with all dispatch, which is why so many letters have been coming and going from Delaware over the last month. I," she added grandiosely, "have been negotiating your marriage contracts. Through my solicitor, naturally, but he couldn't have managed without my help."

"But you said nothing!" Serafina looked down at her worn dress, her muddy boots with sudden despair, knowing she had nothing finer other than her Sunday dress, and that wasn't much better than what she was wearing. "Oh, why didn't you *tell* me, give me some warning? I could have done something to prepare myself!"

Elspeth peered at her over her spectacles. "I can't think

what you could have done, and there didn't seem to be any point in getting you overexcited." She shuffled in her desk, looking for pen and paper. "I'll write and say we'll be arriving Friday next. The wedding can take place Saturday morning. So, my dear, why are you sitting there like a pea-goose? Isn't this what you've been waiting for all these years?"

Serafina mutely nodded, her head still spinning with wonder. "Yes . . . I—I think I must be in shock. You're sure, absolutely certain about all of this?"

"What do you take me for? I'm perfectly *de trop* in these matters," Elspeth said crossly, and Serafina wanted to laugh at the very idea that Aunt Elspeth was *de trop* in anything. And yet she had nothing else to go on but her aunt's word, and since she had never doubted her aunt's good intentions, eccentric or not, she would simply have to believe that Elspeth knew what she was talking about.

Not that Serafina could imagine what negotiating Elspeth could have done. She had nothing to bring to the marriage but herself. Elspeth had probably signed some sort of simple agreement and was just feeling pleased with herself.

Serafina, on the other hand, was elated. Aiden was ready to marry her, and the divine plan was ready to be put into place.

However, given that, there were some practical questions she needed to put to her aunt, and she wasn't entirely sure how to go about them. "Auntie," she said hesitantly, "I was wondering. Do you think perhaps it's time we spoke of what happens after the wedding?"

"Why, after the wedding you live with Aubrey at Townsend, silly girl. What else? You didn't expect to come back here, did you?"

"Of course not, Auntie. That's not what I meant, though. What I was asking is what happens on the wedding night? In bed?"

Elspeth jerked up straight. "Heavens, child. It may be Beltane, but I don't think we should be discussing such things just yet. You'll find out when the time is right, don't think you won't." She turned her back and returned to stirring her brew.

Seething with frustration Serafina shoved her chin on her hands and morosely stared down at the household accounts. She was beginning to think she would *never* know what happened after kissing. As sure as she was that it was marvelous, the technical details eluded her. She realized that a man put seed inside a woman and a baby grew from that. Just how the man put that seed inside aroused her curiosity mightily. She imagined Aiden with a little medicine dropper of the sort that Elspeth used, asking her to open her mouth.

Somehow that seemed unlikely though, and not the least bit thrilling. It had to be something truly extraordinary, she decided, or what happened between men and women in bed wouldn't be kept such a deep dark secret. The only conclusion she could logically draw was that since the two sexes were constructed differently, it had something to do with that, with how they touched each other. She hoped so. She liked the way Aiden touched her in the Dream, how he made her feel, all hot and flushed and filled with love.

She smiled, a rush of excitement flooding through her at the thought that she didn't have much longer to wait to find out everything she wanted to know. And she wouldn't even have to dream it.

Miss Elspeth Beaton had never suffered fools gladly, and as far as she was concerned, Lord Delaware was one of the biggest fools alive. Fostering no illusions about his reasons for belatedly requesting Serafina's hand in marriage to his son, she'd carefully looked into Delaware's affairs and discovered disaster, exactly as she'd expected.

Delaware's financial problems, however, held little interest to Elspeth. Serafina's considerable fortune would bail Delaware out of his difficulties with no trouble, and with the firm restrictions Elspeth had placed on certain of aspects of the settlement, her niece was sure to have a comfortable life regardless of what Delaware did.

It was Delaware's son she was far more interested in, for

she doubted he would go easily to his fate—not that Delaware had left him a choice.

Still, she wanted to know just what frame of mind he was in concerning his upcoming nuptials. "So, Basil," she said, crooning to her beloved parrot, "now that we're alone, I think I'll just have a peek, shall I?"

Basil pulled his head out from under his wing, opened an eye, and ruffled loudly. "Trouble, trouble, boil and bubble," he mumbled, adjusting one long green feather.

"That's 'double, double, toil and trouble; Fire burn and cauldron bubble,' " she said. "I do wish you'd try to get it right, and I don't see why I shouldn't have a little look," Elspeth said defensively. "How else are we to know what to expect from the boy?"

Basil shot her a long, highly suspect look from one beady orange eye and settled his feathers back into place. "Sneaky, sneaky," he muttered.

"Not at all. I am merely gathering information. Now hush and let me concentrate."

Basil turned his back as if to inform Elspeth that he wanted nothing to do with the proceedings and settled his head back under his wing.

Elspeth rubbed her hands together and went to a drawer, pulling out a large sphere wrapped in black velvet. "There now," she said, yanking the velvet off and placing the crystal ball on her little altar. She laid out her circle of stones, then set the censer to smoking and lit the candles.

Raising her arms, she began the ritual chant:

> "Air, fire, water, earth,
> Elements of astral birth
> I call you now, attend to me!
>
> In the circle, rightly cast,
> Safe from psychic curse or blast
> I call you now, attend to me!
>
> From cave and desert, sea and hill,
> By wand, blade, cup and pentacle,

I call you now; attend to me!
This is my will, so mote it be!"

She then placed herself before the altar, her eyes trained on her quartz ball, and waited impatiently. Nothing appeared. "Blast," she muttered. "Come along, we haven't all night." She stared harder into the crystal. Still nothing, but then she'd never been very good at this sort of divining. She was much better at casting spells.

Elspeth picked up the ball and shook it impatiently, and a shadowy image wavered inside. With a shout of glee, Elspeth replaced it on the altar. "There. Now we'll see what's what," she cackled.

Peering as hard as she could, she tried to make out the hazy form, even though it was upside down. She stood and bent over, looking at it from that angle.

So, it was a man. Very good. Dark hair, that much she could tell. Dark hair and blue eyes that blazed with frustration as he unleashed a string of curses, then flung his neckcloth across the room.

"Damn him! Damn him and blast him and damn him again!" he cried. "And I hope he burns in hell."

"Tut, tut," Elspeth said reprovingly. "Wish no harm, silly boy, or it will come right back in your face. It's no wonder you and your family have had so many troubles with *that* attitude."

His face drew into a frown of concentration as he slumped at his desk and flipped through a pile of papers, obviously not for the first time, given the speed at which he went.

Probably promissory notes, Elspeth assumed, bills of exchange, mortgages, debts to various creditors and retailers, all a sad story of his father's general financial mismanagement. And the shipping company by which the family had made its fortune three hundred years before was sadly caught up in the worst of the debts. Well, Serafina's money would fix all those little problems.

Elspeth smiled happily, remembering the day that nasty, ambitious Alice Segrave and her sniveling son Edmund had attended the reading of John's will, only to discover to their horror that while they might have snatched away the title and Bowhill, they had but a small income from the estate to keep the property afloat. Serafina had inherited everything else. Served those two vipers right, too, she thought gleefully.

She was particularly pleased over her handling of Serafina's inheritance, refusing to touch one penny of it, shepherding it to even greater heights. Come to that, she was pleased with her handling of Serafina altogether.

She was an unspoiled girl, respectful of the earth and its creatures, mindful of the goddess, even if Elspeth *had* had to send her to church every Sunday. She was properly dutiful and innocent of the darker aspects of the world. In short, Serafina was a perfect bride.

As if in answer to that thought, Aiden groaned and put his face in his hands, his fingers clenched in his hair. "Poor boy," she murmured. "It can't be easy for you. But never mind, it will all work out, you'll see."

The image blurred and shivered, fading away altogether and Elspeth grunted with disappointment. Still, she'd learned enough about what she wanted to know. And since her part in the matter was nearly done, all that was left was to sit back and watch events unfold. It was not her place to interfere.

She sighed heavily as she covered the crystal again, fully aware of the difficulties that lay ahead. Nevertheless, the marriage was a promising beginning, even if it did chafe at Aiden's pride and independence. It was going to chafe at a lot more than that before all was said and done, but that couldn't be helped.

Clearing nearly a thousand years of karmic debt was no easy task. Elspeth could only hope Serafina and Aiden were up to it.

2

$\mathcal{F}$our days of packing, punctuated by Elspeth running around like a chicken with her head cut off shouting conflicting orders, were followed by the actual loading of the carriages, trunks of odds and ends lashed onto the roof and the back.

Serafina couldn't think where they'd accumulated so much of nothing. She had only a small trunk of clothing for herself and a few personal articles. Her aunt, on the other hand, seemed to have an infinite assortment of possessions that she wanted to take along with her on the trip, and since Serafina knew that her aunt's wardrobe was as limited as her own, she was baffled about what was in the other huge trunk.

Serafina took one last look around the crumbling castle that had served as home for the last eleven years. She was going to miss Clwydd acutely. She remembered the day she'd arrived, numb with grief over her father's death and the strain of the funeral, feeling like a duck out of water, stripped of the only home she'd ever known, reeling from the shock of having been turned out of Bowhill by her detestable cousin and his mother without one kind word.

The memory still hurt after all this time, and Serafina winced as humiliation came rushing back in full force. She didn't really know why she was thinking about that awful day now, except that she felt an immense gratitude to Aunt Elspeth for having taken her in, for having made her welcome in her castle on a cliff when Serafina had nowhere else to turn until her marriage to Aiden.

" 'Ere, come along now, Miss Serafina," Tinkerby said from behind her, startling her out of her thoughts. "Times awasting, and your auntie's loaded up that blasted bird. You know he won't keep his beak shut for more than two minutes, and I'm not inclined to stand about getting my eardrums broken."

Serafina turned and gave him a fond smile. "Coming, Tinkerby. I was just saying my good-byes."

"Aye, well good-bye is the best thing I can think of your saying to this drafty old pile of mortar. I daresay it'll be missing you a good deal more than you'll be missing it."

"Oh, I don't know," she said. "I've grown awfully fond of the place, even though it is falling apart at the seams. It feels strange to be leaving, as much as I can't wait to be married."

"Aye, and your husband-to-be is waiting too." He winked. "Won't have him saying that I held up your nuptials, not when he's so anxious to have you at his side, if you know what I mean."

Serafina blushed; she wasn't exactly sure what Tinkerby meant, but she knew she needed to be better prepared than she was. She hadn't been able to get another word out of Elspeth on the subject and she was no closer to discovering the mystery. Still, if the prelude in the dream was anything to go by, she expected she'd enjoy the conclusion enormously.

"You see, Tinkerby?" she said, gently teasing. "You thought I was making everything up about my destiny with Aiden and it all happened just as it was supposed to."

"I still think that part about destiny is a lot o' nonsense," Tinkerby said. "But I'm prepared to admit I was wrong about his lordship. Mind you, I wasn't to know he was in the Americas all that time. Hard to marry you when he was an ocean away, I'll give you that."

"Thank you," Serafina said, kissing his cheek.

It was Tinkerby's turn to blush. "You save that sort of thing for your husband," he said gruffly. "We don't want you coming up empty on your wedding day."

"I don't think there's a chance of that," Serafina replied with a little laugh. "Oh, Tinkerby, I don't think I've been so excited in my entire life!"

She sobered, longing to ask Tinkerby the question that had been uppermost on her mind the last few days, ever since she'd learned that Aiden had summoned her. "Do you think . . ." she said, hesitating. "Oh, Tinkerby, how do you think he'll find me? Do you think he'll find my face displeasing?"

Tinkerby chuckled. "I'm sure I can't speak for his lordship, Miss Serafina, but you put me in mind of your mother when she first came to Bowhill, that you do. Why do you ask?"

"Because everyone said I was such an ugly child," Serafina blurted out. "I think I've improved a little, anyway, but it's hard to tell."

"Aye," Tinkerby said bluntly. "You were no beauty to be sure, but now that you've grown, your face has made better sense of itself."

"But my eyes are still a funny color and the bridge of my nose is too wide and my mouth is too full and—and my front tooth is crooked." She regarded him gravely.

"I don't see a thing wrong with your eyes, your nose, your mouth, or that tooth, for that matter. It's hardly crooked at all to my way of looking, just a little bit off perfect. You should have seen my wife—now there was a mouthful of teeth. Stuck right out they did, but I didn't love her any less for that."

"Oh," Serafina said with acute disappointment, seeing what Tinkerby was gently trying to tell her. "I suppose he'll find me too skinny as well. I never have been able to put flesh on my bones."

"As for that," Tinkerby said, standing back and regarding her with an assessing gaze, "I'd say you were a slight thing, but not sickening for it, and that's what matters. Don't you worry, missie. You may not be a beauty like one of those statues I once saw in Kensington Gardens, but you have character and that's what counts."

Serafina chewed on her lip. She wasn't sure she wanted

character, whereas she was certain she could have done with a little beauty. But since she couldn't have one, she supposed she'd have to make do with the other and hope it was enough.

Tinkerby chucked her chin. "All young girls worry overmuch about their looks, and you're no different. But beauty is as beauty does, I always say, and you keep that in mind. The good Lord made you just the way you are, and there's not a thing you can do to change it."

"I suppose you're right," Serafina said with a sigh. "I'll do my best with what I have and hope Aiden won't be too terribly disappointed."

At least we'll have love, she thought. *At least we'll have love.*

The journey to Rutland stretched interminably. Elspeth insisted on stopping every afternoon for a three-hour nap, which she enjoyed stretched out in the back of the carriage, snoring peacefully.

Serafina used the time to stretch her legs and take pleasure in the changing countryside. Accustomed to the stormy coastal weather of Wales, she delighted in the more temperate climates of the midlands, the balmy breezes and the differences of topography. They brought her back to her childhood at Bowhill, a far less primitive environment than that of Clwydd, where the rock and scrub were shaped by the harshness of the elements.

But even on the fourth afternoon as they neared their final destination of Townsend, Elspeth insisted on stopping, despite Serafina's desperation to continue.

"Auntie, please?" she begged. "We're so close now! Can't you have your sleep after we arrive?"

"I don't believe in breaking with routine," Elspeth said, gesturing to Tinkerby to clean up the picnic lunch. "I've always slept between the hours of three and six and I don't see any reason to change my schedule. You might try a nap yourself to take the edge off your nerves; you're as jumpy as a cat with a dog barking outside the door."

"Auntie," Serafina said, taking Elspeth's hands between her own, "just this once can't you make an exception?"

"Certainly not—making exceptions only leads to trouble. And if you insist on taking one of your walks rather than a sensible nap, just be sure you're back in time to change into your good dress, and try not to collect too many brambles in your hair or I'll be hours getting them out."

Serafina watched with helpless frustration as her impossible aunt marched back to the carriage and pulled the curtains across the window. Aiden was five miles away at the most, no distance at all, a mere heartbeat after eleven years of interminable waiting, and her aunt insisted on snoring away three hours of precious time. Serafina wanted to scream.

"Go on then, missie, have yourself a nice walk in the woods," Tinkerby said soothingly. "You know there's no changing that one's mind once she's set it. You've a lifetime ahead with his lordship and a few hours isn't going to make any difference."

"Not you too," Serafina said in despair. "I would have thought you understood."

"Aye, I understand well enough," Tinkerby said. "But there's some things as can wait, and I say your auntie has the right of it. It don't do to seem hasty."

"How is Aiden to know whether we're hasty or not?" Serafina said with frustration. "He only knows we're meant to be arriving between teatime and dinner."

"That's it exactly. 'Travel in haste, repent in leisure.' You don't want to seem too eager, now do you?"

"That's 'marry in haste, repent in leisure,' " Serafina said in exasperation. "And I don't think the saying applies in this case, since I've waited forever for this moment."

"Then you might want to think about what you're going to say when the moment arrives," Tinkerby said, climbing onto the box of the carriage and pulling his hat over his eyes. "Go on now, Miss Serafina. There's naught to trouble you in these big woods and you might as well work your kinks out."

Serafina shot him one last resentful glare, then took off at a fast pace through the forest that bordered the post road, determined not to let her vexation get the worst of her, not an easy task.

She wandered for some time through dappled thickets, steadily following the elusive sound of water and finally found its source. A bright, bubbling stream ran along one side of a clearing, wending its way over a bed of rock and climbing around and over fallen wood. Damp moss padded the edge of the slight embankment, and Serafina fell to her knees and drank deeply of the cold water, first remembering to thank the goddess for providing her with refreshment.

When she'd finished, she sat up and stripped off her shoes and stockings, then pulled her skirts up around her knees, paddling her feet in the stream with contentment as she wove a chain from the wildflowers she'd picked along the way. She placed the wreath on her head, humming a little song.

Then, since she had nothing better to do for the next two hours, Serafina curled up on her side, resting her head against her arm, and let the warm sun carry her off into sleep.

Soon. So soon now, and she'd be in Aiden's arms. . . .

Aiden had spent ten aggravating days chasing down first the archbishop of Canterbury to obtain the blasted special license, and then chasing down various creditors and bank managers to determine the exact severity of his father's financial crisis. It had not been a rewarding period of time. And now bloody Miss Serafina Segrave was about to arrive to bail his father out and seal Aiden's miserable fate.

He stormed down the stairs and through the hall, intending to ride into the village and get himself thoroughly drunk. And then his sister's voice rang out from the open doors of the drawing room.

"Aiden? Aiden, where are you going?" she called in alarm.

Aiden's step halted and he swore under his breath, then turned and went to the doorway. "Out," he said shortly.

"But they'll be here at any time," Charlotte said, dropping her embroidery into her lap, her face pulled into a worried frown as she took in his appearance.

"Precisely."

"Oh, Aiden, do be reasonable," she said in a cajoling tone, wheeling her chair forward. "You're not even dressed for dinner yet, and you can't come in smelling of horses. What will Miss Segrave think?"

"I don't give a damn what Miss Segrave thinks, or what her aunt thinks, or what you think for that matter, Charlotte. I'm going out, and you can all consider yourself fortunate if I find my way back by tomorrow morning. And I'm thoroughly fed up with being told to be reasonable, so desist."

Charlotte's hand fluttered at her throat. "You know how it upsets me when you work yourself into a temper, and I do wish you wouldn't swear like that—it's most offensive. Anyway, you've been home for nearly a fortnight, and I've hardly seen you." She smiled brightly.

"That, my dear sister, is because I've been busy trying to save our communal skin," Aiden said tightly. "And since the only way to do that is to slip my head into the noose Father's arranged for me, I'm damned if I'm going to hang myself a minute sooner than I have to. You and Father can look after dear Miss Segrave and her aunt perfectly adequately."

"But—but Father's taken to his bed after your set-to this afternoon," Charlotte said, both hands now aflutter at her throat. "And I *wish* you wouldn't swear."

"Sorry. But Father's disappearing act doesn't surprise me in the least: He's probably too much of a coward to face a situation completely of his own making. As usual."

"I know, but Aiden . . . you can't leave me alone with them. What am I to say? How am I to explain your absence?"

"You can explain it anyway you please," Aiden said, his impatience growing by the second. "Tell them I've gone off to perform my nightly duties as a highwayman for all I care."

"Really," Charlotte said reprovingly. "Don't you want to make a good impression on your fiancée?"

"I somehow doubt it would make any difference," Aiden said with a distinct bite in his voice, a bite that didn't hold a candle to the one in his chest, where he felt as if a particularly sharp pair of incisors had taken hold.

"Look, Lottie," he said, deliberately softening his tone at her wounded expression, "I'm sorry. I'm in a particularly foul mood, which is one of the reasons I'm vacating the premises for tonight. I'll try my best to be on better behavior tomorrow, but you know how I feel about this impending marriage and the parties involved in perpetrating it on me."

"I do know," his sister replied, looking down at her hands, slim and pale, as pale as her face, which never saw the sun. "And I'm eternally grateful to you for your sacrifice. It will be hard on me as well to have such a monstrous, unprincipled woman taking over the household I've managed for so long, but I'm trying to put the best face on the matter that I can. You know I'd do anything for you—anything at all to make your life happier in the face of this disaster."

He crossed over to her chair and took her hand, dropping an affectionate kiss on her hair. "And I realize I'm being a selfish bastard in behaving as if I'm the only one who's going to suffer because of this marriage," he said, giving her fingers a squeeze. "But never fear. If Miss Segrave thinks she's going to take over Townsend lock, stock, and barrel, she has another think coming, and I'll be the first to set her straight. I won't let her put you aside, Lottie, I promise. It's your family home, after all, and you've had the running of it all these years."

"Thank you," she said quietly. "You have no idea how much it means to me to hear you say it."

He looked down at her, guilt wracking him, knowing he was responsible for her being in that damned chair to begin with. Miss Serafina Segrave would interfere with Charlotte over his dead body.

"Life will go on as it always has," he said, forcing a smile to his lips. "Everything will stay just as you like it, so please don't trouble yourself."

He turned quickly and left, thereby missing the answering smile of triumph on his sister's face.

Aiden saddled his horse himself, since the one groom left to them was busy with other duties. He was glad that at least his father hadn't sold off Aladdin along with everything else. God, he found it depressing to see what had become of

Townsend in the three years he'd been away, evidence of neglect everywhere.

But he supposed that now some of that would change, once he finished successfully rebuilding the shipping company. If there was any money left. It was going to take hundreds of thousands of pounds to undo the damage his father had done, but at least he could start immediately, thanks to bloody Miss Segrave's bloody inheritance.

The thought didn't do anything to lift his troubled spirits, nor did it erase any of his anger. But on his last night of freedom he refused to dwell too heavily on his miserable future with Miss Serafina Segrave for fear that such black thoughts would drive him straight to the river to drown himself.

He turned toward the west and kicked Aladdin into a fast canter, choosing to head cross-country rather than take the road, mainly because he didn't want to risk being spotted by Miss Segrave and her approaching entourage.

The sunlight had softened into gold as late afternoon approached, and Aiden cut across Townsend's meadows, slowing Aladdin's gait to a walk as they approached Rockingham Forest.

Here the sunlight dimmed and diffused into patches, lending a sense of timelessness, and he breathed deeply, drinking in the familiar tang of new leaf and brush, the rich loam of earth, his ear attuned to the gentle call of birds hidden in the trees, the babble of the stream that ran as a tributary from the river.

He steadily followed the bank, the surest guide through the forest to the path leading to the village. It was easy enough to become lost in the vast sprawl of wood where not too many ventured, other than the occasional poacher. And yet this was a place Aiden had always loved, where as a child he had often come to escape the stifled atmosphere of Townsend, to claim a piece of magic, to live his fantasies before the exigencies of adulthood had stripped him of even those.

In these woods he had dreamt of places long ago and far away, of the legends of King Arthur and his Knights of the Roundtable, had imagined himself to be Lancelot, or Gawain, or even, in his more inflated moments, Arthur himself.

He smiled and shook his head, remembering how he'd once talked to the fairies, believing they could actually hear him, had confided his most private hopes and dreams to them, had even dreamed of one day finding true love. What a joke. Even poor, cuckolded King Arthur had finally been dispossessed of that delusion, he thought wryly.

He'd never forget the day at the age of ten that he'd realized exactly what it was that Guinevere and Lancelot had done together. He'd been curled up under the great oak tree at Townsend reading Malory's *Morte D'Arthur* for at least the twentieth time when the terrible truth had struck that Arthur had been ignobly betrayed by both his wife and his best friend.

Aiden had cried for hours, heartsick, utterly disillusioned. And had sworn that day he would never marry, never leave himself open to that kind of betrayal.

In that afternoon the idealistic boy who thought dreams really could come true disappeared forever, and just as well. Life was hard enough without viewing it through rose-colored glasses. Life, when it came down to it, was a damned travesty.

He gazed up at the lacing of branches forming a canopy over his head that now resembled more of a jail cell to his eyes than a protective bower. The irony of it all was that in the end he had been betrayed in the name of marriage, although the betrayal had been dealt by his father's hand.

Aladdin suddenly snorted and shied and Aiden came back to reality with a jerk, bringing the gelding back under control with his legs and a gentle restraining pull on the bit. He looked around to see what had startled Aladdin and nearly unseated himself.

Just off to the left of the stream lay a body. A woman's body, curled onto its side, the face down, a mass of dark hair tangled around one arm, a bedraggled wreath of flowers on her head. Her feet were bare, her skirt hitched up about her knees. She made no movement.

"Sweet Christ," he whispered in real alarm and brought Aladdin to an abrupt halt, quickly dismounting. He approached the body with trepidation, hoping against hope that he hadn't stumbled across the scene of a murder.

He didn't really feel like getting tied up in a police investigation—with his luck, he'd instantly be accused and find himself hanging from the gallows—the real ones. Not that it wouldn't be a backhanded blessing.

He knelt and reached out one tentative hand, gingerly touching a shoulder, expecting it to be stiff and cold. The next thing he knew the body heaved itself up to a sitting position with a very lifelike squeak and he found himself looking into a pair of wide, startled eyes the most extraordinary shade of light green, surrounded by a thick fringe of dark lashes.

He stared, for once in his life speechless.

She stared back, her rosy mouth slightly open, her small high breasts rising and falling in a rapid rhythm, but other than her initial squeak she made no sound, just gazed at him with those arresting eyes. Aiden vaguely registered the impression that she was one of the most enchanting creatures he'd ever seen.

It's Titania, Queen of the Fairies, he thought irrationally, sitting back on his heels, thoroughly discomposed.

"I—I beg your pardon for disturbing you," he stammered. "I thought you were dead, you see." *Oh God, I really am losing my mind,* he decided as he tried to gather his scattered thoughts.

She blinked, looking exactly like an owl startled out of its sleep. "You thought I was dead?" she said, cocking her head to one side. "What an extraordinary idea."

"Yes, I know," he said, thinking that her voice sounded like liquid music. "I see that now, but one doesn't usually trip across sleeping maidens in the middle of the woods." He glanced around. "Especially sleeping maidens with no visible chaperones."

"What do I need a chaperone for?" she asked, as if he had just posed the silliest question on earth.

"To protect you from men like myself," he said, unable to resist a wolfish grin. "I'm precisely the sort of rogue they're designed to guard you against."

She regarded him with open curiosity. "Ah," she said after a moment of examining him as if he were an interesting scientific specimen. "I've always wondered what a rogue looked like."

"I hope I don't come as a disappointment," he said with amusement, still half convinced she was a fairy, even though the worn, muddied state of her dress indicated she was simply a girl from the village. Still, she was utterly captivating and refreshingly unsophisticated. He didn't think—no, he was certain—that he'd never met anyone like her in his life.

"Well . . . I haven't anyone to compare you to, but I don't find you disappointing at all," she said, chewing on her lip thoughtfully. "You're very handsome. Am I supposed to be afraid of you?"

"Probably," he said, thoroughly gratified and entertaining the most roguishly impure thoughts. "Are you?"

"I'm terribly sorry, but I'm not," she said apologetically. "I know that rogues are supposed to ravish young women, but I don't think you'd be interested in ravishing me."

"Why not?" he asked, thinking she was way off-target with that notion. He knew exactly where he'd start. A deep kiss on those sweet, rosebud lips, followed by a trail of kisses down her long, white neck . . .

"Because you don't love me," she said perfectly calmly. "Surely you don't ravish people you don't love?"

Aiden smothered a laugh. "You really are an innocent, my dear. What makes you think love has anything to do with it?" he asked, unable to resist pursuing this extraordinary line of conversation.

"But of course it has," she said in astonishment. "I can't imagine it would be very interesting any other way, and why else would it be called lovemaking? To be truthful, though," she said with a little sigh, "nobody's ever told me much of anything when it comes to the subject, and I confess I long to know."

"Do you feel your education has been neglected?" he said, not entirely believing his ears.

She regarded him gravely. "I'm not sure. After all, it seems as if it must be such a natural process that one ought to be able to work it out without instruction. It's just the details that trouble me, you see, and I haven't anyone to ask." She looked at him with a little gleam of curiosity. "I don't suppose . . . no. That probably wouldn't be proper."

"Decidedly not proper, but I wouldn't let that trouble you." Aiden ran his hand over his chin, desperately trying to keep a straight face.

"Well, I suppose we'll never see each other again, so it doesn't really matter," she said with a decisive nod.

"Exactly." Aiden sat down and stretched out his legs, crossing them at the ankles, and leaned his weight back on his hands. "Er, are you planning on being ravished at some point in the future? Perhaps you have a rendezvous in mind that leads you to this line of inquiry?"

"Oh, yes!" she said brightly. "How did you know?"

"Just a lucky guess," he replied. "In that case, maybe I could give you one or two helpful pointers."

"I'm very fortunate to have run into you," she said, beaming at him. "I'm not usually allowed to talk to strangers, and I can't think of anyone else to ask. The only person I know well who could tell me is Tinkerby, but he'd be shocked if I brought the subject up. He's very conventional."

"Oh, no, you mustn't shock Tinkerby," Aiden said, enthralled. "Ask away. I'll tell you whatever I can."

"Well . . . I would like to know if lovemaking is a pleasant experience." She regarded him expectantly.

"Hmm. I would have to say very pleasant," Aiden said, his eyes dancing with suppressed hilarity.

"As nice as kissing?" she asked earnestly, looking as if she found kissing the most marvelous thing in the world.

"Decidedly better than kissing." His gaze dropped to her rosy lips again and lingered there, mentally tracing their outline, wondering what it would be like to feel them beneath his own. Extremely nice, he decided. No—better than nice. Like a little piece of heaven.

"Oh, how wonderful," she said with satisfaction. "That is exactly what I was hoping for. Umm—can you tell me what actually happens? When one seals a vow in the flesh, I mean?"

Aiden bit the tip of his thumb, stifling a surge of laughter. "I—I suppose the best way to put it is that a man and a woman become very close, as close as it's physically possible to be."

"But *how*?" she asked, her face a delicious riot of confusion.

"Well . . . they go into each other's arms," he said, trying to find words that wouldn't shock her. "And they kiss and caress, and then, when both are feeling completely delighted with each other, the man joins his body with the woman's."

"How does he do that?" she demanded insistently.

"Hmm," Aiden said, sure that he ought to be prevaricating wildly at this point, but too interested in seeing her reaction to let his conscience interfere. "Let's see. You know, of course, that men are built in a different fashion to women?"

"Yes, of course," she said impatiently.

"Good. Because the man takes that part of himself that makes him male and he places it in that part of herself that makes her female. Do you understand?"

He watched in fascination as she digested this vital piece of information, her eyes focused in concentration at a point somewhere in the middle of his chest. God in heaven, he knew he was being wicked, talking to an innocent girl like this, but he'd never enjoyed being a reprobate more in his life.

She raised her eyes to his after a minute. "I think so. Do they take their clothes off?" she asked, her brow puckered. "I can't see how else they might do this thing."

Aiden wasn't sure he could take much more of her questioning without losing his self-possession. "Generally speaking they do, unless they're in a terrible hurry. But it's the sort of thing you want to take your clothes off for."

"Oh. Like bathing," she said, her face lighting up.

"As far as I'm concerned, it's much more fun than bathing," he replied, his lips quivering. "But you'll have to decide for yourself. The only thing I must caution you about is the possibility of conceiving a child," he added, feeling he did need to inject a note of practicality into the discussion before she decided to go and thoroughly ruin herself. "You do understand this is often the result of lovemaking?"

"Of course I do," she said indignantly. "Isn't that the whole point?"

Aiden stared at her, nonplussed. "My dear girl, with that attitude I think you might seriously consider the option of marrying this gentleman. Unless, of course, he is already married."

She stared back at him, her mouth half open, and then she suddenly burst into peals of laughter. "Oh! You are funning with me. I'm sorry—I don't go out much in the world, so it is not always easy for me to tell."

"Yes, I can see that you've lived a sheltered life," Aiden said. "Which makes me wonder, Titania, what you were doing sleeping in the middle of the woods all alone? Waiting for your Oberon perhaps?"

"Oh, do you think my true love is king of the fairies?"

She laughed merrily again, and Aiden's heart lifted at the sweet, pure melody. She really was like someone from another world, untouched and completely natural, a sleeping princess who only waited to be wakened by a princely kiss. He noticed that she had one very slightly crooked front tooth, which he found rather beguiling.

"I think you must have been waiting for someone," he said, feeling an absurd stab of envy.

"Not at all," she said with a shake of her head, and Aiden watched transfixed as her thick shiny hair, the color of chestnuts in the autumn, swung like a curtain of silk over her back. "I was sleepy, so taking a nap seemed the most sensible thing to do." She yawned. "What time do you suppose it is?"

"Fairy time," he said foolishly. "Actually, I think it's about five o'clock. Why?" He was suddenly terribly worried she'd disappear, vanishing into a cloud of silver mist.

"Oh, that's all right, then," she said and yawned again, and Aiden caught a glimpse of white teeth and the pink tip of a tongue that curled up in the most entrancing fashion. She belatedly clapped her hand over her mouth. "I'm not expected back for a little while still."

Aiden exhaled with relief. "Good. I'm not expected anywhere either—at least not until tomorrow morning when I have an appointment with the noose." He'd never seen eyes grow as wide as hers did then, nor a color change so swiftly from sea foam to the gray of a stormy sky.

"No!" she gasped, her hand creeping to her mouth. "Oh, no—you can't mean they're going to *hang* you?"

Tears sprang to her eyes, and Aiden found himself ridiculously touched that she cared; it had been a long time since anyone had bothered.

"But why?" she said, her voice thick with distress. "What have you done?"

He was tempted to weave a dramatic story of a jealous husband and a duel gone wrong just to wring a little more sympathy out of her, but he decided that the truth would sadly have to serve.

He shifted his position to lean back on his elbow. "Oh, I've done all sorts of dreadful things in my time, but actually, I was only speaking metaphorically," he said, pulling up a piece of grass and placing it in his teeth, nibbling on the stem. "The truth of the matter is that I'm about to be married. And if you bring the notion of love into it, I think I might well strangle you."

She clasped her hands in her lap. "Oh . . . I see," she said, lowering her gaze. "Well, you shouldn't joke about such things as the hangman's rope. And if that's how you feel about marriage, I don't see why you're being married at all."

Aiden shrugged. "Because I've been coerced into it, Titania, and in a very nasty way. The nastiest way possible."

She was silent for a long moment. "Did you ravish her?" she finally asked in a low voice.

"Ravish her?" he said indignantly. "I never laid a finger on her—if anyone's been ravished, it's me. She knew I was in a bad way financially and she happens to have more money than Croesus. So she set up a situation to ensnare me, bloody little schemer, and I have no way out."

"But surely you don't have to go through with the marriage, do you, not if the idea is so repugnant to you?"

Aiden threw away the piece of grass in disgust. "Yes, I'm afraid I do. I gave my word to my family, and that's that. So I'm to be tied to a harridan—an ugly harridan on top of it—for the rest of my days." He dug his fingertips into the earth as if he could ground himself against the fresh rush of anger that surged through him. "As God is my witness, I'll do my duty, but I'll despise the witch until the last minute she draws breath. And believe me, that can't be soon enough."

"Oh, dear," she said, looking infinitely sad for him. "You don't have a prayer for happiness you know, not with that attitude. Can't you think of your marriage as a challenge, perhaps, an avenue through which to grow to love your wife?"

Aiden shot her an ironic glance. "My God, you're even more innocent than I first thought," he said, reaching out a hand and stroking the outside of her arm with one finger.

To his delight she didn't pull away. "I don't see what innocence has to do with anything," she said. "Surely you could try to love her just a little?"

"I'm afraid that there's no hope for peaceful coexistence, never mind love, from a union based on duress." He dropped his hand and sighed. "The best I have to hope for is to live my own life independent of hers as much as possible. I'll get the obligatory heir on her, then establish a string of mistresses and hope they provide me with a little oblivion." He cocked an eyebrow. "Have I shocked you to your core?"

"Shocked me? No, not really. But I can't imagine what it would be like to live in a loveless marriage. Perhaps I'm just a simple person, and I don't understand these things." She looked up then, her expression sweetly fierce. "At least I will have love when I marry, and there will be trust and honesty between my husband and myself. And when we bring our children into this world they will be born from that."

"I think I begin to see," he said, rubbing the side of his nose, unaccountably disappointed that she was to be married, and relieved at the same time that she wasn't heading into ruin at the hands of an unprincipled rake. "Those questions you were asking earlier—they are in anticipation of a wedding, is that it?"

"Yes," she said. "A wonderful wedding that I look forward to with all my heart, unlike yourself."

Aiden shook his head with a wry smile. "And I suppose his name is Prince Charming?" he asked with a soft chuckle.

Her eyes flashed up to his, the green sparking like phosphorescence in a moonlit sea. "I think you're very unkind to mock me. I happen to believe in true love."

"And I hope for your sake that you manage to hang on to that fairy tale. It would be a terrible thing to have it shattered by the reality of a houseful of crying children and a husband who beats you when he comes home tired and drunk and disappointed with life."

She colored angrily, a lovely pink shade like the tinge of the inside of a Caribbean seashell, and Aiden wanted nothing more but to put his hand out and stroke her cheek just on that spot.

"That will never happen," she said adamantly. "And it's unfortunate that you regard all marriages in the same light as your own. I'm beginning to think you're entirely unfeeling."

"A rogue to be sure," he said, unexpectedly hurt that she would draw that conclusion. "One can't afford inconveniences such as feelings."

"Then you really don't believe in love at all," she said, chewing on her bottom lip, her brow drawn together.

"I'm afraid not," he answered. "I'm a pragmatist, Titania. Unlike yourself I've been out in the world, and I learned very quickly that the best way to survive was on one's wits, not on a pocketful of dreams."

"That may be," she said softly. "But a life without hopes and dreams, without someone to love and to love you in return sounds very empty."

He smiled. "But then I'll never have my heart broken, will I?"

"Maybe it would do you some good," she said tartly. "Just to prove to yourself that you do have a heart after all."

He covered his chest with one hand and looked down in concentration. "Sorry," he said, looking back at her after a moment. "Not a single beat to be felt."

She laughed, and he was pleased to see the smile back on her face. "You are impossible," she said.

"Another prerequisite for a rogue," he replied, matching her smile.

She stood then, surprisingly tall and so slender that he knew he could span her waist with his hands. And wanted to. But he managed to keep his hands to himself as he rose to face her. The top of her head came to his shoulder, and he looked down at her. "Are you going now?" he asked, infinitely sorry at the prospect.

"Yes, I must leave," she said. "I truly am sorry for your predicament, and even sorrier that you hold such a pessimistic attitude. But as foolish as it sounds, I wish you all happiness despite it." She held out her hand, her palm sideways as if she were a man.

He took it gently and turned it over, feeling the fragility of her bones, yet the strength in her grip as her fingers clasped his. "Thank you," he said quietly. "It's a hopeless wish at best, but appreciated."

And then, in one of the more misguided moments of his life, he pulled her to him and kissed her exactly as he'd wanted to from the moment he'd first looked into her eyes.

She didn't pull away at first, probably from sheer surprise, and he had the satisfaction of feeling her parted lips soft and sweet under his, her breath mingling with his own, her mouth warm and receptive before she came to her senses and wrenched herself out of his grip.

"You really *are* a rogue," she said furiously, rubbing her hand over her mouth as if she could wipe away his touch. "I'm beginning to think you deserve everything coming to you." Her entire body trembled with indignation.

"I'm sorry," he said, not really meaning it. That kiss, as brief as it had been, was the sweetest he'd ever experienced. "I didn't mean to do that."

"Oh yes, you did," she said, her eyes sparking with anger. "It didn't happen just by accident, did it? And if you ever try such a thing again, I—I'll have my husband call you out, and you'll be very sorry." She picked up her shoes and stockings and marched off, her head held high, her back straight.

Aiden watched her disappear into the forest, her stride long and graceful, putting him in mind of an enraged nymph. An inexplicable longing burned in his chest. He felt as if life itself had just walked out of his grasp.

3

"Serafina, what is the matter with you?" Elspeth asked crossly when Serafina failed to answer her the second time in as many minutes. "You look as if you've seen a ghost, you're so pale. Nothing happened out there in the forest, did it?" she asked, her eyes suddenly narrowing. She shook out Serafina's Sunday dress and stood on tiptoe to reach Serafina's head.

Serafina was saved an immediate answer as the dress fell around her. "I suppose I'm just anxious about arriving," she said, emerging from the folds.

"And here you were telling me that you couldn't get to Townsend fast enough. You're too high-strung for your own good, dearie. I'd better give you a tonic to settle you down or Aubrey's going to think he's marrying a rattle."

"I don't need a tonic," Serafina said, adjusting her dress, her fingers shaking. "I just need a little time to prepare myself."

"Oh, three hours on your own wasn't enough for you?" Elspeth handed Serafina her good slippers. "Well, I hope at least you managed a little sleep. All right, Tinkerby, you may come out now."

Tinkerby came away from the other side of the carriage. "Very nice," he said, looking at Serafina approvingly. "But I think mayhaps you should pinch your cheeks. Nerves are making you pale."

"There, didn't I tell you?" Elspeth crowed. "Nerves. Just so, Tinkerby. Sometimes you can be uncommonly clever."

She dug in her bag and brought out a bottle and a spoon. "Open wide, dearie, and it's no good making a face. A little valerian root is just what you need. Very calming."

Serafina suffered the tonic, wishing nothing more than to be left alone. She'd rarely felt so shaken. She climbed into the carriage and stared out the window, trying to concentrate on her upcoming meeting with Aiden.

But she couldn't get the kiss or the man who'd bestowed it on her off her mind. When she'd come suddenly awake and seen him kneeling in front of her she truly thought she still must be dreaming. And yet he was far more real than any dream, so solid, all flesh and blood and magnificently shaped muscle and bone and height and breadth.

She felt horribly ashamed of herself. It was bad enough that she'd thought him beautiful, bad enough that she'd actually enjoyed his company. But that she had sunk so low as to enjoy his kiss—that was the worst, most appalling thing of all.

He was lucky she hadn't slapped him senseless, she thought rebelliously. She ought to have done. It would have given her immense satisfaction to see her handprint on his lean cheek, proper payment for having caught her by surprise and taken his advantage.

He was probably a master at seduction—he'd practically said so. She'd certainly unwittingly succumbed to his charms, not even knowing she was being seduced, silly girl that she was. In her own defense she hadn't been around men other than the vicar and Tinkerby in a very long time, so how was she to know how they went about such things?

This man had seemed perfectly pleasant, perfectly safe, not inclined to do anything dangerous or unsettling. He had even been helpfully informative, telling her everything she wished to know in a most satisfactory manner, confirming her highest hopes. He'd made lovemaking sound glorious, a true joining of heart and body, and it really had been most obliging of him to offer the information simply because she'd asked, and in such a straightforward fashion.

It was such a relief to finally know, and she would have been grateful to him if he just hadn't grabbed her at the last moment and—and kissed her like that.

But oh, how she had felt when the rogue's mouth had come down on hers, his fingers pressing lightly behind her ears, his body hard and strong against hers, the rapid beating of his heart matching the sudden pounding of her own. For one split second she'd been lost, ready to throw away everything, even her impending marriage, just to have more of him.

Abandonment was a sensation she'd never felt before, not even while dreaming. Dreams and reality were two entirely different things she'd just discovered, as different from remembering a beautiful song as to actually singing one. For a moment she'd felt as if the Dream had never existed, as if it were no more than a gossamer thread that had bound her hopes together for so long, something insubstantial, insignificant in the face of a real mouth on hers, a real body pressed against her own.

Serafina stared out the window, unable to enjoy the scenery, knowing she'd unwittingly betrayed the man she was about to marry. She tried to pull the Dream into her mind, tried to remember Aiden's face, the look of love on it, but she couldn't bring the image into focus. Instead, all that met her inward gaze was the rogue's glossy black hair, his brilliant blue eyes, the dark eyebrows slanted like a satyr's above them.

Oh, how appropriate, she thought angrily, wondering if satyrs also had such broad shoulders and sculpted cheekbones, such full, beautifully shaped mouths that knew how to touch in that tantalizing fashion.

Serafina put her head in her arms and shuddered in self-loathing. Eleven years of waiting for Aiden, never mind a number of lifetimes, all spoiled by thirty minutes in a forest with a complete stranger.

Townsend's front door was the most enormous door Serafina had ever seen. The sound of the knocker still echoed hollowly in her ear. "Oh, Auntie," she whispered, "I think I'm suddenly afraid." Her future lay behind that door, and she had no idea of what to expect now that she was actually faced with it.

"Nonsense, child," Elspeth said. "There's nothing to fear. Isn't this what we've planned for all this time?"

Serafina nodded and swallowed hard. "I know I'm being foolish."

"More valerian root for you, dearie," Elspeth said, patting her arm as the door creaked open. "Miss Elspeth Beaton and Miss Serafina Segrave to see Lord Aubrey," Elspeth intoned to the startled butler as if she were the queen of England herself.

The next thing she knew, Serafina found herself swept across a huge marble hallway in Elspeth's wake, led into a drawing room, and announced by the butler, who promptly disappeared.

She looked around nervously as if she might find Aiden hiding in a corner, but there was no one to be seen other than a beautiful blond woman who sat in a chair near one of the long windows, a rug over her lap, her dark blue dress high necked and long sleeved.

Her hands jerked in her lap as if she'd been taken by surprise, and the embroidery frame she was holding tumbled from them and fell to the floor. "Good evening," she said, ignoring it, her blue eyes fixed on Serafina in an expression Serafina could only interpret as horror.

"Good—good evening," Serafina stammered miserably, knowing what the woman must be thinking, and feeling uglier than she ever had. "I hope we haven't come at an inconvenient time. . . ."

"Not at all," the woman said, quickly hooding her eyes. "I am Lady Charlotte Delaware, Aubrey's sister. Forgive me for not rising, but I am crippled."

"Oh—oh, I'm so sorry!" Serafina said, startled. She walked quickly across the room and picked up the embroidery, handing it to Charlotte. "How very distressing for you."

" 'The bread of adversity, and the waters of affliction,' " Charlotte said coldly. "Isaiah thirty, twenty. Please do not waste your sympathy on the cross that the Good Lord in His wisdom has given me to bear."

"I beg your pardon," Serafina said, feeling as if she'd

just been slapped. "I didn't mean to offend you. I do hope we will be the best of friends," she said, kneeling by the chair and taking one of Charlotte's hands in her own.

Charlotte pulled her hand away. "That remains to be seen," she said. "And I am not a lap dog to be petted."

Stung, Serafina stood, swallowing hard. Lady Charlotte Delaware was obviously displeased with her in the extreme. A cold knot of fear took hold at the thought that her brother might have the same reaction. She stared down at the floor, wanting to drop directly through it.

Elspeth, who had been unusually silent, stepped forward. "Where is Aubrey?" she demanded and Serafina glanced up, wanting to know the very same thing.

Charlotte shifted her gaze past Serafina to Elspeth, and both her eyebrows raised high as she looked Elspeth up and down. "I'm afraid my brother was called away on business at the last minute. He asked me to convey his regrets."

"Oh, I see," Serafina said, not sure if she was disappointed or relieved. Her confidence was already badly shaken, and she wasn't sure if she could bear for Aiden to look at her with the same measure of disgust. "Well, I'm sure his business must be very important."

"Naturally," Charlotte said, her voice dripping with frost.

"Then where, may I ask, is Delaware?" Elspeth said, hands planted on her hips. "I find this a very odd greeting for the woman about to become the new countess of Aubrey."

Serafina wanted to curl up into a ball, since she didn't think Charlotte needed any reminding of a topic she obviously found distasteful. "Perhaps he has also been called away on business?" she said tactfully.

Charlotte's chilly gaze returned to Serafina. "Actually, Miss Segrave, my father is in his bedchamber. He is indisposed this evening, as he often is."

"Oh, how unfortunate," Serafina said, thinking that the Delaware family seemed to suffer from ill health. She hoped Aiden was not similarly inclined. "I hope he will recover soon. Perhaps we could make him a posset or an unguent. My aunt is very skilled with herbs."

Charlotte ignored her. "I ordered dinner trays for you both upstairs on the assumption that you would be exhausted from traveling."

"As it happens, a light supper of cheese, bread, and fruit will suit us perfectly," Elspeth said with one dismissive nod of her head. "Come along, Serafina, it has been a long day." She took her firmly by the arm and guided her toward the door. "I am sure a footman will conduct us to our quarters. I expect we will see you, Lady Charlotte, in the morning."

"I have gone to a great deal of trouble over arranging my brother's wedding. I am certainly not planning on missing it." Charlotte bent her head back to her embroidery as if they'd already left the room.

Serafina trailed after her aunt through the Great Hall, her head twisting and turning in every direction as she took in the specifics of her new home. The exterior had been imposing enough, the great house standing on a terrace above a river, surrounded by gardens, woodlands bordering vast lawns on both sides of the drive.

The house itself, a huge square structure of yellow stone fronted by long rectangular windows on all three stories, was magnificent, but Serafina's gaze had automatically fallen on the gardens, which obviously at one time had been carefully tended, but now struck her as unkempt.

Great stretches of daffodils and narcissus ran over the lawns, a beautiful display of yellow and white that needed no care, yet the lawns themselves, save for a small stretch in front of the house, were unmown.

Well, she was happy enough to see to the care of the lawns and gardens herself. It would give her something to do, and she was used to outdoor work. The interior of the house presented a complete contrast, however. Adorned with beautiful antiques, it reflected loving attention to every detail. The furniture glistened with constant applications of beeswax, the marble floors shone with constant scrubbing, every portrait, and there were hundreds adorning nearly every inch of wall, hung precisely straight.

And yet there was a subtle air of shabbiness that Serafina couldn't put her finger on, other than that draperies hung frayed, the silk shredding from the touch of the sun, and rugs appeared worn.

She frowned as she followed her aunt up the imposing central staircase. Even the footman who led them up looked correct but beaten down. He was tired, she decided, as if he had too many duties to perform and not enough time to perform them in. Not that Serafina knew anything about footmen, or at least what she had known about them from Bowhill she'd mostly forgotten, but she did know something about human nature, having worked at her aunt's side among the villagers and tenants of Clwydd, administering to them when they were ill, encouraging them in times of trouble.

Townsend was embroiled in times of trouble, she was certain of that. But she had no idea what was behind it.

Even the chambermaid who brought up their supper looked exhausted, dark circles under her eyes. She barely spoke; she certainly didn't smile, even when Serafina politely thanked her. She merely ducked her head, gave a swift curtsy, and fled like a dog who was afraid of being kicked.

"Auntie," Serafina said, tentatively approaching the subject as soon as she'd finished eating, "do you think there's something a little odd about Townsend?"

"I can't think what you mean," Elspeth answered through a mouthful of apple. "If you're worried about Aubrey not being here, don't trouble yourself. It's perfectly proper for him to keep his distance on the eve of your wedding. He's obviously respectful of good luck, dearie." She reached behind her to where Basil sat on the back of her chair and handed him a chunk of fruit.

"Oh," Serafina said, watching Basil throw it on the floor. It was the first time she'd heard of that particular custom, but she supposed her aunt knew better than she did about these matters. "But what about his sister? She behaved as if she couldn't be rid of us fast enough."

"That one's nurturing a viper in her bosom," Elspeth said, scowling darkly. "But never mind Charlotte. We'll deal with her when the time comes. I have other matters to talk to you about, dearie, and it's time I addressed them."

"Oh?" Serafina asked, coloring hotly against her will. She had a sinking feeling that she knew what was coming, and after the unsettling events of the afternoon, she could only hope her aunt would divine her blush as simple nerves.

"Now, my dear, normally your mother would be giving you this little talk, but as she's not here, it is my job to do it in her place. You know, of course, that tomorrow night Aubrey will sleep in your bed with you."

Serafina turned two shades redder, her ears beginning to burn, not with embarrassment, but with shame. How could she tell her aunt that she'd already had it all explained to her, and that even worse, she knew exactly how it felt to be held in a man's arms?

"Serafina? Are you attending me, child? This is no time to go off into a daydream. I thought you were breathless for information."

"Yes, I'm listening," Serafina choked, wishing she'd never laid eyes on the rogue.

"Good. There's nothing worse to my way of thinking than having a girl go uninformed to her marriage bed, but it doesn't do to inform her before the fact." Elspeth peeled another piece of apple. "So, to begin. I'm not to know how much you understand and how much you don't, but if you've seen the livestock going about nature's business, the mechanics of the act aren't all that different for humans." Elspeth chewed thoughtfully, looking off into the distance. "I suppose that it's simply a matter of refinement," she eventually said.

"Refinement?" Serafina repeated, for lack of anything better to say. She burned with mortification, thinking that refinement had absolutely nothing to do with it. She was obviously no better than an animal in the barnyard, given her physical reaction to a man she didn't even like, let alone love.

"Indeed. You see, my child, when a man comes to a woman, his body goes from a state of sleeping to complete wakefulness."

This statement caused Serafina's gaze to lift to her aunt's in fascination, hoping she was going to fill out the pieces of the puzzle the rogue had left unstated. "What do you mean, Auntie?"

"Well, you must understand that a man's private part changes when he's aroused. It grows hard and stiff in readiness, not unlike a flagpole. Do you understand?"

Serafina stared at her. A flagpole? The rogue hadn't said a thing about a flagpole, and Serafina found the image alarming in the extreme.

"Excellent," Elspeth said with satisfaction. "So now you have a man in a state of full arousal, his sexual organ ready to enter your body."

Serafina nervously touched the tip of her tongue to her upper lip. The rogue had mentioned the part about joining bodies, but he'd made the whole thing sound so pleasant, so enjoyable, male coming to female in a perfectly harmless way. What Elspeth was telling her didn't sound the least bit harmless.

"But Auntie, how does this happen exactly?" she asked desperately. "I can't imagine being impaled by a flagpole—it must be the most awful thing!"

To her surprise, Elspeth crowed with laughter, slapping her knees. "Oh, my dear child," she said, wiping her eyes on her napkin, "it's no different than putting a cork into a bottle."

Serafina gazed at her aunt suspiciously, wondering if maybe the lecture was another one of Elspeth's flights of fancy. She'd never been married after all, so how was she to know? "Not all corks fit into all bottles," she said nervously.

"Oh, it will fit all right, although it will probably hurt. But that's only because of your maidenhead, and one quick thrust puts an end to that. It's a bloody process, but virgin blood is a sacred sacrifice, so you should be pleased about it."

Serafina's mouth dropped open in horror. *Blood*? First Aiden was going to pierce her with a part of himself that resembled a flagpole, and then he was going to draw her blood? Her hands gripped her skirts, sweat beading her palms. "You're sure about all of this?" she said faintly.

"Naturally I'm sure. Really, Serafina, how do you think babies are born? What comes out has to be put in, and there's only one way to go about it." She hopped to her feet. "So now that we have that straight, it's time for you to go to bed. You have a big day ahead of you tomorrow."

Serafina mutely nodded.

"You're a good girl, and I know you'll be a fine, willing wife," Elspeth said, giving her mouth one last wipe.

She picked Basil up off the chair, parking him on her shoulder where he proceeded to twirl her earlobe with a little croon. "And don't you worry about tomorrow night," Elspeth said, swatting him away. "Aubrey will know exactly how to go about things. You'll become accustomed in no time at all."

She vanished through the door.

Serafina sank onto the bed and covered her face with her hands. As much as she loved him, marriage to Aiden looked less appealing by the moment.

Aiden lifted his mug of ale and took a long swallow. "I swear to God, Rafe, there she was, straight out of a book of fairy tales. If I didn't know any better, I'd think she'd lived in the forest all her life, drinking dew from buttercups."

"*Buttercups*?" the Duke of Southwell said in disbelief. "You, my friend, have windmills in your head." He regarded his cousin with amusement. "But I suppose it's your right to be as addled brained as you please tonight."

"She had a little crown of flowers on her head," Aiden

continued dreamily. "And bare feet. And a simple little dress the color of ripe apricots."

"A rare beauty, obviously." Raphael crossed one leg over the other and rested his cheek on his fist. "An Artemis, complete with fawns prancing and rabbits hopping about her feet, I suppose."

"No—no. Nothing like that." He frowned, wondering how to describe her. "She's not beautiful in the classic sense, with perfectly ordered, chiseled features. She's . . . unusual looking. Delicate. Soft." He realized he was babbling, but he couldn't help himself. "She's . . . striking," he said, sitting up straighter, his palms pressed together. "Striking in the way that takes your breath away, as if you've just come around a corner and unexpectedly stumbled across a field of brilliant flowers, wild and—and unordered, just as nature designed them. Do you see what I mean?"

Raphael grinned. "She's a departure from your usual cultured rose garden?"

"That's it exactly," Aiden said, delighted that Rafe had grasped the point so quickly. "You can't help looking at her and seeing sunshine. And innocence. My God, I've never come across such an unaffected woman in all my life."

He paused, remembering her shy smile, the way her sea-green eyes had regarded him steadily as he dodged his way through a hazy explanation of lovemaking, and later, the way she regarded him with profound pity when he told her that he didn't believe in true love or fairy tales either. He hoped to God that her chosen husband wouldn't hurt her too badly, disillusion her too swiftly, that he would at least be careful with her. Jealousy coursed through his veins at the thought of the man she was going to marry, lucky bastard. And for one wistful, absurd moment, he wished it could have been him.

"Now what's running through your convoluted brain? You look a hundred miles away," Raphael said.

"Rafe, you live on the other side of the forest," Aiden

said. "You haven't ever run across a dark-haired nymph in your wanderings, have you?"

"Oh, dear God. What am I going to do with you?"

"Order another round of ale, I think." Aiden sighed. "I asked the innkeeper if he'd ever seen anyone of her description, but he came up blank, said there was no one who looked anything like that and he's lived here all his life. I'm beginning to think I imagined the entire thing."

Raphael raised an eyebrow. "It's not out of the realm of possibility, although I've never known you to be prone to hallucinations. Still, it is the eve of your wedding, and you haven't been yourself since your father delivered the grim news. Which reminds me—I'm delighted to have bumped into you entirely by accident, but surely Miss Segrave must have arrived at Townsend by now?"

Aiden shuddered. "Don't remind me. That witch is probably touring her new home as we speak, making a mental appraisal of everything in it."

"Tell me. How is Charlotte taking your approaching nuptials? I haven't had a chance to visit her in the last fortnight to find out for myself."

"Oh, you know Lottie. She's a saint. She can't be pleased about my marriage, naturally, and she's concerned for me, but she's doing her best to be stalwart." He fell silent while Raphael called the barmaid over.

"What may I bring your grace?" Betsy said, dipping a curtsy and flashing Aiden an inviting smile as Rafe ordered two more mugs of ale.

Aiden looked away. Betsy was a pretty girl, and a few years ago he'd enjoyed a night in her bed, but he was in no mood for tumbling barmaids tonight, especially when he had the image of a fairy queen burning in his brain. He really was beginning to question his sanity.

There wasn't another village for miles and miles around, and young women didn't just disappear into nowhere, especially when they had nothing but their feet for transport. She'd have to have walked for hours to arrive anywhere but here in Dundle, and it was a small village where everyone knew everyone else. She was a mystery to be sure.

"Charlotte will manage," Rafe said, leaning back in his chair. "It's a damned shame that she hasn't any hope of a marriage for herself. She doesn't even have a life outside the house with the exception of attending church on Sundays, as much as I've tried to persuade her to get out and about, do a little socializing. Her wheelchair is easy enough to transport, but she insists that she's happier at home."

"You know how Lottie feels about her condition," Aiden said, ignoring the display of bosom being offered to him as Betsy returned and plunked down the mugs. "She doesn't like people to feel sorry for her, and I can't say I blame her." He raked his hands through his hair. "I shouldn't have left her alone tonight, but I swear, I couldn't stomach the thought of dealing with the scheming Miss Serafina Segrave or her equally scheming aunt. I have a lifetime ahead of me for that."

"Don't worry, Charlotte will manage. She'll fix Miss Segrave and her aunt with one of the stern looks she gives a misbehaving parlormaid, then read them a passage from the Bible about the consequences of avarice."

"Very funny," Aiden said, staring down into his mug.

"I'm perfectly serious," Raphael replied. "You know what your sister is with her lectures on morality. Godliness is above cleanliness, or something like that."

"Nothing is above cleanliness in Lottie's eyes," Aiden said with a short laugh. "I live in fear of tracking in a speck of mud onto her polished floors. I can't tell you how I relished being away the last three years, able to throw my boots where and how I pleased with no one to scold me like a child in leading strings."

"Ah, well, she means no harm by her lectures," Rafe said. "Charlotte really hasn't anything else to do with her time, poor girl. Maybe now she can bend her attention to reforming your wicked wife, and that just might distract her from trying to reform us."

Aiden grinned. "That would make a welcome change, wouldn't it? Lottie would have made a brilliant mother superior. 'Mother Charlotte, the scourge of God.'" His smile faded. "But it's unkind of me to poke fun at her. You and I are nearly all Lottie has in this world, and I should be more tolerant of her idiosyncrasies."

"As should I," Rafe said, rubbing an eyebrow. "I confess, sometimes I grow impatient with her, and I shouldn't. She's lonely and she has no one else for company, save for the vicar and his unfortunate wife." His mouth twitched at the corner. "Speaking of which, how does Reverend Liddle feel about your bringing in a bishop to marry you?"

"Not displeased, actually. I think he secretly believes it will be a good political connection, pompous fool. Lottie's over the moon, naturally, since she expects suitably lofty conversation at the wedding breakfast." He grimaced. "As much as Lottie might loathe the idea of the marriage, she's determined that the proceedings be flawless, appropriately respectful of both the Church and a future marquess. Hence the bishop. I'm lucky it wasn't the bloody archbishop, but fortunately, due to such short notice, he was previously engaged."

Raphael burst into laughter. "Oh, dear. Trust Charlotte to give it her best effort, though. If I'm ever unfortunate enough to find myself facing marriage, remind me to be sure that your sister has nothing to do with the arrangements."

"You can marry when and whom you please, your magnificence, with no one to interfere. If you choose to be married in a barn, all you have to do is wave one imperious ducal finger and not a murmur will be heard. I only hope that you will marry someone you actually have a small degree of fondness for," he said glumly.

"It's not my marriage we're facing at the moment, it's yours. And as much as I don't envy you the situation, Aiden, it's no good getting yourself worked into such a state."

Aiden just groaned, and Raphael slung a reassuring

arm around his shoulder. "I wish I could be of more help to you. I have to confess to surprise that I wasn't able to discover anything about Miss Segrave from my sources in London."

"That," said Aiden succinctly, "is because she hasn't been to London."

"But why?" Rafe asked with considerable surprise. "She's an heiress, after all, and most young girls of marriageable age make their come-out, eligible heiresses especially."

"As for that, I spoke briefly with her cousin Edmund Segrave when I was in town. He informed me that the one time they'd met he found her the most hideous child he'd ever laid his eyes on and, furthermore, she was a nasty little sneak, which confirmed everything my father told me about her."

Aiden blew out a long breath. "It was Segrave's opinion that her aunt whisked her away to Wales and kept her hidden there so as not to offend the eyes of society. And you wonder why I'm in a state of despair. Oh, *God*, I think I'm going to be sick."

"Drink your ale, and tell me more about your mysterious wood nymph. Maybe that will take your mind off your troubles. . . ."

4

$\mathcal{S}$erafina rose the next morning, troubled, her eyes scratchy from only three hours of sleep. She'd spent much of the night tossing and turning, trying to reconcile herself to the marital act according to Elspeth.

She fervently prayed that her aunt didn't have the vaguest idea of what she was talking about, and yet Serafina found it difficult to dismiss her aunt's words—Elspeth was well versed in matters of a physical nature, often doctoring the villagers, and Serafina had not once seen her falter.

She swallowed hard, the knot in her chest tightening as she thought of what the coming night had to hold. Obviously god and goddess had bestowed the ability to receive the pleasures of kissing on women so that they could endure what transpired after.

It was no wonder a veil had been drawn over her eyes in the Dream as to what followed, for if she'd been able to see that, she'd probably have taken the next boat to France.

She went to the window and threw it open, thirstily drinking in the fresh air, sweetly scented with the wisteria vine that grew outside. It was a beautiful day, the sun shining brightly, not a cloud in the sky, a perfect day for a wedding.

The Delaware family chapel sat on a little knoll, a pretty fifteenth-century building with stained-glass windows and a square bell tower. That particular stretch of lawn had been mown and the path trimmed in preparation for the wedding, a sharp contrast to the rest of the landscape.

She leaned her elbows on the sill, wondering where Aiden

was and what he was doing. In only two hours she'd be facing him at the altar, speaking her marriage vows.

And she felt unworthy.

Here she was, already dreading the night ahead, terrified that he would hurt her, that he would do all the awful things Elspeth had described.

The rogue had said it was nice, that she'd like it, but she couldn't imagine liking being helplessly torn asunder, bleeding like a poor, stuck pig. The rogue hadn't said a thing about blood. And he hadn't said a thing about pain. When it came right down to it, he'd lied to her—no real surprise. He probably lied to all the innocent women he seduced.

That didn't help her with the crippling fear that had taken hold of her. She could only hope that love would carry her through, that Aiden, being the dear, principled man that he was, would make everything all right, wouldn't hurt her too terribly.

She closed her eyes and brought his golden image to mind, tried hard to remember how she had felt in the Dream when he whispered sweet promises to her of sealing his vow. The problem was that it all looked different to her now, not something to be looked forward to, but to be dreaded.

"Oh, goddess, help me," she whispered desperately, wiping away a film of tears from her eyes. "Give me strength in my hour of need. I love Aiden, truly I do, and I want to give myself to him, but I'm very frightened."

A light scratch came at the door and Serafina jumped. But it was just two chambermaids who entered with a large brass tub, followed by two more chambermaids carrying pails of steaming water. They first lit the fire, then filled the bath and disappeared as swiftly and silently as they'd entered with the exception of one, a plump girl of about Serafina's age.

Serafina instantly took a liking to her, for she had a sweet, open face, little shoe-button eyes, and a simple manner about her.

"Your bath, miss," she said, bobbing a curtsy. "I'm Janie, and her ladyship instructed me to assist you. I'm not a lady's maid, miss, just an ordinary housemaid, and I'm brand new here, but I'll do my best for you. Your aunt ordered the bath for you and said to tell you as she'll be coming in a moment, and you're not to get into the tub until she does."

She gave Serafina a look of undisguised curiosity, then vanished as swiftly as the others had, softly closing the door behind her.

Serafina hadn't been in a hip bath since leaving Bowhill, bathing instead in the cavernous underground baths at Clwydd fed by a hot spring. The tub looked awfully cramped to her, but she was nevertheless happy for it. She might as well go clean to Aiden, even if she was scared out of her wits.

"Ah, good morning, dearest," Elspeth chirped, coming into the room with a large mahogany box that Serafina knew contained her aunt's oils and herbs. "Come along, Janie," she called over her shoulder. "Bring in the chest."

Janie reappeared, this time pulling along the mysterious trunk that had come from Clwydd. "Here you are, miss," she said, placing it in the middle of the room and lingering over it, clearly longing to see what was inside every bit as much as Serafina did.

Serafina shot her a bewildered smile and shrugged her shoulders, and to Serafina's delight Janie actually smiled in return, her rosy cheeks plumping up like two apples in her round face.

"The dress your mother wore for her own wedding," Elspeth said, rummaging in her box. "It's my little surprise for you. Do open the chest and have a look—I've altered the dress slightly to make it more stylish, even though you're the same size as your mother was. There are underthings and shoes and gloves, and the family veil to go with it all."

"Oh, Auntie!" Serafina exclaimed, a flood of infinite relief washing over her. She'd thought she'd have to wear her Sunday dress, for each time she'd asked her aunt about a wedding dress, Aunt Elspeth had only said, "We'll make do with what we have, dear, we'll make do."

Janie helped her undo the clasps on the trunk, both of them as excited as children unwrapping a present.

"Oh, miss," Janie breathed, pulling out a white and silver embroidered dress with a panel of lace that ran down the front, a fashionably high waist, and small puffed sleeves. She shook it out and held it up.

Serafina had never seen anything so beautiful in all her life. She lovingly ran her fingers over the soft batiste material, then hugged it to her chest.

"Look, miss, look!" Janie dove into the trunk again and produced a long veil of ivory Belgian lace, worked in a pattern of flowers. "Isn't it just the finest thing you ever did lay your eyes on?"

Serafina admired it, sighing with happiness. "Thank you, Auntie," she said softly. "It's a wonderful present."

"Nonsense, child, it's yours by right. I've been waiting for this moment for a good long time. Now be off with you, Janie, and see to the flowers I picked this morning," Elspeth said, waving a bony hand in dismissal. "I'll look after Miss Serafina. Oh, and don't forget to leave the tray I asked for outside the door. We're not to be disturbed for any reason."

"Yes, miss," Janie said, casting one last admiring look at the dress she'd laid out on the bed. "You just ring if you need me."

Elspeth beckoned Serafina over to the bath, which now smelled deliciously of various herbs. "Now, my child. It is time for your purification. Put yourself in the proper respectful frame of mind, and once you have, in you hop, and be mindful to keep your eyes closed no matter what," she said, lighting two candles that she'd placed on the floor at both ends of the tub. Then she took her censer and lit that too, and the rich, smoky smell of frankincense filled the air.

Accustomed to her aunt's fondness for rituals, Serafina wasn't surprised that she'd come up with one for a wedding. There seemed to be one for every season of the year, as well as various events in between. Why should this be any different?

She removed her dressing gown and night rail, and after taking a moment to still her thoughts as her aunt had taught her, she stepped into the warm water, slipping down as low as she could go in the confined space. She dutifully closed her eyes, as Aunt Elspeth always told her to do when she was invoking a rite.

Serafina was never sure why that was so important, but she did as she was told, not wanting to disappoint her aunt, who probably had some wonderful fantasy about her beloved deities appearing and thought them not appropriate for Serafina's eyes. She never let Serafina attend any of the coven rites, either, but Serafina had no complaints. She was perfectly happy honoring god and goddess in her own way and steering well away from the magic and potions and spells that Elspeth was so fond of.

But Serafina didn't mind indulging Elspeth in those either. Her aunt had few enough pleasures, and magic was her all-consuming passion.

She let her mind drift while Elspeth cast her circle of stones around the tub, then began the usual incantation:

> "May the powers of the one
> The source of all creation;
> all pervasive, omnipotent, eternal;
> may the goddess,
> The lady of the moon
> and the god, horned hunter of the sun;
> may the powers of the spirits of the stones,
> rulers of the elemental realms;
> may the powers of the stars above and the
> Earth below,
> bless this place, and this time, and I who am
> with you."

She droned on and on in her usual fashion, calling on the god and goddess in different prayers, and Serafina listened for a short time, but eventually drifted off, lulled by the warm water and the sweet scents that emanated from it.

She floated, her thoughts aimlessly wandering in and out of the babble her aunt's words had become. A lovely golden haze surrounded her, shimmering and shifting, and then pinpricks of lights pierced through the glow, growing in brightness until Serafina realized they were torches, burning in a magnificent church crowned by arches, the stone walls covered with paintings of saints.

People filled the church, dressed in elaborate, richly colored costumes. Before her stood an altar, a priest in front of it, his robes encrusted with gold, his beard dark and long, a bishop's mitre on his head. He looked achingly familiar to her, and yet she didn't know him.

His arms were raised above him and his words at first sounded like nonsense. But then somehow she knew that they were Greek and she was listening to a marriage ceremony. Her own marriage ceremony.

With a dreamy sense of surprise she realized that Adam stood next to her, her hand held firmly in his. She felt the beating of his pulse through his warm skin, the reassuring pressure of his fingers on hers, heard him speak the marriage vows, his voice strong and certain.

She turned to look at him and he smiled down at her, his dark eyes shining with love, and Serafina knew that all was right with the world and she was where she truly belonged. . . .

"Serafina? Child?"

She started as her aunt's voice penetrated through her haze and the picture rippled and distorted, as she came fully awake. She brought her hands to her forehead, not sure of where she was for a moment. "I—I'm sorry, Auntie. I must have been dreaming," she said, still disoriented. The images had been so clear, as real as the room in front of her now.

"Come child, we're finished here. Out you get. It's time for you to dress."

Serafina stepped out of the bath, letting her aunt wrap her in a towel, feeling strangely weak and light-headed.

Elspeth said very little as she helped Serafina into her clothes, and she said very little as she brought the tray in and prompted Serafina to eat.

Serafina was grateful for the silence. She felt as if she were still in a dream state, hovering between that other world and this one, caught in a nebulous web of time, not one place or the other.

But somehow she knew that the two places were directly connected, that she went to her marriage to Aiden today as she had gone to him in that long-ago time. She was sure of it, as sure as she'd been of the other dream that she'd had for so many years, and the knowledge filled her with a peace and sense of security.

All of her doubts and fears vanished as if they'd never been, leaving her with a simple happiness, as if she'd been washed clean of doubt, of hesitation.

She said a silent prayer of thanks to the god and goddess for having touched her briefly with their wisdom, given her their blessing for her marriage. *Time will run back and fetch the age of gold. . . .*

Elspeth arranged the veil on Serafina's head, pinning it in place with a wreath of roses mixed with lily of the valley and baby's breath. "So, my child," she said when she was satisfied. "Look. Look upon yourself and be glad for Aiden."

She turned Serafina to face the looking glass, and Serafina inhaled sharply when she saw her reflection. Surely this woman could not be she?

She appeared a stranger to herself, the dress clinging to her form as if it had been made for her alone, the veil falling softly over her shoulders, trailing nearly to the floor. Her hair coiled neatly beneath at her nape, dark against the ivory lace. Her eyes, wide and smoky, gazed back at her bright with happiness, filled with wonder.

She turned from the mirror. "Oh, Auntie—I actually think I might be pretty today. Do you think so?" she asked anxiously.

"Pretty?" her aunt said, pursing her lips. "No. I don't think I'd call you that."

"Oh." Serafina looked away, crushed. "I suppose it was too much to hope for."

"Don't be absurd. Today, dearie, you remind me of your mother on her wedding day. She looked as you do now, full of happy expectation."

Serafina considered. Well, looking full of happy expectation wasn't so bad. At least she didn't look thoroughly offensive.

"I was one of her bridesmaids, you know; this dress I am wearing now is the very same I wore then."

"It's lovely," Serafina said, smiling. Elspeth's white gown was better suited to a girl of eighteen than a scraggly old woman. But she wouldn't hurt her aunt's feelings for the world by telling her that. "Auntie . . . I've always wondered. Why did you never marry?"

Elspeth snorted. "Marry? Whatever for? I had everything I needed, including Clwydd from my mother, thanks to the inheritance laws in Wales. There was nothing a man could add to that as far as I was concerned." Her face softened. "Marriage has never been my way, child. I'm better suited to other aspects of life."

Serafina bit her lip, wondering anew about the experience she'd just had. "Just now when I was in the bath, Auntie, I had the most extraordinary dream," she said tentatively. "I saw something that seemed so real, so right—"

"Hot water has always addled your brains, my girl," Elspeth said, interrupting her. "But never mind that. The hour grows late and we have a wedding to attend." She placed Serafina's posy of flowers in her hands. "You don't want to keep Aubrey waiting, do you?"

And then she pressed a rare kiss on Serafina's cheek. "You've made me very proud," she said gently. "Come now. It's time."

Elspeth preceded Serafina down the stairs, her outdated dress flapping around her ankles as she went. Serafina paused on the middle landing of the massive central staircase to adjust her gloves and was surprised to hear her aunt's voice float up to her from the great hall. She knew that tone of rebuke well, although she didn't often hear it.

"So, Delaware. You finally decided to show your face. I assume your son has done the same?"

"Aubrey returned late last night," Lord Delaware said, clearing his throat. "But that's why I wanted to speak to you, Miss Beaton. I—er . . . I think I owe you a word of explanation as to what to expect."

"Whatever you have to say can wait until after the ceremony," Elspeth said testily.

"But this is important," the marquess persisted. "Aubrey is perhaps not as—that is, he's not exactly . . . Well." He cleared his throat again.

"What do you mean, he's not well?" Elspeth hissed. "Are you telling me he's taken a chill?"

"Yes, that's it exactly," Lord Delaware said in a tone of relief. "He's taken a chill. A severe chill."

Serafina's heart nearly stopped at the thought that Aiden might have succumbed to the family tendency of poor health. "Oh, no!" she exclaimed, running down the last few stairs. "Lord Delaware, is it serious? Have you sent for the doctor?"

He abruptly turned, and another shock wave ran through Serafina as she took in his appearance, nothing like the hearty man she remembered from long ago. His complexion was a chalky gray, with the exception of a very red nose, and Serafina thought that maybe he'd been weeping. She stifled her alarm, wondering if it wasn't fear for his son's life that gave him such distress.

"Good God," he said, staring at her. "Good God. *You* are Serafina?" He slowly rubbed one hand over the back of his head as if he'd never seen her before.

"Yes, my lord," she said, moving toward him, hoping she didn't prove too much of a disappointment. "It is I, Serafina. But tell me, what of Aiden?"

"What of Aiden?" he asked, sounding bewildered. "Why, nothing at all."

"But—but you said he was ill?" she stammered, now thoroughly confused, although relieved.

"Ill? Aiden? Aiden has always enjoyed perfect health." An unexpected smile broke out on his face. "My goodness. Won't he be surprised to see you. Yes, indeed."

"I don't think he'll be too surprised," she said, entertaining the unfortunate possibility that it was not Lord Delaware's body that was ill, but his mind. "I believe he's expecting me," she said. "In the chapel."

"Yes, in the chapel," he said, still looking dazed.

Serafina nodded reassuringly. "That's right. For the wedding," she said, prompting him.

"Yes, for the wedding," he answered, clapping his hands together. "Isn't it marvelous?" And then his smile suddenly faded, replaced by a worried frown. "But we had better hurry, my dear. For all I know Aiden's vanished into thin air. He looked as if he might disappear at any moment."

"I'm sure." Serafina's heart broke for the poor man. She couldn't imagine how awful it would be not to be able to hold one's thoughts together from one minute to the next. "Do let's hurry," she said, taking his arm before he could forget where he was going. "It's only a short walk, isn't it?"

"Only a short walk," he agreed, nodding fervently. "Thank God for that, eh? Oh, and speaking of walking, perhaps you'll allow me to walk you down the aisle? Aiden might look on me more kindly when he sees what I've brought him."

"Out of the question," Elspeth snapped, before Serafina had a chance to answer this last muddled comment. "You can't give the bride away to your own son; that would smack of greed. Oh, dear, I hadn't thought of this aspect. We can't have Serafina give herself away, can we?"

"Why can't Tinkerby give me away?" Serafina supplied helpfully, not wanting to confuse Lord Delaware any further. He was already confused enough that he was bringing his son a bride. "I know he'll be there. He said he wouldn't miss the ceremony for anything."

"Tinkerby?" Elspeth said thoughtfully. "Well and why not? It's not as if he hasn't acted as a father to you for all these years. Not like some," she added, scowling darkly at Lord Delaware.

"Er, who is this Mr. Tinkerby?" Lord Delaware asked. "Have I met him? I can't seem to recall . . ."

"I don't see how you could have when you were in bed when we arrived," Elspeth said, a wicked gleam in her eye. "Yes, I think Tinkerby will do beautifully. I'd do the job myself, but I had my heart set on being a bridesmaid."

"Oh . . ." Serafina said, trying not to think of what Aiden was going to make of a seventy-three–year–old bridesmaid traipsing up the aisle. "Well, as you wish, Auntie," she said valiantly.

"And it's not as if your father didn't give you away years ago," Elspeth said. "I'm sure he wouldn't mind Tinkerby standing in for him."

"Quite right, quite right," Lord Delaware agreed. "Well, as Aesop said, 'the gods help them that help themselves.' I'll see you in the chapel." He tore across the hall, the door slamming after him.

"No one could possibly accuse you of not helping yourself," Elspeth remarked caustically.

And on that last pronouncement, which left Serafina feeling as if she'd either lost her mind or had walked into someone else's madhouse, her aunt took her by the elbow and shepherded her out of the house and toward the chapel.

Aiden paced the chapel's side room, seriously entertaining the notion of taking the next packet to China. But duty kept his feet glued to the floor—duty and Raphael's firm hand on his shoulder.

"Sorry, Cousin, but I indulged you last night while you cried into your ale. Today it is my gloomy responsibility to see you married. No bolting, no last minute reprieves."

Aiden stared down at the cold stone floor, his hands shoved low on his hips. "If you love me, shoot me now," he muttered. "Better yet, if you really love me, *you* marry the cow."

"Thanks for offering, but I think I'll decline. In any case, I'm not the one who needs her money."

Aiden glanced up at him. "No, you have more than enough of your own and no father to go throwing it away for you. It's a hard, cruel fate, Rafe, to be brought to this. Have you considered the horrors of the act I'll be forced to perform tonight?"

"You were more than eloquent on the subject last night. I believe I have a clear picture. My advice to you is to drink a decanter of brandy, do what you have to, and pass out." Raphael poked his head out the door. "Your father's finally arrived, but still no sign of the bride."

Aiden groaned. "Soon enough. Just shove me out there

when the time comes, will you? I don't think I have the courage to go of my own accord."

"Are you sure you wouldn't like a blindfold?" Raphael asked with a chuckle. "It might help to get you through the ceremony."

"The only thing that's going to get me through this ceremony is if the bride drops dead at the door. Which will also help me get through the rest of my ill-begotten life."

"Come along, Aiden, buck up, there's a good lad. It will all be over before you know it, just like getting a tooth pulled."

"What would you know about it? You've never had a tooth pulled from your head in your life," Aiden retorted.

"Yes I have, when I was six. My governess tied my remaining front tooth up with a string, tied the string to the doorknob, then slammed the door hard. I howled my head off, more from shock than pain." He grinned. "It wasn't even loose, but she wanted me to have a matching smile."

Aiden stared at him. "You can't be serious."

"Well, maybe it was just a touch loose. The problem was that the first tooth came in right away and there wasn't a damned thing she could do about the other one."

"And you are a filthy liar," Aiden said. "You expect me to believe that?"

"Maybe not. But the story took your mind off your troubles for a moment, didn't it?"

Aiden slugged Rafe's shoulders. "You are truly a sorry excuse for a friend."

"And you are a sorry excuse for a bridegroom," Rafe retorted. "But listen—I think the bride has arrived. The music has started."

Aiden leaned his head against the wall and covered it with his arms, wishing he were ten thousand miles away. Rafe took him by the shoulder and forcibly pushed him through the door, Aiden feeling as if every step brought him closer to his doom.

He took his place at the altar and steeled himself to glance down the length of the nave, attempting to meet disaster in the face and wondering just how awful it was going to look.

He nearly fell over. A little woman well into her seventies pranced toward him in a white gown, a big toothy smile on her wrinkled face. Aiden blinked in disbelief. Even his father wouldn't be so cruel as to send him an ancient bride. Would he?

And then he realized his mistake as he caught a movement behind her. Another woman, a young woman this time, thank God, walked up the aisle, an elderly man at her side. She was dressed in a cloud of white and silver, a wreath of roses and lily of the valley on her head, but her face was cast in shadow and he could make out nothing of her features. And then she stepped forward into a shaft of sunlight that streamed through one of the windows, illuminating her face.

"Oh, dear God," he whispered, his hand slowly lifting to his chest in shock. "Oh, dear God."

For what he was looking on was not a gorgon, but the mysterious fairy queen he'd never thought to see again.

5

$\mathscr{S}$erafina's heart beat so fast in her throat that she thought it might choke her as she walked through the heavy wood door of the little stone chapel. Here she was finally, about to meet Aiden, to become his wife, fulfilling the sacred vow they'd made to each other in that time long ago.

It took a few moments for her eyes to adjust to the dim interior light, and she strained to see. There were not many people in the chapel, but she passed over their vague forms, looking toward the altar alight with candles.

She could barely make out a thing other than a man who appeared to be a bishop, judging by the mitre on his head and the long, white, gold-encrusted robes that he wore. For a brief moment the sight transported her back into that other place. But the bishop had no beard, she realized with a surge of disappointment as her eyes slowly adjusted. And he stood alone. Aiden was nowhere in sight.

Tinkerby, who despite his fervent protestations had been summarily summoned from his back pew by Elspeth to do his duty, nervously touched her shoulder. "Are you ready, miss?" he asked gently, and Serafina managed to nod, thinking her legs might collapse at any moment.

"Good," Elspeth said, nodding. "I'll go first." She set off down the nave and Serafina followed on Tinkerby's shaking arm, concentrating on putting her own shaky feet one after another.

And then, just as she'd managed to regain her poise and

look up, two men stepped out of the shadows to the right of the altar, the first moving into the groom's position.

Serafina held her breath in anticipation as he slowly turned to look at her.

The expression on his face was anything but loving; it wasn't even warm or welcoming. It could best be described as stone cold. But that was the least of her worries. Serafina's step halted, then came to a complete stop, dragging Tinkerby to a stop next to her. She stared in disbelief, her body going numb with shock.

He couldn't possibly be Aiden.

His hair was so dark as to be nearly black, his cheeks were chiseled, his eyebrows slanting over a pair of startled blue eyes that widened in incredulity as he stared back at her. She knew those eyes, that look of astonishment, but they were the last eyes in the world she expected to see.

Her aunt had mistaken the direction and brought her to the wrong chapel, she thought wildly. It was the only explanation. She'd stumbled into the rogue's wedding entirely by mistake. It was no wonder that he looked so surprised. He was expecting his wicked harridan of a bride and she'd popped in completely by accident.

Tinkerby looked down at her in alarm. "Miss Serafina?"

She was about to explain the mistake when an even more terrible realization came to her. Lord Delaware sat at the front of the chapel, his daughter beside him, both looking at her as if they fully expected to see her there, Lord Delaware positively beaming. And Aunt Elspeth continued to march up the nave as if everything was exactly as it ought to be.

Serafina swallowed hard against a knot of disbelief. Her entire world spun in front of her eyes—not as it had done in the bath when she'd been transported into a state of bliss, but in sheer horror.

This was Aiden, for whom she'd waited more than half a lifetime? The rogue, who had blithely kissed her even though he was to be married to another woman in the morning—a woman he professed to hate?

Serafina's heart froze like a lump of ice in her chest and she swallowed again, this time against a wave of nausea. She tried to tell herself that perhaps the rogue had his position reversed and was standing up for the man hidden more deeply in the shadows. Or he was an accidental guest who had come in late through the wrong door. But when would he have had time to see to his own marriage?

I have an appointment with the hangman in the morning, he'd said bitterly. *And if you bring the notion of love into it, I think I might well strangle you.*

All the rest of his vitriolic words against his forced marriage came pouring unbidden into Serafina's head. And yet they made no sense. She was no rich schemer. She hadn't a penny to her name. And she'd done nothing, nothing at all, to cause him to despise her. Nothing except wait for him for eleven long years. No. It couldn't possibly be Aiden, she decided.

"Miss Serafina?" Tinkerby asked again, pulling out his handkerchief and mopping his damp brow. "Is there a problem?"

"Oh yes, a terrible problem," Serafina started to say, but just then Elspeth's hand fastened around her upper arm, shaking her hard. "Child—what's come over you? Aubrey's waiting—look, there he is at the altar."

Serafina shook her head, dazed. "That's the wrong man," she whispered. "We've made a mistake, Auntie."

"No mistake," her aunt said firmly. "That's Aubrey sure enough. And he's going to think you're the biggest cork-brain that ever came along if you don't hop to and join him up there."

"But—but how do you know it's Aiden? You've never met him before!" Serafina said desperately.

"Never mind that," Elspeth said, peering into Serafina's face. "Is it nerves, dear? Brides experience these sensibilities, you know—it's really most correct. Even your dear mother had her moment of doubt in the face of her wedding, but she never regretted her marriage, not for an instant."

Doubt? Serafina had never doubted anything so strongly in her life. "Auntie, I'm telling you, that's *not* Aiden," she hissed adamantly.

"And I'm telling you it is," her aunt hissed just as adamantly. "And furthermore, whatever foolishness has entered your head, you might as well chase it right out again, because you're going to marry him *right now*! I don't want to hear another word about it. Tinkerby, step lively!"

Elspeth propelled both Serafina and a shaken Tinkerby toward the altar, one bony hand digging hard into Serafina's tender spine, and she had no choice but to go and drag Tinkerby with her. But she felt as if she was being forced to a fate worse than death, her entire world crumbling about her with each step that she took.

She managed to negotiate the three steps up to the altar, Tinkerby struggling at her side, and Elspeth practically dragged her posy out of her hands. Serafina turned to face the rogue, who was now regarding her with a broad smile, as if they both shared a private joke.

"What's your name?" she demanded in a whisper, leaning close to his ear, still refusing to believe she was at the right altar with the right man.

"Aiden Delaware," he whispered back, confirming her worst fears. "What's yours? I'm beginning to think it might not be Titania after all."

His brilliant blue eyes held a hint of laughter, and Serafina wanted to plant her fist on his nose every bit as much as she wanted to burst into tears. "Serafina Segrave," she said. "And there's been a terrible mistake."

"No mistake," he replied in the same low undertone. "Except for mine, which I'm about to rectify."

"There's nothing to rectify, really there isn't," she said in a panic, knowing he referred to the stolen kiss. "You don't have to worry—I'm not going to marry you."

"Oh, yes you are," he said, taking her hand and ignoring the bishop's hemming and hawing. "You have no choice."

She snatched her hand away. "I'm not," she insisted. "You don't even want me to!"

"But I do. And you, Miss Segrave, have absolutely nothing to say in the matter except 'I will.' "

Serafina threw Tinkerby a desperate look, but saw nothing but confused panic in his face. She looked frantically over her shoulder at her aunt, only to be met by two little eyes boring fiercely into hers and promising swift retribution if Serafina misbehaved. No help there. She glanced beyond Elspeth to the first pew. Lord Delaware still beamed happily. Lady Charlotte merely looked furious.

She turned back to Aiden, who simply shrugged his broad shoulders. "As you can see, short of breaking a very complicated legal contract and some firm promises, there's nothing to be done except marry me."

Serafina looked as a last resort to the man standing behind Aiden. He was tall and broad, of a height with Aiden and nearly as fair as Aiden was dark, his hair the color of spun gold. His gray eyes looked into hers with a gleam of cynical amusement. He nodded toward the bishop with one eyebrow raised expectantly.

She bit her lip and looked down, knowing she had no alternatives left to her. With an excruciatingly sharp pain in her chest born of hurt and disillusionment and anger at her own naïveté, she slowly raised her gaze to the bishop's and nodded her faltering assent.

He instantly leapt into action, speaking as if he couldn't get the words out fast enough. "Dearly beloved, we are gathered together here in the sight of God, and in the face of this company, to join together this Man and this Woman in holy Matrimony. . . ."

With the grim fall of those condemning words Serafina knew that the dream she'd held on to for so long had been exactly that—a dream.

As soon as the ceremony was finished and Aiden had planted the obligatory ring and revolting self-congratulatory kiss on her, he took her arm and led her out into the sunshine.

"Well, Titania," he said, turning to her, "it's a fine pickle we've found ourselves in, isn't it, although I can't say I'm feeling any regret." He grinned down at her. "And who in God's name was that man you traipsed down the aisle with? He reminds me of our last under-butler."

She wrenched her arm out of the crook of his elbow. "You may find this amusing, but I assure you, I do not."

"That much I can see," he said lightly. "I'm sorry. I'm a little confused myself at how all this came to pass, but I assure you—"

"You can assure me of nothing," she spat. "However, I can assure you that I dislike you acutely. You are nothing but a miserable lying cad, who would take advantage of anyone to achieve your own ends."

"I'm wounded," he said, pressing a hand over his heart. "No, really I am. I came into this marriage as innocently as you did."

"Innocently?" she said furiously. "You're anything but innocent in this—this travesty!"

"But how was I to know when I met you yesterday that you were who you are?" he replied reasonably. "It was a case of mistaken identities, no more."

"Do you always kiss women whose identities you've mistaken?" she said, her eyes flashing fire.

"No . . . at least not often," he said, appearing highly entertained by her anger. "I generally formally introduce myself first. It didn't seem necessary at the time. As I recall, you didn't introduce yourself either."

"Oh!" she cried. "I won't be bullied by a man I married under false pretenses."

"I don't see why you feel misled any more than I've been." He straightened as the first of the wedding party trooped out of the church. "We'll have to take this up later," he said in a low voice, lightly resting a hand on her shoulder.

She violently shrugged it off, taking three steps away from him. "I loathe you," she snarled.

"Well try to keep it to yourself for the next few hours," he said, his eyes alight with laughter. "Hardly anyone here believes for an instant that this is a love match, but we might as well not add fuel to the fire. We have a wedding breakfast to attend and there's no point in creating more gossip—tongues will be wagging fast enough as it is after your performance at the altar."

Serafina glared at him. "My performance was nothing compared to yours. But I agree, there's no point in making a bad situation worse. Your father doesn't deserve to be upset when he's addled enough, poor man."

"I couldn't agree more," Aiden said, "although I don't know why you're championing him when he's the one who put both of us in this situation."

"I'm sure I don't know what you mean," she said, strongly tempted to slap his arrogant, smiling face.

"Serafina, my sweet, I think you know exactly what I mean, so it's no use pretending. You have some explaining of your own to do, but this is neither the time nor the place." He ran a finger under her chin. "Suffice it to say that when we met yesterday I thought you were a girl from the local village, and you said nothing to change that assumption. How was I to know you were on your way to marry me?"

"Oh, and that made what you did acceptable? You only go about kissing girls of low birth?" she said, stung to the quick.

"No," he said considering. "I wouldn't say that's true. But it *was* only a kiss, and I did apologize."

"I should wrap that noose you talked about right around your neck." Serafina glowered at him.

"Please don't. I haven't even had my wedding night yet."

"Oooh, you really are a cad," she sputtered as the thought of her wedding night, already a terrifying issue, struck her with the appalling realization that she would have to experience it at this man's hands. Nothing could be worse. Nothing.

"Being a cad I never denied," he said, grinning down at her, and she wanted to die from mortification that she had asked him all those questions and listened to his lies, let him lead her astray with sweet promises of bliss. She knew now exactly whose side the bliss would be on. He'd left the woman's part out entirely.

"Yes, and now I'm married to you," she said darkly. "Of course, it's always been my deepest desire to be married to a cad. Can you imagine how happy I am in this moment?"

He threw his head back and hooted. "Obviously ecstatic," he said, taking her hand. "Never mind, sweetheart. I feel confident that we can work out the misunderstanding."

Elspeth came beetling up to them before Serafina had a chance to formulate a reply. "So, Aubrey, we meet at last." She beamed at him as if she were greeting a long-lost son, and Serafina wanted to cry with frustration. Her aunt had no idea what a scoundrel Aiden was. If she'd had, she'd have pulled out one of her bone hairpins and skewered him with it through the heart.

"Miss Beaton, I assume?" Aiden said, bending over her hand. "I must thank you for bringing Serafina to me in such a timely fashion. And you made a very fine bridesmaid," he added, his face perfectly straight.

"I did my best," Elspeth said with satisfaction. "And a very pretty ceremony it was, most satisfyingly dramatic. I'm sure we are all wondering what that little conversation at the altar was about." She looked at Serafina expectantly.

"It was nothing," Serafina said, coloring. "I was only attempting to ascertain this man's identity before I was tied to him for life. Since we'd never met, I mean."

Aiden laughed. "Ah, yes. A confusing state of affairs to be sure. Had I thought of it I would have carried a piece of identification on my person to present to my bride, but I was sadly ill prepared." He shrugged. "Still, all's well that ends well, and I think it's ended very well indeed. My dear, may I take you to the house? Our guests await. Do accompany us, Miss Beaton."

Serafina had no choice but to take his arm and let him lead her away, but she treated him to stony silence the entire way back.

Aiden had no such problem. He busied himself with talking to Elspeth as if she were a relative he held in exceptionally high regard, regaling her with stories of Townsend, quizzing her in turn about their life at Clwydd, listening to her responses as if he hung on every word. Serafina wanted to kick him.

He carried on in the same vein at the wedding breakfast, seating Elspeth at his left and Serafina at his right where she studiously ignored him, talking instead to the boring bishop, who banged on about theological dictums that Serafina found baffling. But she heard every honeyed word Aiden spoke to her aunt.

He finally got around to the subject that had obviously been burning on his mind. "And do tell me, my dear Miss Beaton, about the gentleman who was kind enough to escort Serafina down the aisle to me?" He regarded her with a slight tilt of his head. "An old family friend, perhaps? I have not yet had the pleasure of making his acquaintance. I was wondering why he is not in attendance at the breakfast."

"Oh, that wouldn't be proper since Tinkerby is my man of all work. He's eating in the servants' hall," Elspeth said, regarding Aiden with what Serafina could only construe as adoration.

"Tinkerby?" Aiden said.

He shot Serafina an incisive look, filled with amusement, and she wanted to crawl into a little ball, remembering far too well how it was that Tinkerby's name had come up in conversation the day before. She tore her gaze away from his, blushing hotly.

"He has been with you a long time, then?" Aiden asked Elspeth, as if he had no idea of Serafina's embarrassment. She truly wanted to kill him.

"Oh, yes, Tinkerby has known dear Serafina since the day she was born and was with her father for many years before that. He's a good man, if a bit misguided in his opinions."

"Oh, yes?" Aiden said, looking as if he was trying not to laugh, which only infuriated Serafina more. How dare he make light of Tinkerby? He probably thought himself too good for the man. He probably thought himself too good for her too, given the cavalier way he'd treated her in the woods. Apparently Aiden was a snob on top of everything else.

"Yes," Serafina said disdainfully, turning to him. "Tinkerby comes from a long line of men of all work. His father blacked the boots at Bowhill. That's where I used to live before I was forced away, but you probably know that."

She speared a forkful of chicken livers that had been sauteed in a sherry sauce, even though she despised chicken livers and had just discovered that she didn't like the taste of sherry either. But it was one of the only dishes that she recognized on the table. She was far more accustomed to simple stews and roasts. "Tinkerby came with me to Clwydd and taught me everything he knew from gardening to scouring the pots and pans," she said, waving her fork in the air for emphasis. "And I can black the boots as well as anyone can." She twisted the fork in her hand and shoved the revolting stuff into her mouth.

"How useful," he said, not missing a beat, although he regarded her with an odd expression. "I'm sure you'll teach my valet any manner of things, once I can afford one."

"Whether you can afford a valet or not is none of my concern," Serafina replied through her mouthful, forcing herself to swallow. "Of course, if you are so hard done by I suppose I can always manage the task for you. I won't require much of a salary."

Aiden met her gaze evenly as if she hadn't said anything untoward and leaned his cheek on his hand. "Would five guineas a year be acceptable?" he asked lazily. "I think I might just be able to manage that, although the wage does seem extravagant."

"At that price, I think I'll have to throw your boots at your head each morning, my lord, and consider that my extra compensation." She narrowed her eyes. "But then maybe it's the most effective way to wake you up."

Aiden chuckled. "I can see I have a stormy ride ahead of me. Perhaps I'd better break out my spurs."

Elspeth, who had been leaning on every word, gave a loud crack of laughter. "And your crop too, I should think," she said gleefully. "You've a green one on your hands, Aubrey."

Serafina blushed beetroot and glared at her aunt, willing her to keep her mouth shut. Knowing Elspeth, she was next going to offer Aiden her virginity for dessert. Blood pudding.

"Oh, but I never use a crop," Aiden said. "I believe in the art of friendly persuasion."

Serafina wanted to slide under the table in mortification. She shot Aiden a filthy look and turned back to the bishop and his boring conversation.

She couldn't wait for an opportunity to escape, desperately needing solitude and time to sort out her confused thoughts. But to Serafina's dismay the company moved into the drawing room when the meal was finally over.

The man who had been introduced to Serafina as the Duke of Southwell, which had only made her feel even more inadequate, pushed Charlotte's chair over to the window and engaged her in conversation, his back turned away. She knew they were both studiously ignoring her, which didn't help to alleviate her sense of alienation.

But she'd already divined what Charlotte thought of her, and since the duke had done nothing but fix her with chilly looks all throughout the breakfast, she wasn't particularly surprised. Had Elspeth said Charlotte had a viper in her bosom? It seemed to Serafina that she'd landed in an entire nest of vipers. She scowled darkly, looking around the room.

Lord Delaware and Elspeth had vanished somewhere between the dining room and the drawing room, taking Aiden with them. Aiden had excused himself prettily enough, saying only that he would be back shortly. If she had her way, he would never return at all.

The bishop and the vicar were involved in arguing over some silly theological point, a conversation Serafina had no interest in joining. Their God was low on her list at the moment.

That left Serafina with only the vicar's wife to hold conversation with, and she quickly found her a singularly stupid woman, full of pretensions and nauseating obsequiousness. She prattled on and on until Serafina wanted to wring her fat neck.

"Oh, my lady, I must say I find it thrilling that you are married to your childhood sweetheart at long last," she trilled. "The village is all in a tizzy about it."

"My childhood sweetheart?" Serafina said, staring at her in horror. "Where did you come up with that idea?"

"Why, from Lord Delaware, of course. He said you were engaged to each other when Lord Aubrey was all of seventeen. How deliciously romantic," she cooed.

"Not at all, Mrs. Liddle," Serafina said. "It is my understanding that peers and future peers of the realm never marry for love, nor are they foolish enough to choose wives who would expect it of them. Such saccharine sentiments are reserved for those of the lower classes."

"Oh . . ." Mrs. Liddle said, her fatuous smile fading. "But I thought—"

"You must have misunderstood," Serafina said calmly, even though her heart felt like breaking at the irony of Mrs. Liddle's assumption. "The marriage was an arrangement made between our fathers, nothing more," she continued. "I am sure Lord Aubrey will go his own way soon enough, with no need to perform his matrimonial duties once he has his heir."

The Duke of Southwell's head slowly raised from his conversation with Charlotte. He turned and gave Serafina a long assessing gaze, meeting her eyes evenly, his own as cold as slate and filled with obvious dislike.

Serafina dropped her gaze, overcome with a desire to burst into tears of despair. She felt as if she had just married into the enemy camp through no devising of her own. It was more than obvious to her that neither Aiden's sister nor his cousin considered her a suitable bride, and she could hardly be surprised, since Aiden shared the sentiment. Aiden would have been much better off with a woman like himself, someone cold and unfeeling, someone who didn't care about being loved or about giving it. He'd told her that much already. As well as a great deal more.

She really couldn't bear another minute in the company of strangers. "Please excuse me," she said, blinking hard to contain her tears. "I find I am exhausted from the festivities." She nearly ran out of the room, not caring in the least that everyone was staring at her.

Serafina changed into one of her old dresses and slipped out through the back of the house, unwilling to face another person. She didn't know where to go, only that she wanted to disappear as fast and thoroughly as possible.

But she'd only walked a few yards when a voice came from behind her, stopping her in her tracks.

"So, here you are, Countess," the Duke of Southwell said smoothly, and Serafina spun around in alarm.

"Oh . . . it's you, your dukedom," she said stupidly, not knowing how to address him properly, wishing Elspeth had prepared her better for this sort of thing.

"It is indeed. But please, do call me Raphael, now that we're family." He said it as if the thought disgusted him.

"Yes—yes, I suppose we are," she said, her fingers catching nervously at the edges of her skirt, not sure why his being Aiden's friend made them anything but enemies.

"I'm delighted we agree. So, since we're family, I'd like to know why it is that you look at Aiden with daggers in your eyes and murder in your heart." He fixed her with his level gaze.

"I—I can't speak of it," she said, desperately wishing to escape. "It's for Aiden to tell you, if he will."

"What is there for him to tell me that he hasn't told me already? He's made his feelings about the marriage clear to me."

"In that case, I can only suppose he told you that I coerced him into the agreement. I assure you, I had nothing to do with it." Serafina wrenched her gaze away from his, the taste of bile bitter in her throat.

"Didn't you?" Raphael asked calmly. "It's not unheard of for a woman to use whatever tools she has at her disposal to elevate herself in the world. So maybe you'd like to take this opportunity to explain yourself."

"There's nothing to explain," Serafina said miserably, knowing there was no way to explain anything, least of all to herself.

"No? Then if you don't wish to tell me your motives for marrying Aiden, maybe you'll explain your behavior at the wedding breakfast. Or there's always the particularly vitriolic condemnation you made of Aiden's intent to the vicar's wife. Are you trying to make a fool out of him, now that you've secured his title?"

Serafina shook her head frantically. "I don't care about his title. It means nothing to me, just as Aiden means nothing to me. Oh, *why* can't you leave me alone?" she said in sheer desperation.

"Not until I get some answers from you. You see, I do care about Aiden, very much, and I won't see some manipulative little hussy malign him, not when he doesn't deserve your scorn."

"Is that what he told you, that I'm a manipulative little hussy?" she said, angry tears starting to her eyes. "I suppose I shouldn't be surprised. He's probably told half the world the same thing."

"And I wonder what you've told the other half of the world, my lady. That is what I call you now, isn't it? 'My lady?' How very clever of you, to have secured rank and privilege at the price of Aiden's soul."

"He doesn't *have* a soul," she cried. "He's cold and unfeeling, and—and a blackguard!"

"Thank you. That answers my question quite nicely," Raphael said, folding his arms across his chest. "In which case, you've just made it very clear why you married him. A charming picture, don't you agree?"

"You think—you honestly think that I *planned* all of this, that I meant to mislead Aiden into this marriage?" she said furiously. "Oh, you are just like him!"

"Since Aiden is the most honorable man I know, I wonder if I shouldn't take that as a compliment," Raphael replied coolly.

"Honorable?" Serafina said, glaring at him. "That's an interesting definition for your friend. I'm beginning to think that all men of rank and privilege have the same overbearing, superior attitude. With the exception of my father," she added loyally. "At least he was kind and gentle and honest. And if he'd known the nature of the man he agreed to marry me to, he'd have instantly rescinded his offer, of that I can assure you. He *never* would have consigned me to Aiden's protection, not when he knew that I had nothing else and no one else in the world other than my Aunt Elspeth."

"Oh?" Raphael said, his eyes conveying an expression of boundless cynicism.

"Yes, and if you think you know any better, you're badly

mistaken. My father cared about my well being, which is far more than I can say about Aiden. He thinks I'm bringing him a fortune. Ha!" she said in perfect imitation of her aunt. "He's going to have the shock of his life."

Rafe fixed her with a hard look. "Either you've completely lost your mind, or I've lost mine. Or you're lying. The third possibility seems most likely, since I know my sanity is intact, and you appear a little too bright to be delusional."

Serafina drew herself up indignantly. "I *never* lie," she said. "That would go against the most basic principles of god and goddess."

"Oh, that's it then, to be sure," Raphael said, drawing one hand over his face. "You're mad."

"I'm most certainly not," Serafina retorted, realizing that she'd said a little too much about her beliefs, but refusing to back down now. "What makes you think you have the right of it?"

To her surprise Raphael burst into laughter. "Oh, I'm just a God-fearing Englishman who happens to believe in the dictates of the Church, that's all."

"There's nothing wrong with the Church," Serafina said, planting her hands on her hips. "I sing in the choir every Sunday without fail, as it happens. But that doesn't mean that there's anything wrong with honoring the ancient ways, which have been around far longer than Christianity, I'll have you know."

"So you're a little pagan, are you?" Rafe said, looking highly entertained. "I suppose I shouldn't be surprised, given that you've been living in Wales for so long with that queer aunt of yours."

"My aunt is a perfectly acceptable woman of good breeding, and her religious practices are none of your concern. And it's very rude of you to call her queer. She is merely eccentric."

"I beg your pardon," Raphael said, his smile broadening. "I suppose now you're going to tell me that the reason you balked at the altar was because you didn't have a high priestess in attendance? No wonder you looked at the bishop with such displeasure."

"I did not look at the bishop with displeasure," Serafina said in her own defense. "I'm sure he's a very fine bishop, and it was no fault of his that I didn't want to marry Aiden."

Raphael stared at her. "Now you're saying that you didn't *want* to marry Aiden?"

"No, I did not," she said adamantly. "I thought I did until I saw him, but I changed my mind."

Raphael stroked the high bridge of his nose with one finger. "Then perhaps, since I'm such a muddled, misdirected fool, you will tell me why you changed your mind upon seeing him. Does his appearance displease you?"

"Don't be silly. Anyone can see that Aiden is a very handsome man. But he doesn't love me," Serafina finished flatly.

"I daresay he doesn't. Like myself, Aiden happens to be of sound mind."

"What's that supposed to mean?" she said indignantly. "Do you think I'm not worthy of Aiden's love?"

Raphael regarded her steadily. "I have absolutely no idea," he said. "Given your behavior this morning, I'd have said absolutely not. But I confess that now I'm confused. I think I'll withhold judgment until I have a clearer understanding of this rather peculiar situation."

"Well, it's a moot point because Aiden doesn't even believe in love."

"He doesn't?" Raphael said, one corner of his mouth curving up. "Whatever gave you that idea?"

"He told me so himself in no uncertain terms at the very same time that he informed me precisely what he thought of his marriage," she retorted, goaded out of caution. "It was *not* a pretty description, I can tell you. I am sure you can understand why I'd be disillusioned with him after hearing that."

For the first time Raphael's cool control slipped. "Good God . . ." he said slowly. "You really are a little pagan, aren't you?" He looked her up and down with a sharp, assessing gaze as if he'd just seen her for the first time.

Serafina colored in embarrassment, folding her arms around her waist as if that might protect her from his penetrating examination of her person. "I am *not* a pagan," she said. "I just told you—"

"That's not what I meant," he said, running his fingers back through his hair. "Serafina . . . I may call you Serafina?" he asked.

She nodded, wondering at his sudden change of tone and expression. He almost—almost—looked pleasant, but she wasn't prepared to lower her guard for an instant.

"Tell me something," he said, his gaze direct. "Today in the chapel wasn't the first time you met Aiden, was it?"

"I don't know what you mean," she said, her heart leaping in panic that he might have somehow divined the truth.

"I think you do, and since you say you never lie, I assume you're going to be honest with me. You didn't have that particular conversation at the altar, did you?"

"I told him at the altar that he didn't have to marry me," she hedged. "And he said he did."

Raphael's face lit up with a sudden flash of amusement. "Somehow I'm not surprised. But I'm referring to the other conversation you and Aiden had, which I believe you conducted yesterday afternoon in Rockingham Forest."

Serafina paled. "He told you about that?" she whispered, horrified.

"He did indeed," Raphael said, his eyes alight with humor. "He told me all about it, and I think I'm finally beginning to understand what happened today."

"If he told you all about it," Serafina retorted hotly, "then you ought to understand why I had a change of heart when I saw whom I was to marry. Your friend is an unprincipled rakehell."

Raphael threw his head back and roared with laughter. "Oh, I don't know. Aiden's done his fair share of adventuring, but I think you're going a little too far to describe him so harshly."

"Then the version of events he gave you must have been heavily weighted in his favor," she said. "I assure you, he did not behave like a gentleman."

"Well . . . perhaps not entirely, but what *were* you doing

sleeping alone in the woods? I'm puzzled by that, especially since you were so close to Townsend."

"I went for a walk. I fell asleep. I thought I was perfectly safe," she snapped. "It never occurred to me that a man would come along and try to seduce me, especially when he knew I was going to be married to someone else, and he was too. Which is why I had such a terrible shock this morning."

"If I'd tried for a hundred years, I never would have come up with such an unbelievable explanation. Whoever would have thought it? No wonder Aiden looked so taken aback in the chapel, poor man. The last person he was expecting was his village girl."

Deeply offended, Serafina drew herself up with all the dignity she could muster. "I'm sorry if your friend feels I'm only good enough to black his boots," she said, wanting to slap Raphael's handsome, aristocratic face. "But I assure you, his opinion is of no concern to me, and neither is yours. Good day, your dukedom."

"Your grace," he said with a broad grin.

"Oh, I may be a countess now," Serafina said disdainfully, "but there's no need to give *me* airs and graces."

She turned and fled, the sound of his laughter echoing after her.

6

"Rafe, thank God—have you seen Serafina?" Aiden asked frantically as Raphael appeared in the hall. "She's vanished. Charlotte said she went upstairs, but she's not there either. I've looked everywhere I can think of . . ."

"Your bride," Raphael said, examining his fingernails, "has taken off in the direction of the stables. Or so I observed. You might want to go after her before she abducts one of your only remaining horses."

Aiden blew out a long breath of relief. Serafina's abrupt disappearance had alarmed him more than he cared to admit. "Thank you. I don't think she's feeling particularly comfortable with her new circumstances."

The corners of Raphael's mouth quivered. "No, I would imagine not," he said. "She appeared a little upended to me."

"Damn! I wouldn't have left her for so long, but my father insisted on my signing the blasted marriage contracts immediately, the greedy bastard."

"Hmm," Rafe said. "I trust they provided everything you were hoping for?"

"Yes, of course they did. Why do you ask?" Aiden said, wondering with distraction whether Serafina was capable of sitting any of the mounts. He didn't even know if she could ride. There was only his gelding, one old nag used to pull the gig, and an unbroken stallion his father had been unable to sell.

"No reason in particular," Raphael said.

"What?" Aiden said, his attention snapping back to his cousin. "What are you talking about?"

"I said I only asked about the marriage contracts out of simple curiosity. Your wife's not exactly what I expected. Not what you expected either, I daresay."

Aiden lifted a shoulder, trying his best to look nonchalant. The last thing he wanted Rafe to know was that the woman he'd made such a cake of himself over the night before was now his wife, especially when Rafe was familiar with every last detail of their encounter. And on top of that he felt like a fool for having complained so bitterly about his prospective bride, only to be delivered what he'd been longing for. "She's certainly an improvement over what I anticipated," he said neutrally.

"Anything would be an improvement over a gorgon," Raphael replied, his face perfectly straight. "She's a pretty girl, actually, if a little untutored about social matters," he continued, regarding the toe of his boot as if it held some particular fascination. "But that can be remedied easily enough."

"I rather like her the way she is," Aiden said, then realized that might sound too close to his ravings in the inn. "What I mean is that she's not the witch I was expecting."

"Possibly not," Rafe agreed. "Of course, only time will tell. One can only hope for the best."

"Yes," Aiden said, relieved that Rafe accepted his unexplained change of heart without a lot of unwelcome questions.

"It's a pity, naturally, that we can't always have what we want, but then wood nymphs are hard to come by." Raphael rubbed the corner of his mouth.

Aiden's eyes narrowed suspiciously. "See here, Rafe, if you think to poke fun at me just because I was in my cups and waxing a bit poetic last night, think again."

"Poke fun at you, man? Would I do such a thing, especially in this, your time of travail? No, indeed, you were allowed a bit of fantastical rambling in the last hours before your execution, and I was happy to listen." He regarded

Aiden with an expression of deep sympathy that Aiden suspected wasn't entirely genuine.

"Thank you for your understanding," Aiden said caustically, wanting to rip Rafe's complacent head from his shoulders. "It's kind of you to be so supportive."

"Only my job," Rafe replied with a wave of his hand. "But you ought to be concentrating on the present and go find your wife before she gets completely away from you."

"Yes—yes, I'd better," Aiden said. "Look, Rafe . . . thanks for everything you did today. And last night."

"Not at all, Cousin. I'm sure you'll do the same for me should I ever need your services." He swept a gracious bow, then straightened with a grin. "Of course, since I have every intention of letting my younger brother provide heirs for me, you might be waiting a lifetime or two to repay me."

Aiden laughed and slung an arm around his shoulder. "All right then. Let me go and chase down Serafina."

"That, I think, is an exemplary idea," Rafe said. "I'll see to the ushering out of your guests."

Serafina ran as fast as she could away from Townsend Hall and all it contained, Aiden and his friend included. She would never fit into their world, didn't even want to fit into their world, not if it was peopled by men and women who regarded virtues like love and honesty as if they were something to be mocked and disdained, who looked down their noses at anyone who wasn't as elevated as them.

All of her life she'd believed that it wasn't one's station of birth that was important, but rather integrity of character; that kindness to others was as much a guiding principle as honoring all living things and acting honorably in accordance.

And yet in twenty-four hours, she had been exposed to an entirely different way of thinking and behaving. In this world, hypocrisy was acceptable; in this world, people were bought and sold as if they were items to be bartered over at a marketplace.

She couldn't believe that Elspeth had allowed such a thing

to happen to her—Elspeth who followed the old ways to the letter, who had always told her that love and faith would carry her through anything.

The only conclusion she could reach was that Elspeth hadn't had any idea of what she was consigning Serafina to, that she truly believed, as Serafina had, that Aiden and his family were honorable people who wanted only the best for her.

It was a lie. Her entire life had become a lie the moment she'd set foot in the chapel and seen Aiden's face.

Tears streaming down her cheeks, she headed toward the wide stone bridge with three arches spanning the river. On the other side of the river a hill rose gently from the bank and she stumbled up it, her feet slipping on the slick grass.

It flattened out at the top, a small pond sitting in the middle, two swans, one white, one black, floating on its glassy surface. And off to one side of the pond stood an oak tree. Serafina stopped dead in her tracks and stared in wonder.

It was the most magnificent tree she'd ever seen, rising majestically toward the sky, its huge leafy branches forming a protective ceiling overhead. The gnarled trunk would have taken at least five men's outstretched arms to span its circumference.

The tree of life, symbol of the Goddess Hestia herself.

Serafina moved toward the oak, wanting to feel its massive trunk beneath her hands, as if it could somehow give her solace, could steady her, could help her make sense out of the chaos that whirled inside her head. She pressed her flattened palms against the bark, her fingertips rubbing over the rough surface seeking the life force contained within the wood.

"Dear Hestia, keeper of hearth and home, source of all life," she whispered, "please, *please* help me to understand why you have sent me to this awful man, why you took my beautiful Dream from me?"

Oh, her beautiful Dream. Adam. Gone forever. Replaced by the truth, which was that Aiden didn't love her and never had. She had filled her head with fantasies, turning a marriage contract into a beautiful fairy tale of undying love. She was nothing more than a fool—a silly, romantic fool, loving a man who didn't exist outside of her imagination.

She fell to the ground, burying her head in her arms, her shoulders shaking with heartbroken sobs as all the shock and disillusionment and misery of the last few hours came pouring out unchecked.

In that moment Serafina thought she might die of grief.

Aiden stopped briefly at the stables to inquire about Serafina's whereabouts, learning to his infinite relief that she had gone directly past them in the direction of the river. He hoped to God that in her despair she hadn't decided to throw herself in. He'd had the same impulse himself only the afternoon before.

Incredibly, today he felt entirely different about life. Instead of black misery, he was filled with exhilaration and gratitude that the one thing he had so desperately wanted the day before had, against all expectation, been delivered directly into his hands.

He'd nearly keeled over at the altar when Serafina had appeared, and for a moment he'd thought he was hallucinating when he saw her face, for it hadn't seemed possible that the abhorrent bride he was expecting had miraculously transformed into his fairy queen.

It had occurred to him in that split second that there might be a God after all, a benevolent God who wasn't intent on punishing him with one blow after another, but had actually shown some mercy. Serafina, on the other hand, looked at him as if he had undergone the exact opposite transformation, her expression of shining expectancy changing into undisguised horror as she registered who her husband was.

He'd wanted to laugh, knowing exactly what she must have been thinking. He still had a thousand questions to put to her, but those could be answered all in good time. All he wanted at the moment was to find her, to reassure her that she hadn't married the devil himself, even if he wasn't the Prince Charming she'd been hoping for.

He crossed the bridge, his gaze scanning the riverbanks just to be sure he wouldn't find her floating among the weeds. But the river and its banks thankfully held no bodies. He knew there was only one direction for her to have followed if she had crossed the bridge, so he climbed the hill toward the pond and the oak tree.

Serafina sat huddled beneath its great branches, her body hunched over, and he knew by her bent head and the shaking of her shoulders that she was crying.

He wanted to cry himself. Of all people in the world whom he didn't want to see hurt it was she, and yet by the simple fact of being who he was, he had inadvertently wounded her deeply, delivered that blow of disillusionment that he'd expected to be dealt by a different man.

He walked quietly over to her and kneeling, he gently rested his hands on her slight shoulders.

She stiffened and her head shot up, her eyes wide and swollen with tears. "You!" she gasped, "oh, no—please, go away. L-Leave me in peace, I beg of you. . . ."

"Why do you cry, Serafina?" Aiden asked in the low, quiet voice that he used to calm a frightened horse. "Is it really so dreadful to be married to me?"

She shuddered at his touch, and he dropped his hands. "How—how did you find me?" she said, gulping back a sob.

"I was concerned when you vanished so suddenly. I thought you might have taken one of the horses, so I went to the stables. The groom told me you'd come this way."

Serafina rubbed her fists over her eyes, leaving smudges of tears streaked with dirt on her cheeks. "I want n-nothing from you," she said, trying to catch her breath. "I certainly wouldn't steal one of your horses."

Aiden smiled, thinking that she looked endearingly like a lost child. "You wouldn't have had much of a selection to choose from, but I wouldn't begrudge you. Were you running away?"

"Where would I go?" she said, hanging her head in misery. "You made me a prisoner when you forced me to marry you."

"Ah, straight to the crux of the matter," he said, handing

her his handkerchief. "Here, wipe your eyes and blow your nose. I think we'd better talk."

He arranged himself in a sitting position opposite her and drew up one knee, resting his arm on it. "Serafina, I can only assume that your distress is because of what I said to you when we met yesterday. I'm sorry about that, truly I am. I wasn't in the best of moods."

"Your mood had nothing to do with it," she said, blowing her nose resoundingly. "You told me exactly what you thought of me in vivid detail."

"Yes, but then I didn't know I was speaking to you, did I?"

"It makes no difference to whom you thought you were speaking," Serafina said, twisting the handkerchief into a tight knot. "You spoke the truth about what you felt. You said that I was a scheming harridan. You said you were only marrying me because you'd given your word to your family and that there was no hope for happiness or love. And—and you said I was *ugly*."

Aiden couldn't help grinning. "I did, didn't I? Well, I was wrong—very wrong. Let's just say I'd been given some misinformation. Quite a lot of it, actually."

"Yes, and you've been taken for a fool, my lord, on top of that," she said, glaring at him. "If you think for one minute that I'm going to rescue you from your financial difficulties, then you're going to be sorely disappointed. I haven't a penny to my name, so you've married me for nothing."

Aiden's smile faded as he absorbed this extraordinary statement. "My dear girl," he said slowly, "are you telling me that you honestly don't know what your position is?"

"Yes, I know perfectly well. I'm married to you, and now you can hate me for being penniless on top of everything else. And if you think I care," she added belligerently, "I don't. I'm perfectly accustomed to being poor, which you apparently are as well. So now we are poor together, and I hope you're satisfied, because I'm miserable!"

Aiden frowned, realizing that she really didn't know about her money, which only confused him more. "Serafina . . . tell me something. Why did you agree to marry me?"

"I'm beginning to wonder that exact thing. I thought I loved you. I thought you loved me." She untwisted his handkerchief and blew her nose again.

"But how in God's name could you think we loved each other when we'd never even met?" he asked incredulously. "I know when we spoke yesterday that you said you loved the man you were going to marry, but love is something that can't exist unless two people actually know each other. It doesn't happen as a result of an agreement between families, not when the two immediate parties have never had any contact."

Serafina rubbed her forehead hard, looking equally confused on that point. "I—I suppose the idea had been in my head for so long that I simply assumed it was true," she said. "I couldn't conceive of two people marrying unless they did love each other, so I made up my mind that we did."

"I see," he said, rubbing the back of his neck, not seeing at all. "Well, that's an interesting concept, to say the least. You—you were very much alone in Wales, weren't you?"

"Well, I had my auntie, and Tinkerby of course."

"Ah, yes, the inestimable Tinkerby. But did you have no one else? No friends, no other relatives who visited?"

Serafina shrugged. "No. I don't believe I have any relatives other than Aunt Elspeth and . . ." She hesitated, obviously not wanting to speak of her cousin.

"Yes, I know," he supplied for her, beginning to understand what might be behind her reluctance, given what her cousin had said about her. "You're referring to Edmund Segrave and his mother, and I also know that you haven't had any dealings with them since your father died. So my point is that you lived an isolated life."

"Well, yes," she said, "but I didn't really mind, because I always knew that eventually you would summon me. You were only three years late."

Aiden slowly shook his head. "Serafina, I'm sorry. Please don't interpret this the wrong way, but the truth is that I didn't know you existed until eleven days ago."

"What?" Serafina exclaimed sharply. "You can't—but it's

not possible. . . . Oh, *Aiden*," she said, looking appalled, "did your poor father's memory fail him on even this point?"

"You could say that," he replied with an ironic twitch of his mouth. "But his memory was jogged a few weeks ago. And then I returned home and he informed me that I was to marry a woman I'd never even heard of, that it had all been arranged. I told you the reasons for that yesterday."

"Oh," she said, frowning heavily. "So you agreed, even though you held me in the lowest regard."

Aiden ran his hands over his face, then heaved a sigh, trying to negotiate his way through this tangled web of mis-understandings. "Never mind that for a moment. Suppose we really hadn't met, at least not until this morning? Suppose I'd never made any of my ill-advised statements or given you that even more ill-advised kiss? Would you have come to me with a different attitude?"

"Perhaps," she said, looking not entirely sure herself. "But it would only have taken me a little more time to realize what a heartless cad you are, so in the end we would have been in the same position. I don't see what real difference it makes."

Aiden just nodded, although her words cut him to the quick. "So you think I'm a heartless cad?" he said after a long moment.

"What else can I think of you?" she said desperately. "You told me exactly what you thought of the woman you were affianced to, and yet you were prepared to go ahead with the wedding. You kissed someone you'd never met before when you were going to be married to someone else in the morning."

Aiden grabbed her hands. "You little idiot, I was speaking of a woman whom I believed *had* coerced me. And I didn't just kiss any woman, I kissed you!"

"The point," Serafina said, pulling away from him for the third time that day, "is that you ought not to have been kissing anyone at all, not on the eve of your wedding. I find that despicable behavior. And you certainly shouldn't have been kissing me, knowing I was going to be married to someone I thought I loved."

Aiden raked his hands through his hair. "Listen to me," he roared in frustration. "I kissed you because I wanted to kiss you, no more, no less than that. And if a man ever regretted a kiss more, I'd like to find him and commiserate with him. But you can't possibly be foolish enough to hold that against me for all time?"

"I don't see why not," she said, crossing her arms over her chest. "You kissed me out of lust, not love. You said so yourself, that love had nothing to do with it, that you don't even believe in love."

He closed his eyes for a moment. "Why don't we just put the kiss down to a momentary loss of sanity?" he said, desperately wishing he had never given in to the impulse. "I was there, you were there, and kissing you felt like the thing to do."

Serafina regarded him smugly. "You see, you've just made my point—you're an unfeeling rogue. I suppose you still plan to get your heir on me and go off to establish your string of mistresses?"

Aiden groaned and rested his forehead on his fist. "No," he said, eventually looking up at her. "No. I was only speaking out of bitterness when I said that, although to be perfectly honest, if you'd turned out to be what I expected, that's probably exactly what I would have done."

"Precisely," she said. "Which makes you immoral on top of everything else. I'm sorry, but I cannot help but despise you."

He pulled up a handful of grass and stared down at it as if he'd never seen the stuff before. "And why shouldn't you? You have every right," he said, a bite in his voice. "You obviously came to this marriage completely innocent—and ignorant, for that matter. And yet I've done nothing but malign you, even though it was unintentional, and bully you, and topple all your dreams." He dropped his hand onto his knee and curled it into a fist, hating himself. "I made you cry, damn it."

She touched her tongue to her upper lip. "Well . . . to be fair, you can't help it that I was foolish enough to hold on to an impossible dream," she said after a long pause, raising her eyes to his, the green softer now. "And I suppose you can't help it that you don't love me."

"But Serafina," he said reasonably, "how can you expect me to love you? I don't even know you, for God's sake." He took her hand and held it lightly in his own, and this time, to his relief, she let him keep it. "And yet I swear to you, when you showed up in that chapel today, I was overjoyed, because at least I knew I *liked* you, which is a damned sight better that loathing the ground you walked on."

"You like me?" she said with a surge of surprise. "How can you possibly like me? As you just said, you don't even know me."

"All right. Let's just say that I like what I do know about you," he said with a little smile. "I know that you're honest, anyway."

"But I haven't been the least bit nice to you. I didn't even want to marry you."

Aiden laughed shortly. "You have been a little hellion, I'll admit. But I deserved every minute of your scorn—well . . . most of it," he amended. "Look, Serafina, why can't we put all of this behind us? After all, we're married now, and that can't be undone. Don't you think we should try to make the best of things?"

"What do you mean?" she said, renewed suspicion narrowing her eyes.

"Just that," he said, treading very carefully. "I'd like to be your friend, if you think that's possible."

Serafina's mouth dropped open. "My *friend*?" she said in disbelief. "How can you want to be my friend when you already know what I think of you?"

"Ah, well," he said softly, rhythmically stroking the palm of her hand with his thumb. "That's something I'll have to try to change, isn't it?" He looked directly into her eyes. "But you have to be willing to let me prove to you that I'm not what you presume I am. Is that too much to ask?"

"I don't know how you think you can change my mind," she said with strong confusion, looking down at his hand.

"Oh, I can think of a number of ways without straining myself too hard," he said, his thumb making another sensuous circle, his fingers closing on hers.

"I should have known," she said, angrily disengaging her hand from his. "Now that I've had a little experience with seduction I know exactly what you're about. You're trying to make love to me, aren't you?" she demanded, wiping her palm on her dress.

Aiden smiled lazily. "Not just at this moment," he said. "I thought I'd save that for later."

Serafina blanched, then jumped to her feet, and he silently cursed himself for having spoken so directly. He belatedly remembered what she'd said, that she thought she would go to her marriage bed with her Prince Charming, and even though the practicalities of the matter escaped her, she'd been enthusiastic. Until now.

He wanted to kick himself.

"I can't," she said baldly. "I—I mean, you can't. We can't."

"We can't?" he said, wondering how in hell he was going to recoup the situation. "Why not?"

"Because . . . because it would make me cry again." She looked away, her mouth trembling.

"Tell me, Serafina, do you think you'd cry because you assume you won't enjoy it, or because you truly can't bear the sight of me?" He wasn't sure he wanted to hear the answer.

"B-Both," she stammered. "And because I know that you wouldn't come to me in love."

"Oh, so we're back to this damned love thing, are we?" he said, caught in his own trap but unwilling to fill her head with a lot of romantic nonsense, as tempting as it was. "Well, I'm not going to lie to you, since I can't tell you that I love you—you already know how I feel on the subject. But I will promise you that I'll come to you in tenderness and with the desire to please you. Is that not enough?"

"No," she said tenaciously. "It's not. And you shouldn't think it is either, although you're so unprincipled that it obviously doesn't matter to you what I feel."

Aiden, hurt that she could think him so callous, stood to

face her, his height forcing her to look up at him. "You're wrong, you know," he said tightly. "I care very much about how you feel. You do realize that many marriages have been made from less than this, that most men would insist on taking the rights legally due them?" He rubbed a hand over his eyes.

"Is that what you're asking of me?" she inquired, meeting his gaze directly. "You want me to be your friend, to change my opinion that you're a typical high-born cad who takes whatever he feels is his due at the expense of the woman he means to seduce, and yet in the same breath you ask me to capitulate to you as if I had no feelings of my own?"

"Is letting me make love to you really such an appalling prospect?" he asked, already knowing the answer.

Serafina nodded adamantly. "Yes. It is." She regarded him warily as if he were a snake in the grass, poised to bite.

"All right," he said, praying he wasn't consigning himself to a living hell, but knowing he'd be a fool to push the situation any further if he ever wanted to win her over. "If you feel that strongly, then I won't ask it of you."

She stared at him. "Are you saying you don't intend to sleep with me?"

"I'm saying that I won't make love to you unless you wish it, but I did hope you wouldn't be adverse to sharing my bed," Aiden answered quietly.

"Oh. But I don't want to share your bed," she said, fiddling with her dress. "Not at all."

Aiden turned away from her, clasping his hands behind his back, his head bowed as he thought his way through her latest blockade of defenses. He turned around again. "What, may I ask, do you propose instead?" he asked, a brilliant idea dawning on him.

Serafina, stymied by the question, frowned. "I hadn't thought that far," she replied.

"Apparently not. What do you think our respective families, never mind the servants, are going to make of an arrangement whereby you sleep in one room and I sleep in another night after night, year after year? Don't you think it's going to give them all cause for speculation?"

"I—I hadn't thought of that either," Serafina said, one hand creeping to her mouth.

"Then do think about it," he said, knowing perfectly well that he was manipulating her in a thoroughly disgraceful manner, but unable to help himself. He longed desperately to have her sweet, slim body pressed against his, hoped that maybe he could change her mind about lovemaking with a well-placed arm, a seemingly artless kiss.

"Well," she said slowly, "you do have a point. I wouldn't want to upset anyone. I suppose we could share your room."

"Oh?" Aiden said, seeing a glimmer of hope on the horizon and pressing his advantage at this unexpected capitulation. "And where do you expect me to sleep, may I ask? On the floor?"

"I don't suppose there's a comfortable sofa?" she asked hopefully.

Aiden looked at her in disbelief. "Now you want me to sleep on a lumpy sofa and wake up with kinks in my back every morning?"

Serafina flushed. "No, of course not. That would be very distressing for you, I can see that."

"I'm so pleased that you're sympathetic to my plight."

"Well, it is your room after all, and you've probably slept in the same bed since you were a child. It would be less than fair for me to throw you out of it, and I confess that I have no more inclination to sleep on the floor or the sofa than you do."

"I'm beginning to think you a highly practical woman. So are we agreed?" he said, sensing victory within his reach.

"Oh, very well," she said. "We can share. Actually, I've read about a practice in America called bundling. A board is placed in the middle of the bed, and the two people sleep on either side—"

"Serafina," Aiden said dangerously, "if you think for one minute that I'm going to sleep with a board running down the middle of my bed, you can think again. If you don't want me to make love to you I won't, and that I will swear. But I won't be tossed onto the floor like some piece of discarded baggage, and neither will I turn over in the night and meet with a cold, splintered piece of wood."

"Oh," she said. "Yes, I can see that might be uncomfortable. But how do I know you will keep your word?" she asked, clutching her hands together in a tight fist.

Aiden wondered the same thing, but he wasn't about to admit that to her, not when he'd come so far. "Because I've given it to you," he said simply.

"Yes, but for all I know you will be overcome by your male appetites and do something awful to me," she persisted.

"Serafina," he said, trying very hard not to collapse into laughter, "I have never had my lovemaking described as awful, I'm happy to say, with the one exception of my indoctrination when I was seventeen. And that was with a woman who was paid handsomely not only to put up with me, but to make sure it never happened again. Rest assured, when the time comes, I'll make sure that you won't apply that adjective to it either."

"When the time comes?" she said nervously.

"You can't think that I'm going to lie in a state of wanting for the rest of my life? Sweetheart, I'm willing to accede to your wishes up to a point. But if you don't want me to run off to those mistresses I mentioned, you're going to have to come around eventually. I'm only a man, and men, such low beings as we are, do have physical desires."

Serafina looked away. "You're saying that if I don't submit to you that you will break your marriage vows?"

Aiden, pushed to his limits, would have happily strangled her. "What I said, you little fool, is that I want you. I'm prepared to wait until you want me too. But if you decide you'd rather behave like a nun for the rest of time, then yes, I will take myself elsewhere and not bother you with my attentions."

Astonishment and shock crossed her face.

"What troubles you, my Titania?" he asked. "Is it that you really don't want me as I want you? Or is it that you're afraid you might want me after all, and that terrifies you?" He touched a hand to her cheek, lightly stroking her skin.

Serafina jerked away. "You are truly impossible!" she cried. "How can you in one moment try to make things better between us and in the next behave like a—a libertine? You blithely tell me of your past conquests, of your experience, you imply that you have been lover to many women, and yet you haven't loved a single one of them."

"That's true. But then none of them has been my wife," he said softly.

"What do you mean?" she whispered uncertainly, her eyes suddenly wide and vulnerable.

"What I mean is that you and I are now bound together," he replied, gently taking her face between his two hands. "Vows are important to you, aren't they?"

"They're everything," she whispered, meeting his gaze.

"Then know that I don't intend to break my marriage vows. But I need your cooperation."

"Oh," she said, blinking.

He smiled at her, a long, promising smile that he hoped conveyed his message. And then he dropped his hands. "It's up to you now. I won't go back on my word."

"You—you really won't?"

"No, I really won't." He stepped away. "Despite what you think of me, I have never taken a woman against her will and I don't intend to start with you. I'll wait for your invitation."

"I will honor your wishes to share a bed," she said. "But," she added adamantly, "as for the rest of your desires, I cannot accede. If you ever manage to change my mind about you I might reconsider. But I think the chances of that happening are as likely as—as snow in July."

Aiden grinned. "One step at a time," he said. "I'd better get back. Oh, and Serafina, just for your edification, you really are a bloody heiress. You'd better speak to your bird-witted aunt. It seems she forgot to tell you."

7

The butler jumped back as Serafina flew through the front door, out of breath from having run all the way back. She was determined to find her aunt and force some answers out of her. Somewhere along the line Elspeth had some accounting to do, for Serafina felt certain Aiden wouldn't lie about such an important thing as money, not when he needed it so badly and said he'd only married her because of it.

"My lady?" the startled butler said, blinking rapidly at her as she stormed across the hall. "May I help you in some way?"

Serafina nodded decisively. "Yes, you most certainly may. Where is Miss Beaton?"

"Your aunt is in the library with his lordship, my lady."

"And where is the library?" Serafina asked impatiently.

"Naturally I will conduct you, my lady," he said, drawing himself up with dignity, and Serafina felt a stab of guilt that she'd upset him by her lack of manners.

"I beg your pardon," she said, softening her expression. "Of course you may conduct me. What is your name?"

"Er, Plum, my lady."

"Well, Plum, I am happy to meet you," she said, shaking his hand enthusiastically. "Have the guests left?"

"Yes, my lady," Plum said, looking down at his hand as if he'd never seen it before. "The duke was the last to leave, and that was an hour ago."

"Good," Serafina said with satisfaction. "I hope that wherever he's gone, he stays there permanently."

"Did you not enjoy the duke's company?" Plum asked with no change of expression.

"I found him arrogant and overbearing. I think he likes being a duke a little too much and is accustomed to ordering people around. I'll bet he orders you around all the time, doesn't he, Plum?"

"Er, yes, my lady," Plum replied with a small twitch of his lips. "But then it's my job to take orders."

"Oh, well that's true, I suppose. But it's not my job to take orders, and between his dukedom and my husband I think I've been ordered around enough for one day. Please, I'd be much obliged if you'd take me to the library now."

"Certainly, my lady," Plum said with another twitch of his lips. Serafina followed him, wondering if poor Plum wasn't affected by an unfortunate tic. She would have to remember to ask Elspeth if she didn't have something to help it.

Plum bowed her through a door on the opposite side of the drawing room. She found her aunt sitting legs akimbo in an armchair opposite Lord Delaware, drinking a glass of sherry and smacking her lips loudly with relish.

"Oh, there you are, dearie," Elspeth said, waving her glass in the air. "I wondered where you'd gone to. Do join us. Delaware and I were just celebrating our good fortune." She swigged down the remains of her sherry.

"Oh, *Auntie*," Serafina said with exasperation, seeing that her aunt was halfway to being pickled. Elspeth rarely drank, but when she did, she became thoroughly unreliable. "How many glasses of sherry have you had?"

Elspeth's brow puckered in concentration. "Four?" she said, holding her glass out for more.

Serafina sighed and pulled it out of her hand. "Three too many," she said. "Auntie, I need to speak with you. It's urgent."

"You always were too stiff-principled, girl. What's a little celebration between families?" Elspeth said with annoyance. "Nothing worse than a prig, I say."

"But a fine-looking gel," Lord Delaware intoned, his voice slurred. "Who would have known, eh, Elspeth? Thought Aiden was going to murder me when I told him he was going to be leg-shackled, truly did, but he looked pleased enough today, don't y'think?"

Elspeth chortled and slapped her thigh. "Could have knocked him over with a feather when he saw her, but I always knew it would be a fine match, didn't I tell you, Delaware?"

"Auntie!" Serafina bellowed. *"I need to talk to you."*

"No need to shout, child, I'm not hard of hearing," Elspeth said churlishly. "What's got you worked up into a lather now?"

"It's about the money," Serafina said, placing her aunt's glass on the sideboard well out of reach. She sat down on the sofa. "My money. Does it ring a bell?"

"A bell?" Lord Delaware laughed uproariously. "Hell's bells, wedding bells, we'll ring any bells you like, my dear. We're saved, salvaged, delivered, all thanks to you—er, do have a glass of sherry," he said, regarding her uncertainly. "Or are you a teetotaler? Well, never mind, most appropriate in one your age, but now that you're a married woman you can indulge a little."

"Thank you, but I won't," she said. "However, now that I am a married woman, I think I am owed the truth about how that came about."

Lord Delaware's eyes lit up. "A married woman, did you hear that, Elspeth, my dear? It has a nice ring to it, eh?" He burst into another fit of laughter. "Bells. Oh, yes, bells," he said, wiping tears from his eyes. " 'If ever been where bells have knoll'd to church, if ever sat at any man's good feast.' Shakespeare, I think, or was it Milton . . . ? Oh, dear, such a shame when the mind goes."

Serafina covered her eyes with one hand, appalled that her aunt had so forgotten herself as to lead a senile old man astray with drink. "Auntie," she repeated, looking up. "Do you think we can talk? Privately?"

"Privately?" Elspeth huffed. "What need do we have of privacy? Delaware is privy to any information you might want. So what is it, dearie—not more nerves at this late date?"

Serafina wanted to scream with frustration. "It's nothing to do with nerves," she said, trying desperately to remain calm. "It's about my being an heiress. Is it true?"

Elspeth turned her gaze to Serafina, eyes squinting as she attempted to focus. "Well, of course it's true. Are you a complete sapscull, girl?"

Serafina felt like wrapping her hands around her aunt's neck. "No, I'm not a sapscull, Auntie. It's only that you led me to believe I'd been turned out of Bowhill without a penny to my name and we've lived on a shoestring ever since. I'm having a bit of trouble understanding why you perpetrated this myth if it has no basis in fact."

"Oh, yes," her aunt said, "that's right. I forgot for just a moment that you didn't know about the inheritance. Well, easy come, easy go I always say, and better easy come than the other way around, isn't that right, dearie? Surely you're not blaming me at this late date for keeping your fortune safe for you until it was needed?"

"My fortune," Serafina said, anger growing stronger by the second. "*What* fortune, Auntie? Just what fortune is this that you bargained me away for?" She planted her hands on her hips and glared at her aunt. "All this talking about destiny over the years was really about how much I was worth?"

"Oh, well . . ." Elspeth said, pulling out a hairpin and scratching her head, "that was merely an incentive. Aubrey will come around, you'll see." She winked at Lord Delaware. "One night is all it will take if your son knows his stuff, isn't that right?"

Lord Delaware chuckled. "Oh, Aubrey knows his stuff, never fear. He's always had a string of high-steppers, that one. Women flock around him like bees to honey, begging for a taste, and he's a generous lad."

Serafina's cheeks burned. She knew all about Aiden's lecherous behavior, but it didn't help having it confirmed by his own father. She turned back to Elspeth. "Why didn't you tell me?" she demanded. "Why did you let me think that Aiden wanted me?"

"Well, of course he wants you, child. Has he told you any differently?" she said, suddenly sitting up straight, her eyes narrowing.

"What he has told me, Aunt Elspeth, is that he was forced to marry me. That he knew nothing of me until only days ago. That he only consented to the marriage because it brought a badly needed fortune with it."

Elspeth turned to Lord Delaware, her eyes shooting sparks of fury. "Do you mean to tell me that you never even informed the boy of his destiny?" she screeched. "What were you doing for the last eleven years? Waiting for him to work it out for himself?"

"Auntie," Serafina said softly, shaking her arm. "It's not Lord Delaware's fault. He didn't *remember*."

"Didn't remember. Ha! You think it just slipped his mind, do you?"

Serafina nodded vigorously. "Sometimes these things can't be helped. Please don't blame him."

"You see," Lord Delaware said, regarding Serafina fondly, "I told you she was a good girl. It's nice that somebody understands my problems."

"You're not to worry yourself in the least," Serafina said reassuringly. "I realize how difficult your situation must be for you, and I will do anything I can to make you feel comfortable."

"Oh, a good, tender-hearted child to be sure, Elspeth. She makes a delightful change from my own two children, who never have a kind thing to say to me." He drained his glass and refilled it from the bottle on the table next to him.

"Your son is not a kind-natured man, but I shall try to speak with him," Serafina said. "He should at least treat you with respect."

"I couldn't agree with you more," Lord Delaware said, his eyes tearing up. "But he's never given me any respect, that one, even though he is my only son and heir. He goes his own way, does as he pleases with no regard to my feelings." He covered his eyes with his hand.

Serafina's heart went out to him. "I know how that is,"

she said, dropping to her knees next to his chair. "But he promises that he's going to try to reform."

Lord Delaware's hand fell away and his eyes shot open in surprise, the tears vanishing. "He does?" he said, his mouth hanging open.

"Yes, he does. And I shall do everything I can to encourage him, for I can see that his behavior has upset you deeply."

"And Charlotte?" Lord Delaware asked anxiously. "What are you going to do about Charlotte?"

"Do about Charlotte?" she asked, perplexed. "Do you mean you think something can actually be done for her?"

"I doubt it," he said, shaking his head. "But if you think you can turn Aiden around, who knows what miracles you might be able to perform with his sister?"

Serafina looked at Elspeth. "What do you think, Auntie?" she said, her brow furrowed. "Do you think we can help her?"

Elspeth scowled. "It's nothing to do with me," she said. "You're the one who has to live with her for the next fifty years."

"Yes, that's true. But I thought you might have some thoughts on how to treat her."

"An ice-cold shoulder would be my advice," Elspeth said, retrieving her glass from the sideboard and helping herself to Lord Delaware's bottle.

Serafina rolled her eyes. It was no good trying to get information out of Elspeth when she was in her cups. From what she'd observed, there wasn't a thing wrong with Charlotte's shoulders. Her legs were clearly the problem, since the duke had had to carry her from the chapel back to the house.

She'd think the situation over and consult with Elspeth when her aunt was back in her right mind. Maybe some exercises and treatment with herbal oils would be helpful.

"Well, Aiden, and here you are at last. How could you have deserted your guests like that today?" Charlotte asked, pushing her chair through the door of Aiden's study. "I've never been so mortified! It was bad enough having that woman run out on them with barely a word of explanation, but for you to go chasing after her? Have you lost your mind?"

Aiden looked up from the letter he was writing. "What are you going on about, Lottie?"

"You heard me perfectly well, so it's no good pretending that you didn't. You abandoned the dear bishop, not to mention the vicar, his wife, your cousin, and your sister. You even left Raphael to see to your excuses."

"That's right," Aiden said, tapping his quill against his cheek, trying to tune his sister out.

"But Aiden—your manners were appalling. And this after all the trouble I took to see that your day, if not a happy one, was at least fitting for your station."

"Serafina was upset, Lottie. I wasn't going to leave her to wander all over Townsend like a lost lamb."

"A lost lamb?" Charlotte said with disgust. "That girl is no more a lost lamb than I am—I'm sure she only wanted to draw attention to herself, since no one was paying her any. And why should they have, when everyone knows what a selfish shrew she really is?"

Aiden carefully put his quill down before he snapped it between his fingers. "Lottie, I love you dearly, but I will not have you speak of my wife in that manner."

Charlotte's jaw dropped open in shock. "You—you can't mean you have already been taken in by her? No . . . Aiden, I don't believe it. I won't believe it." She clenched her hands together in her lap, staring at him white faced. "How could you have anything but repulsion for her after the way she treated you in the church, at the breakfast? And—and you should have heard the terrible things she said about you afterwards in the drawing room. She said—"

"I'm really not interested," Aiden replied, cutting her off. "Serafina had a difficult day and I'm sure she was entitled to whatever she did say."

"I think not," Charlotte said sharply. "She was *most* unchristian in her words. The girl is—is a spoiled, badly mannered hussy, and I am horrified that you are defending her. She is not fit to be countess of Aubrey, and you for one should know it."

"That's enough!" Aiden roared, his temper snapping. "I don't give two pins what you think, Charlotte. Serafina is my wife, and I won't have you malign her."

Charlotte raised her chin. "I—I see," she said coldly. "Yesterday you were prepared to think all those things of her and more, and yet today, now that she has actually shown her face, you have reversed yourself, simply because that face is not as hideous as you were anticipating? I should have known that you'd be led astray by lust, Aiden Delaware, for hasn't it always been the way with you?" Her mouth tightened into a thin line, censure written all over her face. "Don't think I haven't been told by the housemaids about your request to move your wife's belongings out of our mother's old bedroom and into your own."

Aiden stood, his fingers gripping the edge of the desk. "If you think to start in on one of your morality lectures now, Lottie, think again. There is nothing immoral about wishing to share a bedroom with my wife. And yes, although it is true that Serafina is an attractive woman, that has little to do with my annoyance with you or my desire to see my wife treated with kindness." He released a sharp breath. "And furthermore, I deeply resent your assumptions about her character and mine, for that matter, simply because you are displeased with our sleeping arrangements."

Charlotte's hands flew to her cheeks where two spots of red burned. "Oh, you are cruel," she cried. "Here I am, looking after your best interests as I have always done, and all you can do is malign me, when none of this is my fault! I did not bring that scheming, deceitful woman into this house, you did—you and Father both. And now I am to be subjected to your scorn when I have done nothing to deserve it?"

"All I have subjected you to is a simple request to keep your tongue and your opinions to yourself," Aiden said more quietly, feeling guilty that he'd upset her so badly. "As for scorn, that is exactly what you have subjected Serafina to without even giving her a chance. I'm only asking you not to judge her until you've had an opportunity to know her a little better. Is that really so difficult for you?"

Charlotte tore her gaze away. "Very well," she said, staring down at her lap. "Since I can see that you refuse to hear me and my company is clearly repugnant to you, I will take myself away. Since both Father and that Miss Beaton have already retired for the evening, you and your—bride—can dine alone, without me to distract you from your amorous thoughts."

"Don't be a little fool," Aiden said impatiently. "It's no good flying up into the boughs over a small disagreement between us."

"A small disagreement?" she said tightly. "You cast me aside in favor of a new wife, and you call it a small disagreement?" Tears flooded her eyes and she dabbed at them with her handkerchief. "I never thought you would turn on me, Aiden, never in a hundred years."

Aiden moved over to her side and took her free hand, overcome with remorse that he'd lost his temper with her, something he rarely did. Lottie deserved better than the sharp edge of his tongue, and he knew better than to upset her when her health was so fragile. "I'm sorry," he said gently. "I'm not casting you aside, I promise you. I'm merely trying to ensure that we all get along, and a little charity on your part will go a long way toward making that happen."

"I have never been accused of being uncharitable," Charlotte sniffed. "Have I not always seen to the welfare of the villagers, even in my condition? Have I not sent baskets of food to those in need, since I could not go myself? Have I not seen to the religious education of the staff, concerned myself with keeping them on a godly path?"

"Yes, of course you have," he said, privately wishing that she'd concern herself a little less with the state of people's souls. "That's not what I meant. I just ask that you try to make Serafina comfortable in her new home, since her change of circumstances is overwhelming to her at the moment."

"I will naturally do what I can since I would hate for you to think me lacking in charity," Charlotte said, dabbing at her eyes again. "Please excuse me. I feel one of my migraines coming on and I would like to retire to my bedchamber."

"Of course," Aiden said, feeling guiltier than ever. He knew how Charlotte suffered from her headaches, and it was all his fault she was having one now.

He bent over and kissed her cheek. "Sleep well. I hope you feel better in the morning."

"I will do my best," Charlotte said. She turned her chair and wheeled herself out of the room.

Aiden swore softly as the door closed behind her. He crossed the room and poured himself a large glass of wine from the decanter, calling himself every kind of fool he could think of.

Serafina changed into her Sunday dress, Janie fussing over her as she did up the buttons on the back. "There you are, miss—my lady, that is," she said as she finished. "Probably as hard for you to get used to the title as it is for me. But you look just like a countess, sure you do."

"Thank you," Serafina said shyly. "That's very kind of you. I don't think the Delawares or their friends would agree with you, though. They look at me as if I was something the cat dragged in."

"I don't know why you'd be thinking that," Janie said with astonishment. "Lord Aubrey certainly doesn't look at you that way, not if the way I saw him smiling at you earlier is anything to go by."

"He was smiling at me? When?" Serafina asked.

"When you were on your way upstairs with your poor, indisposed auntie. He was standing in the door of his study."

"He did—I mean, he was?" Serafina said. She hadn't stopped to think how Aiden might actually view her—not the real Aiden, anyway. It wasn't that he'd made any secret of his desire to throw her into his bed and ravish her, but she assumed that was because he was a rogue, and from the sound of it, rogues would bed just about anyone.

She glanced around the room again, Aiden's room, where he'd wasted no time in depositing her, her gaze falling on the dressing table where his silver-backed hairbrushes sat, on the writing desk by the window where a pile of books was stacked haphazardly, on the wardrobe where his clothes hung, finally lingering on the huge canopied bed where she would sleep that night. With him.

Her stomach churned sickly. She had no way of knowing if he'd keep his word not to touch her. Aiden was a mystery to her, one minute saying one thing, the next doing something else entirely. And yet he seemed sincere about his promise. But then, he'd seemed sincere in the woods too, and look what had come of that.

She tore her gaze away from the bed back to Janie, not wanting to think about Aiden's true intentions a moment longer. It was bad enough that she had to spend the rest of her life with him without working herself into a state over the next few hours.

"Are you ready to go downstairs?" Janie asked, standing back, her hands resting on her plump hips. "Mr. Plum said dinner at eight and it's already five to."

The last thing Serafina wanted to do was descend the stairs to face Aiden and his family again, but she knew she had no choice. She'd already behaved badly enough for one day. "I suppose so," she said despondently. "Although I'd far rather hide away in here and never come out again."

"Pshaw," Janie said. "You're experiencing bridal nerves, that's all. My mum says it's natural when you've just been married. She told me you might be in a bit of a state tonight, that she did, this very morning when I left home to come look after you."

Serafina forced a smile to her lips. "It was very kind of you to do so. I have to confess, I'm not accustomed to being looked after, Janie."

"Well then, and I'm not accustomed to looking after ladyships, either, so we're in the same boat. The last job I had was doing for nice Mr. and Mrs. Kirkland, until Mr. Kirkland was carried off by a bad heart. His poor wife died just last month, so when word went out that they were looking for a lady's maid for the new countess, I brought myself straight up here, thinking there was no reason I couldn't look after a countess as well as I could a plain missus."

She grinned. "Better, maybe, since I don't have to do all the cooking and cleaning and carrying on my own, and that's a blessing to be sure, even though I do have to live up here now."

"Won't you miss your family?" Serafina asked.

"Sure enough I will, but I'll see them on my half-day off, won't I, and they can do with the extra money in their pockets. The only thing that troubles me is that I'm used to having laughter about me, and the servants' hall is fairly glum, miss. My lady, I mean."

"Oh . . ." Serafina said, glad someone else had the same impression. "I noticed that last night. Nobody seems to smile."

"No indeed, they're all stifflike and shut up like corpses in a coffin, except for that Mr. Tinkerby of yours. I like him, I do. We had a jolly chuckle over supper when we discovered we have relatives in common over Leicestershire-way— distantlike, but still . . ." She clapped her hands over her mouth. "But here I am prattling on when his lordship is expecting you downstairs. My mum always said I did run on at the mouth, and I reckon she's right."

"Oh, Janie, I'm awfully glad you do prattle on," Serafina said sincerely. "I'm feeling most alone at the moment, and it's nice to know someone is willing to talk to me."

"I'll talk at you all you want, my lady. You'll probably want to shut me up soon enough. But you'd better run along and make your first appearance as lady of the house."

Serafina drew in a deep, shaky breath. "Oh, Janie, I don't know the first thing about being lady of the house, let alone a countess! I'm sure I won't be any good at it."

"You'll do well enough, you'll see. Nothing's so bad as it first seems, and that's the truth right enough. I had a case of the butterflies myself this morning when I left home, wondering if I wasn't going to be out of place with you, but I think we're going to march along nicely together, so it only goes to show, doesn't it?"

Serafina laughed. "I think we're going to march along nicely indeed, Janie, and I'll take your words to heart."

"There you go, my lady," she said. "Now off with you, and try to enjoy yourself."

Serafina nodded. She left the room, squaring her shoulders, and started down the stairs.

8

Charlotte sat in her chair next to her bedroom window, staring sightlessly out into the dark night, her thoughts turned inward.

She still stung from Aiden's harsh words. He'd never talked to her so before, so cruelly, so brutally insensitive to her feelings. She'd known the night before that there was going to be trouble—oh, yes, she'd known it from the moment Miss Serafina Segrave had appeared in the drawing room—not the unsightly monster that Aiden had described, but a beautiful girl with a comely figure and sweet voice.

Charlotte had been stricken with shock, for the first thought that occurred was that her brother might not be so adverse to his bride after all. That had proved out sure enough at the altar, sudden delight written all over Aiden's face as if he was actually pleased to see her, even when she had behaved in such a disgraceful fashion.

And then at the wedding breakfast he'd hardly taken his eyes off her. Oh, he might have pretended his attention was elsewhere, but Charlotte knew. She'd seen lust before.

She remembered well the time that Peter the footman had been smitten by Martha the parlor maid, his eyes following her everywhere with undisguised craving. And hadn't Charlotte taken care of that? She had indeed, catching them together in a disgusting embrace, pawing at each other in the pantry when they thought no one would be about, Martha's dress hitched up about her hips, Peter's breeches undone, his male organ exposed to Charlotte's view.

Charlotte shuddered in memory, the sinful, loathsome image ingrained on her brain for all time. But had she dismissed them? No. She, Christian that she was, had instead given them both a double load of work, never taking her eyes off them, reading tracts from the Old Testament while they labored side by side, not allowed to look upon each other.

God had seen to the rest, giving Martha her just desserts for her wicked wantonness when she died from influenza two months later. And the lascivious footman who had been led astray consigned himself to eternal hell two weeks after that, taking his life in the stables at the end of a rope.

Now her beloved brother was caught in the same web of lust, blinded to his wife's true nature. He hadn't even cared to hear the dreadful things Serafina said about him, had turned a deaf ear to Charlotte's pleas to be heard. And he had even gone so far as to change the sleeping arrangements without even consulting her, all because he knew what she'd have to say about his motives.

Aiden, sleeping with that woman, not because he had to do his duty, but because he wanted to—to . . .

Charlotte squeezed her eyes closed, her fist pressed to her mouth, trying to stifle a rush of nausea. It wasn't as if she didn't know that Aiden had long indulged his male appetites. She'd overheard the stories of his philandering when he and Raphael spoke in the evenings, not aware that she could hear every word through the knot in the library paneling.

She'd learned a great deal over the years, her ear pressed carefully against the wall in her bedroom next door. She'd prayed long and hard that Aiden would outgrow his lamentable habits. But to have him now carnally indulging himself under her own roof with a woman Charlotte was convinced was Satan's handmaiden was more than she could bear.

She'd always dreaded the prospect of Aiden's marriage, knowing that another woman would move into her house, but she had hoped that he would at least marry someone biddable, someone who would sit in the evenings with her, appropriately submissive as Charlotte instructed her in the ways of the Lord.

She had even gone so far as to hope that the dreadful woman Aiden was forced to marry would be trainable, that by virtue of Aiden's disgust of her, she would turn to Charlotte for advice. And Charlotte had planned that advice carefully, had worked out exactly what to do and say to keep the woman under firm control.

But all of her planning had gone astray, simply because Aiden could see nothing in front of him but a desirable body. Why else would he have so quickly turned against his own sister? He didn't even know what the woman really thought of him. But Charlotte did, and her heart broke for her misguided brother.

Everything she had ever done she'd done for Aiden. She'd kept the house going, ensured that even when their fortune fell everything was cared for as it should be. She'd looked after their pathetic father, seen to the servants, the tenants, the villagers, all in Aiden's name. And he had no gratitude, cared nothing for her labors. Cared nothing for her.

Charlotte turned her chair away from the window, her head bowed in despair. At least she still had Raphael, she thought, wiping tears away from her eyes. He saw straight through her brother's wife, his eyes unclouded by lust. Raphael loved her, loved her deeply, even though a marriage between them was impossible. Raphael needed an heir that Charlotte could never give him, but if it hadn't been for her crippled condition, they would have been married years before.

She sniffed into her handkerchief. Poor Raphael, consigned to a hopeless love, never marrying, solely out of loyalty to her. He was so devoted, visiting her every chance he had, and although they could never speak of their love for each other, it was there, a pure, chaste, beautiful thing that sustained her lonely days and nights.

Raphael understood how devastated she was by Aiden's marriage. He was devastated himself, on Aiden's behalf as well as her own. Hadn't he told her just today to be brave, to be of strong heart?

Well. She wouldn't let him down. She would make the best of a terrible situation. She would see to it that Aiden wasn't led too far astray by that witch of his. It might take a little time and patience, but Aiden would surely soon realize what his bride really was beneath that pretty surface.

And Charlotte would be there, waiting to pick up the pieces of his broken heart. All she had to do was to find a way to speed the process along.

Charlotte lifted her head, stiffening her resolve. This was no time for self-pity. If she was to set the situation right, she would have to put all of her energy and intelligence to the matter.

All she had to do was to find a way to catch Serafina out, prove to Aiden that she was not worthy of his compassion or his attentions.

She wheeled herself to her desk and began to prepare a list of how she might go about just such an important task.

Aiden impatiently waited in the drawing room for Serafina, watching the clock on the mantelpiece tick away the minutes. He was going to give her five more and then go upstairs and bring her down himself. The only cause he could think for her delay was a strong desire not to appear at all, and he couldn't say he blamed her. If the situation had been reversed, he'd be hiding in his bedchamber too. But then, he was the party who had made out well in this arrangement. Serafina hadn't been so fortunate.

He felt like an utter fraud. He'd as good as stolen her at the altar against her will, dragged her into a marriage she wanted nothing to do with, and why? Because he was a selfish bastard who had seen something he wanted and taken it. He didn't regret what he'd done for a moment, but he'd been searching his conscience for the last hour and he didn't like what he'd found there. For if he was truly to be honest with himself, he was every bit the cad Serafina had called him.

Oh, he needed her money, and badly, but he didn't want her because of that. He wanted her because she was everything he'd never thought to find in a woman—sweetness and innocence and artlessness. He could have let her walk away from him today, given her freedom and the chance to find someone who could love her the way she wanted. But he hadn't. In the one split second at the altar that he could have changed everything for her, he'd decided that he'd never wanted anyone more in his life.

And now Serafina was paying the price.

Aiden rubbed his forehead. The only thing he could do now was to try to find a way to make it up to her. If he couldn't be the fairy-tale prince she wanted—and that was a joke in itself—he could at least give her a decent life. A happy home. Children to fill it, if he could ever persuade her into his arms, that was.

He had no idea how to go about the process of seducing Serafina. She obviously wasn't interested in what he had to offer her as a husband, and she was sure proof against the charm that had never failed him in amorous pursuits. The problem was that he'd never really cared before whether he succeeded. The pursuit had always been a game, the prize a night or a week or even a month with a woman who knew the game as well as he. No tears and recriminations—or at least nothing that couldn't be handled with a parting gift of expensive jewelry and a few well-chosen words.

Serafina was entirely a different matter. Not only was she his wife and therefore a permanent proposition, he also desired her as he'd never desired before. But this was a different kind of hunger, born not just from strong physical attraction but also from some nameless longing that struck a chord deep in his being, as if it had always been there, but he had never known it.

That alone was enough to scare him out of his wits, but apparently not enough to stop him.

He cared about what she thought of him, a dangerous thing in itself. He wanted her to like him as much as he liked her, a fool's mission. He wanted her to smile at him again, that sweet, wide, gamine smile, to hear her bright laughter, to see her eyes light up with amusement at some ridiculous comment he made.

And he, idiot that he was, had gone and ruined it all in one careless encounter in the woods, spoken words that couldn't be unspoken, given her a scoundrel's kiss that couldn't be unmade. He was probably going to spend the next twenty years or so making up for that alone.

He glanced up at the clock again. Another five minutes gone by and still no sign of her. He marched over to the double doors and pulled them open. Only to find his wife standing at the bottom of the stairs, chatting away to one of the footmen.

"Really," she was saying, "seven children? How marvelous for you, William! Your wife must be very happy with her good fortune."

"Happy indeed, my lady, although she says she'll beat me over the head with a broomstick if I give her one more. She has enough on her plate and washing that never ends. The youngest is only two and that's enough trouble, although the older ones are good about looking after their little brothers and sisters."

Aiden leaned against the door, listening to the exchange with fascination.

"Oh, that is help indeed," Serafina said. "I'd always hoped to have a houseful of children. They make life so cheerful, even if they are a lot of work."

"Yes, my lady, and we're truly grateful for every last one. But sometimes I think it's just as well that I only have one evening out a week and one day a month or we'd probably have a handful more."

Aiden felt unreasonably jealous that not only did the footman have a wife in his bed who was obviously welcoming, but Serafina was bestowing on him that sunny smile he pined to have turned on himself.

But her smile faded. "That is all the time you're allowed off?" she said, her brow puckering.

"That and a half-day on Sunday when her ladyship takes us all to church, but I'm not complaining, mind you. I'm lucky to have the position here at all, since married servants aren't encouraged."

"I can't see why not," Serafina said. "That doesn't seem fair at all."

"Too many distractions from doing their work," Aiden said straightening and coming forward, intending to claim his wife.

The footman looked up with alarm and turned white as a sheet. "Begging your pardon, my lord, I—I . . . I wasn't meaning to step out of place."

"No need to beg my pardon, William. You are very kind to entertain my wife. I imagine the subject of your children is of the deepest interest to her."

He didn't bother to add that he'd never known that William had any children at all, let alone that his name was William to begin with, although the man had been at Townsend for a good ten years. Serafina, naturally, had availed herself of this information at the first opportunity, and he strongly suspected she'd soon dig out the deepest secrets of the laundry woman as well.

"Are you planning on joining me at any point this evening, Serafina, or were you going to leave me to dine alone?"

"I hadn't realized you were so anxious for my company," Serafina retorted. She shot a parting smile at William as he swiftly bowed and disappeared. "I'm sorry if you felt I was ignoring you. I am merely trying to acquaint myself with the household. Or is speaking in a friendly fashion to members of the staff not done in your elevated circles?"

"You may speak to whomever you please in any manner you wish," Aiden said, seeing by her chilly expression that he'd gotten off on the wrong foot once again. "I was merely lonely."

"Lonely? Oh, dear. And I thought you found yourself the best of companions."

Aiden couldn't help grinning at her prickly attitude. "I'm a far better companion when I have someone to share myself with."

One finely etched eyebrow shot up. "That comes as no surprise at all."

Aiden sighed. "Serafina, do let us try to be friendly tonight, shall we? Come into the drawing room. Perhaps a glass of sherry would help."

Serafina shook her head. "I think there's already been

enough sherry consumed in this house this afternoon to sink a battleship. It certainly did so to your father and my aunt, who both went to their beds in a state of inebriation."

"Yes, I'd heard," Aiden said, showing her to a chair. "I'm not surprised in the least about my father, but your aunt didn't strike me as being a boozer."

"My aunt is not a boozer," Serafina said indignantly. "She is simply enthusiastic by nature, which does her no good on the rare occasions that she does drink, for she tends to over-do it. I am sorry to say that she passed out when I delivered her to her room."

"Since I already know that my father did the same, and since my sister removed herself to her apartment with a headache, that leaves us in a singularly advantageous position."

"I'm not sure that 'advantageous' is a word you should be using around me, my lord," Serafina said, her eyes flashing dangerously.

Aiden inclined his head. "Very well. Let me amend that to 'fortunate.' We have the evening to ourselves, and for that I can only be grateful."

And oh, how he meant it. To have Serafina to himself without the interference of various family members was a stroke of good luck. "We can use the time to good account— to get to know each other better," he added for clarification. Serafina looked as distrustful as a hapless worm about to be descended on by a hungry robin.

"Very well," she said primly. "If you wish to hold con-versation, I cannot object."

"Really, Serafina," he said, struggling not to laugh, "how else are we to learn about each other? Especially when you leave no avenue open to me other than conversation?"

"I suggest that if you wish to hold conversation at all that you refrain from certain unpleasant subjects."

Aiden couldn't help himself. He burst into laughter. "Oh, very well," he said. "We shall stick strictly to the weather, your health, and my detestable traits."

"If we stick to your detestable traits, we might very well be here all night," Serafina replied tartly. "Perhaps the weather might be the safest subject, since my health has always been unexceptional."

"I hear that storm clouds are gathering over Rutland," he said, his grin widening.

"Really? Rain is always good for the flowers," she replied neutrally.

"Is it? It helps them bloom, I assume?" he said, equally neutrally, but wanting to laugh.

"Flowers generally bloom when the weather is fine, my lord, as much as they need rain to nurture them. But I doubt very much that you know much about the cultivation of flowers, given the state of your gardens."

"Yes, the gardens," he said, longing to span the distance between them, take her into his arms and put an end to this silly conversation. "I'm afraid they've been hardest hit by our reduced circumstances. The gardeners were the first to go. I hope the gardens aren't too badly suffocated by weeds."

"Weeds I can manage. Gardens I can also manage. What I find a little more difficult to manage is you."

Aiden cocked his head to one side. "Ah, and now you wish to manage me. Well, I can't say I blame you, although I doubt you'll have much luck. I've never been a very manageable sort."

"So I gathered from your father," she said, giving him a hard look. "But Aiden, speaking of that . . . don't you think you might try to be a little kinder to him? He is an old man, after all, and not—not in the best of condition."

Aiden regarded her curiously. "What makes you think I'm unkind to him? I can't think of a single objectionable thing I said to him all day."

"Because he told me so. He said that you don't respect him, that you are not careful of his feelings."

Aiden drew one finger down his cheek and rested it on his chin. So, he thought with annoyance. His father was already at work, once again sticking his nose where it didn't belong and making a hash of things as usual, this time with Serafina.

"Did he happen to tell you why he thinks I ought to treat him with respect?" he asked, trying not to let his anger show.

"What a terrible thing to say," she replied, looking shocked. "He's your father, and you're very lucky to have one at all. He can't help what he is, you know, and I think you should have some sympathy for him."

"I suppose you went to him to ask about your money, then. Did he tell you the truth?"

"My aunt told me the truth, although she wasn't making much sense. But she did confirm that I have an inheritance—which is now yours, of course," she added darkly. "And I can just imagine what you plan to do with it."

Aiden thanked God that at that particular moment Plum appeared at the door to announce dinner. "We'll talk about it later," he said, seeing they were heading into another potentially explosive situation. "Here, give me your arm, Serafina, and let me take you in. We might as well try to behave like a happily married couple for the sake of the servants."

She hesitated, then took the suggestion as he knew she would. Serafina might not be the least bit interested in his own sensibilities, but apparently she had a healthy respect for those of the staff.

Her fingers slipped into the crook of his arm, warm fingers, their light pressure sending an unexpected physical shock through him. He realized this was the first time Serafina had voluntarily touched him, and he enjoyed the sensation hugely.

"Plum," he said when he saw that Serafina's place had been laid at the far end of the table, "would you be so kind as to have her ladyship's setting moved next to mine? I have no intention of making myself hoarse by shouting halfway across the room."

"Certainly, my lord." Plum quickly changed the arrangement as Aiden stood in the middle of the room, unwilling to so readily relinquish Serafina's fingers.

"Thank you." Aiden pulled out the chair on his right and deposited Serafina in it as Plum vanished and immediately reappeared with a tureen of carrot soup.

He brought it to Serafina's side and she looked at him, as if she wondered what he expected her to do with it. Plum gazed pointedly at the ladle, and Serafina brightened, then dipped the ladle in the tureen and promptly splashed half the contents on the table.

"Oh," she said with dismay, looking at the mess she'd made. She dabbed at it with her napkin. "I—I'm afraid I'm not accustomed to doing things this way. At home we serve the food directly onto the plates and then put them on the table." She flushed a deep red.

"Ah," Aiden said, seeing that Serafina was going to need a great deal of instruction. He'd had an inkling of that at the wedding breakfast, given the way she'd gone about things then.

He nodded at Plum, who promptly took the ladle from her and filled her bowl. Aiden then helped himself, murmured a word of instruction into Plum's ear, and waited until Plum had poured two glasses of claret and vanished.

"I hope you don't mind my breaking with tradition," he said, trying to ease her embarrassment, "but I really would rather have you where I can see you." He picked up his soup spoon. "You're much too pretty to have your face obscured by an overstuffed epergne."

"I know nothing about tradition," Serafina started to say, and then her gaze crept up to his, her expression startled, eyes wide. "You think I'm pretty?"

He thought she was a great deal more than pretty, but he wasn't going to go too far, lest she question his motives and treat him to that leveling look of disgust she was so good at. "I think you are exceedingly pretty," he said, watching with fascination as a delicate flush rose from her neck and spread into her cheeks.

She bent her head, concentrating on her soup, and his gaze wandered to the soft little wisps of hair on her nape, the long sweep of white throat, the delicate curve of ear. A jolt of desire surged through him as wicked thoughts of what he'd like to do to that throat, that shell-like ear danced in his head.

"I think you say so only because you wish me to look more kindly upon you," she mumbled, lifting her glass and half draining it.

"Not at all," he said in surprise. "Have you never been told it before?"

She shook her head, staring down at her bowl. "I wish you wouldn't fun with me, Aiden. I know perfectly well that I'm not pretty, and telling me I am isn't going to further your cause."

Aiden, taken aback by her mistaken assessment of her looks, stared at her. "Serafina . . . I don't know what has given you the idea that you're unattractive, but I assure you it's not true." *Anything but true,* he thought, wondering angrily who had put the notion into her head that she was in any way lacking and ready to take his head off.

She looked up then. "If that's the case, why is it that you're the first person who has ever told me so?"

"Could it be because there's never been anyone else who's had the opportunity?" he said. "From what you've told me you've lived a life of seclusion."

"I don't see what that has to do with it. Tinkerby and Aunt Elspeth looked at me every day, and there was the vicar on Sundays, and the people from the village when we went to doctor them. The most anyone said was that I'd do, which is a polite way of saying that I should make do."

"I see," he said, his gaze traveling over her heavily fringed sea-green eyes, her dear little nose, her wide, sensual mouth all set in an enchanting heart-shaped face, and deciding the vicar, the villagers, Tinkerby, and Elspeth Beaton were all either blind or mute. Serafina was a woman of unearthly beauty, and he was going to put his mind not only to seeing that the rest of the world knew it, but that she realized it for herself.

Which gave him an idea, and the more he thought about it, the more he liked it. "Serafina," he said, trying to sound casual, "I have to go to London tomorrow. I'm sorry, but it's a matter of the utmost urgency. How would you like to accompany me?"

Serafina's hand stopped halfway between her bowl and her mouth. "No!" she exclaimed, the soup spilling off the side of her spoon. "Thank you, I mean, but I think not." She put her spoon down abruptly and took another large gulp of wine.

"Why not?" he asked, regarding her steadily. "From what I've observed you need a trousseau, and I have a good dressmaker in mind. You've never been to London, have you? Wouldn't you like to see a whole new part of England?"

"No," she said, panic chasing over her face. "I've only just arrived here. I—I think it's best if I settle in. And I can't desert Aunt Elspeth—she'd never know how to go on."

"Oh, I think your aunt would know how to go on under any circumstances. She'll be perfectly comfortable here on her own."

"But I still don't think I can," Serafina said miserably. "You don't understand, Aiden. I'm not suited to your world. I wouldn't have the first idea of how to behave in it."

"But that's my point, sweetheart. I don't wish to do anything to unsettle you unduly, but at some point in time you'll have to become accustomed to being my wife, and that involves having contact with my world. It's your world too, you know. You were born into it."

"I may have been born into it, but I haven't experienced it ever, not really. I lived a quiet life at Bowhill and an even quieter one at Clwydd. I don't know the social customs, not even the simplest formalities, and those I once did I've since forgotten from lack of practice."

"I'll remind you," he said, thinking her thoroughly adorable.

"Oh, Aiden," she said miserably, "it's no good. I know you want me to fit in so that I don't disgrace you, but I don't think I can change who I am at this late date."

"I don't want you to change who you are," he said, looking at her over the rim of his glass. "I only want to make it easier for you to be a countess."

"But that's just it," she cried. "I never even thought as far as being a countess. Perhaps I should have done, but the only thing I cared about was being your wife. *That* was what I wanted to be good at."

Something in Aiden's chest twisted painfully. "And now you no longer care about that, either," he said quietly.

She looked up at him, her eyes shining with tears. "I won't lie and tell you I want to be your wife. All I wish is to live the way I'm accustomed to. This marriage is difficult enough to accept without being forced into something completely foreign to me."

"I understand," he said, wishing he'd never brought the subject up. "But you can't live in a protected bower forever, as much as you might wish it. Sooner or later the real world will intrude. It's already begun to, hasn't it? Today was difficult for you—aside from the shock of having to marry me."

She nodded, wiping her eyes on her napkin.

"I'm sorry for that, and I'm sorry for your distress. I wish to hell that your aunt had prepared you better for this marriage, but she didn't."

"She prepared me perfectly well for marriage," Serafina said. "She just didn't prepare me for you."

"That is more than clear," Aiden replied, trying to keep his face impassive as anger battled with hurt. "But you can't blame me for that."

She looked down, her lashes heavy on her cheek, glistening wetly. "No. I can't. I have only myself to blame for expecting someone else."

Aiden pressed his palm against his forehead as if he could suppress his frustration. "Serafina," he said, "neither of us is to blame. We were both unwitting pawns in someone else's game. But we might as well make the best of what we have. And to that end I'm trying to find a way to make you comfortable."

"How?" she said, raising tear-stained eyes that pulled at his heart. "How can you *possibly* make me comfortable, knowing how I feel?"

He wasn't sure himself. He felt more helpless than he ever had in his life. He knew almost nothing about her, only that she came to him ignorant in the ways of his world, that if it wasn't for the station of her birth she might easily be a simple village girl after all.

How did one go about training a young woman for her position without making her feel impossibly inadequate in the process? How did he gain her trust so that at least he could make some headway? What he desperately needed was information about her, and he wasn't going to get anything sensible out of Elspeth Beaton, that much was certain.

In that moment Tinkerby unexpectedly stumbled through the door like a God-given solution, carrying a platter of lamb and vegetables.

9

"Tinkerby!" Serafina exclaimed in strong relief, thrilled to see an ally suddenly appear out of nowhere. She quickly wiped her eyes so that he wouldn't see she'd been crying. "What are you doing here?"

"Don't know where else I should be, my lady," he said with a big grin. "I'm not accustomed to being idle, you know, and there's not enough staff about this great big place to keep it going as it should."

He placed the already carved platter of lamb on the sideboard and removed the soup bowls, groaning a little as he bent over. "So I told that Mr. Plum that I'd been serving you all my life and I wasn't about to stop now, especially when you needed a friendly face around you in your new home. Got myself a suit of livery and took the platter right out of his hand, I did."

"Well, I'm very happy to see you," she said, qualifying the thought in her head as she took in his costume, the green and silver uniform of the Townsend footmen looking ridiculous on his bent old body, his legs even more obviously bowed in the clocked stockings, his balding head covered in powder.

She was about to formally introduce Tinkerby when Aiden did the job himself. "I confess I'm pleased to have an opportunity to meet you at last, Tinkerby," Aiden said, standing. To Serafina's astonishment he warmly shook Tinkerby's hand.

"And I can say the same to you, your lordship. Thought

you was never going to send for Miss Serafina—her ladyship as she is now, and high time too."

"There was a little mix-up in communication," Aiden said smoothly, sitting down again. "But now that that's all been taken care of, I expect everything will progress as it should from here on out."

"It does my old bones good to hear you say it, my lord," Tinkerby said, shooting a satisfied look at Serafina. "We don't want anything more going amiss, especially not on this happy night. I thought for a moment that you wouldn't have a bride at all from the way she was carrying on this morning. Nearly gave me heart palpitations, it did." He glared at Serafina as if she were a naughty child.

"Oh, I wasn't too concerned," Aiden said. "I expect the sight of my face just gave her a shock. Serafina tells me she was anticipating someone a bit more, um, *docile* in appearance."

Tinkerby gave a great crack of laughter. "Nothing docile about you, my lord, that's for certain. Took her right in hand, you did, and that's as it should be."

If Serafina could have reached him, she'd have given her dear friend a swift kick. Instead she looked expectantly toward the lamb, hoping Tinkerby would remember his duties and refrain from making any more ill-advised remarks.

Much to her relief, Tinkerby shuffled back to the sideboard and prepared two plates, depositing them in front of Aiden and herself, and she heaved a small sigh of relief that she hadn't been expected to serve herself during this course. The soup had been disaster enough, but really, she couldn't think how she was supposed to manage at that angle.

Tinkerby refilled Aiden's glass and pushed the decanter close to his hand. "There we go, my lord. I'll leave you in peace now. Enjoy your meal and you just ring if you require anything else."

"Actually," Aiden said, regarding Tinkerby with an expression that Serafina couldn't read to save her life, "there is one thing. I'm in need of a valet, and my wife informs me that you have worked in all capacities. Since you obviously plan to stay on here at Townsend, I wondered if you would be willing to take on the job?"

Serafina gaped at Aiden, looking for the trick in his offer.

"Me, a valet?" Tinkerby said after a moment. "I've never been a valet, although I can probably pick up the way of it soon enough. But are you sure you don't want to hire someone more practiced?"

"I think I'd be a disappointment to anyone more practiced," Aiden said. "I'm not in the habit of changing clothes more than once or twice a day, and I don't live a very social life. What I really require is someone who can perform a decent shave and keep track of my belongings."

"Oh, I can shave you well enough, I expect," Tinkerby said with a grunt. "After all, I've shaved myself every day for the last fifty years or so. You might have to put up with a nick or two in the beginning, though."

"A small price," Aiden said equitably. "Good. Why don't you begin this evening? Let someone else play footman and take yourself up to my bedchamber. You'll find everything you need."

"Will you be wanting me to lay out your nightclothes, my lord?" Tinkerby asked blandly, and Serafina nearly choked.

"Just my nightshirt. You'll find it in the dressing room off the bedroom."

"Very good," Tinkerby said. "I'll tell Mr. Plum about your orders and get right on with the task at hand."

"Thank you." Aiden turned his attention to his food.

Serafina watched him for a moment, thoroughly confused. Aiden looked as if he hadn't done anything the least out of the ordinary, as if he asked weathered old men with no experience to be valet to an earl every day of the week. She was thrilled for Tinkerby, since a position as valet would lighten the old man's chores considerably, but she knew perfectly well that Aiden would have been better off with someone trained.

He glanced up and met her eyes with a gleam of amusement. "Why are you staring at me?" he asked. "Do you have a problem with my employing Tinkerby in this capacity?"

"No . . ." Serafina said, tearing her gaze away from his. "I'm grateful, actually. But why did you do it, Aiden?" she said on a rush. "What possessed you?"

He shrugged. "As I said, I need a valet. I left my own behind in Barbados and I'm lamentably bad at looking after myself."

"But Tinkerby? I love him dearly, but you must know he's not suited to the job."

"How would you know?" he asked, his eyes alight with laughter. "You've never had a valet."

"No," she retorted sharply, "nor a lady's maid either. But that's not the point. I remember enough from my life with my father to know that Tinkerby isn't the usual sort of gentleman's gentleman."

"But, sweetheart, you keep telling me I'm no gentleman," he pointed out reasonably, his brilliant blue eyes dancing. "Doesn't it then follow that I don't need a gentleman to look after me?"

"Oh, you are impossible," she said. "You know exactly what I mean." She raised her glass to her lips and drank, still wondering what Aiden was really up to.

"Yes, I believe I do. Suffice it to say that I like Tinkerby; he's a refreshing change from the usual pompous sort who hire themselves out as valets. I imagine we'll do very nicely together as long as he doesn't scar me in the process of educating himself."

Serafina couldn't help smiling. The idea of Tinkerby taking a razor to Aiden's infuriatingly handsome face was hugely appealing. She could just see Aiden now, little bits of bloody paper stuck all over his lean cheeks. "You are brave, my lord," she said. "I hope you don't regret your decision."

"I'll let you know." He tilted his head and regarded her intently. "Seriously, Serafina, I thought you'd be pleased. Tinkerby is obviously very close to you if he walked you down the aisle," he said, stifling a smile in his napkin. "And I honestly think he'll be a great deal more attractive in his own clothes. I'm not sure I could keep a straight face looking at him every day dressed up like a clown in the circus."

Serafina burst into laughter. "The thought occurred to me

too. Poor Tinkerby. He did look a little silly." Her smile faded as an alarming thought struck her. "You really did hire him to please me, didn't you?"

"Yes," he said simply. "I did. I thought you'd be happier knowing that he'd be looked after. I'm really not very demanding, and this way Tinkerby will have a little position downstairs. He's too old to have to deal with the hierarchy of the household, and on top of that he deserves a reward for having looked after you so loyally for so long."

Serafina almost—almost—found herself liking Aiden. "Thank you," she said, the words sticking in her throat. It wasn't easy to have to be grateful to Aiden for anything. But she was willing to accede the point to him for Tinkerby's sake.

"My pleasure," he said easily, reaching for the decanter.

Serafina watched him as he lifted it, the candlelight flickering over his strong profile, his eyes lowered, focused on his task. Her gaze fell to his well-shaped hand, the fingers long and slender, the curve of his palm gripped around the crystal as he refilled her glass. She barely remembered drinking the first one.

She'd never consumed wine before, which probably accounted for the increase in her heartbeat, a breathlessness in her throat. And she felt light-headed, as if her focus was slipping away from her.

He placed the decanter back on the table and picked up his knife and fork again. Serafina's eyes hypnotically followed the movement of his hand as it lifted a forkful of lamb, watched as he brought his glass to his full, sensual mouth and drank. Her gaze lifted to his lean cheeks, covered in the finest of dark shadow, only made more dramatic by the sharp slant of the light that played on them.

Serafina drew in a quick breath and forced her attention to her own plate. But the food had lost its appeal. Her hands drifted to her lap, caught up the napkin placed there, squeezing it hard as she tried to still the erratic beating of her heart.

Aiden glanced up, meeting her eyes, and images flooded her mind involuntarily, images of another time, another place when a man she had loved had lifted a glass in just that manner, when his hand, just as finely made, had reached out to clasp hers in his own and stroked her fingers.

Only then the glass had been a goblet of gold. And the face that had smiled down on her own had been different, his eyes dark and clear. But they held the same expression as Aiden's did now, a sensual expression of promise.

She realized that Aiden held her hand in his, that he was stroking her fingers in the same manner.

Something hot came over her, flooding her body with molten fire and she felt dizzy, disoriented. She passed a hand over her face, trying to bring herself back into the present, trying to still the familiar, longed-for voice she heard inside her head. "Sarah? Sarah, what is it, my love?"

She shook her head hard, thinking she was losing her mind. It was Aiden's voice. Just Aiden's voice, coming to her from a distance. "Serafina?" he repeated, and his words rung in her ears. "What is it, sweetheart?"

She managed to look up at him, his face swimming before her eyes, the gold hair shading into black, his brown eyes transfigured into sapphire blue.

"Nothing," she managed to gasp. "It's nothing. I think I must have had too much to drink."

"You've only had one glass, but then wine always did go to your head," he said with a little smile.

Serafina's head shot up. "What?" she said, jolted. *How could he know that?* she thought with true alarm, still caught in the fog that threatened to engulf her.

"I said that you've never been able to drink very much. . . ." He shook his head hard, then passed a hand over his face as if he was as confused as she was. "What I meant is that you must have lived an austere life up until now. You're obviously not accustomed to spirits of any kind."

She nodded, her head swimming, trying to make sense of his words. "I expect you're right."

"I know I'm right," he said, standing. "You're looking pale. Would you like me to take you up to bed?"

She nodded, pressing her fist against her forehead. "I'm— I'm sorry. Silly of me, I know. I feel most dreadfully dizzy."

He helped her to her feet and without bothering to ask

her permission he picked her up in his arms, carrying her out of the dining room, through the hall and up the stairs. Serafina rested her head against his shoulder, her arms holding fast around his neck as her dizziness only increased.

She heard his voice again as he laid her down on the bed and she struggled for a moment, not sure where she was, even who she was.

"Be still," he murmured. "I'll look after you. You have nothing to fear."

You have nothing to fear. She knew she'd heard the words before somewhere, somewhere when she'd been safe and protected, truly loved.

Time will run back and fetch the age of gold. . . .

He moved away and she pressed her cheek into the pillow, the fog beckoning to her, calling her to a place of sanctuary, and she finally stopped fighting and gave herself over to the peace of surrender, to Adam who stood like a shadowy figure in the swirling mist. She'd been waiting for so long. Love and longing welled up in her, bringing her closer, ever closer to him. There was no Aiden any longer, only Adam, Adam who waited for her too.

Time will run back and fetch the age of gold. . . .

She heard the sound of the door closing, a muffled thud. And then Adam's hands turned her easily, deft hands, familiar hands, sliding her dress over her head, stripping her of her chemise just as easily. She thought she must be ill, for he touched her as gently as if she were a child, his deep voice murmuring soothing words she couldn't make out.

Something else came over her head, a drift of cotton. Her hips raised naturally as the material smoothed around them, cool covers pulled back, her body lifted in strong arms and deposited beneath their comforting depths. *You have nothing to fear.*

Then there was quiet, broken only by the sound of Adam moving about the room. A few minutes later a weight settled in next to her and arms came around her, holding her close, sheltering her.

She sighed in contentment. Home. She was finally home at last.

"Thank you, Adam," she murmured, drifting off into blessed sleep, dreams already tugging at the corners of her mind.

Time will run back and fetch the age of gold. . . .

She sat in a great hall in the middle of a long table that stretched from one end of a dais to the other. Below her the hall was filled with gaily dressed people as far as the eye could see, the sounds of celebration booming around her in a great, happy din.

"Are you as pleased as your people seem to be, my love? I think that all of Kyrenia has turned out for our wedding party."

She turned her attention from the scene of revelry to Adam, who held his gold goblet up toward her in a salute.

"I am well pleased for your sake, my lord," she said, her heart filled with love for him. "It is not every day that a prince is married, and your people do you honor."

"As they do honor to my bride. Look upon my parents' faces, Sarah, and know they too are well pleased with you, although none is as pleased as I."

She glanced down at the end of the dais where Adam's father sat next to his mother, both of them smiling, although she didn't think the queen looked quite as pleased with her as Adam would like to think.

Clio of Curium was a regal woman who took her aristocratic lineage seriously, and there had been much original dissent on her part to Adam's proposal to marry Sarah, who was only of minor noble blood, and not even from the island but from Antioch on the mainland. But eventually an agreement had been reached, and Sarah's considerable dowry had finally placated Clio, who was equally intent on refilling Kyrenia's coffers.

Sarah had an uneasy feeling that she would have to tread carefully with Clio. The king, on the other hand, she liked enormously, and he had always been kind, if perhaps led a little too easily by his ambitious but beautiful wife. Sarah also had an uneasy feeling about the way Clio's gaze wandered a little too often to handsome Michael Angelus, who was a captain in the army and Adam's closest friend.

Michael sat across the table, laughing and telling outrageous stories, his eyes flashing with sharp intelligence. Sarah had the impression that Michael didn't miss much, but she couldn't escape the feeling that he was oblivious to the queen's close scrutiny.

There's trouble in that direction, she thought, then wished she could snatch the thought back as a chill of premonition ran down her spine. Sarah had always had an overdeveloped sixth sense, which rarely proved wrong, and she didn't like the direction it led her in now.

Bishop Margolis, who sat on her right, turned to her. "What troubles you, Sarah? A cloud just passed over your face, a strange thing to see on this happy day."

She shook her head. "Nothing, Father. Just a passing thought. But tell me; how long has Captain Angelus been back from the fighting?"

"Oh, only a month I believe. The last Arab raid was brilliantly rebuffed, and I don't believe there will be trouble again from that direction. Were you fearful of an attack, my child? I know your city has been under constant pressure from the Seljuk Muslims." He stroked his beard thoughtfully.

"No, I'm not afraid," she said truthfully. "Adam believes that the constant raiding is over now, thanks to the efforts of the emperor." She smiled. "And being Adam, he is pleased because peace is good for business."

"That many more ships to build and load for trade? And why not? The West is as hungry for our goods as we are for theirs, and despite the troubles, trade is strong with the East as well. More money for Kyrenia, which we will all applaud."

Adam leaned over, having caught the tail end of the conversation. "Indeed, for the fighting has hurt us badly in terms of financial loss. But it shouldn't be too long before everything normalizes and we can make up the damage. I thank God that this city-state is located in an inconvenient position for raiding—look at what Famagusta has had to endure, being a direct target on the southern side."

The bishop nodded. "Yes, but then in times of peace Famagusta has considerable advantages over you. Tell me, Adam. Do you hold the same view that your parents do?" he asked, lowering his voice.

"Oh, do you mean my mother's resentment of the killing har-

bor fees that the king imposes on every ship going out and coming in?" Adam grinned. "If I had the principal port on the island, I would probably do the same. In any case, there is nothing to be done."

"I am pleased to hear you say it," the bishop said quietly, lacing his fingers together.

"What else could I say?" he said with a shrug. "Famagusta has a stranglehold over us and we'd be unwise to object to their policy. All a protest would do is raise the tariffs even higher. We learned that lesson twenty years ago, and I have no intention of learning another one, no matter what—"

Sarah intercepted a subtle look of warning that Michael threw at Adam, and Adam's instant curtailing of his response. A thrill of alarm ran through her, something reinforcing her sense that danger threatened. But the moment vanished as Adam took her hand and gently squeezed her fingers.

"Forgive me, beloved. This no time to be discussing politics," he said smoothly. "Drink with me to our future, for this is the beginning of our life together, and it will be one filled with joy from this day forth, I swear it to you, even if it has taken three long years to reach this point."

She laughed. "If I have even one more sip of wine I shall fall off my chair. All these toasts are enough to make my head swim as it is."

"It is true, you have never been able to hold your wine in all the time I've known you. But then if you swoon, I will be able to carry you off to our marriage bed that much sooner."

"Much good I will be to you then," she said with a chuckle. "Oh, Adam, this is the happiest day of my life."

"And will be the happiest night as well, I hope," he said with a mischievous gleam in his eye. He cupped her face in his hand and gave her a lingering kiss that sent another thrill through her, this time of pleasure. "But you can tell me yourself come morning."

"My lady? My lady, rise and shine. It's nearly gone ten."

Serafina was about to tell the annoying voice to go away so that she could resume her conversation with Adam, but it came again, pulling her up and up, the image before her eyes wavering and finally, to her heartbroken disappointment, disappearing altogether.

It was the nicest dream she'd had so far and the longest, and she wanted nothing more than to be back with Adam, even if she knew now that he was nothing more than a fantasy.

And yet she couldn't help feeling a terrible surge of grief at having to relinquish him, relinquish the beautiful dream that had sustained her for so long. Fantasies might be exactly that, but they had so much more appeal than reality. She already missed Adam acutely, knowing he was lost to her, gone back to that imaginary place where he and she had existed so happily. And loved so fully.

Serafina reluctantly opened her eyes, squinting against the bright light as the draperies opened and let in a flood of sunshine. She sat up in bed, disoriented, not sure of where she was, sure only that she was back, and she didn't like it.

And then a rush of panic swept over her as memory came flooding back. She was married to awful Aiden, and he was as different from Adam as could be. And sadly, she couldn't wake up from Aiden.

She looked around the room, her panic only increasing. She was in Aiden's bed, and she didn't even know how she'd arrived there. But at least Aiden was nowhere to be seen. Only Janie moved around the room.

"Oh, Janie," she said hazily. "What happened?"

"You were lost deep in dreamland, and a happy place it must have been if the smile on your face was any telling. I thought you were never going to wake up. I called and shook you and called and shook you, and you just turned over and ignored me." She grinned. "But then you probably had a long night."

Serafina rubbed her eyes, wishing she could remember anything at all about the night. One minute she'd been talking to Aiden about . . . about Tinkerby, that was it. And the next she was here with the morning light pouring into the room. She looked over at the other side of the bed.

The pillows were indented, the sheets tousled and thrown back, and her blood ran cold.

Had it happened after all? Had Aiden done that terrible thing to her while she slept, without her even knowing? Or had a veil truly been drawn over her eyes so that she wouldn't remember?

She quickly did a mental assessment of her body. She wore a nightdress. That was a good sign, although she couldn't think how she'd come to change into it. And she felt no pain, no bruises, no soreness anywhere. She waited until Janie turned away to pour hot water into the basin, then slid over and pulled the covers back. No rivers of blood either.

Serafina breathed a deep sigh of relief. So he had kept his word. But then *why* couldn't she remember anything?

A knock sounded at the door, and Janie smiled knowingly and opened it, disappearing. Serafina started as Aiden came through, carrying a tray, and she quickly snatched the covers up to her chest as if that could protect her from him.

"Good morning," he said. "Did you sleep well?" He walked over to the bed and placed the tray down, then sat down next to it. "I thought I'd bring you breakfast up here this morning as it's so late, and I have to leave for London shortly. Tea?"

She nodded, her lip caught between her teeth, wishing he'd vanish.

"Milk? Sugar?"

She shook her head.

"Has the cat got your tongue, or is your head hurting too badly to allow for speech?" he asked wryly, handing her a cup and pouring one for himself. "I would have ordered you chocolate, but I don't know if you drink it."

"Tea is perfect," she said, gulping the hot liquid, her throat parched.

He leaned back and gave her a long, assessing look. "So, Titania. I think perhaps you'd better stick to drinking dew-drops after all. How is your head? Sore?"

"Why should my head be sore?" she asked suspiciously, thinking that would be the last thing she'd expect to hurt.

"Only, my dear innocent wife, because that's generally

where one feels the effects of overindulgence. You were three sheets in the wind last night. Don't you remember?"

Serafina stared at him. "Are you saying that I drank myself into a stupor?" she said, horrified that she might have done such a thing. "I—I don't remember. Oh, *Aiden,* I don't remember anything!"

He raised an eyebrow. "Nothing? You remember nothing at all? Do you mean to say all my spectacular talents went for nothing?"

"Oh . . . oh, no," she moaned, nearly dropping her cup in her lap. "You wicked, evil man! You took advantage of my inebriated state, didn't you? Oh, I should have known." She bowed her head, a flush of embarrassment and dismay covering her from head to foot.

Aiden laughed. "You really don't remember, do you? Actually, I was merely referring to picking you up and carrying you to bed."

"You—you did? Oh, and then Janie must have changed my clothes," she said with infinite relief, that puzzle answered.

"No, actually, I did that. You were in no state to have the servants see you. I think they assumed when they saw me convey you upstairs in my arms, your head lolling in my shoulder, that impending nuptial matters were well on their way, and I saw no reason to disillusion them. So I took the task of undressing you upon myself."

Serafina wanted to die from mortification. "Oh, no . . ." she said, her hand creeping to her mouth. "Oh, how dreadful."

"I didn't find it so," he said wickedly. "Actually, I rather enjoyed it. And I thought we orchestrated the situation perfectly, even if completely by accident. Everyone will now assume that the marriage stands where it should, which will spread like wildfire through the servants' quarters and back upstairs where it most needs to be heard."

"Yes . . . yes, I can see that," Serafina said, still mortified, not only by her behavior, but also that he'd seen her unclothed, even though that was her own fault entirely. "Aiden,

I swear to you that I'm not in the habit of drinking myself into a stupor, truly I'm not. I've never even had wine before, except a sip at Communion."

"I suspected as much," he said, clearly amused. "Not to worry. I imagine you just drank too much too quickly on a mostly empty stomach."

"I—I must have been overcome by nerves. I don't even remember having more than a glass." She managed to look up at him. "Did I make a terrible fool of myself?"

"Not at all, and actually, you didn't have more than a glass. You merely went from complete coherency into a near swoon in the blink of an eye. And you didn't make a fool out of yourself, other than calling me by the wrong name." His eyes glinted with amusement. "If I were a jealous man I might have taken exception, but I put it down to a slip of the tongue."

Serafina's hand crept to her mouth. "What did I call you?" she asked, not wanting to know the answer, terrified that she knew what it was.

"Adam," he said. "Close enough, and rather appealing, actually, the way you said it. Now if you'd called me Oberon, I really might have flown into a jealous rage."

Serafina blanched, utterly undone. She truly must have been out of her mind to make such a terrible mistake. "I— I'm sorry," she said, desperately relieved that nothing else had come out. Had it? "I didn't say anything else, did I?" she forced herself to ask.

"No, nothing. Why? Is there an Adam in your deep dark past?" he said, regarding her curiously. "I can hardly think so, but I have to wonder why you're looking so guilty."

"I have nothing to feel guilty about," she said, swearing she'd never drink another glass of wine again. She couldn't bear it Aiden ever found out about her foolish dream, and wine apparently not only made her tongue loose but her senses go wandering. "You know perfectly well that Aunt Elspeth kept me locked away all these years."

"Yes—a little too much so, I think." He buttered a piece of toast and handed it to her. "Here, eat this. It will help with your head."

"There's not a thing wrong with my head," she said, but she took the toast and hungrily bit into it, feeling as if she hadn't eaten in days. "I feel perfectly well," she mumbled through the mouthful.

"Then thank God for your good fortune, for I've had enough sore heads for us both in my time."

"Why am I not surprised?" she said tightly. "I suppose that's another prerequisite of being a rogue."

"Just put it down to asinine youthful indiscretion like so much else. Look, Serafina, I really do have to leave if I'm to arrive in London in decent time," he said, buttering another piece of toast and putting it into her hand. "Tinkerby has offered to drive me in your carriage, which I consider most generous of him."

"Oh, but Aiden . . . he only arrived two days ago. I don't want you to exhaust him by having him drive all the way to London."

"Nonsense. I can share the driving. I'd take my own carriage, but I don't seem to have one at the moment." He smiled. "That, however, I plan to remedy in no short order along with a number of other matters—which is why I have to leave today. Are you sure you won't reconsider and come with me?"

"No. I won't." The very idea of going to London struck fear into Serafina's heart. It was bad enough to be ridiculed at Townsend by the duke and Aiden's sister, but to have an entire city of fashionable people look upon her with mocking disdain was truly more than she could bear.

"I can see you're not going to budge. Very well. I think I have a fair idea of your size."

Serafina glared at him, thinking that he'd probably memorized every miserable feature of her naked body the night before when he'd stripped her. "I'm sure you have an excellent idea of my size, my lord, although that's not going to get you anywhere."

"I thought I'd give your measurements to the dressmaker I mentioned," he said, ignoring her barb. "She's fast, faster if I give her a little extra incentive."

"I wonder what that might be?" Serafina said, unaccountably jealous that Aiden would exert his considerable charms on a dressmaker. She could just see him now, tumbling her in bed while whispering his wife's measurements into her ear. "Haste is everything, Colette, even if my wife is a wretched creature." And Madame Colette cooing in return in a fine French accent, "Such a pity, my lord, that she isn't more amply endowed. But never worry, your wish is my command. I will turn her out in a fashion fitting for your countess, even if she is not worthy of the title. For you, your worship, anything at all."

Serafina angrily set her jaw. "I do not need a trousseau, my lord. I will do well with what I have. What need do I have for pretty dresses when I plan to spend my days here, working in your gardens with no one to see me?"

"You may work in the gardens to your heart's content, but you will be dressed appropriate to your station in life, like it or not," Aiden said, his eyes narrowing dangerously. "In the garden or out of it. We will compromise, Serafina, so it's no good throwing your temper up at me. I am not asking of you all that I might, so I expect you to meet me halfway in this matter, especially since I'm giving up far more than you at the moment."

Serafina opened her mouth to object, but realized that he had a point, and one that she didn't care to push. "Very well, my lord," she said demurely, wanting to throw her teacup at him.

"And you will desist from calling me 'my lord,' " he added, his voice tinged with severe annoyance. "I have a name. I'd appreciate your using it."

"Very well, if you desist from calling me 'sweetheart,' " she replied with cloying sweetness. "It irritates me in the extreme, since it's obviously not the truth."

"It's less of a mouthful than Serafina," he said, the humor returning to his face. "I suppose I could call you 'bloody harridan' since that's how you're behaving, but I think you'd take to that even less kindly."

"It's also one more syllable than Serafina," she said tartly. "And I don't wish to be a harridan, but you give me little choice when you try to push me into your way of doing things."

"I don't wish to push you anywhere." He put his cup back on the tray. "As I told you last night, you can't avoid moving forward. You can do it at your own pace, but you can't put it off forever. And I intend to dress you in a fitting manner while you get used to the idea of being my wife."

Serafina saw that there was little point in trying to argue, since he had no intention of listening to her. "Dress me as you will, but just keep in mind that you can't make a silk purse out of a sow's ear. I am what I am, Aiden, and no manner of dressing me up is going to change that, no matter what you might wish."

"Stubborn, but not entirely intractable," he said with a little smile. "I'd say we were making progress. I'll have a willing wife on my arm yet."

"You may have a wife, but I'm certainly not willing," Serafina retorted.

Aiden stood abruptly, his smile disappearing. "Maybe intractable after all. Very well, Serafina, have it as you wish. I'll be back in a month."

"A month?" she gasped. She thought he'd be gone a few days at the outside. A month seemed like an eternity.

"Yes, I'm afraid so. I have a company to rescue and some outstanding debts to pay, as well as a number of other pressing affairs to put into order."

"Oh . . . oh yes, of course. I can see that would take some time. Well, please don't rush home on my account," she said, telling herself that she couldn't wait for him to take himself away. A full month of sleeping alone, of not having to worry about what he might do to her would be a balm to her battered soul—and she should count herself lucky that was the only thing that had been battered. So far, she added glumly to herself.

"I was about to tell you that I'll miss you, but after that last remark, I'd be a fool. It's a lucky thing for you that I'm a patient man, Serafina, but don't try my patience for too long. It's liable to wear thin."

She shot him a look of poison. "Maybe you should start lining up your stable of mistresses now," she said. "I'd hate for you to feel deprived any longer than necessary."

To her surprise, Aiden burst into laughter. "Ah, well. If you really hated for me to feel deprived, you'd come over here and give me a sweet parting kiss. But since I don't really think you care how I feel one way or the other, I won't hold my breath."

Serafina crossed her arms over her chest. "You know what I think about kissing you."

"A fate worse than death, or something like that? Can you honestly tell me it was really that bad, Serafina?" he asked softly.

She colored, remembering exactly how nice it had been. "It's the principle," she said, refusing to meet his eyes, for fear he'd see the truth.

"Oh, yes—the principle. The principle being that I shouldn't have kissed the woman I was going to marry, simply because I didn't know I was going to marry her. A lot of prospective marriages would be scuttled if that was the operating principle, Titania. I wonder if you realize just how many illicit kisses are exchanged every single day with no harm done?"

"That's different, and don't try to confuse me, because you know exactly what I object to."

"As far as I can gather, you object to anything to do with me." He moved around to her side of the bed, and Serafina shrank back against the pillows in alarm.

"Relax. Despite what you think of my morals, I'm not a wolf who's about to devour you on my way out the door. I only want to say good-bye." He bent down and dropped a light kiss on her head, the faint scent of lime and sandalwood mixed with his own unique masculine smell drifting down to her. "There. That wasn't so bad, was it?"

Serafina couldn't answer. The truth was that every time he touched her she felt hot and flustered and started to tremble uncontrollably. Which was an unfathomable reaction when she didn't even like one square inch of his beautiful male body.

"Be happy," he said softly. "Or at least as happy as you can manage under the circumstances. And Serafina—believe it or not, I really am going to miss you."

And then he was gone, leaving Serafina alone in his big bed.

She didn't understand why she wanted to cry.

10

Serafina pruned another stem from the dormant rose-bush, then rubbed her hand over her cheek and gazed up at the sky with a heavy sigh. As much as she enjoyed toiling in the gardens, the constant work wasn't enough to take her mind off her troubles, and they were considerable.

The last week had been more difficult than she'd ever imagined. The wedding had been disastrous enough, but the reality of her marriage had truly sunk in over the last few days, and all she could see ahead was a life of misery.

The days weren't so bad, and at least the weather had been fine. She took breakfast in her room and chatted with Janie, which helped to alleviate her loneliness. She walked in the mornings, then settled down to work outside. She ate a simple luncheon with her aunt in Elspeth's quarters and returned to the gardens, digging and weeding for hours on end, trying to forget about the unhappy fate that had been doled out to her.

But then inevitably came dusk, and after going to her room to wash and change and find numerous excuses to delay, she was faced with the drawing room and Charlotte, an inescapable presence, always watching and listening and judging.

Charlotte behaved as if she and Elspeth had brought a communicable disease into the house, for although Charlotte sat quietly in her chair before dinner, working on her ever-present embroidery, her tight-lipped expression spoke worlds of disapproval.

Serafina had no illusions about what Charlotte disapproved of; she clearly thought that her brother's new wife was uncouth and ill-mannered and not suited to an elevated life at Townsend. Her expression turned particularly sour if Serafina addressed any of the staff in a friendly fashion. It turned even more sour if Serafina was ill-advised enough to speak kindly to Lord Delaware on the rare occasions that he appeared, and sourest of all when Elspeth and Lord Delaware embarked on one of their convoluted conversations, which Serafina enjoyed mightily even though they rarely made any sense.

Then came dinner which Serafina truly dreaded, for that was Charlotte's appointed hour to speak, and she never failed to speak of God. Hers was a God Serafina wasn't acquainted with, and didn't wish acquaintanceship with. Even the vicar at the little church in Abersoch hadn't droned on in such an alarming manner about sin and salvation.

So far Elspeth had kept her lips buttoned, but Serafina knew that state of affairs wouldn't last long, not with the way that Elspeth glowered across the table, noisily chewing her food as Charlotte banged on and on, Elspeth looking as if she were ready to do murder to the woman, or at least cast a spell of silence on her. Thank God her aunt hadn't tried that, for it was bound to go all wrong and Charlotte would end up preaching twice as much as before.

There were times when Serafina actually wished Aiden back, hoping he would know how to silence his impossible sister. Aiden of all people wouldn't put up with such nonsense—she doubted he even believed in God. But since she'd never seen Aiden interact with his sister, she couldn't know how he behaved around her.

All she did know was that she couldn't go on day after day, night after night like this, her appetite fleeing in the face of Charlotte's diatribes. She'd even taken to dashing around corners when she heard Charlotte's chair approach, hiding in rooms or even closets until she could be sure Charlotte had vanished again. It was no wonder that the servants all looked so cowed. Charlotte was a hard taskmaster, ever demanding perfection, her eyes and ears everywhere. Serafina felt as if she were living in a prison, the only reprieve between the hours of four and six when Charlotte took a nap.

Even dear Elspeth was no help. "I don't like Charlotte Delaware, and I don't want to discuss her beyond saying that I intend to stay as far away from the woman as possible," she'd informed Serafina in no uncertain terms. As a result, with the exception of dinner, Elspeth spent her time holed up in her own quarters, happily concentrating on making a mess with her magic potions now that she had nothing else to distract her from what she considered to be her life's purpose.

Janie, ever curious, had asked Serafina what was in the various jars and bottles that Elspeth had stacked all over her room, and Serafina, stumped for an answer, told her it was medicine, which was true enough, depending on how one chose to view Elspeth's hobby.

The explanation satisfied Janie easily enough. "I'll just pass the information on down to the chambermaids who are concerned about the smells," she said in her cheerful fashion. "They believed they might be coming from that bird of your auntie's, sickening for something, you know, so they'll be relieved to know he's not catching. And hasn't that bird just got a mouth on him! Says the most peculiar things, he does. Called me a saucebox the other day when I told him to stop his screeching. . . ."

Serafina shook her head. Eccentric Aunt Elspeth and her equally eccentric parrot were the least of her worries. She didn't even have the comfort of escaping her miserable life in her sleep, for she hadn't dreamt since the night she'd had the wonderful vision of Adam and herself at their wedding feast.

She wished her dreams would return, for at least they would help to stave off her loneliness, make her feel loved and appreciated, even if for only an hour or two.

A shadow fell over Serafina, and her head shot up in alarm. The imposing figure of the Duke of Southwell hovered over her, his golden hair glinting in the sunlight.

"Your—your dukedom . . ." she stammered, trying to collect herself. She pushed away a lock of hair that had fallen over her eyes and blinked up at him. "You're back."

"I am indeed. How are you getting along, Serafina?" he asked pleasantly enough.

She shrugged, thinking that she needed to ask Aunt Elspeth for a spell to make people disappear. "I'm managing. But you've wasted a trip. Aiden isn't here."

"I didn't come to see Aiden; I came to see you. And Charlotte, of course."

"Oh yes . . . Charlotte," Serafina said with an inward sigh. "She said you lived nearby."

"That's right, Southwell is five miles away, on the other side of the forest. So, Serafina, how do you find life at Townsend?"

Serafina considered. She sincerely doubted that he wanted to hear the truth, and since she wouldn't lie, she decided to use a little selective editing in her reply. She really didn't think she could bear to be subjected to another reprimand about how ungrateful and unworthy she was.

"Townsend has its merits, I suppose. It's a pretty place, and I'm enjoying my work in the gardens."

"That I can see," he said, removing a fine linen handkerchief from his pocket and handing it to her. "Here. You have mud on your cheek."

She took it from him and rubbed it over her face, wanting to throw the handkerchief at him. She supposed he expected a perfectly turned-out lady, even though she was laboring in the dirt. "Why did you come to see me?" she asked bluntly. "I thought you made your feelings about me perfectly clear last week."

"I had a letter from Aiden. He asked that I look in on you, make sure you were comfortable."

"How very thoughtful of him," she said caustically. "I suppose what you really mean is that you wanted to make sure I wasn't disgracing him again."

Raphael chuckled. "That's not what I meant at all. I honestly do want to know if you're comfortable." He reached a hand down to her to help her to her feet.

Serafina reluctantly took it and stood. "Comfortable enough," she said. "Did Aiden really write to you, or was that just an excuse for you to come by and spy on me?"

"He really did write, and I have no reason to make excuses, or to spy. You're Aiden's wife now, Serafina, and I have every wish to see that you're happy. So I ask again. Are you?"

She looked away, hoping her face didn't betray her.

"Answer enough," he said, taking the secateurs from her hand and placing them in the basket on the ground. "So my next question is obvious. What is making you unhappy? Is it Aiden's absence?"

Serafina stared at him, nonplussed, for she assumed he'd understood the situation. "Aiden's—Aiden's absence? No! That is, I hardly know him, so how could I miss him?"

"You have a point. But on the other hand, I find you and Aiden eminently well suited to each other, and I assumed you must have discovered that for yourself, given the tone of Aiden's letter."

"What tone?" she asked suspiciously, not believing for a minute that Raphael thought them well suited. "What did he say?"

"Oh, just that he was concerned that he had to be away during a trying time of adjustment for you, and he worried you'd be at sixes and sevens in his absence. Can you blame him? Actually, you are looking a little peaked."

Serafina colored hotly. "I can't think my appearance is any concern of yours. But I suppose Aiden told you he was intent on improving it since he finds me sadly lacking as I am now. That's something else the two of you have in common."

"He only mentioned that he planned on buying you some new clothes, since you didn't have many of your own. Serafina," he said, gazing down at her intently, "I wish you wouldn't view me as your enemy. I swear to you that I come in friendship, whether you believe it or not. I admit that I wasn't as pleasant as I might have been to you initially, but that stemmed from a lack of understanding of your situation."

"Oh, you mean that you thought I was hanging after Aiden's title," she said bitterly. "And that I purposely meant to demean him. And that—"

"Enough," he said quietly. "I was wrong and I freely admit it. Aiden filled in all the bits and pieces in his letter, about how you had no idea of what his father had done, that you had no involvement in the matter. He absolved you absolutely, said that you'd come to the marriage in good faith. Actually, I gathered that much the last time we talked, so the news came as no surprise."

"What—what else did he tell you?" she asked with a gulp, wondering if the duke knew how truly awful things were between them.

"Only that you'd lived a very simple life with your aunt, that you were unprepared for your new circumstances. He's concerned, Serafina, as I am. It is no easy thing to be thrown into a life where expectations of you are high and you've had no training."

"Aiden has already given me this speech. I told him I wasn't interested in being trained. I'm not a dog."

"No, my dear, you most certainly are not. You're a sweet girl who has found herself placed in a very difficult position with nowhere to turn."

Serafina covered her face with her hands, trying desperately not to cry. The last thing she'd expected was a friendly voice, for compassion to come from a man she thought hated her. To her utter dismay, the tears came anyway. And so did Raphael's arms around her, pulling her close. Too overwrought to pull away, she let him hold her, grateful that at least someone showed a shred of caring.

"I'm sorry your situation gives you so much distress," he murmured. "What can I do to help you?"

"N-Nothing. It's—it's just so awful . . . everything is awful," she sobbed, taking comfort in the refuge of his hard shoulder, all of her unhappiness pouring out like a dam released. "Ch-Charlotte is impossible, treating me like a piece of vermin that's entered her house, and—and she reprimands me every time I don't get something right, and—and," she added, with a hiccup, "I don't know whether I can bear to hear another word about sin. I think she believes me the most sinful person who ever walked the earth and I don't even know why," she cried.

Raphael's chest rumbled with laughter against her cheek. "I wouldn't let Charlotte upset you unduly. It's only her way, Serafina. She dedicated her life to God as a way of coping with her situation, and if she does it a little too brown, it's only because she has nothing else to do with herself and no other company to speak of."

Serafina raised her tear-streaked face to Raphael's. "But— but why does she keep reading scriptures about Sodom and Gomorrah and Lot's wife being turned into a pillar of salt? I keep thinking that she means me, but I haven't done anything to warrant her disregard, other than being forced to marry her brother." She hiccupped again. "I think she'd like to turn me into a pillar of salt herself."

"I'll have a word with Charlotte," he said, stroking her back in a comforting manner. "You have to remember that she has been very much on her own at Townsend. It can't be easy for her to have her world turned topsy-turvy because Aiden took a wife."

"I know, I thought of that. But I haven't interfered in any way with her household management. I wouldn't even know how to go about ordering people around."

"No, you probably wouldn't," he said, his voice kind. "And that's something we need to change. Not that I expect you to start issuing orders right and left, but there is a subject we need to address." He released her. "Serafina . . . I think this might be an area I can help you with."

"How?" she asked, wiping her eyes on his handkerchief. "I don't know anything about dealing with position. Charlotte despises me for that too, and yet she'd hate me even more if I interfered. And Aiden thinks I'm hopeless, as polite as he's tried to be about my inadequacies." She blew her nose. "I don't want to live my life forever feeling inferior to everyone around me, just because I don't know how to go on in their manner. But I don't know what to do about it."

He fell silent for a long moment. "I think I might have a solution," he finally said. "Do you know how to ride?"

"Of course," she said, wiping her eyes yet again.

"Good. I'll have a decent mare sent over to you first thing in the morning. You can ride over to Southwell every afternoon, and you and I can proceed from there."

"What do you mean?" she asked in confusion.

"What I mean is that we have only three weeks before Aiden returns. I think—I can't be sure, of course—but I think that I can teach you much of what you need to know in that time about being a countess. If we go about the lessons at my house, no one will be the wiser, Charlotte included, and furthermore, my staff is well trained and they wouldn't think to ask questions."

Serafina gaped at him. "But what do you think you can possibly teach me? I'm hopelessly backward."

"Let me be the judge of that. All I ask is that you appear at lunchtime tomorrow."

Serafina gazed up at him, looking for the trick in his offer. But he appeared totally sincere, his gray eyes filled with warmth and a touch of gentle humor. For the first time since she'd landed at Townsend, Serafina felt accepted for who she was. She felt as if she'd found a friend.

And yet she couldn't bring herself to accept his invitation, mostly because she had no desire to make even more of a fool of herself than she already had. She knew he could never make a countess out of her, as much as he wished to. "I cannot, your dukedom, although I appreciate your kindness in offering."

"But this is my point exactly," he said. "I don't want to put too fine a point on it, but you actually address dukes as 'your grace.' "

"Oh," she said, feeling incredibly foolish, realizing that was what he'd been trying to tell her the last time they met. "Your grace, I mean."

"Very good, although you should call me Raphael, since we're second cousins by marriage."

"Cousins? How are we cousins?" she asked, thrown into confusion again. "I thought you and Aiden were just good friends."

"That is easy enough to explain," he replied. "My mother

and Aiden's mother were cousins. Since they married men with adjoining estates and Aiden and I were born only a year apart, we grew up more like brothers."

"Oh, how nice," she said wistfully. "I always wished for brothers and sisters. Have you any? Real ones, I mean?"

"I have a younger brother who is a complete scapegrace," he said ruefully. "My sainted mother routinely suffers heart palpitations on his behalf, since he has a fondness for getting himself into trouble and working his way out of it by dueling."

"Dueling?" Serafina said, her eyes lighting up with delight. "Do you mean pistols at dawn?"

"Pistols, swords, whatever comes to hand. Hugo so far has managed to avoid actually killing anyone, mostly because he's usually too foxed to do any real damage."

"But aren't you terrified that he'll be killed?" she asked breathlessly. She'd only read about duels in books, and they sounded the most romantic thing, a man fighting for a woman's honor by the gray light of sunrise.

"No," Raphael replied dryly, "because his opponents are also either too foxed or too frightened to kill a duke's brother—retribution and all that. But just to be safe I sent Hugo out of the country for a time on the theory that a continental tour might cool his blood. So far I've only had to bail him out of gambling debts, an easier proposition than clearing him of murder."

"Has Aiden ever fought a duel?" she said, sure she knew the answer. She could just see Aiden now, stalking down his adversary, murder in his eyes.

"*Aiden*? You must be joking. He's far too sensible." He picked up the basket. "We'd best start back, given the hour. I've secured a dinner invitation from Charlotte." They walked for a moment before he spoke again. "I think you should know that Aiden only pursues what he knows he can win, which is what makes him such a good businessman."

Serafina considered his statement, turning over its meaning, hoping he didn't intend her as his target. "If he's such a good businessman," she said after a minute, "then why is his family in such bad financial straits?"

This had been a subject of considerable concern to her. She hadn't managed to ferret out another single piece of information from Elspeth, who had only said that since the Delawares were now saved by Serafina's fortune there was no point in worrying about the problem.

At least Elspeth had finally gotten around to explaining about Serafina's inheritance, that it had been separate from the entail that bound Bowhill to the closest male heir. When Serafina had questioned her as to why Elspeth had kept the fortune such a secret, Elspeth merely said that she hadn't seen any need to mention it and turn Serafina's head when she was going to be married to Aiden anyway.

"You really are in the dark, aren't you?" Raphael said, regarding her curiously. "The family problems are no fault of Aiden's. He was away overseeing the shipping business in various parts of the world when his father nearly managed to lose everything they owned by making some singularly poor business decisions."

"Oh, how difficult for Lord Delaware," Serafina said with heavy sympathy. "But surely Aiden oughtn't to have let his father make any decisions at all, not in his condition."

"What condition is that?" Raphael said, glancing down at her.

"*You* know—his mind wanders," she said, frowning. "He can't help it."

"It's not his mind that wanders, it's his hand. He'd do a great deal better if he kept it away from the bottle," Raphael said matter-of-factly. "And Aiden could hardly do anything about his father's drinking, especially when he was thousands of miles away, so you can't blame him for what happened. If Delaware had bothered to inform Aiden when the trouble first began, Aiden might have been able to salvage the situation. As it was, he knew nothing about the disaster until it was nearly too late."

Serafina's mouth fell open in shock as she finally understood what was at the root of Lord Delaware's constant confusion and prolonged absences in his bedroom. "Do you mean to say Lord Delaware is *not* senile?"

Raphael burst into laughter. "Senile? I should say not, or

at least not until he's consumed a bottle of burgundy by mid morning. Is that really what you thought?" he said, his smile fading. "That Aiden was responsible for this entire mess?"

Serafina bowed her head. "He said nothing to explain."

"And why would he? Do you think he'd come right out and say his father was a drunkard, especially when you'd already had enough shocks? I imagine he hoped you would divine the situation for yourself, but then I suppose you've never been exposed to tosspots before."

"No . . . only Aunt Elspeth when she overcelebrates, which is limited to the sacred days when she honors the god and goddess. Oh—poor Aiden," she said as another, even more awful thought occurred. "He must have been truly horrified when I swooned the other night after drinking a glass of wine."

Raphael stopped in his tracks. "Did you?" he said, his face returning to that neutral expression that betrayed nothing.

Serafina, deeply ashamed, nodded. "I didn't mean to— it's just that I've never had anything alcoholic to drink before and the wine went to my head. Aiden must think he's married another drunkard, since he had to carry me upstairs and put me to bed." She colored in hot embarrassment. "I think I know how Lord Delaware feels. I couldn't remember a thing. It was awful."

Raphael scratched his cheek, gazing down at the ground. "Oh, well, as for that, it's perfectly normal to be forgetful after overindulging. I wouldn't worry yourself overmuch. You just have to learn how to pace yourself."

"No, I think I'd rather not," she said.

He looked up. "Oh, dear. Then we might have a problem."

"What I meant was that I think I'd rather stay with my usual fare of water. But—but what about Lord Delaware?" she asked, returning to her initial concern. "He can't go on muddling up people's lives just because he drinks too freely. No wonder Charlotte goes on and on about the evils of alcohol the few times that her father has been in attendance. I thought Aiden must have told her how I'd disgraced myself and she was trying to set me on the right path."

"I'm sure she's trying to set you on the right path, much as she's always done with Aiden and myself to no avail. But in Delaware's case, I think he's bound and determined to evade his daughter, which probably explains why he spends so much of his time in seclusion. I don't think he wants to be reformed, certainly not by Charlotte."

She sighed. "Then I suppose the only thing to do is try to help him find something else to do with his time. He's probably just lonely, since he really doesn't have anyone to love or to love him, from what I've seen. Maybe I can persuade him to help me in the gardens, where he wouldn't have time to drink." She looked up at him. "Do you think that might work?"

Raphael picked up her hand and held it in his own, gazing down at her fingers. "Serafina . . . I think you might be the best thing that's happened to this family in a very long time."

"You do?" she said, shocked to her core. "I—I thought you believed the exact opposite."

"Initially, but that was before I spoke with you privately. Suffice it to say that I believe you might be a godsend. There's been too much unhappiness at Townsend for too long."

"I don't see how I can help with that. Charlotte can't bear the sight of me, Lord Delaware can barely see me at all, and Aiden doesn't love me in the least. Even the servants find me a trial, for they vanish the instant I appear."

Raphael smiled. "That's what they're trained to do."

"Oh. Well, I find their behavior very disheartening, for I'd like above anything to have someone to talk to. The only person who speaks freely is Janie—she's my maid, but she only came to Townsend when I did, so Charlotte hasn't trained her to silence yet. Janie talks nonstop, which I find comforting."

"And let us hope she continues do so if she's giving you some comfort. I know Townsend is a gloomy, depressing place, Serafina. My mother says that when Lady Delaware died, all the life went out of the place; Delaware never really recovered from his wife's death. Apparently he loved her deeply and was devastated when he lost her."

"How did she die?" Serafina asked, suddenly wanting to

know as much as she could about Aiden's family in the faintly dawning hope that she could somehow make a difference to them, give a purpose to her own life.

"She died giving birth to Aiden," he said flatly. "She'd had Charlotte, followed by a few stillbirths, and she'd been warned against another pregnancy but she kept trying, knowing how badly her husband wanted a son. Delaware's son and heir was produced at the expense of his wife's life." He shook his head. "I think Aiden has always felt responsible for his father's deep grief, which is probably why he hasn't ripped him limb from limb before this."

Serafina's eyes filled with unexpected tears as she absorbed the significance of his words. "How sad that Aiden never had a mother—and his father must have resented him for appearing at all, even if he was the heir he'd wanted."

"You're right about that. Delaware never had any time for Aiden as a boy, devoting himself to his grief rather than his children. And then there was Charlotte's accident six years after Lady Delaware's death, which didn't help matters any."

"I've been longing to ask," Serafina said hesitantly. "I don't want to intrude, but I am curious about what happened to her."

Raphael sighed heavily and pushed a hand through his hair. "God, that was a terrible day. We were out riding, Charlotte in charge of us, when Aiden's pony bolted and Charlotte took off after him on her horse. In her haste she took a jump badly and fell." He squeezed his eyes shut for a moment, as if he could erase the scene he described. "Charlotte broke her spine."

"Oh . . . oh, how terrible!" Serafina pressed her hands against her cheeks, reminded of her mother's accident on a runaway horse. But her mother's accident had been fatal. At least Charlotte's life had been spared, even if she couldn't walk.

"Yes, it was. Nothing's been the same for Charlotte since. She was such a bright, cheerful girl, only twelve, her head filled with plans for marriage and children, talking incessantly about her come-out, the usual feminine prattle that used to drive Aiden and me crazy." He released a long, hollow breath. "And then in one split second all her hopes were destroyed when she took that fall and lost the use of her legs. She's been in severe pain ever since."

"I—I'm sorry," Serafina said, overcome with shame. "I should never have said anything nasty about her, especially if she's suffering."

"You weren't to know," he replied. "And Charlotte can be trying, I do realize, but I find it helps if you remember what difficulties she faces every day."

"Poor woman, how dreadful for her," Serafina said, filled with a newfound compassion for her sister-in-law. "And yet she never complains, which says worlds about her bravery. What a hard life she has had."

"Aiden's life hasn't been much easier," he said quietly. "Between feeling responsible for his mother's death and Charlotte's accident, never mind dealing with his father's problems, Aiden has lived his own life of hell."

For the very first time Serafina's heart went out to her husband. She could just imagine him, a motherless child, living at Townsend with a crippled sister and a drunken father, shouldering the weight of responsibility on his shoulders from an early age.

And to have to marry her only because his father, no longer capable of making rational decisions, had forced Aiden to it—that explained a very great deal to her about Aiden's bitterness.

Serafina made a decision then and there. She might be terribly disillusioned about their marriage, but Aiden didn't deserve her disdain or her anger, not after what she'd just heard. If he wanted a proper countess, then a proper countess he'd have, even if she could give him nothing else.

"Very well, your grace," she said, standing very straight. "I will allow you to teach me whatever it is you think I need to know."

"You will?" he said, catching up her hands in his, his expression delighted. "I must confess that I'm relieved to hear it. Shall we begin tomorrow?"

"Tomorrow," she agreed, wondering just what she was getting herself into. "But first we have to get through dinner, and I assure you, it will not be a pretty picture."

"Oh, I can make anything pretty," he said cryptically, then left her at the door with her basket of rose prunings.

Aiden crossed his legs in front of him, pondering the array of fabrics that Mme. Bernard had spread out in front of him, wishing dearly that he was not in London, but at home with his bride. He tapped his finger against his mouth, feeling at a complete loss. He wasn't in the habit of ordering women's clothing, only looking at it.

"Hmm, let's see. As I explained, my wife will need everything from the inside out. I trust you can see to the chemises, nightdresses, stockings, all that sort of thing without my help."

"Naturally, monsieur." Mme. Bernard inclined her head. "Of the highest quality, of course."

"Of course," he said, thinking he really ought to have brought along one of his old mistresses to advise him. Tinkerby wasn't going to be much use if the bewildered expression on the man's face was anything to go by.

"And Monsieur will be wanting morning dresses, walking dresses, carriage dresses, evening dresses?"

"Yes. Four of each—no, make that five. You know the sort of thing—but nothing too frilly. My wife is best suited to simplicity." He brought Serafina's image to mind, trying to imagine her dressed like a lady of fashion, not an easy picture to conjure up, since he'd far rather imagine her without anything on at all. Now *that* had been an appealing picture. Beautiful Serafina, just as God had created her, a shining example of womanhood.

"Monsieur?"

Aiden reluctantly dragged his attention back to the matter at hand. "What I want is . . . is elegance," he said. "And comfort."

"Comfort?" Mme. Bernard said, taken aback by this preposterous request. "But, monsieur . . ."

"Comfort," he repeated firmly. "The countess has a perfect figure, so there's no need for whalebone all over the place. And no scratchy materials. I won't have her itching like a monkey."

Mme. Bernard regarded him as if he were a lunatic. "Whatever your lordship wishes," she said doubtfully.

"Good. Oh, and I'll need two ball dresses as well. That should do it. I'll leave the styles up to you." He craned his head and looked at Tinkerby. "Colors, Tinkerby," he commanded.

"Colors?" Tinkerby said, scratching his chest. "Do you mean her ladyship's? Well, her hair is dark brown and her eyes are—"

"I know her ladyship's coloring, you cods-head. I meant her favorite colors."

"Oh right, your lordship," he said, shifting his weight from one foot to the other. "Can't say as I've ever noticed. She's always outdoors though, so you might want to make her blend in like a nice piece of spring grass."

"Never mind," Aiden said impatiently, turning back to the dressmaker. "Pastels. Nothing simpering like pink or blue, though. Rose, peach, sea-green, that sort of thing."

A light laugh came from behind him. "Aiden, darling, I can see you're as useless as ever when it comes to understanding the finer details of a woman's wardrobe."

Aiden looked over his shoulder. "Good heavens. Harriet!" He stood and kissed her hand, thinking that God had taken care of the matter after all and provided him with the perfect help. Harriet always had been overly fond of expensive clothing, but she was also one of the most impeccably stylish women he'd ever known. "How are you, my dear? It's been an age."

"Well over three years," she said, but she didn't look the least upset, a relief since at their parting she had created one of those emotional scenes he so despised. "Do I understand correctly that you have married?" she said, tapping her fan against her gloved fingers. "I couldn't help but overhear." She cast a curious look at Tinkerby, her lips trembling with amusement.

"Very recently," he said, watching her warily for any signs

of jealousy. Lady Harriet Munro might have a husband of her own, invalid that he was, but she preferred her lovers unattached.

"Why, how wonderful for you, darling! Town has been abuzz with the news that your father ran up some terrible debts and put you in the River Tick. May I assume the marriage brought with it a hefty compensation? Otherwise I don't think you could afford to be patronizing dear Mme. Bernard's superior establishment."

"My marriage bailed us out of our difficulties, it is true," he said cautiously, unwilling to give Harriet too much information that she could use to spread gossip.

"What good news. Is she anyone I know? I must have missed the marriage announcement."

"I haven't had a chance to notify the papers, but I don't believe you can have met Serafina. She's the only daughter of the late Lord Segrave, but she's lived in an isolated part of Wales these last eleven years."

"Segrave . . . Segrave—oh, yes of course. She must be related to Edmund, then." Harriet nodded, filing away Serafina's pedigree in the tidy place in her brain where those things belonged. "Well, darling, I do commend you for wanting to see to your wife's wardrobe, but I do think Mme. Bernard might find my suggestions a great deal more useful than yours, and I'd be happy to help."

"An excellent suggestion," he said, relieved that someone else was willing to take over the task. "I've already told Madame what sort of thing I want, but I'll leave you to sort out the details. Thank you, Harriet. I appreciate your offer."

"Nonsense. I have nothing better to do with my afternoon and it would amuse me to attire your wife. You do know how I like to spend money," she said with a little smile. "I gather money is no object?"

"None. My only concern is that my wife be suitably attired for her position. Oh, and I need everything finished and delivered in three weeks."

"Three weeks, my lord?" Mme. Bernard looked as if she might keel over with shock. "But this is impossible!"

"Nothing is impossible," Harriet said. "Three weeks and you can double the bill, isn't that right, darling?"

"What?" Aiden said, having already dismissed the matter. "Oh, fine. Whatever it takes to see the job done. Good day, Harriet, and thank you again."

He was about to walk out when another thought occurred to him, and he turned back. "You have my sister's measurements on file, haven't you, madame?"

Mme. Bernard nodded, dazed.

"Excellent, throw in a few morning and evening dresses for her—nice and sober. Come, Tinkerby, let's go. I have a meeting with a moneylender."

"But, monsieur—my payment?" Mme. Bernard said, suddenly panicking at that ominous word.

"Send the bill to Grillion's Hotel. Not to worry, you'll be paid promptly and in full."

He marched out, feeling inordinately pleased with himself. Serafina had been unexpectedly easy to dress. He hoped she wasn't going equally difficult to undress, but he had a sinking feeling it was going to be a long time before he got the chance.

Serafina appeared for dinner, apprehension heavy in her heart. She walked into the dreaded drawing room, only to find Raphael chatting with Charlotte, who was actually smiling. Serafina could scarcely believe her eyes.

"Serafina, here you are at last," Raphael said, standing. "I've just been telling Charlotte what marvelous work you're making of the gardens."

"You—you were?" she said, glancing over at Elspeth, whose her face was twisted into the usual scowl she wore whenever she was subjected to Charlotte's company. She'd buried her head in a book as if she could shut out Charlotte's presence.

"Indeed," Raphael replied. "I noticed the difference in front of the house as soon as I arrived. The beds are tidy for the first time in two years. You've made a big difference in Townsend's appearance."

Serafina couldn't help but be pleased that someone had noticed her efforts. "Thank you," she said. "I'm hoping when Aiden returns that I can persuade him to hire a full complement of gardeners. There's so much more that needs doing."

"If Aiden is going to spend money on anything, it will be the interior of the house," Charlotte said, her eyes sharpening at Serafina's suggestion. "Too much has fallen into disrepair to be neglected any longer. And the household staff needs to be considerably enlarged. I had to dismiss a full fifteen servants when my father squandered the family fortune."

"I'm sure Aiden will take your requests under advisement," Raphael said tactfully. "For the moment he has enough to do trying to get everything else in order."

"I meant no criticism of my brother," Charlotte said, her mouth thinning. "Aiden will turn his attention to Townsend as soon as he possibly can. I was only saying that the gardens can wait, but the furnishings cannot for they will continue to deteriorate and it will cost twice as much to refurbish them. But then my sister-in-law can't be expected to know about the running of large houses."

Raphael cast a brief glance at Serafina over Charlotte's head, his expression sympathetic. "I am sure Serafina will learn very quickly," he said, looking back at Charlotte. "With your help," he added hastily as Charlotte's face darkened ominously. "To be sure, no one knows as much as you about managing Townsend, Charlotte."

"I would think not," she snapped. "But then Serafina has shown no signs of listening to anything I have to say."

Serafina forced herself to remember that Charlotte was in constant pain. "I'm sorry if you think I don't listen," she said, deliberately making her voice gentle. "Perhaps that is because I am unused to a great deal of conversation. I will try harder to attend in future."

"That would behoove you well. It is a virtue to attend to those older and more experienced," Charlotte said tightly, but at least she looked slightly mollified.

"May I offer you a glass of wine, Serafina?" Raphael asked,

his eyes dancing wickedly. "Plum has decanted a particularly fine claret and you might find it just the thing."

Serafina cheerfully could have punched him. "No, thank you," she said, not giving him the satisfaction of a reaction.

Charlotte nodded approvingly at her for once. "Wise of you. 'Woe unto them that rise up early in the morning that they may follow strong drink.' Isaiah, chapter five, verse eleven."

Serafina sighed. It wasn't the first time she'd heard Charlotte quote that particular piece, even if Lord Delaware wasn't present to hear it. At least Serafina understood better now why Charlotte plagued him with her quotations.

"Ah, but what about 'A man hath no better thing under the sun, than to eat, and to drink, and to be merry,'" Raphael quoted straight back at Charlotte. "Ecclesiastes, chapter eight, verse fifteen."

"Raphael!" Charlotte said in extreme disapproval. "You mustn't take the Bible's words out of context." Her expression softened. "Even if you are teasing me. At least you know your scriptures."

"How could I not?" he said. "You have quoted them at me for nearly as long as I can remember. And in this instance, I believe Ecclesiastes was right, for he was commending the enjoyment of life, was he not? I couldn't agree with him more, and it wouldn't hurt you to practice a little more enjoyment yourself."

Charlotte colored hotly. "God did not put me on this earth to enjoy myself, but to toil in His cause. He made His wishes perfectly clear by putting me in this chair."

Raphael lifted his gaze to the ceiling, then looked back down at her. "Since I am not nearly as good at interpreting the Good Lord's wishes as you, dearest, I will not argue, although if His intent really was to keep you locked away in this house, I would feel quite out of favor with Him. Why don't you go out into the sunshine tomorrow, see what Serafina has done with the gardens? That was my point in bringing up the subject in the first place, to get you into the fresh air a little."

Charlotte gazed down at her slim hands. "You know my

health is uncertain, Raphael. I dare not risk catching a chill from the outdoor air for fear of what might happen as a result."

Raphael clapped one hand against his thigh. "I give up," he said. "You can risk a chill once a week when you go to church, but not on any other day?"

"The Lord's day is a different matter entirely. That I cannot neglect, and if I should become ill as a result of venturing out, then it is His will that I should be so."

Serafina glanced over at Elspeth, who was practically tearing the pages out of her book, her pursed lips working soundlessly and no doubt rudely.

At that moment Lord Delaware came through the door, his steps carefully measured as if he expected something to jump out and trip him up at any moment. Now Serafina understood that too, as well as the constant glowing of his nose.

"Delaware," Elspeth said curtly, "it's about time. Look, man, you have company."

Lord Delaware searched the room, his bleary gaze finally locating the duke. "Ah. Southwell." He scratched his head and looked around again, his eyes lighting on the decanter. He toddled over and poured himself a measure, downing it quickly. "Good evening all, and a fine evening it is," he said, as if the wine had fortified him for speech. "Good to see you, boy, good to see you. What brings you our direction?"

"A simple desire for company," Raphael said, raising an eyebrow at Serafina as if in confirmation of Lord Delaware's condition. "It's been a dreary fortnight of planting and I wished for a change."

"Oh, have your tenants harnessed you to the plow now?" Lord Delaware said, then chortled with laughter as if he'd made a particularly fine joke. "Well, if you will be a farmer, what else can you expect, eh? Yoke and plow, yoke and plow."

Raphael inclined his golden head, his face perfectly straight. "Indeed. Fifteen thousand acres of arable land makes for a long day's work. Have you managed any planting this year?"

"Not a single furrow. No money, you know." His head swiveled and he fixed an eye on Serafina. "Oh, but that's right," he said, a pleased smile breaking over his face. "We're rolling in the stuff now. Should have thought of that. Should have thought. Is it too late, d'you think?"

"Not to put in the late summer crop, I don't imagine. Of course, you'll have to begin to till the fields now to prepare them."

"Hmm, yes, but best wait for Aiden, or he might take my head off for not consulting him. The boy's a bit touchy on the subject of my interference at the moment. It's not easy feeling useless, not easy at all when I've been accustomed to managing things." He scratched his head again. " 'Course, I did make a bit of a hash of matters."

Serafina decided to jump in with both feet, since she'd just been given a perfect opening for her proposition. "Lord Delaware—Papa," she added for effect, "I can think of something you could do that would be most helpful, and I'm sure Aiden would have no objections."

"Eh? What's that, girl?" he asked, squinting his eyes at her as if he could bring her into better focus.

"You can help me."

"Help you? Help you do what?"

"Help me put the gardens in order. I have no one else at the moment, and I'm making such slow progress on my own. Would you be willing? I'd be so grateful."

Lord Delaware stared at her, as did his daughter. "You want *me* to dig in the garden?"

"Yes . . ." she said, steeling herself for disapproval. "I think Aiden would be so happy to know you were making an effort to put things right. It might make up for—for other things that have gone wrong."

The disapproval she expected came instantaneously from Charlotte. "Are you mad?" she said, her tone biting. "You can't mean that you expect my father to work in the gardens like a common laborer?"

"Why not?" Raphael asked reasonably. "Working at something might actually do him some good, and furthermore, I believe Serafina has a point. Aiden would be pleased to see your father making himself useful about the place."

Lord Delaware frowned at Raphael. "Do you really think so? I would so like to have Aiden look on me kindly. He doesn't at all, y'know."

"I think he would look on you very kindly indeed." Serafina wasn't at all sure that would be the case, but she'd deal with that problem when the time came. Right now her will was bent toward seeing her purpose fulfilled, and she was grateful that Raphael championed her cause with Charlotte, who clearly worshiped the ground he walked on. At least she'd buttoned her lips in the face of Raphael's approbation.

"Do you think you might want to try?" she said. "Just think, you really might enjoy yourself."

"Well, I—I don't know. Maybe I would enjoy myself. My dear Isabel always did love her gardens," he said, his eyes suddenly welling with tears. "I might feel a little closer to her out there. And if you think Aiden will be pleased, that would be all to the good, wouldn't it?"

"I believe it would, nearly as much as it would please your wife to see you taking care of something she loved." Serafina smiled at him, but her heart broke to see how deeply he missed his wife, how truly lonely he was. "You can do it as a tribute to her memory."

He reached his hands out and grabbed hers up, clasping them in a tight embrace, squeezing them until Serafina thought her blood might be cut off. "Then I will," he said, his voice rough. "It's a magnificent idea, my dear, a magnificent idea—I can't think why I didn't come up with it myself. When do we start?"

"Tomorrow morning at nine o'clock," she said, hugely pleased with his capitulation and surprised it had been that easy to convince him. "I'll meet you in the rose garden. I've been trying to put the bushes into order, but there's so much more to be done."

"I will be there," he said. "Isabel was particularly proud of her roses. Perhaps together we can bring them back to their former glory." He wiped his eyes with the back of his hand.

"I am sure of it," she said as Plum announced dinner.

"A tribute," he murmured. "Yes. Maybe she will look down on me from her place in heaven and know I love her still."

"Oh, yes," Serafina said, deciding to plant one more idea in his head and praying it would take root. "And just think how happy she'll be to see you outdoors, living a healthy, productive life, celebrating the earth's blessings with clear eyes and a glad heart in her honor."

"Yes. Yes, indeed," he replied, scratching his head. "She would like that, wouldn't she?"

"Very much," Serafina said as she tucked her hand into the crook of Lord Delaware's elbow and led him into the dining room, wondering if the goddess didn't have a divine plan for her after all.

Maybe she had been sent to Townsend to make it a happy place again.

11

$\mathcal{A}$iden pulled off his jacket, loosened his neckcloth, and threw himself onto his bed at the Grillion, where he had taken up residence until he could buy a house. His so-dependable father had sold their own.

"Bloody idiot," Aiden said with disgust, cupping his hands behind his head. He hadn't been so tired in a long time, but he felt a great deal better than he had a month before.

Serafina's money had seen to all his financial problems, as much energy as it had taken to clear them. He'd spent virtually every waking hour of the last month dashing around London and Southampton, doling out huge sums to various creditors, charming bankers, hauling around letters of credit.

He'd managed to regroup the fleet of ships, many of which had fallen into disrepair and been consigned to dry dock. He'd arranged for cargo and more people to be paid, even more to be hired since so many had been laid off. But the task was done, the company back up and running, ships sailing all over the world again.

And all of this thanks to his wife, the wife he hadn't wanted in the first place.

Serafina. He closed his eyes and brought her sweet face to mind for the hundredth time that week. God, how he wished she were with him. He wanted to show her London, see her light up with pleasure at the sights and sounds of a city, take her to the opera, dance with her, introduce her to his friends—if he had any left. It had been a long, long time since he'd been back, and the few people he'd run into hadn't been overflowing with warmth.

It was probably just as well that Serafina wasn't with him this time, he decided, since not only wouldn't he have been able to entertain her, but he also obviously had some damage to undo on his father's behalf. But still . . .

He breathed out in longing, remembering the feel of her body pressed against his own through the one night they'd had together. Serafina had slept soundly, but he'd hardly closed his eyes, drinking in the fragrant scent of her hair that reminded him of walking through a herb garden in the warm summer sun. Her soft, supple limbs had curved so naturally into his own, the rise and fall of her breathing soft and even against his chest, inciting waves of desire in him as he held her protectively into the small hours before dawn.

He'd been absurdly touched by her performance at dinner, which had run the gamut from defensiveness to fear to gratitude—if he could call it that—for his having hired Tinkerby. And then had come the final act, when Serafina's eyes had blinked and blurred, and she'd actually looked at him with something akin to affection. Even tenderness, if he was stupid enough to believe that.

That had been the finest moment of all. Maybe he ought to ply her with wine more often, he considered. Well, maybe not, given the disastrous effect it had on her other senses. But all in all, he really couldn't wait to get home, and that was not an emotion that had occurred in the past with any frequency.

A pounding started at the door and Tinkerby appeared carrying an armload of clothes. " 'Ere you are, my lord, all cleaned and pressed, just the way you like them. And her ladyship's trunks have been delivered downstairs. Won't she be pleased tomorrow when she sees all the finery you've bought her?"

"I hope so, Tinkerby," Aiden said, sitting up. "I sincerely hope so. On the other hand, she might well bash me over the head. Your mistress doesn't strike me as being interested in the finer things in life."

"Aye, well I reckon that's only because she hasn't had them for so long. Like I told you, Miss Serafina's an unspoiled girl."

"Yes, you've told me a great many things, not the least of which is that my wife has lived a highly unusual life for a long time, thanks to her aunt."

"You mustn't go misunderstanding about Miss Elspeth, or I'll regret every word I ever said," Tinkerby said, throwing Aiden's neatly pressed clothes into a heap on the chair. "She's a good woman she is, and I won't have you taking her wrong, even if she does have some odd ways of looking at things. She brought Miss Serafina up with the sole idea in mind that she'd be your wife, and I have to give her credit for that, anyway, even if she did go about it in a different fashion. At least she did it with love."

Aiden shot a disbelieving look at Tinkerby. As he'd intended when he took Tinkerby on, he'd gleaned a great deal of highly useful information from the man, which more than made up for Aiden's having to tolerate wrinkled linen and creased jackets, not to mention a constantly nicked face. But for Tinkerby to sing Elspeth Beaton's praises really did stretch his credulity, since Tinkerby was usually starchy on the subject of Serafina's aunt. But then again, Tinkerby was starchy on almost every subject and he strongly suspected Tinkerby's starchiness hid a heart of gold.

"As you say," Aiden replied. "At least she did it with love." He wished, not for the first time, that he was able to offer Serafina the same thing. But even if he could, he doubted very much that she'd have anything to do with him.

Still, maybe there was yet a shred of hope that he could convince her to like him, as much of an uphill battle as that appeared.

Serafina watched carefully as Raphael demonstrated the proper carving of a wood pigeon, his deft movements punctuated by continuous commentary, most of which had her in stitches.

"Down the middle, sword wielded with courage, carcass

split like so. And so, the dastardly deed is done, the swords-man victorious and hungry, ready to consume the con-quered. The only problem is avoiding choking on the bones of the unwilling victim." He popped the meat into his mouth, chewing, then took hold of his throat and coughed wildly.

An alarmed footman leapt instantly to his side, and Raph-ael had to wave him away with an apology.

Serafina pealed with laughter. She'd vastly enjoyed the last three weeks of Raphael's daily tutelage, even though the first afternoon that she'd arrived at Southwell she'd been horribly cowed, feeling like an impostor at his magnificent door.

But he greeted her with ease, inviting her in as if he were asking her into a small, comfortable cottage instead of the hugest house she'd ever seen. He made the lessons more like a game, taking her through one step and then the next, mak-ing fun of it all, never once allowing her to feel silly or ig-norant.

They covered table manners, appropriate forms of ad-dress, practiced taking tea, pretended to make calls and hand cards to butlers, various corners turned to indicate the form of call. He taught her about bowing and scraping, or not bowing and scraping according to the order of precedence, and was deliciously irreverent about it all.

Through everything Raphael had been nothing but a friend to her. Serafina had never had a friend before, and she liked the experience enormously.

The only thing she found unsettling was the way that Raphael talked nonstop about Aiden, telling her about their life together, their boyhood exploits, their time at university where they got into all sorts of scrapes. She wouldn't have minded hearing about Aiden so often, except that Raphael made Aiden sound positively likable. She couldn't help but wonder if Raphael had ever seen Aiden's darker side, the side that took advantage of innocent girls, the side that charmed while it tried to seduce.

And yet, if she was to be truly honest with herself, she had to admit that her opinion of Aiden was slowly changing, shaped by the stories Raphael told that filled out his character, shaped also by her growing understanding of the unhappy life he'd led at Townsend.

It couldn't ever have been easy for him, and there were times that her heart ached for him, for she knew what it was like to grow up without a mother, and his father had been as good as absent. He must have been as lonely as she during his childhood. Only instead of dreaming fairy tales about true love and make-believe castles, he had gone in the opposite direction, seeing life as a harsh reality to be survived. And who was to say Aiden wasn't right? Her version of life hadn't had much basis in truth.

"Conversation, please," Raphael said, watching carefully as Serafina attempted to dissect her wood pigeon in the manner he'd demonstrated. "You must be able to talk at the same time as eating, although not with your mouth full. How is Lord Delaware today?"

"He's fine," she said, struggling with her knife.

"No sign of backsliding?"

"Not so far. As I told you, he has a glass or two of wine with dinner, but other than that he seems reasonably clearheaded. He goes out to the garden first thing in the morning and stays there until four o'clock practice."

"Ah, yes," Raphael said, the corner of his mouth quirking up. "Practice. Are you making progress with the staff?"

Serafina finally managed to spear the pigeon in the correct manner with her fork. "Yes, they're doing very well, and they're actually enjoying themselves."

"I'm sure they're having an unusually good time," he said, his smile broadening.

"But they do take their work very seriously, so I don't *think* Aiden will be offended," she added, pushing down with her knife.

"I'm sure Aiden will be delighted, and not just by the surprise you have planned. Have you heard anything as to when he returns?"

"No, not a word, although I expect it will be any day. Oh, no!" she exclaimed as half the pigeon went flying off the plate and into her lap. She looked down at it despondently. "I'm not sure I'm ever going to have the way of being a countess," she said mournfully, picking the piece up with her fingers and putting it back on her plate.

"Nonsense. You're doing beautifully," Raphael said in a muffled voice through the folds of his napkin.

"Are you laughing at me?" she demanded.

"Certainly not. I was—I was just clearing my throat. Try holding your fork and knife a little more firmly—that's better," he said. "Now press down hard but with steady pressure, and try not to look as if you're tackling a rhinoceros. And countesses generally do not poke their tongues out of the side of their mouth when they're carving their food."

Serafina looked up with a grin. "I can't help it. This requires tremendous concentration."

"So I can see," he said dryly. "Concentrate all you wish, but please converse. How is Charlotte?"

"Well . . . I thought she'd be pleased about her father's progress, but she's still annoyed that he's behaving like a laborer." Serafina finally managed to successfully slice the bird in quarters and she popped a piece into her mouth with relief. "She doesn't think Lord Delaware's new occupation is suitable for a marquess," she said through her mouthful, belatedly remembering not to talk with her mouth full as one of Raphael's eyebrows rose.

"At least she is being more cordial to you," Raphael said, politely filling in the conversational gap while she chewed and swallowed.

"Much more cordial," she said, nodding.

"Do you think Charlotte might be adjusting to the idea that you're Aiden's wife and therefore a permanent fixture at Townsend?"

"Oh, no. I don't know if she'll ever adjust to that idea, but I do think she might be feeling better."

"Feeling better?" Raphael said, both eyebrows shooting up in surprise. "What do you mean?"

"Well, I didn't want to say anything until I was sure that it was working, but I managed to talk a potion out of Aunt Elspeth for Charlotte's back."

"A potion?" Raphael said, staring at her in disbelief. "What sort of potion? Oh, lord—is this some kind of witch's brew your aunt has concocted?"

"It's perfectly safe, I assure you. Aunt Elspeth is actually very clever with medicines, even though she can seem a little muddled at times. Charlotte's footman rubs it on twice daily and helps her do some exercises that will stretch out her knotted muscles, part of what causes her pain, I think."

"Her *footman*? What in the name of God do you mean?"

"Well, I don't know what else to call him," she said. "He's the one who carries her up and down the stairs and puts her into bed."

"Frederick," Raphael said impatiently. "But do you mean to say that he's rubbing this stuff all over Charlotte's body?"

"Yes," Serafina said, puzzled by his astonishment. "Elspeth said Charlotte had to have someone with strong hands to do the job properly, and Frederick seemed the logical choice."

"And Charlotte is actually putting up with this?" he said, resting both arms on the table and leaning forward, looking at her skeptically.

"She didn't like the idea very much at first," Serafina admitted in a gross understatement, "but when I told her about how the oil helped Tinkerby's rheumatism, which can get so bad that he has to go to bed for days on end, she finally changed her mind."

"Fascinating," he said. "What's in this magic potion?"

"I have no idea. I know there are oils of rosemary, juniper, and something called lemongrass, but the rest is Aunt Elspeth's closely guarded secret. She only perfected the recipe last year."

"Tadpole tails, no doubt," he said dryly.

"It's lizard tails," Serafina replied absently. "But Auntie hasn't ordered any of those for ages, so they can't go in this blend."

Raphael smothered a laugh. "I hope you're not serious."

"Oh, yes. You have to realize that some ingredients can be very expensive and hard to obtain," she said, wiping the corners of her mouth. "Aunt Elspeth kicked up a terrible fuss when I asked her for a bottle of her precious oil—you know what she thinks of Charlotte—but I persuaded her that not only would she be unkind not to help someone in pain, but also that Charlotte might not resort to quoting the Bible so often if her back didn't hurt all the time. She gave me two bottles."

Raphael laughed. "Very clever. I don't know if anything will stop Charlotte from her Bible quoting at this late date, and I sincerely hope for your sake that Charlotte never discovers what practices your aunt's medicinal background is based on, for there would be hell to pay if she thought she was in the presence of a witch."

"I have worried a little about that. Aunt Elspeth's patience is not her strongest suit, and Charlotte is severely trying it. But Auntie returns to Clwydd soon, so I think her secret about being a Wiccan will remain safe."

"Good, unless her feathered familiar spills the soup," he said with a wicked gleam in his eye.

"Oh, Raphael, don't be silly." Serafina looked at him with exasperation. "He's not a familiar, he's just an ordinary parrot who talks too much for his own good."

"Mmm. Has Charlotte found out yet?"

"I'm afraid so. One of the housemaids unwisely mentioned him, and Charlotte became terribly agitated, convinced Basil would soil the rugs and chew the furniture and spread vermin everywhere. I promised her Aunt Elspeth would keep him confined to his cage and that he really was very clean, and she eventually capitulated, although I can't say she was happy."

"No, I should think not. Charlotte's ordered life at Townsend has been set on its ear, even more than she realizes. But the change is good for her. It's been good for Lord Delaware, too. Aiden will have much to be grateful to you for when he comes home."

Serafina pulled her gaze away, not having any idea what Aiden would think.

"Are you still concerned you won't be up to scratch?" Raphael asked, regarding her closely.

Serafina didn't know how to reply. She'd carefully steered away from the subject of her feelings toward Aiden, not even sure she knew what they were anymore. "I am a little nervous," she said truthfully. "You'll keep your promise, won't you? I'd rather he didn't know you've been teaching me."

"I'll keep my promise, but do you really think Aiden's going to believe you suddenly learned everything out of the clear blue sky?" he said, amused.

"Maybe he'll think I've picked up my newfound knowledge from Charlotte," she said. "I hope so, because I don't want him to ask any questions." She peeped an embarrassed little look up at Raphael. "I have to confess that when Aiden suggested I had things to learn, I dug my heels in and told him I wanted nothing to do with his world. I wasn't very nice about it."

"Weren't you?" Raphael asked gravely.

"No, and I feel ashamed of myself for being so intractable, since I have come to think that Aiden was only trying to be helpful. I know I'm being proud, but I—I'd rather Aiden didn't know that I changed my mind about learning to be a countess."

"Aiden is not an unreasonable man. Why would he be anything but happy that you changed your mind?"

"I can't explain," she said, desperately searching to find an acceptable explanation for her reluctance to have Aiden know what she'd been doing. She couldn't possibly tell Raphael the truth of the matter. "It's just that we got off on the wrong foot with each other and—and I want to start over, to make things better between us. But I don't want Aiden to think I'm trying too hard, or he might mistake my intentions again."

"Ah," he said, rubbing the corner of his mouth. "I think I begin to see."

"Do you? Do you really?" she said, infinitely relieved.

"It sounds to me as if you want to please Aiden, but you don't want him to know it in case he returns to thinking that all you care about is being a countess. Is that what you're trying to say?"

"Yes! That's it exactly." There was more to it, far more, for her greatest concern was that Aiden might misinterpret her desire to give him a happy home as a willingness to capitulate to him in every way, the one thing she wasn't prepared to do to further his happiness.

"I can't say I understand completely," he said slowly, "but far be it from me to judge your reasoning. I'm pleased that you're willing to make an effort at a marriage you were unhappy about to begin with. Perhaps you'll even find that Aiden makes a good husband."

Serafina didn't answer, mainly because there was nothing to say.

"Well, let's not put the cart before the horse. You know I hold Aiden in high esteem, and I hope one day you will discover the reasons why. In the meantime, you needn't worry about me; you have my word that my lips are sealed as to my part in your education."

"Thank you," she said with relief. "I appreciate your help as well as your silence."

"Not at all. Now let us practice peeling fruit with a knife and fork."

Aiden pulled up at the front door of Townsend absurdly proud of himself. He'd not only brought home three trunks' worth of clothing for Serafina and his sister, but he'd also brought home a fine carriage embossed with the Delaware coat of arms and a team of four high-stepping horses. On top of that, he'd put the family finances to right.

He alighted from the carriage and ran up the front steps, taking them two at a time, wanting nothing more than to see Serafina's smiling face greeting him, a harmless piece of fantasy he'd indulged himself in over the last four weeks.

But instead of Serafina, Plum met him at the door. Well, nothing unusual in that, he thought through his disappointment.

"Where is her ladyship?" Aiden asked as soon as Plum had finished his usual welcoming speech.

"Which ladyship, my lord?" Plum inquired. " Lady Charlotte is in her study, and your wife is out for the afternoon."

Aiden experienced another surge of disappointment. "Do you know where my wife has gone?" he asked, trying not to show his impatience.

"I can't say, my lord. Lady Aubrey leaves every day at noon and doesn't return until four 'o clock."

"Does she?" Aiden replied with surprise. "Does she go walking?" he asked, thinking he might find her somewhere nearby.

"I believe not, my lord. Her ladyship takes a horse."

"A—a horse?" Aiden said, sudden panic coming over him at the thought of Serafina atop an ungovernable mount. "Can she ride?"

"I have no idea, my lord, but as she comes back in one piece every day I assume she can, unless she walks the beast on foot."

Plum actually smiled at him, and Aiden thought he must be hallucinating. The Townsend staff never smiled, certainly not Plum. He'd never even known Plum had teeth. "I see," he said, doing his best not to stare at the man in open astonishment. "Very good. I'll—I'll see if I can't track her down. Will you see that the trunks are brought in from the carriage and taken upstairs?"

"Very good, my lord."

Aiden turned on his heel and went back out the door, deciding to go and saddle up Aladdin. He'd waited a month to see Serafina, and he didn't intend to wait a minute longer. He headed toward the stables, wondering where Serafina went for four hours every afternoon on horseback.

As he passed the burgeoning rose garden he vaguely noted that it looked considerably tidier. An elderly man dressed in shabby clothes was busily trimming the hooped bower. Aiden was under the impression that all the gardeners had been dismissed, but he supposed Serafina might have taken it upon herself to hire help, devoted gardener that she was.

And then his step slowed and he stopped, his head turning to look harder at the man. He stared in disbelief, thinking for the second time in nearly as many minutes that his eyes were playing tricks on him.

He strode quickly toward the bower. "Father?" he croaked, nearly speechless with astonishment, "is that you?"

Lord Delaware turned, his face lighting up with pleasure.

"Aiden, my boy—you're home! We thought you might be any time now. How did your trip go?"

Aiden slowly shook his head, taking in his father's appearance. He looked . . . healthy. Cheerful, even, but not the befuddled sort of cheerfulness that came from drinking. This was a man he might never have seen before, his eyes clear and alert, a man who thrived on his work.

"Oh, dear," his father said, his smile fading. "Did you not manage to recover our losses? I'm so terribly sorry." The hand that held the clippers dropped to his side. "I made a terrible mess of things, didn't I?" He hung his head.

"No—no, everything went well," Aiden said, still in a state of shock. "I'm merely surprised to see you here."

"Thank heaven," Lord Delaware said, his face clearing again. "I thought for a terrible moment that you'd been too late in getting to London. I didn't hear from you, and I kept telling myself no news was good news. And I suppose it was after all."

"Yes—yes, it's all good news." Aiden looked at him closely, baffled. "I didn't write because I didn't think you'd be interested in hearing the details. And speaking of that, I've never known you to take any interest in gardening. Why now?"

His father laughed, his eyes bright. "I decided that it was high time I made myself useful. Isabel would have been appalled at the state I allowed her beloved gardens to fall into, so I thought I might remedy matters." He pulled out a handkerchief and mopped his face. "Serafina has been most helpful in instructing me—a most knowledgeable girl. What do you think, Aiden? Looking much improved, isn't it? I think your mother would be happy."

Aiden glanced about him, trying to regain his balance. His father had hardly mentioned his mother's name in all the time Aiden could remember. And yet now his father spoke it as naturally as if it came tripping off his tongue every day.

Aiden hadn't even known that his mother had loved the gardens. He swallowed hard against the knot that had formed in his throat, thrown off guard by the sudden mention of a woman he'd always wanted to ask about but hadn't dared. Aiden's mother had been a subject completely off-limits.

"Yes," he answered, speaking with an effort. "I'm sure she would be happy." He passed a hand over his face, assailed by emotions he hadn't even known he'd possessed. "I—I'm pleased that you're making an effort," he managed to say.

"Are you, my boy? I'm so happy to hear it. I don't think I've pleased you in a very long time, if ever, and I'm sorry about that." Lord Delaware fidgeted with one of the buttons on his jacket. "I hope I can find a way to make it up to you, and if it's only by lending a helping hand about the place, I'll be content."

Aiden didn't know what to say. He felt as if he'd just entered an alternate world where his father had always been sane and sober and accessible. But images flashed through his mind that grounded him in reality, memories of a man who had locked himself away, drinking himself into a regular stupor, a man who had flown into ungovernable rages at the drop of a hat, a man who had even married his son off without his consent just to save the family name.

"Work where you will," he said, hardening himself against a treacherous urge to be sentimental. "It's as much your house as mine, and more so when it comes down to it. I'm hardly likely to stand in your way."

His father colored, his gaze dropping away. "I had hoped you would be a little more forgiving. But you have every right to your ire. I am sure I deserve it."

Aiden was about to respond to that understatement when a cry went up and he turned to see a woman flying across the lawn on a beautiful chestnut mare, her hair loosed, legs astride, her hand waving, a handful of flowers grasped in it.

His heart lurched as he realized it was Serafina—riding bareback as if she'd been born on a horse, the most welcome sight he'd seen in a very long time, although he didn't have the first clue where the horse had come from.

For one wonderful moment he thought she was waving at him, but that hope was quickly dashed as she rapidly dismounted, running toward his father instead, leaving her horse to graze.

"Look!" she cried. "The foxgloves are out! Won't Aunt Elspeth be pleased? She can make—" She stopped abruptly, her eyes widening, the flowers dropping from her hand as Aiden stepped out of the shade of the bower.

"Hello, Serafina," he said softly, his heart filled with joy to see her like this, the wild wood nymph he'd longed for, looking natural and simple and full of life itself. She even had a twig caught in her hair.

"Aiden," she said, taking a step back, her gaze falling to the grass. "I didn't—that is, I wasn't . . ."

"Expecting me?" he said, walking up to her and retrieving the fallen bunch of flowers. "I was bound to reappear at some point."

She raised her head and met his eyes, her own filled with a dismay that crushed his heart and his hopes.

"Hello," she said in her sweetly musical voice, and he knew she forced the smile to her lips. "Welcome home."

"Thank you. It's good to be back." But he was beginning to wonder. She resembled a doe about to bolt into the woods, her sea-green eyes filled with alarm.

Serafina cast his father a beseeching glance, as if rescue might come from that direction, and Aiden wanted to laugh. His father was the last person likely to rescue anyone.

"I think I might amble back to the house now," Lord Delaware said, missing his cue as Aiden knew he would. "I'll see you shortly."

Aiden simply nodded, focusing his full attention on Serafina. "I hope I don't come as too much of a surprise," he said, handing her the flowers. "I'm actually very happy to see you, even if you don't return the sentiment."

"Oh—but I'm happy to see you too." She ran her tongue over her lips, lips that Aiden longed to take under his own but which were unavailable to him.

"It's just that I didn't expect to greet you in this manner," she finished, flustered.

"And what manner did you plan to greet me in? Maybe with a hatchet at the front door?"

To his delighted surprise, Serafina burst into laughter. "Nothing so diabolical," she said. "I planned to greet you properly in my Sunday dress, curtsy nicely to you, and *then* run for my life."

Aiden tilted his head to one side, scrutinizing his wife. If he wasn't sure he was making it up, he'd have thought Serafina really did look pleased to see him. In that moment she reminded him far too acutely of the queen of the fairies he'd met that first day in the forest, her cheeks flushed, no wariness in her eyes. "What's this—an actual smile for me?" he asked.

"And why not? Isn't that how wives generally greet their husbands?"

"Begging your pardon, but the last time I saw you, I had the impression that you would have been perfectly happy to slit my throat."

Her smile abruptly faded at his comment, and he felt as if the sun had just disappeared.

Clod pole, he told himself furiously. *When are you going to learn to guard your tongue with her?* "What is it?" he asked gently. "Why do you suddenly look so somber?"

"Aiden, I—I have an apology to make to you," she said, glancing down.

"An apology?" He studied her hard, trying to decide what sort of trouble she'd gotten herself into during his absence. Maybe a guilty conscience explained the warmth of the smile she'd given him, he concluded with disappointment. "For what? What have you done?"

"I—I've had some time to think while you were away, and I've come to the conclusion that I was perhaps a trifle unreasonable in my behavior toward you."

"You were?" he said, caught off guard. This type of apology was the last thing he'd expected to hear.

"Yes. I was angry and frightened and unhappy." She tugged on her bottom lip with her teeth in a sweet gesture of confusion. "But I've come to realize that you were right. Since we can't change the fact that we're married, we might as well try to be friends."

Aiden couldn't believe his ears. "You want to be friends," he repeated. "Despite everything."

"I would," she said shyly. "It will take some time to grow to know each other well, but since we have to live in the same house, I thought we might at least try to get along."

"Do you have any particular idea in mind as to how we might accomplish that?" he asked, regarding her with supreme curiosity. He'd long since discovered that Serafina's brain did not follow any standard logical pathways, so he had no idea what might be coming.

"Yes, I do," she said. "I think we should start the way all friends start and spend some time together. If the suggestion is agreeable to you, of course."

Agreeable? Oh, he found her suggestion extremely agreeable. He could hardly believe his good luck. "How would you like to spend this time?" he asked, all sorts of wickedly delicious ideas occurring to him.

She touched a finger to her chin. "I thought we might start by walking together, but only if you have the time. I know you are busy with your work."

"Not at all," he said, contemplating all the possible opportunities isolated walks presented. "I enjoy walking. What else?" He reached out and gently disentangled the twig from her hair as he spoke, pleased that she didn't pull away from his touch.

"I'm not sure," she said. "Maybe we could read aloud to each other?"

Not so promising, but not without possibilities, he considered. "I wouldn't be adverse to that. I like books."

"Oh, you see?" she said, clapping her hands together gleefully. "I do as well, so perhaps we have a few things in common after all."

What Aiden saw was that the one thing he most wanted to have in common with Serafina might be a long time coming, given her idea of amusing things to do. But he wasn't going to throw away a golden opportunity, simply because she hadn't come around to that particular suggestion yet.

"Yes, I believe we might have few things in common," he

said carefully. "And I'd be more than happy to explore any avenues of possibilities that might lead us closer together." He felt like a wolf masquerading in sheep's clothing.

She beamed. "Really? Oh, that is most amenable of you."

"I'm nothing if not amenable," he replied, picking her hand up and dropping a kiss on its back, then hastily returned it to her before she found a reason to object. "I am yours to command."

"Then I command you to return to the house with me," she said, smiling at him in a manner that threatened to undo him. "I have a surprise for you. Wait just a moment."

She fetched her horse, then started toward Townsend, leading the mare by the reins. Aiden followed at her side as readily as if she were leading him by the bit.

12

Charlotte dropped the fold of draperies in disgust. She'd seen enough of her brother's performance with his wife. So. Aiden had returned and his blood was no less hot than before. Typical. She'd hoped his month away would have put some sense into his head, but apparently nothing had changed.

Bile rose in her throat. How could the man be so blind? How could he not realize that he was being played for a fool?

Charlotte had worked it all out: Serafina must have known that Aiden came to the marriage filled with contempt for her, feeling entrapped and embittered. So the heiress did the one thing guaranteed to change his mind. She played the unschooled, reluctant virgin and her scheme had instantly borne fruit, Aiden practically falling all over himself to please her. Of course, the minute he'd left, Serafina had suddenly acquired all sorts of polish.

Oh, she was clever, very clever. Serafina had already wrapped their foolish old father around her finger, and now she was setting out to do the same to Aiden. Charlotte had seen that display of pretended devotion and she knew exactly what was behind it, even if Aiden didn't.

The witch intended to take over everything. She'd already started trying to sway the servants, fluttering her eyelashes at them, smiling at them, speaking to them as if they were her equals. All of Charlotte's hard work, her careful training was slowly being undone. Serafina had even had the gall to take over conversation at the dinner table—traditionally

Charlotte's time to speak, encouraging her father and that awful woman to babble on about stupidities.

Soon enough, Serafina would convince Aiden to put Charlotte out into the cold.

Well, Charlotte knew how to deal with that. She would find a way to ensnare Serafina yet. She'd been slowly putting her plan into effect, being nothing but sweet and kind to her sister-in-law, pretending affection, even allowing Serafina to persuade her to use the oils.

Although she had to admit, she found that she liked her rubs, a pleasant respite from the demands of the day, and it was time for her afternoon treatment. That would help to settle her mind and relax the tension that had set in when she'd seen Aiden and Serafina together again.

She wheeled herself over to the bell pull and summoned Frederick.

"My rub," she commanded the second he appeared.

"Certainly, my lady," Frederick said. He picked her up from her chair in his strong arms and deposited her face down on the bed, opening her dress at the back and slipping her arms out of the sleeves. He pulled her chemise over her head, leaving her back naked.

Charlotte waited impatiently for Frederick to fetch the oil. And then his hands began to move in slow, comforting circles, working the oil into Charlotte's skin, starting at her shoulders. Charlotte breathed a deep sigh as the heat began to penetrate. She closed her eyes, giving herself over to the exquisite sensations that Frederick's fingers induced as he worked, rhythmically kneading her muscles.

She drifted off, imagining Raphael's hands doing the same, touching her in just such a way, rubbing and stroking. She moaned a little in pleasure as Frederick reached the small of her back, pressing down hard.

She'd never really looked at Frederick before, seeing him as just another servant, but he was really most presentable, with good teeth, a thick head of brown hair, and a broad pair of shoulders. But his hands were what she liked most of all, for they were strong and sensitive and steady, although she was sure she ought not to like their touch quite so much.

A man's touch. Wicked. So terribly wicked, even if she let him touch her only to soothe her pain-wracked body.

And yet the constant pain she'd been plagued with for the last twenty-two years had nearly vanished, a different sensation taking its place, one that she wasn't familiar with at all. All she knew was that a new part of her felt awake, a part that centered deep in the pit of her stomach, that burned and ached even lower down. And the new sensations she felt tormented her. Each day her imagination went just a little farther as to what Frederick might do in the course of her rub, secretly wishing that he'd touch her more intimately, loathing herself for entertaining the thought at all, but unable to help it.

She sighed again as Frederick pulled up her skirt, starting again at her feet and working his way up the back of her legs, stroking her tight muscles into relaxation. Oh . . . so nice. So very nice. She wondered what would happen if she eased her legs apart just a little, inviting him to go just a little higher. . . .

But to her disappointment he pulled her dress down over her legs again. "All done, my lady."

And then he was gone, leaving Charlotte alone in her bed, trembling with frustration and disgust that she could even entertain such a lustful fantasy.

Serafina tied her horse to the hitching post, then turned to Aiden. "Stay here for just a minute," she said, and ran up the front steps, hoping Lord Delaware had done his job in time.

She'd nearly had apoplexy when Aiden appeared out of the blue, no warning to give her a chance to prepare. But his timing couldn't have been better, for it was past four o'clock now, and Charlotte would be safely upstairs sleeping, unable to interfere with Aiden's surprise.

She pushed the door open, filled with excitement. This was the moment they'd been practicing so hard for. Lord Delaware and Plum had gathered everyone in the front hall, and they all looked nervous. She smiled reassuringly, her finger to her lips, then turned and beckoned to Aiden. He wore a puzzled expression, but he came up the steps obligingly enough.

Serafina lifted her hands, then dropped them.

The entire staff of Townsend Hall burst into rousing song, Serafina and Lord Delaware joining them.

Aiden stopped dead in his tracks as he came through the door, his face blank at first. His gaze swept from one side of the hall to the other. He slowly shook his head in disbelief, then turned to Serafina, his eyes brilliant with something she almost might have thought were tears, except that men like Aiden didn't cry. Did they?

The last strains of the song fell away, and Aiden rubbed one hand over his face. "Thank you," he said hoarsely after a long moment, looking up at the beaming staff. "That's the nicest welcome I've ever had."

The servants shuffled their feet, nudging each other, their faces showing their pleasure.

"We practiced every day," Lord Delaware said. "Back in the kitchen so your sister wouldn't be woken from her afternoon sleep. Did you like the harmony? Serafina arranged it—and doesn't your wife have a lovely voice?"

"Beautiful," Aiden agreed, looking over at her, his face schooled back into composure. "Thank you, sweetheart. I'm truly touched by your surprise."

She blushed with pleasure. "I'm so pleased, Aiden. I chose an old Welsh song traditionally sung when a lord returned from battle. I thought it appropriate, since in a way you have."

"Victorious, I'm happy to say. Who was to know Townsend held such musical talent? You have a proper chorus here."

"They are good, aren't they? I thought that maybe I'd ask the vicar if he wouldn't like a choir for the church, since he doesn't have one. I think music makes Sunday services so much nicer, and we can practice here just as we have been doing, so nobody's duties will be affected."

"It's a wonderful idea," Aiden said, smiling down at her. "Actually, if you have room, I wouldn't mind being in the choir myself."

"Really?" she said with delight. "Of course there's room. But can you sing?"

"You'll have to be the judge of that, but I don't believe I'll set the dogs to howling."

"Then we'll be happy to have you. Won't we?" she said to the others. They all nodded and murmured they would, but they didn't look very comfortable with the idea of having the grand Lord Aubrey in their midst. Lord Delaware was a different matter, for his wasn't an imposing presence, but Aiden did have a certain quality that spoke of authority and breeding, something that set him apart from ordinary people.

Well, Serafina considered, he'd get over all that soon enough, and it would be good for him to mingle with his servants.

Aiden reached his hand out and cupped her chin. "Thank you, Serafina," he said softly, so that only she could hear. "Thank you for giving me a chance."

"If you're not any good, I'll toss you out," she replied with a light laugh. But she knew what he really referred to. And it occurred to her that in giving him a chance, maybe she had given herself one too.

"Oh, my lady, look at what his lordship's brought you!"

Janie turned from the trunks, her arms full of dresses and petticoats, her face flushed with excitement. "Everything you could possibly dream of!"

Serafina stared at the array of clothing that tumbled over the bed, the chairs, everywhere she looked. "Good heavens," she said in wonderment. "It's an entire dress shop. . . ."

Aiden appeared behind her shoulder. "I hope everything meets with your approval," he said. "When I left you weren't at all pleased with the idea of being dressed like a countess."

She turned to him, her eyes shining. "Oh, Aiden—Aiden, I was only being silly and stubborn. I didn't really mean it."

"You didn't?" he said, rubbing his hand over the back of his neck. "You sounded very sure to me."

"Well, I was at the time, but that was before I realized that you were right, that I need to learn how to fit in. I appreciate what you've done, truly I do. You're very generous to have bought me so many nice things."

"Not really," he said with a gleam of irony in his eyes. "Your money paid for them, after all."

"It's not my money, it's yours now, and you're welcome to it. What would I do with a fortune?"

"I have no idea," he answered. "But I doubt you would do any of the usual things." He looked around the room. "Janie, I think you'd better put everything next door in the other bedroom. The hanging wardrobe will never accommodate all this clutter. And give me a little time alone with my wife, will you?"

"Yes, your lordship," Janie said with a breathless curtsy. "As you wish. Right away." She scooped up as much as her arms could hold and went through the connecting door, closing it behind her.

Serafina regarded Aiden nervously, not sure why he wanted to be alone with her. But he went straight to the point.

"Serafina," he said, clearing a space on the bed and sitting down, "I don't know what happened while I was away to change your attitude toward me, but I want you to know that I'm hugely relieved—and grateful to you. As much as I looked forward to seeing you again, I dreaded living in a constant battle zone. This place is dreary enough as it is."

Serafina nodded, feeling ashamed of herself for having made his life so miserable on top of everything else he'd had to deal with. "I know," she said. "But I do think Townsend is slowly improving."

"If the sight of a houseful of formerly dour servants merrily singing to me is any indication, I'd say there's been a vast improvement. Even—" He paused for a moment before continuing. "Even my father seems improved, although I hesitate to trust that judgment."

"Oh, but he is improved, Aiden," she said earnestly. "He's not as lonely as he was, which helps. He and Aunt Elspeth have become good friends, and we hold long conversations while we garden. At least he's making an effort to change."

Aiden rested his forearms on his knees and folded his

hands together. "I don't know if the change will last, but I thank you for caring enough to try to help him. I've never had any luck."

"Maybe it's easier for me because I don't have an argument with him. And I honestly like your father. All he needed was a little encouragement and some attention paid to him. A little love goes a long way."

Aiden gazed at her, his expression undecipherable. "Well, as I said, I appreciate your efforts. But to go back to the original issue, I also appreciate your willingness to put an end to the hostility between us. I'd like to return the favor if I can."

"I don't see how," Serafina said, puzzled. "You were always much nicer to me than I ever was to you."

Aiden smiled. "I wasn't the one with an argument. I told you I was perfectly happy to be married to you. You might not believe that, but it's the truth."

Serafina pressed the palms of her hands together. "Maybe you look at marriage differently than I do. You're a man."

"That was never in dispute," he said, quirking an eyebrow. "And that brings me to my point. Sweetheart, if you'd rather not share my bed, I'll understand."

Serafina stared at him. "You will?" she blurted out, stunned. "But—but why? Why would you change your mind now?"

"Because I know you didn't like the idea of sleeping with me to begin with, and I probably should never have asked you to strike that particular bargain, not when I deliberately coerced you into it." He sighed. "I'm sorry for that, I truly am. You deserve far better than me, Serafina, and I'm trying to make up for my shortcomings the only way I can think of."

Serafina's hand slipped to her mouth. She could see by his vulnerable expression that he was being completely honest with her, that he meant every word. Something deep inside her shifted and eased, a tightness she hadn't even realized was there, as if a wound that had been inflicted a month before was finally healing.

He spoke the truth to her, she was sure of it. She began

to wonder how many other times he had spoken the truth and she simply hadn't believed him. Perhaps Raphael really was right about Aiden—he was an honorable man. And perhaps the difference between holding on to a dream and living in real life was the willingness to accept that dreams could never be fulfilled, whereas life was an endless source of surprise and possibility.

She moved across the room and lightly rested a hand on his shoulder. "Maybe," she said, meeting his eyes directly, "maybe you're really not such an awful rogue after all."

"Well, that's a relief, considering that you'd made up your mind I was a rogue through and through, thoroughly unscrupulous and without any feelings." He slanted a glance up at her.

"I had, but offering to rescind our agreement is the most generous thing you could have done. Aiden . . ." She bit her lip, determined to repay his generosity with her trust. "I think I'd—I think I'd rather stay right here."

Aiden stared at her, thrown completely off balance. "You would?" he managed to stammer.

"Yes. I haven't changed my mind about—about the other thing, but I understand all the reasons you asked me to sleep with you in the first place. I don't want you to be embarrassed by household gossip."

Aiden rubbed a finger over one eyebrow. "Well, maybe I lied a little. There's a perfectly good bed next door, and it is common practice for husbands and wives of our social position to have separate bedrooms." He looked up at her from under half-lowered lids. "Oh, all right. The truth of the matter is that I lied thoroughly and completely to you in order to have my way."

A little smile crept to Serafina's lips. She was discovering much to her surprise that she actually liked this side of Aiden. "I know," she said. "Janie told me that the other room was supposed to have been mine before you changed the arrangements."

Aiden groaned. "I should have known. Hoisted with my own petard. Caught out for the scoundrel I am."

"What did you think you'd accomplish by lying to me?"

she asked curiously. "You'd already promised not to touch me."

To her surprise, Aiden actually flushed. "To be perfectly honest, I thought that maybe if I inundated you with my close physical presence night after night you would decide I wasn't such a poor proposition after all. I was depending on your feminine instincts to kick in, you see."

"Oh, I see," she said, not really seeing at all. "Did you decide I didn't have any? Is that why you changed your mind?"

"Not at all." Aiden leaned back on his elbow. "I already know your feminine instincts are perfectly intact. I just thought you might look more kindly on me if I gave you your privacy."

Serafina looked at him long and hard, suspicion rising fast. "And just how do you know my instincts are intact?" she asked, her voice chilly. "You swore you didn't touch me that night."

Aiden burst into laughter. "You are a skeptical creature, aren't you? I didn't touch you, other than putting you to bed. Oh, and I did hold you, since you seemed to need holding. But other than that, my dear, you are still a complete virgin."

He sat up and took her by the hands, pulling her down next to him with a tug, and taken off guard, she landed on the mattress with a soft plop.

"What did you do that for?" she asked breathlessly, finding herself practically nose to nose with him.

"Because I refuse to crane my neck to look up at you a moment longer while we have this discussion." He brushed a strand of hair off her cheek, his fingers light as a feather. Serafina couldn't help shivering.

"Serafina, I told you I would never take a woman against her will. I would also never take a woman who wasn't completely aware of what she was doing." He flashed a devilish smile at her. "But if you're still wondering how I'm sure that your instincts are fully operational, I'd be happy to show you."

"Thank you, but I think not," she said, inching away from

him. Aiden may have been away for a month, but the alarming physical effect he had on her hadn't lessened one iota. Already she felt warm and flushed by his near presence.

"As you wish." Aiden's expression suddenly grew serious and he picked up her hands, holding them loosely between his own. "Listen to me, sweetheart. Since we're being completely honest with each other, I won't deny that I'm powerfully attracted to you. I'm not inclined to pretend otherwise." He stroked the back of her hands with his thumbs. "But I'm determined that you come to me of your own accord. Anything else would be unsatisfying to both of us. Will you trust me to keep my word?"

Serafina reluctantly dragged her eyes to his. They blazed into hers, azure fire, his expression intent. "Yes. I trust you," she croaked, no proof against his fixed, determined gaze. "I do. I told you, I want to be friends."

"And I want that too, but I also want to be your husband in every sense of the word, even if the thought strikes terror in your heart at the moment. I told you that I'm prepared to wait, but to that end I also need you to trust me when I do touch you. It bothers me when you shrink away."

"I'm sorry. I can't help it," she said, not knowing how to explain the effect his touch had on her, how frightened she was of what it might lead to. She no more wanted to be impaled now than she had a month ago.

"Hmm. I think the best solution to that problem is if you become more accustomed to being touched. I'd be happy to teach you, but again, you're going to have to trust me."

"What—what kind of touching do you have in mind?" she asked nervously.

"It's actually very simple. I'd like to to kiss you, but with the assurance that I'll go no farther. Do you think you could manage that?"

"You—you want to kiss me?" she said with severe alarm.

"I do, very much, especially after what you did today in arranging that extraordinary welcome for me. I wanted to kiss you then, but I didn't want to be rebuffed in front of the entire staff. Do you think I might properly thank you now in the privacy of our room?"

Serafina thought about his request. It wasn't entirely unreasonable, she decided, although she wasn't very comfortable with the idea of voluntarily submitting to his kiss. "I suppose I can manage that," she said, trying hard to be agreeable, since Aiden had been so circumspect about asking.

"Good," he said, regarding her steadily, but he didn't move. Serafina imagined he must be waiting for her.

She released a long breath, closed her eyes, and screwed her face up, preparing herself for the onslaught.

All she got for her trouble was Aiden's laughter. "I might as well be kissing a goat's bottom."

Her eyes shot open. "A goat's bottom?" she said, offended.

"Well, yes. A kiss is meant to be enjoyed. If you'd just relax a little, I think we might be able to make this a pleasant experience." He stroked her cheek. "A kiss, Serafina, is a naturally occurring phenomenon. It doesn't require much beyond two willing parties and a mutual meeting of the mouths. I thought you'd grasped that concept in the woods, although I must confess our kiss in the chapel left something to be desired."

"What was wrong with our kiss in the chapel?" she asked, thinking that she'd done a fine job with the business.

"For one, you screwed your mouth up just as you did now. It's hard to do much of anything with. Here, look." He pursed his lips together as if he was about to whistle.

Serafina had to smile at his contorted expression. "Yes, I see your point."

"All right. Now I suggest that you come a little closer so that I can hold on to you. You don't want to fall over, do you, since I'm likely to fall on top of you?"

She shook her head, absolutely certain she didn't want that to happen. Aiden held out his arms, and Serafina warily moved toward him.

His hands came down to rest on her shoulders, his touch light. He looked into her eyes for a long moment, then picked one hand up and ran a finger down her cheek. "You're so pretty," he whispered. "So soft and sweet."

Something pulsated in Serafina's chest, a hot thrill of excitement that only grew as his finger traced the line of her jaw and slipped under her chin. A pounding started in her ears as he bent his head toward hers.

His mouth came down with a gentle pressure, his lips moving over hers, so warm, his touch so enticing. Her own lips parted involuntarily under his and her fingers twined of their own accord into his thick hair, sensation flooding through her body, turning her limbs to water. A tiny moan escaped her throat and he pulled her even closer, his arms tightening around her, his mouth opening on hers as he deepened the kiss.

She was drowning, lost, disappearing into mindless pleasure, fire erupting deep in her belly, coursing through her blood like quicksilver. She couldn't think, could only press harder against his hard body, wanting something more.

An electric shock ran through her as his tongue invaded her mouth, tasting her, his hot breath coming fast against her open mouth and she tentatively responded, touching her tongue to his.

He suddenly pulled away, burying his face in her hair with a groan, his hands moving over her back. "Sweet Christ, Serafina," he murmured. "You're enough to tempt even a saint, and that I'm surely not."

Serafina wriggled out of his grasp, her cheeks on fire, appalled with herself. "I—I don't know what happened," she whispered. "I didn't mean to do that. . . ."

Aiden laughed lazily, slanting a look down at her. "I don't know why not. You did it very nicely." He rubbed his hands over his face, then gazed up at the ceiling. "Well, that should answer two questions," he said.

"What questions?" she asked shakily, gripping her hands in her lap.

"That your feminine instincts are entirely operational." He abruptly stood and turned his back to her, one hand digging into his hair, his breathing still rough. "And that I'm a bloody gentleman. No self-respecting rogue would have stopped things there."

A little bubble of laughter escaped Serafina's throat. "Thank you," she said, meaning it. She knew he could easily have ravished her then and there.

"I should think you would thank me." He turned around and regarded her with a flash of humor. "I think I'd better leave you before I change my mind and move on to the next lesson."

Serafina longed to ask him what the next lesson was, but quickly decided it was a question best left unasked. She'd had enough of a shock for one afternoon. "I should dress for dinner," she said instead.

"You do that. Pick out something nice. I'm going for a walk—a nice, long walk."

He cast one last curious look at her, shook his head with a little laugh and left, softly closing the door behind him.

Serafina buried her face in her hands, her head swimming with confusion.

Elspeth finished her experiments for the day, happily stoppering up the various bottles and piling her notes together. She washed and changed, looking forward to dinner, for she had a prodigious appetite and a chess game to win from Delaware afterwards.

She was also mightily curious to see Aiden, for the chambermaid had told her he'd returned. High time, too. To her way of thinking Serafina was spending far too much time with the duke—oh, yes, she knew all about it, she thought darkly, skewering her hairpins firmly into place.

"There's only trouble that can come from it," she said over her shoulder to Basil. "Don't we just know it? Serafina's reasons for popping over there might be as innocent as the day is long, but she belongs with her husband, and Aiden's a fool for leaving her alone so long with nothing else to do."

"Silly man," Basil squawked in agreement.

"Just so," Elspeth said with satisfaction. "If matters are going to go differently this time around, Aiden needs to keep his eyes open and his head up. At least Serafina has finally started to see that he might have some merit after all, or so she says. Goddess, but she gave me some bad moments there last month, kicking up such a fuss." She scowled. "Don't know what got into the girl when all she's ever wanted is that man. It's not as if I didn't do everything in my power to see that she got him. And then what does she do? Practically spits in his face, and who knows why?"

"Bad girl," Basil crooned lovingly.

"Simply misguided," Elspeth corrected. "Maybe she expected an exact double for all I know. But never mind, we're back on the right track. It's that Charlotte who worries me now—she'll take anything and twist it to get her own way, just like before, and we both know what a disaster *that* ended up. I'm telling you, the duke had better watch his step all the way around."

Elspeth dug in a drawer and pulled out a biscuit. "Here you are, dearest. This will have to be your supper, since that dreadful woman won't allow you at the table. I don't know why I let Serafina talk me into giving Charlotte my special potion. I ought to have doctored it, I really should have done, put stinging nettles into it."

"Do no harm, do no harm." Basil grabbed the biscuit in one foot and started to munch on it, crumbs flying everywhere.

"Don't you go telling me," Elspeth said with annoyance. "I'm doing my best to stay out of the way, and don't think it's easy. But you and I both know that the lot of them have to sort out their own problems, or it's no good."

She returned to her dressing table and liberally scattered a puff full of powder on her face. She peered into the mirror. "Not bad for an old woman," she said cheerfully, her spirits restored. "Now back to business. I'm going down to see what's what with those two. Heavens, people can be blind to what's right under their noses."

13

Aiden paced the hall, anxiously waiting for Serafina to make an appearance. He still couldn't believe his good fortune. She had let him kiss her. Actually let him kiss her. And dear God, but that had been an extraordinary experience, even better than he could have imagined. He felt as if he'd been waiting for that kiss all his life.

And it had nearly driven him out of his mind. He was still amazed that he'd managed to put a stop to it, but securing Serafina's trust was far more important to him than physical satisfaction, even though he was fairly certain he could have persuaded her straight under the covers if he'd put a little effort into it.

He couldn't think what had come over him. He'd never let a woman get under his skin like this, causing him to lower his carefully constructed defenses, ready to do anything to please her. If she asked for the moon, he'd probably start climbing trees in an effort to catch it for her. He'd even gone so far as to offer her a separate bedroom, throwing away all of his carefully laid plans in one foolish moment of truthfulness.

And yet she'd refused his offer. That confused him more than anything. She said she had no interest in letting him make love to her. So why in the name of heaven did she want to share his bed? And how was he ever going to keep his vow not to touch her until she asked, when he had to lie side by side with her every night?

But still, given the way she'd responded to a simple kiss,

maybe he wouldn't have to wait too much longer before he actually managed to convince her that lovemaking was a good idea.

"There you are, Aubrey. Home at last and not a moment too soon."

Startled, he turned to see Elspeth Beaton hopping down the stairs like a schoolgirl. "Oh . . . good evening, Miss Beaton," he said, watching her come off the bottom step with a little skip. It wouldn't have surprised him if she'd decided to slide down the bannister. "I trust I find you well?"

"What else would I be? Never had a sick day in my life and I'm not about to start now. Did you like your concert, boy?"

"My—oh, yes. Yes, very much. I've always been fond of music, and Serafina did a fine job of teaching the staff the song. I was impressed. And touched."

"Of course you were. Serafina has an unusual talent. She could probably teach a cow to sing if she put her mind to it."

Aiden couldn't help smiling. Elspeth Beaton might be the most peculiar woman he'd ever come across, but he liked her enormously. And despite the eccentric way she'd chosen to raise her niece, he couldn't be sorry, although he did find that some of the stories Tinkerby had told him about Elspeth's more unusual practices gave him slight cause for alarm. He didn't relish the idea of finding strange substances floating in his soup bowl.

"I imagine Serafina could accomplish just about anything she put her mind to," he said, wondering with distraction what Elspeth had all over her face, for it clung in clumps to her wrinkled skin. She looked as if she'd fallen into a flour bin. Maybe one of her dubious experiments had gone awry again, he decided.

"Oh, my yes," Elspeth said. "The child has a will of steel. Once she makes up her mind to something, that's that."

That much Aiden already knew. What he wanted to know was how one went about unmaking it. "On that subject, Miss Beaton, I was wondering if you might enlighten me as to something," he said, treading carefully. "Apparently Serafina made up her mind a long time ago that this was to be a love match. Do you have any idea how she got that idea in her head, when you and I both know it was anything but?"

Elspeth's eyes sharpened like a hawk's, and for the first time Aiden saw a keen intelligence lurking there.

"That's your concern, my boy, not mine. But what makes you think it isn't a love match?" she challenged. " 'There are more things in heaven and earth, Horatio, than are dreamt of in your philosophy,' " she added cryptically. "Just insert your own name in there, Aubrey, and take a lesson from Shakespeare. Or are you a religious fanatic like your sister? Someone ought to stuff a sock in that girl's mouth."

Aiden sighed, grateful that Tinkerby had warned him about Elspeth's beliefs. "I think it would be better if we left my sister out of this conversation," he said as patiently as he could manage. "I was asking how Serafina came to believe she was entering a marriage based on love."

"What else do you think would have brought her to you?" Elspeth snapped. "Be grateful for what you have, Aubrey, and don't ask a lot of fool questions, for they won't do you any good or make your job any easier. You have a marriage to get on with, and it's your own fault if you've given Serafina any reason to doubt you. Not many men are fortunate enough to have their destiny delivered directly into their hands without lifting a finger."

With that addle-brained statement Aiden had his answer. Serafina had obviously had her head filled with a lot of El-speth's nonsense, and it was no wonder she'd been so badly disillusioned, although he still couldn't work out why she thought she'd fall into the arms of a man who loved her when they'd never exchanged so much as a letter.

"I'm not caviling against my destiny, if that's what you think. But I think you might have been wiser to give Serafina the truth rather than a bunch of drivel about true love. I'm not a knight in shining armor, Miss Beaton, and I'm not likely to turn into one any time soon."

"No one said the first thing about your being a knight,

shining armor included. But you are a man with a new wife
on your hands, and I suggest you turn your thoughts in that
direction." She pointed at the staircase.

Aiden looked up and his heart nearly stopped in his chest.

"Titania," he breathed, staring at her, overwhelmed.

Serafina stood on the middle landing, attired in one of
the evening dresses he'd brought home, a high-waisted sea-
green net over a slip of white satin that draped her slender
form to perfection. White gloves covered her graceful arms
to the elbow, and her dark hair, arranged high on her head
with artful ringlets brushing her cheeks, was entwined with
flowers throughout.

She appeared every inch a countess, yet she hadn't lost
any of her fairy queen qualities; she was just a more elegant
version. He couldn't help the surge of relief that flooded
through him. For some reason he'd thought that dressing
her appropriate to her station might turn her into a copy of
every other woman he'd ever known.

But he saw now that it didn't matter how she dressed.
Clothes couldn't alter Serafina, they could only enhance her.
Her beauty overwhelmed him, humbled him, left him reel-
ing.

She drifted down the stairs toward him, a hesitant smile
on her rosy lips, her cheeks lightly flushed. "Good evening,
Auntie. Aiden?" She gazed at him, her eyes wide with nervous question. "Are you pleased?"

He could barely formulate a coherent thought. "I—yes,
yes I am," he said, forcing the words out. "You look as if you
walked straight out of a fashion plate. No—better than that,"
he corrected, trying desperately to regain control of his voice.
"You're a vision, Serafina. A true vision," he said honestly.

"That's more like it," Elspeth retorted caustically.

Aiden ignored her. "I—I hadn't imagined you would look
so lovely. You surpass every expectation I had."

"Do you really like it?" Serafina asked, fiddling with her
bodice. "I've never had anything so fine before. I feel a little
foolish."

Aiden's every instinct was to take her in his arms and kiss
her senseless to reassure her of just how lovely she was, how

impossibly desirable. But he obviously couldn't do that, so all he did was smile and hope he didn't appear as much of a dazed idiot as he felt. "You look anything but foolish," he said, wishing Elspeth away so that he could tell her what he really thought.

"Thank you," she said returning his smile shyly. "Thank you for taking the time to order me such nice things, and thank you for not being disappointed with me—I was afraid you might be. I took ages trying to decide what would please you most."

"You would please me in anything," he said, taking her arm. *You would please me more in nothing,* the rogue's voice inside his head silently added. "Shall we go into the drawing room?"

"Aiden!" Charlotte cried as they entered. "Oh, you're home! I could barely wait for your return. Come over here, dear boy, and give your sister a kiss. How I've missed you— you must tell me everything." She laughed breathlessly and held her hands out to him. "And thank you for my new dresses. I didn't like to say, but I was starting to feel positively shabby."

Aiden crossed the room and dropped a kiss on his sister's cheek. "You're looking well, Lottie," he said, surprised by the new color in her face. She'd lost the pinched look she'd worn for years, and he couldn't think what to attribute it to.

"I am well," she said, smiling up at him. "Your dear wife has given me an oil that helps considerably with my pain."

"Did she?" Aiden said, casting a suspicious look in Elspeth's direction, sure that her hand was behind the oil, but pleased nonetheless that something was helping his poor sister.

"Yes, and I'm really most obligated to her. I am sleeping much better at night. Why Serafina, how charming you look—your dress suits you beautifully. Doesn't Aiden have a fine eye?"

"He has," Serafina said. "I wouldn't have had any idea how to go about choosing a trousseau for myself, but Aiden did a wonderful job." She glanced at him shyly.

Aiden's heart swelled with gratification. He felt like a

puffed-up rooster, even though he'd had little to do with actually choosing her trousseau—he'd have to remember to send a note of thanks to Harriet. But what was important was that Serafina was pleased with him. Almost better than that, it appeared that Charlotte liked his wife. That was a miracle in itself, given Charlotte's antagonistic attitude when he'd left, an attitude that had worried him considerably over the last month.

He listened as Serafina conversed easily with Charlotte, watched as she laughed merrily with Elspeth and his father—still clear-eyed and coherent even though it was past seven. That alone was cause for incredulity.

He observed her all the way through dinner, nearly falling off his chair as she gracefully helped herself from the serving platters the footmen presented at her side as if she'd been doing it all her life, her manners impeccable throughout the meal, not that her aunt's had improved any. He couldn't think where she'd acquired her skill, unless Charlotte had been teaching her.

And miracle of miracles, Charlotte only quoted two biblical verses during the entire meal.

Aiden felt as if he'd walked into someone else's house where goodwill and harmony were the norm. For the first time in memory, he actually enjoyed dinner with his family.

"That was an interesting evening," he said to Serafina as soon as she finished saying good night to her aunt, the last person except for themselves to go upstairs. "I just have one question for you."

Serafina turned from the open doorway, her smile fading. "What is it?" she asked, her expression suddenly nervous. "Did I displease you in some way?"

"*Displease* me?" he said with surprise. "Anything but. I was only going to ask if you've been flinging fairy dust about. I can't think of any other explanation for the profound changes I observed tonight."

Serafina burst into laughter. "Despite what you tell me to the contrary, I think you're secretly fanciful at heart, Aiden."

"I'm beginning to think I must be—either that, or I'm hallucinating. I'm not sure if I care. Four weeks ago I would have sworn on my soul that a pleasant evening like this would have been impossible." He shook his head. "And yet I can't question what I witnessed. My God, my father only had two glasses of wine all night, and believe me, I was counting. I don't think I've ever known him to go to his bed sober."

Serafina clasped her hands together. "I told you he was trying," she said. "He only wants your approval, Aiden. He feels terrible for nearly losing everything and putting you in such a terrible position."

"Not so terrible," Aiden said, crossing the room and taking her hands in his. "I'm beginning to think his stupidity was a blessing in disguise."

A pensive expression came over Serafina's face. "Really?" she asked softly. "I—I think maybe you're right."

Aiden inhaled sharply. He knew he should expect the unexpected from her, but she continuously caught him off guard. "What do you mean?" he asked cautiously, wondering if his kiss hadn't had more of a beneficial effect on her than he'd first realized.

"When I first came to Townsend, I thought everything in my life had gone wrong. But then I realized that there's a purpose behind everything, that nothing happens by mistake. So I looked to see what my purpose was, and I saw that I had a chance to make things a little better, not just for the people around me, but for myself too." She swallowed. "Do you understand?"

Aiden's heart ached anew with that unfamiliar sensation that made him want to draw her to him and hold her, protect her from the harsh world, cherish her, damn it. She was so blasted innocent, her head filled with these idiotic, idealistic notions of predestination. And love. And perfect men on perfect white chargers riding full tilt to carry her off into the sunset.

And the most damnable thing of all was that she inspired a desire in him to do just that. He wanted to cry with frustration because he could never be what she wanted, and he knew better than to let himself get caught up in her dream.

But God, she made it look appealing.

"Aiden? What are you thinking?" she asked, gazing up at him.

"I'm thinking that I'm a bloody fool," he said roughly, taking her face in his hands, tracing the fine line of her high cheekbones. "If I weren't, I'd lie through my teeth to you and tell you that I'm that man you were waiting for, that I've always loved you, that I just didn't know it until now. I'd give anything to hand you that fantasy on a silver platter, just to see you happy." He ran a thumb over her mouth. "And if I were really a scoundrel at heart, I'd also lie through my teeth because I know that way I could take you to bed and make love to you all night long, pretending to be someone I'm not."

Serafina lowered her eyes. "But I wouldn't believe you," she said, her thick lashes shining with what he suspected were tears. "I don't believe that man exists, not anymore. He was nothing but a childish dream."

He tilted her face up to his. "And I'm sorry for that too. I wish to hell I could be him, sweetheart, because you deserve to be happy. I suppose the best I can do is try to not let you down anymore than you already have been."

Serafina blinked, her tears spilling over. "Aiden," she choked. "Don't. Please don't take any more responsibility on yourself. You deserve to be happy too, and you won't be if you're constantly worrying about disappointing me. Maybe I just needed to grow up, to understand that we can't always make things be the way we want them." She ran trembling fingers over her eyes. "The most we can do is accept what life gives us and try to understand the divine reason at work."

Aiden's heart twisted painfully in his chest. "Serafina. Sweetheart," he said, taking a shuddering breath, trying desperately to control himself. He wanted her more in that moment than he ever had, wanted to kiss her tears away, to take her to a place where she didn't care about reason, divine or otherwise. "The way I feel right now, I'm about to lose the little reason I have. I think you might be wise to take yourself up to bed and go to sleep. I'll come up later."

Serafina bowed her head. "I've offended you."

"Oh, God," he said, on the very edge of doing something

outrageous. "Anything but. Get thee gone, woman, or I swear I'll break every vow I ever made to you. I may not be the man you wanted, but I am a man, and you tempt me sorely to prove it to you."

That did the trick. Serafina stepped hastily away. "Good night then," she said, bestowing a wobbly smile on him.

"Good night. Sleep well. And for God's sake don't fling yourself about in your sleep, or I won't be held responsible for my actions."

Serafina absently let Janie undress her, her mind a million miles away. Even Janie's chatter didn't permeate her thoughts, slipping over and around her unnoticed. She answered without even hearing what she was saying, then managed to bid Janie good night. She washed her face and brushed her teeth and slipped under the bedclothes, gazing over at Aiden's place. It looked empty. For some inexplicable reason she wanted to see his dark head resting on the pillow, to see his face turned toward hers, feel his weight bearing down on the mattress.

She wanted his arms around her. And she didn't understand that either. For a month she'd been grateful to have him gone. Hadn't she? For a month she'd been free of his unwelcome attention. But was it so unwelcome? For a full month she'd convinced herself that he had no real place in her life other than being her husband, a man whose happiness she wanted to ensure, even though she didn't even know whether she liked him.

And yet today he'd turned all of that around. He'd shown her what real longing was by the touch of his mouth on hers, inflaming her senses. And she'd discovered that she did like him after all, that he did have feelings, could be heartbreakingly honest when he wanted to be. He'd shown her sensitivity and caring. And he'd also admired her.

Serafina had never had anyone admire her before, but she knew she hadn't mistaken the open appreciation in his eyes when she came down the stairs, so nervous her knees knocked together.

She'd actually felt pretty for the first time in her life, and she almost believed it was true, given the way he'd looked at her all night. It couldn't just have been her new dress. And he had said the very same just before he'd kissed her, even if he had been trying to have his way. He'd even called her pretty before this, although at the time she'd thought he was trying to make her feel better. She didn't know anymore. She felt as if she didn't know anything at all.

Aiden was turning her life upside down, not for the first time, but this time she truly didn't mind, as alarming as she found the experience.

She stretched her hand out and touched the pillows next to her, imagining his head resting just there, her fingers stroking through his soft, silky hair, moving up to trace the outline of his finely sculptured face. She snatched her hand back, dismayed with the direction of her thoughts.

Everything would be different, her instincts acceptable, if she only loved him as she'd once loved Adam long ago in a fairy tale. . . .

She slowly drifted off into sleep, images floating into her mind, then dissolving again, reforming. Aiden, laughing with her at some joke, taking her hand in his. Aiden, stroking her hair, then picking her up and carrying her to the big bed in his room, nuzzling his warm mouth into her neck, whispering words of love against her hair as his hands lifted her nightdress over her head and returned to her flesh, sliding over her waist, smoothing up to the swell of her breasts, shaping them in his palms as he took her mouth in a deep kiss, his tongue tangling with hers, something remembered from somewhere else.

She trembled under his touch, strained upwards as his head bent down and took her nipple in his mouth, gently tugging, one hand skimming down over her thigh, stroking up again as her arms embraced him tightly, pulling him close, even closer as he drove her into a state of impassioned longing. So near now, so near to knowing . . .

Serafina shivered, turning over on her side, her hand reaching out for him, but he wasn't there. She only met space, cold, empty space. A surge of loss jolted through her and her eyes flew open, seeking him through the dark. She didn't know where he'd gone or why.

And then she heard a soft rustle somewhere in the room and she raised her head, hazily focusing through the soft moonlight filtering into the room. He was there after all, his tall, powerful figure silhouetted against the window, his hands stretched out on either side of it as he stared out into the dark.

Aiden. Aiden had finally come to bed. And she'd dreamed the entire encounter. But *how*? How could she possibly have dreamed something she'd never experienced? It had felt so real, so right.

She sat up abruptly, the last fragments of dream fading away, but her body trembled with remembered longing.

"Aiden," she murmured, rubbing her hands over her eyes.

"Who else?" he said, turning from the windowsill, dropping his hands. He wore nothing but a nightshirt, the fine linen covering him to his knees.

"Where have you been?" she asked, stifling a yawn against her palm, but she couldn't help the surge of desire that ran through her at the sight of his nearly unclothed body.

"Out. Walking," he said shortly.

"Walking? At this hour? Why?" She peered through the dark, trying to decipher his expression with no success.

"Why do you think? Go back to sleep, Serafina."

He spoke in a harsh tone, and a stab of hurt pierced through her heart as she realized that she'd somehow unwittingly upset him. "Aiden?" she asked uncertainly, her eyes finally adjusting to the dim light. "What's wrong?"

"Nothing's wrong. I didn't mean to wake you." He moved over to the bed and pulled the covers back, his weight shifting the mattress as he lay down and pulled them back over him. He turned away from her onto his side.

Serafina cupped her cheek in her hand, gazing at his broad back, longing to run her hands over it as she had in her dream. "You look troubled. Can I help?"

"Help?" he said with a short laugh. "Oh, I imagine you could, but you've tied my hands fairly effectively, haven't you?"

"Oh," she said, finally understanding. "I—I'm sorry." She felt stupid and selfish for having created an impossible situation between them.

"No need to be sorry," he murmured. "My fault entirely for being the damned fool I was talking about earlier. Please, sweetheart, go to sleep."

"Aiden?" she persisted, tentatively reaching out a hand and touching his back just as she'd longed to do earlier. His skin burned under her palm, and she snatched her hand back. "I just want you to know that—that I don't think of you as a black-hearted, unfeeling rogue. Not anymore. You've been nothing but generous and understanding to me."

He rolled over to face her, his eyes glittering at her through the dark. "You think I'm generous and understanding, do you? Then you're as big a fool as I am. And if you have any sense in your head you'll leave it there, unless you want to tempt me to take you in my arms here and now and show you the meaning of the word foolish." He turned onto his back and tightly folded his hands over his chest. "Good night."

"Good night." Serafina surreptitiously watched him under her lashes until his breathing finally deepened and his hands relaxed.

She propped herself up on her elbow and thought back to her dream, surprised she'd had it at all. It was Adam she'd always dreamt about in that way, not Aiden. Never Aiden. She could only reason that the kiss she and Aiden shared that afternoon had unleashed a torrent of sensuality, and her imagination had just done some creative enhancing.

Really, she considered, looking down at his nicely made hands, it might not be so bad to have Aiden touch her like that. But that was the problem.

She was obviously capable of making up just about anything. If she'd learned anything from her marriage it was that real life bore no resemblance to fantasies. And as much as she'd liked Aiden's kiss, there was no way of knowing if she'd like what came afterwards, no matter what she'd conjured up. From everything Elspeth had told her, she felt certain it wouldn't be nice at all.

But she now knew she couldn't put Aiden off forever, and that frightened her more than anything else.

14

Elspeth had just finished concocting a recipe she considered a vast improvement on any she'd formulated before for enhancing the memory of dreams. She was making her final notes in her notebook when a knock came at the door.

"Enter, enter," she called impatiently, frowning down at her foolscap, trying to decide if it was cinnamon or cardamom that she'd written. "Cinnamon, of course it's cinnamon," she muttered, then looked up to see what fool had come to disturb her concentration now.

"Miss?" Janie asked, stepping into the room. "May I have leave to speak with you?"

"What is it girl, what is it?" Elspeth said, scratching her ear with her quill. "I'm frightfully busy."

"Yes, miss," Janie said shyly. "But Mr. Tinkerby suggested I speak with you. It's about her ladyship. And his lordship." She took an uncertain step forward. "About their bed, miss."

"Their bed? What's wrong with their bed?" Elspeth said with distraction. "I'm sure it's perfectly adequate. Serafina isn't accustomed to luxury, you know."

"It's not that," Janie said, her brow knotting. "It's that nothing is happening in it, if you see what I mean. Mr. Tinkerby thought you might have a suggestion."

"What in the name of the goddess are you going on about, girl? I haven't all day to listen to your chattering."

"But Miss Beaton," Janie said desperately, "they're not doing anything in it! The sheets are pure as snow every single morning and have been since the day the two of them was married. I asked my mum just to make sure, and she said it wasn't natural, and I remember from when my last mistress was married, before her husband was taken away that is, and I knew to change the bedding when it was stained. Five days now since his lordship's been back, and not a thing, even though they're newly wed."

Elspeth stared, at a loss for words. "Nothing?" she finally croaked. "Maybe the girl's having her time," she said, brightening.

"No, miss. She finished with her courses a week before his lordship returned."

"Bother," Elspeth said with annoyance. "And you say the sheets were the same on their wedding night?"

Janie nodded fervently.

"Oh, dear. Dearie me. This won't do." Elspeth threw her quill down, ignoring the ink that ran over her notes. "It's him, of course. Serafina knows all about doing her duty. It's not as if I didn't instruct her." She thought hard. "Yes. Hmmm. Must be that resentment about his marriage he still has simmering that's keeping him away." She thought some more. "Well, we can take care of that, can't we just."

She jumped to her feet. "You say you discussed the matter with Tinkerby?"

"I did, miss. I didn't know who else to turn to, and with Mr. Tinkerby being his lordship's valet and all, I thought maybe he knew what the problem was. But he didn't have a clue, just said I should talk to you."

"Wise of him," Elspeth said, nodding. "Every now and then the man shows a glimmer of sense. Well, Janie, although I didn't expect it, I am prepared for this day." She marched over to her chest and threw it open, drawing out a precious vial of liquid. "I happened to make this up at Clwydd before the marriage, just in case something unanticipated happened. Forethought is always rewarded, you know." Elspeth held the vial up to the light and admired the cloudy solution she'd so lovingly labored over.

"What's that, miss?" Janie asked, one hand going to her throat, her expression wary.

"Nothing you need trouble yourself over. All you need to

know is that it will take care of Aubrey's reluctance fast enough." She handed Janie the vial. "Don't tell Tinkerby, for he's sure to kick up a fuss. You just make sure that five drops of this go into a glass of Aubrey's wine every night."

"But—but how, miss? I have nothing to do with his lordship's wine." Janie peered at the small glass bottle.

"Oh, that's right. I can't exactly give this to Plum, either. I know—dump the entire contents into the decanter Plum puts out in the evening. Surely you can manage to do that when nobody's about." She chortled. "A day or two of drinking a glass of this in the evenings and Aubrey will be rearing like a stallion."

Janie nodded, but she looked doubtful. "Very good, miss. But won't Lord Delaware be rearing like a stallion too? He drinks from the same decanter as his son," she pointed out.

"Pshaw. Delaware's too old and too befuddled to be affected by an aphrodisiac. This sort of thing only acts on the young. You wait and see, you'll be changing those sheets morning, noon, and night."

Janie's round face broke into a broad smile. "Then it must be for the good. I've seen the way my lady's eyes follow his lordship about. She knows what she wants sure enough, and it'll be mighty pleasing to her when he decides to oblige."

"Exactly," Elspeth said. "Hop to, girl, and slip the stuff into the wine before anyone's the wiser. Shouldn't taste of anything. Deer antler tips are fortunate in that regard."

Janie chuckled. "My mum always did say that women knew far better than men about the ways of love. I think you've just proved that true, miss."

"Your mother is a wise woman. But you just keep your trap shut about what we're up to. We don't want anyone tumbling onto the truth."

"No, miss. You can count on me." Janie scurried out the door and Elspeth settled back into her chair, mightily pleased with herself.

"Bad bird," Basil scolded loudly as soon as the door had closed. "Bad, bad bird."

"Oh, hush your beak—it will all work out for the best. I know I'm not supposed to interfere, but the boy's been stalling in his duty, and that won't do. He had better realize how he really feels about his wife in no short order, or that Charlotte's going to work her poison again, mark my words."

Aiden found his sister in her study off her bedroom, hard at work at the household books.

"Aiden," she said, looking up in surprise, but her smile was welcoming. "What brings you here? I thought you'd forgotten all about me—I've hardly seen you since you've been home."

He kissed her cheek. "I'm sorry about that. I've had rather a lot of work to attend to."

"And here I thought you were busy with your new wife," she said. "Don't tell me you've been neglecting her too."

"Actually, I wanted to thank you for the kindness you've extended to Serafina. I appreciate the effort you've made, especially given how you felt about her when she first arrived."

"Oh, as for that, I thought over what you said and realized you were right." She closed her accounts. "I was being unchristian in my attitude. Dear Serafina might be young and naive, but she's trying to be a good wife to you."

Aiden smiled fondly at his sister, relieved that she had come around so easily. "She is trying," he said, wishing in his heart that Serafina would try just a little harder. He was finding it decidedly difficult to keep his end of the bargain, especially being in such close quarters with her. The truth was that he was finding it nearly impossible to keep his hands to himself, especially after the last kiss they'd shared, so full of promise. Sequestering himself seemed the only solution, which was the real reason he'd spent so much time locked in his study.

"That's all I ask. I only want your happiness, Aiden."

"And I wish the same for you, Lottie," he said, squeezing her hand. "I'm delighted that you're looking in so much better health. The oils really are working, aren't they?"

"I believe they are," she said. "Naturally I am deeply grateful to your wife." She sighed and ran a hand over her forehead. "Now if I could just be rid of these headaches."

Aiden's heart tugged with guilt. He couldn't imagine how hard it was for her to have to live with constant pain of one kind or another, and he was fully aware that it was all his fault. He wished he had a way to make the accident up to her, and he'd probably spend the rest of his life trying, even though Charlotte never cast blame.

"I thought I'd bring you some good news. By next quarter I can afford to put fifty thousand pounds into the refurbishing of the house. Does that please you?"

Charlotte's face lit up. "Really? Oh, Aiden, how wonderful! I can spend it as I please?"

"Exactly as you please, although you might want to speak with Serafina about anything she might like."

Charlotte's smile abruptly faded. "Aiden, dearest, it's a generous idea, but Serafina has always said that she knows nothing about managing a household, let alone decorating one. You don't want to overburden her or make her feel inadequate to the task, do you? Perhaps you could spare a little extra money for the gardens, for that seems to be her area of interest and I'm sure she would be happy for some help."

Aiden was touched by her concern for Serafina. "Yes, it's a good idea," he said softly. "Thank you, Lottie, for thinking of it."

"Well, there's poor Father too. He can't go on struggling away at his age. I worry for his health."

"Father?" he said, surprised at this new area of concern. "I think he's enjoying every minute of his work—he looks better than he has in years, and you have to admit, he's mostly staying away from drink."

"Nevertheless," Charlotte said, faint color staining her cheeks, "I don't think his behavior is seemly. He's a marquess, not a gardener."

"And Serafina is a countess, but she still makes a very fine gardener, don't you think?" he retorted, wishing Charlotte wouldn't put such a fine point on position.

"Your wife was not brought up to be a countess. Father was born to be a marquess, however, and I wish he'd behave like one. What must the servants think, seeing him coming in covered in dirt like one of them?"

"I have no idea," Aiden said, thinking it was a good thing that Charlotte didn't know he and their father spent an hour every afternoon in the kitchen playing choir with the staff. He couldn't imagine what her reaction was going to be in church this Sunday when she discovered what they'd been up to, but he found he didn't really care. They were all having too much fun. He'd never enjoyed life at Townsend so thoroughly, and he had Serafina to thank for bringing them all a breath of fresh air.

"Well, it's simply not a good influence on them, I can tell you that. I'm already having problems with their attitude—I sense a loss of respect."

"I wouldn't worry about the servants, Lottie," he said, suppressing his frustration. "They appear to be going about their work with lighter hearts, and that's all to the good." He ran a knuckle down her cheek. "I have to get back to work. I'll see you at dinner."

"Very well, Aiden. But bear in mind what I've said. Discipline and dedication to God and one's duty is the only way to keep a house this size running, and the servants need to be constantly reminded of that."

Aiden didn't reply. He couldn't without telling her he thought she was as far wrong as she could be.

Serafina waited for the staff to take its place for the daily choir practice. They hadn't lost an ounce of the enthusiasm that had started with rehearsing for Aiden's homecoming, and she took enormous pleasure not only from teaching them, but also from hearing them hum snatches of songs as they went about their work.

"Right, my lady, what's it going to be today?" William asked, picking up his hymnal and leafing through the pages.

"Why don't we wait until everyone is here?" she suggested. "Oh, and William, move behind Alice. You need to listen carefully to the soprano for the next piece of harmony."

Townsend was changing, slowly but surely, and Serafina

was well pleased. More and more often the servants came to her with their troubles and their questions, and whenever she could help or dispense personal advice she did, although she remained careful not to interfere with Charlotte's orders in any way.

Aiden came in at the last moment and took up his position in the rear, his gaze trained on the floor.

She frowned with concern. Aiden hadn't been himself the last few days, jumpy and distracted, and she could barely get five words out him. She wondered if maybe he wasn't suffering from overwork, for he came to bed long after she retired and rose before her in the morning, spending most of his time locked in his study. He'd even taken his dinner alone there the last two evenings.

He looked tired and strained around the eyes, although whenever she asked if his business dealings were still causing him anxiety he claimed that all was running smoothly. Nevertheless, the only time she saw him for any period of time was at choir practice, and even then he barely looked at her.

Serafina had discovered to her amazement that Aiden really could sing. He had a beautiful voice—a clear, rich tenor that blended in beautifully with the others. And although at first the staff had been a little nervous around him, they soon became accustomed to his presence and returned to their customary joking and teasing.

Serafina thought there might be a little too much teasing, a result of spring fever, she decided. Except for Aiden. He didn't seem to be suffering from spring fever at all. His father on the other hand stood much too close to Mary the chambermaid, looking as if he'd like to pinch her bottom at any minute. Serafina couldn't help the stray thought that she wished Aiden would look at her like that.

"You're a fetching creature," Lord Delaware said with a leer in Mary's direction. "Can't think why I never noticed you before, my dear. Charming, absolutely charming."

"Papa, please," Serafina said in a reproving voice. "You need to concentrate on the task at hand."

"Thought that was what I was doing," he retorted with a broad wink at Plum, who winked right back, then returned to puffing out his chest like a proper Lothario and making eyes at poor Janie again.

Janie cast a helpless look at Serafina, who could only shake her head and shrug. Music had a euphoric effect on some people, but she really couldn't think what had gotten into Plum or Lord Delaware, for that matter.

Aiden on the other hand conducted himself with absolute propriety, not looking at anyone at all until they started to sing, at which point his eyes stayed fixed on her as she conducted. But that was as close to any kind of contact that they had. She wished he would contract a little spring fever.

He hadn't even tried to touch her in the last four days, and she thought she knew why. He'd been angry that first night that he'd come to bed, and she was the cause. But she didn't know how to change his attitude. She couldn't just throw herself into his arms and give him what he clearly wished. That would go against every principle she'd ever held regarding the act of love.

Oddly enough, she missed him. She even missed the way he touched her—she didn't think she'd mind at all if he decided he wanted to kiss her again, even though she knew how dangerous a proposition that was and where it would likely lead. Which was why she hadn't done anything to encourage him. But her feelings were hurt nevertheless by his inattentiveness.

"Let's begin," she said, recalling herself to her task. "We'll start with 'Oh God, Our Help in Ages Past,' verses one, four, and five. Remember, this Sunday we'll be singing in church for the first time, so let's put every effort into getting it right. . . ."

An hour later Serafina dismissed her choir, satisfied that they were nearly up to scratch. They filed dutifully out of the kitchen, Aiden taking up the rear.

Serafina screwed up her courage, not wanting him to leave until she'd had a chance to speak to him, come to some sort of understanding about what was bothering him.

She touched his arm lightly, and he looked at her in surprise, but he stopped obligingly enough.

"I think the vicar will be surprised, don't you?" she asked.

"Very surprised," he said, taking a quick step away from her. "It was a nice thought to form a choir for the church."

Serafina gathered up her courage. "Aiden . . . are you avoiding me?"

"Avoiding you?" He appeared suddenly rattled. "Why would you think that?"

"Because I've hardly seen you in the last few days."

"And that disturbs you?" he said, raising an eyebrow. "Why? I was under the impression that my attentions were unwelcome."

Serafina colored hotly. "No—of course they're not. I mean they are in one respect, but how are we to be friends if we never see each other?"

"Serafina," he said, sitting down at the huge kitchen table and resting his chin on his fist, "you are obviously dismally lacking in any understanding of how the male body works. I thought I made things perfectly clear the other night. If you wish to remain a virgin for the rest of your days that's your decision and I told you I'd honor it." He pressed his thumb and forefinger against the bridge of his nose. "But don't expect me to torture myself by constantly exposing myself to your presence."

Serafina scuffed one foot along the floor. "I thought that might be the problem," she whispered, feeling terrible that she was the reason that Aiden felt he had to lock himself away in his own house. "Would you rather I go away?"

"Go away?" he said, his head shooting up. "What do you mean by that?"

"Just that my presence clearly makes you uncomfortable," she replied miserably. "I'm sorry—I wish I could change the way I feel, but I told you that I can't be with you the way you want, at least not yet. It's not that I don't *want* to try, but I can't try if you're never around."

Aiden looked over at her, his gaze hard and assessing. "Then you're saying that you do want to try?"

"Yes, of course I want to try," she cried in helpless frustration. "But I have to love you, don't you see? That's the only way I can be with you with any conscience. And how am I supposed to learn to love you if you lock yourself away from me?"

"Let me see if I have this right," he said, running a hand over his lean cheek. "You've now decided that you might be able to learn to love me, and if you can manage the impossible, then you are willing to be my wife in all regards. I don't have to love you, though. Is that it?"

Serafina chewed on her lip. She wouldn't have put it quite like that, but she supposed he was close enough. "Yes," she said. "That's it."

Aiden burst into wild laughter. "Oh, that's reassuring. That's bloody marvelous. So all I have to do is work out a way to transform myself into a silly, lily-livered prince and we both get what we want." He dropped his head onto his arms with a strangled groan.

Serafina glared at him angrily for a minute, thinking he mocked her. And then a gurgle of laughter escaped and another as she saw the absurdity in the situation, for he certainly had a point. "I don't want a prince," she said. "I certainly don't want a silly prince. I think I want you, Aiden, but I can't be sure, not until I know you better."

His head slowly lifted. "You do?" he said in a strangled voice. "Oh, God. Oh, God, sweetheart. Do you mean there might be an end in sight to this living hell? Come here, you ridiculous girl."

He reached a hand out to her, and Serafina gingerly approached. He pulled her down onto his lap and buried his head in her hair, his arms coming fast around her. "I'm dying," he murmured against her cheek. "Inch by inch. I want you so badly I could scream. It's a damned miracle I haven't killed myself in the last few days."

Serafina's fingers crept up to entwine themselves in his soft hair. "Can you wait a little longer?" she asked, trying to buy herself a grace period. When he held her like this, made her feel so desirable, so needed, her resolve weakened treacherously. "I don't mean to tease you, Aiden, truly I don't, but this is very hard for me. I can't just love you overnight, although I've decided that I do like you very much."

He put her abruptly off his lap and stood, turning slightly away from her. "You can have all the time you want. I don't know how one goes about transforming liking into love since I've never been loved before, but however it happens, could you try to hurry up the process?"

"I'm not sure how to do that," she said honestly. "I don't know anything about it either. Maybe a little companionship would help?"

He glanced at her sideways. "Companionship, as in consigning me to more interminable longing? I suppose I can manage that, if I'm going to try to be the superhuman man you expect. Well, and why not? I've learned more over the last few days about interminable longing than most men learn in a lifetime."

Serafina pressed a swift kiss of gratitude onto his cheek, breathing in his warm masculine scent, so achingly familiar to her now. "Thank you," she said, her knees weak with relief that he'd been willing to hear her out. "I'll try not to let you down."

"Come ride with me," Aiden said, her kiss doing serious damage to his already compromised body. Oh, how he would have liked to ride her instead, but Aiden intended to be good to his word, even though he felt certain he'd lost his mind in making the agreement. He'd been crawling out of his skin for days now, his need for Serafina only growing by the hour.

But Serafina wanted companionship, and he realized that the only way he was going to further his cause was by giving it to her, especially in light of what she'd just said. But the only safe place he could think to give it to her was from the back of a horse where his attention would at least be diverted by the need to think of something else other than his aching groin.

"I'd love to ride with you," she said, her eyes lighting up with pleasure. "Will you give me a moment to change my clothes?"

"Naturally," he replied, resisting the urge to offer to come and watch. Instead he walked her out into the hall, but he did watch as she dashed up the staircase, feasting his eyes on a brief flash of slender ankle.

Even at the tender age of seventeen and plagued by sexual desire nearly every waking minute, he'd never been so obsessed. He was truly beginning to worry about himself. His body stood in a continual state of readiness, one look from his wife ready to send him into renewed agony. He felt as if he'd grown a third leg, but it wasn't one that was of any use to him at the moment.

He walked down to the stables and saddled two mounts, hers with an old sidesaddle, deciding it was time for Serafina to learn to ride like a countess, one lesson Charlotte couldn't teach her.

He looked up as she came into the stableyard, all grace and beauty and elegance in her new riding habit, a beautiful deep green velvet, a jaunty white feather plume in her hat. Mme. Bernard had again done a brilliant job. Serafina had been born to be a countess, he thought in breathless admiration, watching as she came toward him. The tightening in his poor groin started again, and he cursed under his breath, wondering if this had been such a good idea after all.

"Oh, Aiden," Serafina said, looking at the mare, blissfully ignorant of the licentious direction of his thoughts. "You've saddled Rosie . . . but I fear I'm only accustomed to riding bareback."

"Nonsense," he said, thinking with amusement that Rosie was the most inappropriate name she could have chosen for a thoroughbred mare. "You can do anything you put your mind to, or so I've noticed. Anyway, you're dressed for riding sidesaddle, and beautifully dressed, I might add."

"Oh—thank you," she said, flushing with pleasure, distracted for a moment. "It's a very pretty costume."

"Not as pretty as its wearer," he said gallantly, but meaning every word. "And you'll like the way it drapes over the saddle. Here, let me show you. You'll find the saddle easy enough and a secure seat as well." He took her foot and propelled her up onto the mare. "Look, you hook your leg over the pommel like this," he said, helping her. He couldn't help but be aware of the beguiling outline of her slim leg beneath her skirts, and he quickly snatched his hand away. "Now tuck your foot into the stirrup." He watched to be sure she was safely mounted, although she looked endearingly anxious about the unfamiliar position.

"Relax, sweetheart, you're perfectly safe. From what I observed the other day, you're a fine horsewoman. A saddle will give you an even better purchase." He swung up onto Aladdin. "I've been meaning to ask you—where did the mare come from? I was surprised to see her when I returned."

Serafina glanced over at him nervously. "Your cousin sent her as a wedding present."

He moved Aladdin into a walk, and Serafina followed next to him. "So Rafe sent you a mare. That was thoughtful of him. Plum says you take her out every afternoon for a few hours. Where do you go?"

"I go—I go through the woods," she mumbled, the tip of her tongue poking out of the side of her mouth as she stared down at the mare's mane.

"I should have realized," he said with a smile. "And what do you do?"

"I look for flowers and herbs for my aunt. And I try to learn things about my new home."

"You've learned an enormous amount, but I doubt you learned much of it in the woods," he said with amusement. "I don't believe I've told you, but I'm mightily impressed by your improved grasp of etiquette."

Serafina's cheeks flared with the lovely pink tinge he found so appealing. "I'm pleased you noticed, Aiden. I've tried hard to observe what is around me," she said with a shy sideways peep up at him.

"Your powers of observation are keen indeed. I'd never have believed you could learn so quickly and so well in such a short period of time. You make me proud, sweetheart, and not just of your newfound manners, but also because you've made such a difference to my father and sister."

"Thank you," she said, her face lighting with another of her wide smiles. "But you mustn't give me all the credit.

Charlotte has been very generous in making me welcome in her home."

"It's your home too now," he pointed out.

"Yes, that's true," she said. "I've tried to think of it like that. And your father has been kind to me also—but you've seen for yourself how far he's come."

Aiden nodded thoughtfully. Although deep wounds still lay beneath the surface of their relationship, Aiden couldn't fault his father's attempt to make a new start. He still felt skeptical that the attempt would last, but he was willing to give the man the benefit of the doubt. For the moment. Aiden hadn't missed his father's recent lusty behavior, even though he put it down to the diminished effects of alcohol on his father's system—although Plum, who had always been the soul of propriety, was also behaving in a questionable fashion, and Aiden was not only puzzled but concerned. The last thing he needed was to have his father and the butler chasing chambermaids through the house and upsetting Charlotte.

Charlotte. There was another miracle in the making. The bite was gone from her tongue, along with her religious prattle—or at least most of it. Whatever Serafina had given her for her pain was obviously working magic, for the tight lines of pain were gone from her face, letting her natural beauty show through.

"Sweetheart, about Charlotte," he said as he turned toward the forest. "Is this oil some concoction of your aunt's?"

"How did you know that?" she asked in alarm, her eyes widening.

"Tinkerby told me that your Aunt Elspeth is an amateur—ah, chemist," he said carefully, unwilling to call the woman an out-and-out witch. "He said that she likes to dabble in medicines. I assumed that was the case here, and don't mistake my meaning, for your aunt has managed to accomplish for my sister in weeks what the doctors haven't been able to accomplish in twenty-two years."

"Aunt Elspeth can be very gifted in her work," Serafina said, relaxing. "She doesn't always get it right, but I suppose that's to be expected. But she's never harmed anyone, which is why I felt sure it was safe to let her try to help Charlotte." She licked her bottom lip. "But Aiden, I think it's best if Charlotte doesn't know the mixture was made by Auntie— the two of them are like oil and water, and Charlotte might decide against using it if she knew where it came from."

"Where does she think it comes from?" he asked curiously.

"Wales. I told her it was specially made in Wales, which is perfectly true. And the ingredients are safe, just strong herbs I think. You don't mind, do you?"

"Well, you've explained why Charlotte's been smelling like the kitchen cabinet of late," he said with a grin. "But no, I have no objection, Serafina. How could I? Charlotte's a different woman thanks to you and your aunt, and I won't say a word to her about Elspeth's involvement."

"Thank you. I know Auntie can be a little difficult at times, and not everyone takes to her, but she's a good woman at heart."

"I couldn't agree more. After all, she brought you up." He glanced over at his wife, wondering again at what her life with Elspeth must have been like. From what Tinkerby had said, they had lived simply, in near poverty at times, although thank God Serafina had never gone lacking in food, just the basic comforts he'd always taken for granted.

He still didn't understand why Elspeth had chosen such a humble lifestyle for her niece when she'd had a huge annual income at her disposal and could easily have raised Serafina in luxury. He certainly didn't understand why Elspeth not only neglected to tell Serafina about her fortune, but also kept her in isolation against the day that Serafina married him—a marriage that might easily never have come to pass.

But he doubted he'd ever fathom the old woman or what made her tick. One generally didn't fathom loose screws. As Tinkerby said, at least she'd provided a loving home for Serafina, even if she had overlooked some of the finer educational points.

As a result, Serafina was unique and unspoiled, despite her head being filled with fanciful notions. And she was beautiful. And he wanted her.

"You're suddenly very quiet," Serafina said. "What are you thinking?"

"I'm thinking that we should attempt a trot," he answered, as if he could outrun the heat surging through him. "Just sit the way you would if you were bareback and let the horse do the work. Can you manage that?"

"Of course," Serafina said gamely, but she swallowed hard. "It's—it's just that I'm accustomed to using my legs."

"Rafe wouldn't have sent you a horse that wasn't trained to a sidesaddle. Don't worry, she'll know what to do."

He urged his gelding forward, knowing the mare would follow. And then a sharp cry tore from Serafina's throat and he glanced behind him in alarm, only to see the mare tearing into a full-fledged canter, racing across the field toward the forest, Serafina clinging to her mane.

Aiden's heart leapt with sick panic and he kicked Aladdin into a gallop, chasing after her, terrified. The mare's neck lowered and stretched as she picked up speed. The next thing Aiden knew, the horse had taken the stream in a wide jump and to his horror Serafina went flying off her back, landing in a heap on the ground.

Aiden pulled Aladdin to an abrupt stop and jumped off his back, running to Serafina's unmoving form, his heart in his throat, terrible images flashing through his mind of finding Serafina dead, at best maimed. He might have been six years old again, looking at his sister's crumpled body.

"Sweetheart," he cried desperately, bending over her and lifting her limp body in his arms, holding her close against him. "Serafina, speak to me. Please, open your eyes, there's a good girl. . . ."

To his infinite relief she blinked and stirred, then drew in a gasp of air. "Oh," she said, her hand going to her stomach. "I must have knocked the wind out of myself."

Aiden buried his face in her hair, whispering all sorts of mindless stupidities, unbelievably grateful that she hadn't managed to kill herself. "Can you move?" he asked, when he could speak coherently. He ran his hands over her legs, her arms, trying to ascertain if she'd broken anything.

"Of course I can move," she said, wriggling in his grasp. "It's not the first time I've fallen off a horse, you know."

"Oh, God—God, you frightened me," he said, relaxing his hold on her.

She looked up into his eyes, her own wide and soft, the color of leaf buds. "I'm sorry," she murmured, her soft lips slightly parted as she gazed at him. "I didn't mean to."

He couldn't help himself. He lowered his head and kissed her hard, pouring all his relief out as he took her mouth with his, invaded her warm recesses, capturing her tongue with his own as relief changed in a heartbeat to unbridled passion.

Serafina's arms wound around his neck and clung, her small ripe breasts pressing against his chest, inflaming him even further. His hands slid up her sides, gently stroking, his palm slipping over one sweet swell of flesh, his thumb finding her nipple and teasing it until it sprang up small and hard under his touch.

Serafina moaned, pushing up against his hand, and Aiden dropped his head lower, his tongue tracing a line down her smooth throat, his lips settling in the apex of her throat, kissing and teasing her warm skin with his tongue.

His hands moved to the buttons on the front of her jacket and loosened them, pushing aside the material, his fingers slipping inside to caress her breast through the thin cambric of her shirt, the heat of her skin burning into his own.

Her breath quickened as her breast swelled to fit his palm, and her hips pressed against his, as if she instinctively knew what she sought.

Aiden nearly lost his mind at the sudden contact against his erect, throbbing penis. He groaned, his mouth capturing hers again, ravishing her with his tongue the way he desperately wanted to ravish the rest of her body.

And then, before he could register what had happened, she jerked away, fumbling with the buttons of her jacket, her fingers shaking. "Don't—Raphael," she whispered.

"Raphael?" he said in disbelief, trying to gather his addled senses. What the hell was his wife doing speaking another man's name at a time like this? And then his ears registered the sound of hoofbeats and his head shot up.

Raphael was pounding across the field toward them, his horse kicking up clods of dirt in his haste, Serafina's mount held by the reins, galloping along beside. He rapidly dismounted as Aiden jumped to his feet.

"What—what the hell happened?" Rafe said, fear written all over his face. "Is Serafina all right? I saw her horse on the forest path, worked into a sweat and Serafina nowhere to be seen."

"She took a fall," Aiden said tightly, trying to rein in the unwarranted jealousy that gripped at him. He couldn't think why Rafe had turned white when he hardly knew Serafina. Or why Serafina had spoken his name so urgently. Or why Rafe looked at her now with such concern and Serafina looked so embarrassed.

"Oh, dear God," Rafe said, dropping to his knees. "Serafina? You didn't hurt yourself, did you?"

"No, I'm fine. I wish the two of you wouldn't leap to the worst of conclusions just because I was silly enough to take a tumble." She looked up at Raphael with a wry smile that struck Aiden as being far too familiar.

Raphael expelled a long breath and wiped a shaking hand over his mouth. "Thank God," he said, bowing his head. "For a moment there when I saw you on the ground . . . well, never mind. All's well."

"Of course it is," Serafina said, rising and brushing her dress off. "I do understand why you're both a little jumpy after what happened to Charlotte, but disaster doesn't strike every single time someone falls off a horse."

"What happened?" Raphael said, bracing his hands on his hips.

"What happened," Aiden said coldly, annoyed by his cousin's arrogant stance, never mind his curt question, "is that you gave my wife an ungovernable mount as a wedding present. What the hell where you thinking?" His head felt as if it were caught in a vise, all reason fleeing in the face of his even more unreasonable anger. Something tugged at the corners of his mind, as if he'd been here before, spoken similar words of anger.

"But she's a beautifully schooled mare," Raphael said, frowning. "Truly, Aiden, she's one of the gentlest horses I've ever owned."

"It's my fault entirely." Serafina looked around for her hat. "I always race her toward the forest on this stretch, so she expected it. But this time I couldn't use my legs to hold her in, and I didn't want to hurt her mouth by sawing on it, so I let her run, thinking she'd stop. I've never taken a jump on a sidesaddle before, and I lost my balance, that's all." She located her hat in a clump of bush and settled it back on her head. "You can't blame Raphael for something that was my doing," she said, adjusting her plume.

The angry mist slowly cleared from Aiden's eyes. "It's a reasonable enough explanation," he said, regretting his outburst of temper toward his closest friend. "I beg your pardon if I accused you of carelessness, Rafe."

"Forgotten," Raphael said amiably. "Your concern for your wife is commendable. I'm sure I would have felt the same way in the same circumstances."

"Speaking of circumstances," Aiden said, still shaky not only from Serafina's fall, but also from their encounter immediately afterward, "what fortuitous event put you on this path?"

"Actually, I was on my way to see you. I only returned today from visiting my mother in London, and she's come up with the admirable suggestion that you and your wife come to town next week for the end of the season. She'd like to introduce Serafina on your behalf."

Aiden gaped at his cousin, knowing perfectly well that not only was Raphael fully informed as to the unfortunate circumstances of his marriage, but that the dowager duchess also had full knowledge. Further, Raphael had attended the wedding and seen Serafina's lack of manners for himself. "Why?" he asked bluntly.

"Because my mother is a kind woman who happened to be exceeding fond of your mother, and she's even managed a little fondness for you," Rafe answered dryly. "She believes that a brief presentation would go far in stilling the loose gossip running about town. And it would also do you good, Aiden, to make a strong appearance, since the gossip includes the Delaware misfortunes. I believe that you and Serafina can accomplish a great deal in showing your faces now, rather than later."

Aiden considered. Raphael had a point. He'd already had a taste of censure on his last trip to London, and he hadn't enjoyed it. "I'll think about it," he said.

"Not to put too fine a point on the matter, but my mother's patronage as well as my own will go a long way toward mending matters. I wouldn't delay, Aiden. Your father already made a hash of things a few months ago by running about and asking every acquaintance he knew for funds when he could find them nowhere else, and you know how well that washes."

Aiden grimaced, a fresh coil of anger fastening around his heart. "Wonderful." He sighed heavily, understanding Rafe's meaning perfectly clearly and seeing no way out. "Very well. Next week it is."

"Aiden?" Serafina's voice came softly at his shoulder. "May I have a word with you?"

"I'm sorry, sweetheart," he said, Serafina's plight immediately apparent. "I should have asked you first. If you'd rather not go, I won't ask it of you."

"That's not what I wanted to speak to you about," she said, fiddling with her gloves. "I just thought that if we have to go, you might consider bringing your father along. In his improved condition he can probably help to repair the damage."

"Are you out of your mind?" Aiden said incredulously. "Bring my father to London, where one wrong word out of his mouth could sink us?"

Serafina's hand slipped over his, her fingers curling into his palm. "He won't go wrong, I'm sure of it. If there's anyone you should worry about going wrong, it is me. You already know your father wishes to make amends, and what better way to let him than to take him with us?"

Aiden could refuse her nothing, especially when she

looked at him with that earnest, trusting expression that never failed to turn him inside out. "Very well. My father may come along," he said, sure he was sealing his doom.

"And Charlotte?" she said, smiling up at him now, his downfall. "Would you ask Charlotte to come as well? She's so much better, and I'm sure she'd enjoy herself if we were careful about not overtaxing her."

"Charlotte?" Raphael interjected. "Serafina, you cannot be serious. You know how she is—she only leaves the house on Sunday, and that's a chore for her, despite her religious fervor."

"But Raphael," Serafina said brightly, "you haven't seen her for ages. She's so much improved that I do believe she will consider the idea. Don't you think she deserves a chance to see London, to be exposed to people of her own kind? And who knows, she might even meet a man to admire her—she is a beautiful woman, even if she is confined to a chair."

Aiden thought for the hundredth time that Serafina's head was filled with fairy dust. But then, she hadn't been wrong so far. "I'll present the idea to her," he said reluctantly. "But don't be disappointed if she refuses. I suppose you're next going to ask me to invite your Aunt Elspeth along?" He hoped to God that wasn't her intention, for he wasn't sure he could bear the idea.

"Oh, no," she said to his intense relief. "Auntie would hate London. She'll be happiest here, working on her spe— I mean her medicines."

Raphael abruptly turned his back with a smothered cough, and Aiden shot him a suspicious look, wondering if Rafe knew more about Elspeth Beaton's unconventional habits than Aiden realized. But Rafe turned back again, his face a mask of innocence. "Excuse me. A slight cold. I have to say that I think your wife's proposition is wise, Aiden. Your father and sister's presence will only add an impression of family unity."

"Yes. Yes, I suppose it will." Aiden nodded decisively. "Then write your mother. Tell her that we'll be appearing on her doorstep the last week of June. I hope to God that this isn't a mistake, Rafe."

"No mistake," his cousin replied. "No mistake at all. I can't think of a wiser decision you could have made. And I'll be with you through every step of the way."

"Then we'll all be in good hands," Serafina said, smiling warmly up at Raphael, who returned her smile with equal warmth.

Aiden looked at them both hard, assailed again by the faint but persistent sense that there was more between Serafina and Raphael than met the eye.

He quickly dismissed the thought as absurd.

15

$\mathscr{S}$erafina tossed fitfully that night. It didn't help that Aiden lay at her side sleeping peacefully, his back turned toward her, his breathing deep and even while her head spinned with troubled thoughts. She thought it was most unfair that he could sleep at all, especially after everything that had happened today.

She hadn't said a word about her misgivings to Aiden, but she didn't look forward to going to London, certain she was bound to make a fool of herself. She might marginally be able to perform like a lady in the safety of Townsend, but braving society was a far more daunting proposition.

Nevertheless, she saw the necessity if Aiden was to regain his family's honor. She would simply have to find a way to manage. If poor Charlotte, who rarely ventured outside the walls of the house, was brave enough to agree to the trip, Serafina had no right to be nervous.

But an even larger, more terrifying question hung over her. Today Aiden had given her a clear taste of just how nice it could be to submit to his embrace, to the touch of his wicked roguish hands.

Fire sparked low in her belly when she thought of the exquisite sensations he'd ignited in her, sensations that before this she'd only dreamed about. If Raphael hadn't come along when he did, she had no idea of what might have happened. But Raphael's appearing had been a blessing in disguise, for if she were to give herself to Aiden, it had to be for the right reasons, not because she was caught up in a fit of mindless lust.

She'd told Aiden the truth—that she liked him. And she did, enormously. She liked his self-deprecating humor, the way he laughed at the silliest things. And she liked his honesty in the moments he chose to give it to her, even at his own expense.

She especially liked the way he'd looked at her this afternoon after she'd taken her tumble, his beautiful eyes filled with deep concern as he pulled her into his arms, his voice hoarse with worry.

She felt truly cherished for the first time since her father had died, as if her well-being was of real importance to Aiden, even if he didn't love her. But she was beginning to think maybe love didn't matter so much—maybe it was enough that he cared about her and that she cared about him. And she did. Very, very much, more than she'd ever have thought possible when she'd married him.

She felt an affinity with him now, and if she were really to be honest with herself, she'd felt that same affinity from the first day in the woods, as if he were someone she'd always known, had always been comfortable with. It was she who had pushed him away because she'd been in love with a figment of her imagination. She'd since discovered that figments didn't bear up to the light of scrutiny. But Aiden had, contrary to all her expectations.

He was right—he was no prince. But she really didn't want a prince, not anymore. She wanted Aiden, just as he was, flesh and blood. She loved him for the man he was, complete with flaws.

Serafina shot bolt upright in bed. She stared down at the covers, her fingers clutching the blanket as if to anchor herself against the shocks that raced through her, shaking her to the core of her being.

Was it possible that she *did* love him? The idea seemed preposterous. People didn't fall in love just like that. She hardly knew him—they'd only met six weeks ago, and four weeks of that time they'd spent apart. He was a man of the world, she knew nothing at all of it. And yet . . . and yet she couldn't deny that he was constantly on her mind, that she wanted to be with him and missed him when he was busy with other things. And she couldn't deny that she found him tremendously attractive, that he turned her bones to water whenever he touched her.

Serafina shivered, remembering how his warm hand had felt when it cupped her breast, his thumb teasing her nipple until it sprang up under his touch. He'd made her moan with desire today until she couldn't think, could barely breathe. She only knew she wanted more of him, more of his caresses. And she knew that Aiden wanted her too in the same way. He had made no pretense about that from the very beginning.

But tonight, for the first time, she understood what it was to live in a state of physical longing.

She began to see that much of the reason that she'd fought against Aiden so hard had been a result of simple fear, fear that he didn't really care about her, fear that he'd physically hurt her. But Aiden had given her every reason to believe that he did care about her, even if he didn't love her, and that he would be gentle with her. She snuck a glance down at him, remembering what he'd said to her under the oak tree the day they were married.

I promise you that I'll come to you in tenderness and with the desire to please you. . . .

She believed him about that. On the other hand, he had cleverly sidestepped the part about impaling her. The version of lovemaking he'd handed her had included joining bodies, but he'd made it sound like a delightful coupling instead of a violent assault.

Maybe he hadn't wanted to frighten her. Or maybe, since he hadn't realized he was speaking to his future wife, he had simply left out the most important details, reasoning that it wasn't his responsibility to give her the grim news.

She might just have to summon up her courage and ask him for the absolute truth. They certainly couldn't go on like this forever, especially given the way she felt about him, how much she wanted him. It seemed a hopeless situation.

She lay down again and pulled the covers up to her chin, thinking back to her dreams. They'd been so nice . . . always so nice, so full of love and happiness and desire.

Adam, kissing her in the meadow, whispering intimate promises in her ear. *I'll renew my own pledge in the flesh the minute I have you to myself. . . .*

And she had wanted him to. She had desperately wanted him to, at least in a dream. Was real life any different? She wanted Aiden just as much, even if she didn't know anything about the conclusion of the matter, but she expected she'd find out about that soon enough whether she liked it or not. She'd learned the hard way that life had to be lived in the present, attendant with all its grim realities. Nothing could be counted on, nothing foreseen.

Serafina yawned, suddenly overwhelmingly tired. She turned onto her side, tucking her fists under her chin, casting one last look at Aiden's strong back. Her last thought as she gave herself over to sleep was that at least she had love to guide her through.

"My love, my sweet love," Adam said, his hands spreading beneath her, running over her back, cupping her buttocks, raising her to him, his tongue tracing a hot circle on her breast.

She made a gasping sound of pleasure in her throat as his fingers found her female flesh, gently slipped between the moist folds, stroking her into liquid fire until she pushed up against him with a sharp cry.

"Adam! I love you—oh, how I love you," she sobbed, wanting him as she'd never wanted anything. She'd waited so long and now he was finally hers and she was his, and they were free at last to be together as God had planned.

He groaned, his legs moving between her thighs to spread them, the heat of his body scorching her everywhere he touched. His hard shaft moved to her entrance, his shoulders rising and falling with harsh pants as he prepared to enter her. "Sarah . . . you must be the most beautiful woman God ever created."

He pushed into her as he spoke, stretching her wide, then pushed again. "Oh, my sweet love—you're so tight. I don't . . . I don't want to hurt you," he groaned, coming up against the bar-

rier of her maidenhead, and she cried out in pain, reflexively trying to jerk away.

"Sarah, beloved, try to relax." He smoothed his hands over her hair. "My darling, I have to—I have to do this quickly. It will all be over in a moment, I swear it." He thrust hard into her as he spoke.

She cried out, but this time not in pleasure. She felt as if he were going to split her open at any moment, searing pain shooting through every fiber of her being. "No—oh, no!" she sobbed, trying to pull away from him as he plunged deeper, penetrating her completely. "It hurts so! Adam, it hurts!"

He went completely still, holding her tightly. "I'm sorry, my love—I'm so sorry. Wait. Wait just a minute and the pain will ease."

"No!" she cried, terrified that he would move again, break her to pieces. "Oh, Mother Mary, help me!"

"It's all over now, sweetheart—you were just having a bad dream. I'm here. Nothing will hurt you, I swear it. . . ."

She gulped back another sob, burying her head in his shoulder. And then she came awake with a jolt as she breathed in Aiden's unmistakable scent, warm and masculine. Aiden's arms held her tightly, and it was his voice that soothed and comforted her.

"Ai-Aiden," she stammered, tearing herself out of his grasp. She sat up and wiped her eyes, wet with tears. "What—what happened? What are you doing?" For a terrible moment she thought that he had taken her in her sleep and that was what had caused her such pain.

He gently stroked her hair. "You had a nightmare. Better now?"

She nodded, realizing that she'd been dreaming. "I—I think so. Oh, Aiden, it was awful. . . ."

"So I gathered," he said, sitting up next to her. "You were howling like a banshee. Do you want to talk about it?"

"You *lied* to me," she said illogically, wiping her hands over her eyes again.

"I did? In what way?" he said calmly, taking her outburst in perfect stride, as if he listened to anguished outbreaks every day.

"You said it was nice, that I'd like it. And I didn't like it at all. It was painful and horrible, and it's true about being impaled after all!"

"What in the name of God are you talking about?" he said, regarding her with a mixture of concern and puzzlement.

"You *know* what I'm talking about," she said, wrapping her arms around her midriff. "You said you do it all the time."

"I haven't the first idea of what you mean. All I know is that you woke me from a deep sleep, carrying on about Mother Mary." Aiden ran his hands through his tousled hair. "Why don't we start at the beginning? What was painful and horrible, and what on earth do you mean by being impaled?"

"You know perfectly well," she said accusingly. "What you want to do to me. All the fine things you said about lovemaking were nothing more than a device to have your horrible way with me."

Aiden stared at her as if she'd lost her mind. "You're telling me that you had a dream about my making love to you, and *that's* the conclusion you reached?" He burst into laughter. "Ah, sweetheart, you really are difficult to fathom sometimes. Was all of this brought on by what passed between us this afternoon?"

"I have no idea what brought the dream on," she said, still shaken. She adjusted her nightdress around her knees. "I only know that it was the truth."

"Oh, I see," he said with a broad grin. "And now you know all about it, do you?" He shook his head. "You have the most active imagination of anyone I've ever met."

Serafina had to agree with him on that point. But that didn't mean that she was wrong. "My imagination has nothing to do with it. Auntie was right after all," she said, glowering at him. "You do all sorts of nice things to me until it comes to the moment of truth, and then out comes your flagpole and—and you tear me to pieces while you *impale* me with it."

Aiden covered his face with one hand. "A *flagpole*?" he

said in disbelief. "Your aunt told you I was going to impale you with a flagpole?" His voice caught on another laugh.

"Yes. And you're going to draw my blood when you do. I imagine by the time you've finished I'll have nary a drop to call my own. It will serve you right if I expire on the spot."

Aiden threw his head back and howled. "I—I'm sorry," he gasped after a minute. "I don't mean to make light of your worries. But oh, *God* this explains a great deal about your reluctance to be with me. The very idea of your aunt tutoring you in this regard . . ." Aiden wiped tears away from his eyes. "What the devil makes you think your spinster aunt knows the first thing about lovemaking?" He regarded her quizzically.

"She is a highly knowledgeable woman," Serafina said defensively. "She can deliver babies, and as far as I can gather, giving birth is just as painful. I think she knows whereof she speaks." Serafina crossed her arms over her chest and regarded him balefully.

"Oh, really," he said dryly. "And what else has your aunt told you, other than feeding you a lot of tripe about flagpoles?" His face twisted up again.

"She said that it was a bloody process," Serafina replied, wanting to slap his laughing face. It was all well and fine for Aiden to take her plight lightly, but she knew the truth. Now she *really* knew.

"Well . . . that's correct to a small degree," he said, slowly sobering. "Generally speaking, a woman will shed a drop or two the first time she makes love, but that's only because there's a small membrane in the way that has to be broken."

Serafina was fully aware of that fact, memory still acute. "That's easy enough for you to say. It's not your membrane, is it?" she challenged.

"No . . . but it's easily enough disposed of. Mind you, I'm not in the habit of taking virgins to bed, but I think I have the way of it down well enough. And I can sincerely promise you that you won't regret the aftermath, even if you do experience one brief moment of discomfort." He picked up her hand and kissed her palm, then ran his mouth up the inside of her arm.

"How do you know?" she said, trembling at the touch of his warm lips nuzzling the crook of her elbow.

"Well," he said lazily, lifting his head. "I could show you."

Serafina swallowed hard. "What happens if you're wrong?"

Aiden considered. "I could always stop," he said. "If you want me to, that is." He ran a finger down her cheek. "I don't think that will be the case."

Serafina covered his hand with her own. "I'm afraid," she whispered.

"Little wonder," he replied comfortably, entwining his fingers with hers. "I'd be frightened too if I'd had my head filled with a lot of nonsense. No one wants to be impaled. And I'm sorry to have to tell you that I don't possess anything that remotely resembles a flagpole." His lips trembled as if he found the idea hysterically funny.

"I *dreamt* it," Serafina said insistently. "It hurt terribly. And—and I don't want you to do that to me again."

Aiden took her by the shoulders, his fingers caressing lightly over them. "It was only a dream, sweetheart. It's really not such an awful experience as you imagine," he said, gazing at her through the dark.

She felt so confused that she couldn't even tell the difference between Adam and Aiden, dream and reality anymore. All she knew was that she'd had an awful experience, one that didn't bear repeating. She blinked back a fresh rush of tears, looking at Aiden doubtfully.

"I'm not lying to you, I swear it, and I never have, not about this. The act of love is as pleasurable for a woman as it is for a man. You had a taste of it today, didn't you?"

She nodded, wiping her eyes with the back of her hand. "I liked that," she admitted in a small voice.

Aiden smiled down at her. "I know. I liked it too. And it only gets nicer from there." He pushed his fingers through her hair, gently holding her face between his hands, his thumbs stroking over the curve of her ears. "But I only have one way to prove that to you. Try to trust me, will you, sweetheart? We're going to drive each other insane if we carry on like this."

Serafina raised her eyes to his. He gazed down at her, his expression completely sincere. Her heart turned painfully over in her chest, for in that moment she knew with absolute certainty that she really did love him. Nothing but love could make her want to give him anything he desired. Nothing but love was strong enough to overcome her fear. Nothing but love caused her to put her arms around his back, drawing him close.

She rested her cheek against his chest, heard the pounding of his heart, a hard release of breath. "I do trust you," she whispered, running her hands over his strongly muscled back. "I do."

He didn't answer. Instead his hands lifted her face and he kissed her hard, his mouth seeking, tasting, urging her to respond to him. She couldn't help it. She was no proof against his powerful masculinity, no proof against herself and her own fevered response to him. She gave him back everything he demanded, put everything of herself into that kiss, everything she was, had ever been, showing him exactly how much she trusted him.

Aiden groaned, turning her in his arms, lowering her to the mattress, his hands smoothing down over her shoulders, up her torso, and wherever they touched they left flame in their wake. Serafina felt like a piece of clay as he molded her, shaped her, sculpted her into new dimensions. She felt newly made, as if she'd never known his touch before; she felt old as the hills, as if her body had known it forever.

He cupped her breast, lowered his head to it, took her nipple in his teeth between the material of her nightdress, breathing more fire, Lucifer's fire, onto her skin as he tongued the tip, bit lightly down on it.

"Aiden—oh, Aiden," she cried, her hands pulling his head even closer, her back arching up to meet his scorching touch.

Aiden reached down and in one swift movement he slipped her nightdress up her thighs and waist, then over her head, tossing it to one side. He took her breast in his mouth again, but this time with nothing to shield his mouth from her flesh.

Serafina gasped as he suckled her nipple, his damp tongue flicking over the tender, erect nub, his hands wandering over her back, lifting her buttocks, cupping them.

"Serafina—oh, God," he said, his voice strained, taking her other breast now, pulling and tugging, driving her into a frenzy of need.

Her hands explored his back, the chiseled curves and hollows of his magnificent musculature, the shifting contours as he changed his weight, drawing himself up on his forearms. He kissed her again, this time without restraint, nipping on her lower lip, driving deep into her mouth, chasing away any doubts, any hesitations. She couldn't remember why she'd ever been afraid of him.

Serafina twisted against his hips, encountering something stiff, something she was sure hadn't been there before. She gave a little gasp of surprise, and Aiden laughed breathlessly.

"Does that feel like a flagpole to you?" he asked, capturing her wrists, his breathing rough and fast.

"No—not at all," she replied just as breathlessly, shamelessly wanting to look, to gaze upon this remarkable male phenomenon that changed shape so rapidly. She pressed up against him a little harder, trying to get a better idea of his dimensions.

"I should think not," he murmured, rubbing his mouth over her cheek and finding her ear, tugging on it with his lips. "But for God's sake stop squirming or I'll go out of my mind."

"That feels good?" she asked with surprise.

"Yes, it feels good—it feels bloody incredible, but that's the problem, Titania. If it starts to feel too good I won't be able to take my time, so you have to show me a little mercy. Let me give you a small example of what I mean."

He released her wrists and sat up, covering her breasts with his palms, stroking them down over her belly. Serafina drew in a sharp, shuddering breath as he moved lower, his thumbs slipping into her nest of curls, sliding even lower, sending a shock of electrifying sensation through her as he found her cleft.

"Oh, so beautiful," he murmured, stroking now, lightly,

so lightly, back and forth as she writhed helplessly under his touch. "So warm and sweet, just like the rest of you. That's right, open your legs a little. Do you see how nice that feels?"

Serafina couldn't formulate a coherent answer, so she made a wordless sound of assent then sighed, pressing her hips up against his touch as he rhythmically stroked back and forth.

He shifted slightly, coming down to her, his mouth taking hers in a hungry kiss, his tongue following the rhythm of his thumbs until she thought she might lose her mind.

Serafina's fingers twined in his thick hair, sensation shooting through her body and centering in the exact spot that flamed and throbbed where his hand caressed. And suddenly he slipped one finger inside her and she cried out, the pleasure excruciating, a desperate strain building in her body until she thought she might shatter. She clutched Aiden's shoulders, her eyes locked on his face, his eyes so dark a blue now as to appear black, his expression taut as he looked down to where his hands moved on her, in her.

"Aiden!" Serafina's back arched as everything in her body came together and exploded into fire like the sun itself imploding, over and over, finally dying down to a shower of sparks that left her weak and shaking and gasping for air.

"Mmm," Aiden said, dropping a kiss on one throbbing nipple. "Nice." He raised his head and kissed her, his mouth lingering on her lips.

"Aiden—oh, Aiden, I never had any idea," she murmured when she could finally breathe properly. "That felt wonderful. . . ."

"Good." He brushed a damp lock of hair off her forehead. "You're going to like the next part, too."

"I'm sure I should be ashamed of myself for enjoying this part quite so much," she said, stroking her finger down his neck, tracing it over the outline of his powerful pectoral muscles.

"Don't you dare start sounding like Charlotte," Aiden said, sitting up and abruptly pulling his nightshirt over his head, then replacing her hand on his bare chest, his skin hot and damp beneath her fingers. "There's not a damned thing wrong with enjoying yourself, and the more you do the happier I'll be." He lay down on his back, the sheet pulled down to his waist. "Have your way with me, woman," he said with a grin, folding his hands behind his head.

Serafina chewed her lip, and Aiden laughed. "I love it when you do that. It's always a dead giveaway that you have no idea what to do or say next."

"I'm not sure I do," she said shyly. "I'm not accustomed to having my way with a man."

"You can always kiss me," he said helpfully. "I believe you've mastered that technique."

"I have?" she said, enormously pleased that he thought so.

"Oh yes, indeed. I told you this afternoon that I find you a quick learner." He shuddered as she smoothed her palms up his chest and over his hard nipples, and that pleased her too.

She bent over and kissed him as he'd asked, and his arms went fast around her back, pulling her down onto him, his naked flesh burning into hers. Serafina's heart, which had only just returned to a normal pace, began pounding again furiously at the sudden, searing contact.

His erect manhood pressed hard against her belly, but instead of frightening her, its heated touch only excited her more. She shifted a little, rubbing against him, and he made a strangled sound in his throat. "And I thought you were going to be merciful," he choked.

"You didn't show me any mercy," she said with a little laugh. "I don't see why you think you deserve special treatment." Her hand crept between their bodies, and she cautiously touched him with one finger, surprised by how silky he felt.

Aiden drew in a sharp gasp, and emboldened, she slipped her fingers around his shaft, trying to determine the full size and shape of him. Such velvet over steel, pulsing under her fingers. She slid her hand down and up again, eagerly exploring.

"Dear God," he choked. "Dear, dear God . . . oh, sweetheart. Slowly. Please—" He grabbed her around the waist and swiftly rolled her onto her back, his breath labored. He reached under her, cupping her buttocks, his hand reaching farther, his fingers finding her soft folds and stroking her again, bringing her back to furious desire. She moaned, finally knowing what she really wanted. Aiden—it had always been Aiden. . . .

"Please," she whispered, pulling him closer. "Please—now?"

"Are you sure, sweetheart?" he asked shakily, running his warm mouth over her cheek.

"Yes—oh, yes," she said, lifting her hips to him in desperate, mindless invitation, her legs spreading for him.

Aiden didn't waste an instant. She felt his tip push against her entrance, a strange, burning invasion, but she welcomed it. She welcomed all of him, opening wider, urging him to come more deeply into her, wanting nothing more than for him to possess her fully, to truly make her his.

He pushed gently, stretching her, and although she felt a slight sting, it was nothing—nothing at all in comparison to having him inside her. He kissed her deeply as he thrust harder this time, penetrating her fully with his hard length, so strong, so perfect.

Her hips matched his driving rhythm as he thrust over and over again, completing her in a way she'd never imagined possible. He was everything, her entire world, so real, so solid. . . .

Her hands stroked over his back, her body shuddering in furious response as he drove her beyond time, beyond thought, into a place of pure heat and desire where nothing existed except his body moving in hers. Nothing else had ever mattered so much—nothing would ever matter again. She felt like the first woman on earth, and he the first man.

She gasped as waves of release crashed through her, and she cried out his name as she contracted in furious tremors around him, her fingers digging into his back.

Aiden groaned again, his entire body tightening, his head buried against her throat as he pushed hard into her and held. "Oh, God!" he cried hoarsely, shuddering violently, and she felt a surge of heat wash against the neck of her womb. His life in her. His seed. The mystery completed.

He collapsed against her heavily, moaning, and she wrapped her arms tightly around him, stroking his hair, his nape, turned her head and kissed his cheek where it rested against hers, his breath slow and shallow in her ear.

After a few minutes he raised himself onto his forearms and looked down at her, dropping little kisses on her forehead, her eyelids, her nose. He lazily kissed her mouth, then smiled, looking like a cat in the cream pot. "Mmm," he murmured. "Well? Was I right?"

Serafina couldn't help laughing. "You were right, and I'm sure Prince Charming couldn't have done any better," she said, pulling his head back down to hers and kissing him.

"Thank God," he said, rolling over onto his side, taking her with him. "I tried to think of how a prince might proceed and went from there. Although I think you should elevate me to a bloody king. Never in the annals of history has a man exhibited such self-restraint in the face of such insane desire."

"You're awfully pleased with yourself, your majesty," she said wryly, tracing the outline of one strongly muscled bicep.

"I damned well should be. Christ, Serafina, you have no idea what a state I've been in." He idly stroked her breast with one finger. "Well worth waiting for, though. Are you sure you've never done this before?"

"Idiot," Serafina said lovingly, stretching under his touch like a cat. "If I had, I wouldn't have waited so long myself. I think I like lovemaking, Aiden."

"Oh, yes," he agreed. "I think you like it very much, which augers well for me. Just tell me one thing, though. Who the *hell* is Adam?"

16

$\mathscr{S}$erafina's heart nearly stopped in shock. "Wh-What?" she stammered, horrified.

He stroked his finger down her nose. "You heard me. Adam. Who is he? It's not the first time you've called me that, and a man really would rather hear his wife cry out his own name in the throes of passion."

She stared at him, her mind racing to find a plausible explanation, but nothing came. "You—you must have misunderstood," she said, grasping at straws. "Aiden, Adam—they're close enough in sound."

"I think I know my name when I hear it," he replied dryly. "And you look as guilty as can be." He dropped a kiss on her fingers. "Is there something you haven't told me, sweetheart?"

"I—I don't know anyone called Adam," she said truthfully enough, relieved to see that he didn't seem upset or angered by her appalling slip of the tongue, which she couldn't understand. "I really think you must have misheard."

"Possibly," he said. "I might be inclined to make more of a jealous scene if I didn't know for a fact that you believed yourself in love with me when you came to the marriage. That's such an unlikely scenario in itself that no one could make it up." He grinned. "Almost as unlikely as your dreaming that I assaulted you with a flagpole."

"Aiden, I'm sorry about that," she said sincerely, cursing

Adam, the figment of her imagination, for causing her so much trouble. "I'm sorry that I thought you would hurt me, and I'm sorry to have made you wait for so long because of that."

"Ah, well." He stroked his fingers lightly over her back. "The truth of the matter is that some women do have a bad experience their first time."

"They do?" she said, pulling slightly away and looking at him hard. "So you lied to me after all," she said, frowning.

"No, not exactly. I didn't see any point in dwelling on a remote possibility when you were already frightened, and I reasoned that since you've been riding astride and bareback most of your life, you probably had unwittingly taken care of the problem. I was right—you were remarkably easy to deflower."

Serafina thought that over. She supposed he was referring to all the jolting around she'd done, which explained the lack of pain when he'd penetrated her. Another reason to discount anything she'd ever dreamed about Adam.

She was going to have to have a serious word with herself and banish her fantasies for once and for all. Especially now that she had Aiden to love—although she didn't think she'd give him that piece of news just yet for fear of frightening him away.

"You may deflower me anytime you wish," she said, snuggling more closely against him, loving the way he felt and smelled and tasted.

"I'm afraid deflowering is the sort of thing that can only be done once," he said with a choked laugh. "But your enthusiasm pleases me, and I'll be happy to make love to you day in and day out and anytime in between. For example," and he bent his head and took her mouth in a deep, lingering kiss, "I think right now would be a good time to begin. There's so much ground to cover. . . ."

"You're in a fine mood this morning," Tinkerby said, helping Aiden into his jacket.

"I have every reason to be in a fine mood," Aiden said, not inclined to explain any more than that. He didn't think

Tinkerby needed to know that it had taken him nearly six weeks to consummate his marriage. "However I have a few matters to take up with Serafina's aunt."

"Do you now, my lord? Well, I should be careful about going into her chambers, for today is Midsummer, and it's her favorite day in the year to be casting spells—she'll be at it until midnight, mark my words. And mind you, this time last year she blew the cow shed to smithereens, so there's no telling what she'll get up to."

"Hmm. Well, never mind, I'll risk it," Aiden said with an amused smile. "Tell Janie not to wake my wife this morning, will you?"

Tinkerby touched his finger to the side of his nose and winked. "Right ho, your lordship. A girl needs her sleep, 'specially if she's been kept up half the night by her husband."

Aiden shook his head, wondering if Tinkerby would ever learn any respect. He strongly doubted it. He went straight to Elspeth's quarters and knocked.

"Enter, enter, and be quick about it," she called in her high voice, and he pushed the door open, then stopped on the sill, looking about in speechless astonishment.

The room was littered with stones formed into circles. Each circle contained an assortment of objects, or symbols that Aiden imagined were runes. The air reeked of incense, candles burning everywhere, and a cauldron sat near what Aiden imagined to be a makeshift altar, on which sat a cup, a pentacle, a wand, a crystal ball, and a few other objects he couldn't identify. Aiden's gaze traveled to the left side of the altar where a broom rested, and he passed his hand over his face for a moment, then dropped it.

Elspeth Beaton was farther gone than he'd ever imagined.

She knelt on all fours, her backside to him and cocked up in the air as she drew something in the middle of one of her circles.

"What are you waiting for? Bring the wine over here, Janie," she commanded.

"It's not Janie," he said, struggling to keep the laughter from his voice.

She jerked up to an upright position with a loud squeak and turned, her face registering her horror as she took in his presence. "Aubrey! Whatever are you doing coming to my apartment?" She hopped to her feet and shoved her hands on her bony hips, glaring at him.

"Now you've got trouble," a muffled voice said to the left of Aiden's shoulder and he started and turned his head sharply to locate who had spoken. A large green parrot sat on a perch, his head cocked, regarding Aiden with one beady eye.

"Were you talking to me?" Aiden said to the bird, feeling as if he'd just stepped into Bedlam.

"Hush," Elspeth snapped, and Aiden wasn't sure whether she meant him or the bird. "Explain yourself, Aubrey."

"I came to have a private word with you," he said, trying to recover his equilibrium. "It's about Serafina."

"What about Serafina?" she said, cocking her head in a good imitation of the parrot. "Is there something wrong with her?"

"Not at all, but I think there's something wrong with you. What in God's name were you thinking of when you gave Serafina your marriage speech about flagpoles and how I was going to make her bleed half to death? You scared her silly and gave her nightmares to boot!"

Elspeth tapped her finger against her mouth. "So that's the problem, is it? And here I was thinking you didn't want the girl. Well, that changes everything."

Aiden blinked. "You thought I didn't *want* her? Are you completely out of your mind? Did Serafina say something to you to make you think that?"

"She hasn't said a word on the subject. But you said enough the other night. All that business about not loving her."

Aiden picked his way across the room to one of the windows. He shoved it open, desperate for fresh air. "Miss Beaton," he said, turning back to her, speaking as patiently as he could manage. "I might not be in love with your niece, but I never said I didn't want her. Why would you think such a ludicrous thing?"

"Because that's what you told everyone before the wedding, and Janie said not a thing was going on in that bed. What else would I surmise? I thought if you had any interest in Serafina, you'd have enough sense to get on with the matter."

Aiden pressed his fingers to his temples. "Janie has been reporting to you about my private affairs?"

"She's got a good head on her shoulders, that girl."

"And what did Janie think you were going to do about the situation? Have another helpful chat with my wife?" Aiden walked over to the corner of the room and took a deep breath, attempting to control his temper, reminding himself that he was dealing with a madwoman.

A light tap came at the door, and before Elspeth had a chance to answer Janie appeared, carrying the wine decanter from downstairs. "Here it is, miss, but I think we'd better stop doctoring it," she said in a rush, not seeing Aiden standing in the corner. "I've just seen for myself that his lordship did his business sure enough last night, but I think Plum's been tippling at the stuff too, for he just cornered me in the kitchen and tried to plant a kiss on me! Plum!"

"No, no, no!" Elspeth cried, jumping up and down and flapping her arms wildly. "Stop, stop!"

"But it's God's honest truth," Janie insisted. "You thought your love potion would only effect Lord Aubrey, but Lord Delaware and Plum both are behaving like two stallions after the mares."

"That's enough," Elspeth shouted, still flapping like a hen.

Aiden couldn't believe his ears. No wonder he'd been suffering from a permanent erection the last few days. "Are you telling me you've been putting some kind of aphrodisiac in the wine?" he roared.

Janie jumped a foot, nearly dropping the decanter in her shock. "Oh—oh, your lordship! Oh dear, I didn't know you were there!" She stared at Aiden, then back at Elspeth, her eyes wide as saucers and filled with fright. "Oh, merciful heaven . . ."

"What do you think I was trying to tell you, stupid girl!" Elspeth said, grabbing the decanter out of her hands. "Off with you before you say another word and put your foot even deeper in it. I'll finish this with his lordship."

Janie fled the room, wringing her hands and wailing.

"You, Miss Elspeth Beaton, have some explaining to do," Aiden said tightly, ready to strangle the woman.

"I was just trying to help," Elspeth piped sheepishly. "And look there, it worked, didn't it?" she added, brightening a little.

"I'd say it worked a little too well," Aiden retorted hotly, taking forcible possession of the decanter. He marched over to the window and poured the contents out, strongly tempted to throw the damned container after it. He turned back to Elspeth, who stood with her hands behind her back, looking like a chastised child.

"Don't you ever, *ever* do something like this again," he said, biting out the words, his fingers clenched so tightly on the neck of the decanter that his knuckles turned white. "I do not need love potions to enhance my sexual drive, which is perfectly adequate, thank you very much. My *God,* woman, I was already in a bad enough state of frustration, thanks to the misguided information you gave my wife! But you made my life a living hell the last few days with whatever witch's brew you concocted!"

"I'm sorry," Elspeth said, bowing her head. "I was just trying to move things along."

"You were just trying to move things along." Aiden sighed. "Well, you've obviously also managed to play havoc with Plum and my father, never mind with me. How long does it take for the effects of this poison to work its way out of the system?"

"Twenty-four hours, perhaps?" she said in a small voice. "I'm not entirely sure. I've never tried it before."

Aiden rubbed his eyes with one hand. "That's bloody marvelous. You've never tried it before, so you thought you'd experiment on me." He held his hand out. "Give it to me."

Elspeth drew back. "But why can't I keep it if I promise never to use it on you again? It was most expensive to make."

"Give it to me," Aiden shouted, and Elspeth jumped.

"Oh, very well," she said sulkily. She went to a chest that

sat against one wall and pulled out a bottle filled with a cloudy liquid. She held it out to him. "Here."

Aiden put the decanter down and took it from her, pulled the cork out, and sniffed. There was no discernible odor, but he now understood why the wine had looked a little off-color the last few nights. And he'd thought that had been the result of improper storage, idiot that he was. He poured the contents out of the window, watching it splash onto the grass below, wondering if bizarre things would begin to sprout from the spot.

He gave her the bottle back. "See here, Miss Beaton, I don't mind what nonsense you get up to in the privacy of your own quarters, but in the future you keep your meddling hands off me and everyone else who lives at Townsend. I grant you that your oil, whatever is in it, has been helping my sister, and for that I am grateful. But I won't have you going about dosing people with Spanish fly without their knowledge, or giving them anything else that's suspect." He glared at her. "Do I make myself clear?"

"Deer antler tips," she said indignantly. "Spanish fly is an irritant, not an aphrodisiac."

"Whatever," he said impatiently. "And for God's sake, try not to burn the house down. You have enough candles lit in here to set us all aflame."

"But it's the Sabbat of Litha, the day when the powers of nature are at their peak," Elspeth said, scuffing one foot on the floor. "I am celebrating the fertility of the god and goddess and I simply cannot do it without candles."

"I don't give a damn what you're celebrating," Aiden said, ready to tear his hair out. "Just be careful, would you?"

Elspeth shot him a sly look. "Oh, I'll be careful enough. But you had better mark this day, my boy, for magic is also at its peak on the summer solstice, and if I were you I wouldn't scoff at it. You need all the help you can get."

"I've had more help from you than I need," Aiden said dryly. He picked up the decanter, intending to take it downstairs and have Plum scour it out with boiling water. "Oh," he said as an afterthought, "by the by, are you acquainted with anyone called Adam?"

"Adam? Why would I be acquainted with someone called Adam? The only Adam I ever heard of lived a very long time ago, and didn't *he* think he was a fine fellow?" She chuckled as if vastly amused by her wit.

"Never mind," he said, thinking he must have misunderstood Serafina after all. He didn't even know why he'd bothered asking Elspeth, when the woman was the loosest screw he'd ever encountered. "It was a foolish question."

"Not all questions are as foolish as they might seem, Aubrey, and you might keep that in mind when you look to the future. More answers lie in the far distant past than you realize."

"I'm sure. Good day, Miss Beaton," Aiden said, his head beginning to ache from a combination of smoke fumes and sheer frustration. "Enjoy your celebration." He left swiftly, unable to abide another moment of lunacy.

"Good day, Aubrey," Elspeth said, waiting for the door to close behind him. As soon as it had, she gave a little skip of excitement and gleefully clapped her hands together. "The magic is working, Basil," she sang, turning a circle. "He's on his way. Not long now. Not long at all."

Charlotte lay still as Frederick prepared her for her afternoon rub and nap, her teeth gritted in anger. Nothing was working; her brother was becoming more enamored of his wife by the minute. She'd watched them this afternoon from her position at the drawing room window, walking hand in hand, heads bent together. She'd seen the long, passionate kiss Aiden had given Serafina when he thought they were unobserved, and hadn't missed Serafina's equally impassioned response.

Charlotte squeezed her eyes tightly closed, loathing welling in her chest. The very sight of Serafina made her ill. Not only had Charlotte been unable to discover anything about her sister-in-law that might hasten her downfall, but she was also forced to witness the constant ardent glances Aiden cast his wife and Serafina's calculated response, so shy, designed to further inflame him. Oh, yes, Serafina knew the game well. She'd probably been playing it for years, judging by its effect on Aiden. The poor man hadn't been himself since his marriage, his tongue practically hanging on the ground as his wife led him along by the nose—or more likely by his male member.

Charlotte colored hotly as the image of Peter the footman's swollen organ came clearly to mind. Recently she'd been constantly plagued by these thoughts, playing the scene over and over again when she'd found Martha and Peter together, Peter poised to enter Martha's body, his shaft so huge, so powerful.

She quickly forced the image away with a little moan. The erotic currents running between her brother and his wife were obviously affecting her reason. And yet as wicked as she knew the wish to be, her deepest desire was to have the same for herself.

And why shouldn't she? Why shouldn't she, Lady Charlotte Delaware, daughter of a marquess, have a normal life like everyone else? She was a beautiful woman. She'd become aware of that recently, spending hours gazing into her vanity mirror, thinking about how Raphael must see her. For the first time since her accident she actually enjoyed looking into mirrors, knowing that her looks had not been wasted after all.

She had skin the color of porcelain, eyes the same sapphire blue as her brother's, and her features were even and classically arranged. Her figure was good, even better now that she'd been exercising.

And oh, she couldn't wait to surprise Raphael with her news, for his entire life would be changed. That was the sole reason she'd agreed to go to London, to prepare herself for their future, to meet the appropriate people.

But for now it was her secret, her wonderful little secret that she planned to save until the moment was right. And that day would not be long off, the day when she pushed herself out of her chair and walked across the room into Raphael's loving arms.

Her pain had vanished, and with it the weakness in her limbs. The exercises and constant massages had helped to revitalize her muscles, and she could now stand without support, each day for longer and longer. She had even tried taking a few steps, although she still needed to lean on furniture and tired quickly.

But soon, so soon she would be waltzing with Raphael. And soon enough she would be his duchess, the childhood dream that had been shattered by her accident finally realized.

Frederick finished rubbing her back and rolled her over to work on the front of her legs, arranging her dress over her ankles as he always did. But today she reached down and pulled it up above her knees.

He shot her a startled, questioning glance.

"Really, Frederick," she said, smiling at him, "there's no need to be so careful with my modesty. I'd rather you do your work properly, and the higher up my limbs you rub, the better the treatment will work. You've already effected such an improvement in my condition."

"Yes, my lady," he said, nervously licking his lips, but he did as he was told, his hands slipping up under her dress to her thighs, kneading the muscles there. Charlotte sighed with pleasure at the feel of his fingers soothing and rubbing. She really couldn't help herself; she let her knees fall slightly apart so that he could work his hands even higher.

And she couldn't help that her gaze drifted to the bulge in his groin as she imagined what lay beneath. She drew in a sharp breath as she realized that the bulge was shifting, changing, growing stiff, the hard outline unmistakable in his breeches.

The slow throb that had started between her legs turned into a desperate pulsing, and warm moisture trickled from her cleft, soaking her curls. She moaned aloud and tilted her hips up, urging his fingers closer.

Frederick closed his eyes, beads of sweat springing to his brow, and Charlotte knew with certainty that he wanted to touch her there just as much as she wanted to be touched.

She daringly eased her legs open even farther, knowing she was being horribly depraved, but helpless to prevent herself. She burned, desperate for release.

"My lady," Frederick gasped, his breath coming in rapid

pants. "I don't know what . . . do you want me to—that is . . ." He swallowed hard. "Oh, Lord above," he croaked.

"I want you to touch me," she said, her voice low, her chest rising and falling as rapidly as his own. "I want you to touch me there, Frederick. I know you want to touch me and you may."

"Are you—are you sure, my lady? I don't want to lose my job should you change your mind."

"The only way you'll lose your job is if you don't get on with it!" Charlotte cried in frustration.

"Yes, my lady," Frederick said, his expression pained. He brushed his fingers up, leaving a trail of fire on her sensitive skin, and she gasped as he found her nest of curls and cupped it in his hand, rubbing in little circles.

"Oh—oh . . ." she cried as his fingers dipped between her throbbing folds, and rubbed there too, back and forth until she sobbed with unbearable pleasure. "My breasts," she cried. "I want you to touch me there, too."

"Yes, my lady," Frederick barely managed to gasp. With one hand he deftly pulled the bodice of her dress away, exposing her breasts. He cupped one delicate swell of flesh in his palm, then pinched and squeezed the nipple with his fingers, his other hand still stroking between her cleft. Charlotte tossed her head back and forth, her entire body shaking.

"Show me your organ," she panted. "Take it out and show me."

Frederick turned scarlet and gulped, but with one hand he undid his breeches and let the flap loose. His shaft sprang free, and Charlotte thought she'd go out of her mind with excitement. It was big, sticking straight out from a tangle of dark hair, as swollen as she'd remembered Peter's. The blunt tip was red and hungry looking, a drop of moisture beading from it.

Charlotte sobbed and reached out a hand, pulling Frederick closer. "Touch me with it," she whispered. "Don't put it in me, just touch me."

Frederick nodded, and he pushed her skirt up to her waist, exposing her flesh to his wicked, lustful eyes. He came over her, his weight resting on his forearms and the tip of his huge organ slid between her cleft. He rubbed against her as he had with his fingers, but this was different, so wildly electrifying she thought she might scream. His head dropped down and he took her breast in his mouth, sucking and pulling desperately as his hips slid back and forth, back and forth.

Charlotte knew what they were doing was sinful. She'd never intended to go so far, but she didn't care. She couldn't stop, not now. It excited her more, knowing how depraved her behavior was.

Frederick pulled away for a moment, and Charlotte sucked in a sharp breath as something invaded her—his fingers, she realized, diving inside her, driving her into a full frenzy as they moved in and out, his thumb sliding over that hard little nub of sensation he'd found that made her writhe like a madwoman. And then he came back and pressed his shaft just there where his fingers had been.

"Don't worry, my lady," he said hoarsely, "I ain't going to enter you, just bring you off nicely." He pushed against her opening, the tip of his head just inside her. He stayed, rocking his hips ever so slightly, over and over, his thumb rubbing on her nub until she thought she'd go insane.

Charlotte opened her mouth in a silent scream as she climaxed, her flesh throbbing wildly around his blunt head. He groaned and slid away from her, his body falling onto hers. His hips jerked and he sighed, something wet and sticky sliding onto Charlotte's bare midriff.

"Sorry, my lady," he choked. "Couldn't help coming off. I was too far gone. I hope you don't mind—you won't catch a babe this way."

Charlotte touched her fingers to the semen he'd spewed onto her. She brought her fingers to her mouth and rubbed them on her lips with a slow smile, then flicked her tongue over her lips, tasting. She liked the taste, salty and foreign. And she liked the smell. Male. Crude. So erotic.

"I don't mind at all," she said, flicking his cheek with her thumb. "I liked what you did. Did you like it too?"

"Oh, yes indeed, my lady," he said, rising and adjusting his breeches. He shrugged one shoulder. "I've tried to keep my mind off sinful thoughts like you taught us. But the last few days—I don't know, my lady. I've fair been going crazy with lust. It's been difficult touching you and not thinking about other things."

Charlotte smiled slyly. Of course it had been difficult, the poor boy. He couldn't resist her, and why should he? She sighed happily, thinking of all the happy mornings and afternoons they were going to have together. As long as he kept her a virgin for Raphael, he could do anything he wanted to her. She wasn't going to turn back now, not when she'd just discovered how stimulating lust was.

Daily bouts of it were only bound to improve her health.

"You've been daydreaming the afternoon away, my dear," Lord Delaware commented, sitting back on his heels and smiling over at Serafina. "Are you thinking of your introduction to society as Aiden's wife, perhaps?"

"Not in the least," Serafina replied, adding another clump of weeds to her growing pile. "London society holds no interest for me. I'd far rather stay here and tend to the gardens, but I know that Aiden feels strongly that we all make the right impression, so I'll do what I can, even if I do feel awkward." She wiped her hand over her brow. "More to the point, how do you feel about going to London, Papa?"

"Oh, I suppose I feel happy that I can make up for past mistakes, but I share your attitude—I'd be just as content to stay at home and watch the gardens blossom. You don't suppose Elspeth will change her mind and come along, do you? I'll miss her company."

Serafina laughed. "Society will be far better off without my aunt to take it to task. Auntie's more suited to peace and quiet and doing things her own way. She decided a long time ago that she wanted nothing to do with the ways of the normal world."

"Yes, a most refreshing woman," Lord Delaware said with a chuckle. "She has given me hours of pleasure. I dread the day that she decides to return to Clwydd, for the house will seem empty without her."

"I know. I'll miss her too, although she's been so busy with her experiments that she hasn't had any time for conversation outside of dinner."

"Well, my dear, the two of you have brightened our dreary lives considerably. Look at Charlotte, for example. She positively glows with beauty these days, and I rarely hear a harsh word out of her."

"Charlotte is much improved, and you can thank Auntie for that." She dug at a stubborn root with her spade, thinking that Charlotte might be much improved, but she still had the eerie habit of creeping up on a person unannounced. And there was something about Charlotte that still made her nervous, as pleasant as Charlotte was to her. She felt as if Charlotte was always probing and poking, as if she was trying to discover some enlightening secret about Serafina's life before Townsend. Serafina would have loved to gratify her, but there was nothing to tell. But she supposed that anyone might be curious about a life lived with Aunt Elspeth. Fortunately, Charlotte still knew nothing about Elspeth's beliefs, and Serafina planned to keep it that way, which was why she was reticent to discuss her time at Clwydd.

"But I don't think I can thank your aunt for Aiden's improved disposition," Lord Delaware said with a sideways glance at her. "I've never seen the boy so happy. Today he looked as if he might burst out into song, and it had nothing to do with choir practice."

Serafina blushed. She still couldn't believe it was possible to feel such happiness. Maybe magic did exist after all, for Aiden had finally banished her ghosts, brought her into the fullness of her love for him. And she did love him, she was sure of that now. The goddess truly had given her to the man she was meant to be with, and she later intended to thank and honor the god and goddess with all due ceremony on this, their special day. They had brought her a true gift.

Aiden had made love to her most of the night, taking her

to never before imagined heights of pleasure, but the day had held equal delights, for the simple, singing pleasure she took in his company fulfilled her every bit as much as his lovemaking.

Their walk today had brought her nothing but joy, her hand tucked securely in his as he regaled her with amusing stories of his time in faraway places. His physical attentions, once so dreaded, she now welcomed with open arms and a glad heart, the lightest of his touches sending shivers through her.

"Serafina? Have I lost you again, dearest?" Lord Delaware shot her a quizzical glance.

She came back with a start. "I'm sorry. I have been a bit dreamy today. What were you saying?"

"Only that Aiden looks a happy man, and I believe you have everything to do with that. He reminds me of myself when my dear Isabel was still alive."

"Does he?" she said, pleased beyond measure that Aiden's father thought so. "I'm so glad. I wish for Aiden's happiness above all else."

"Why . . . why, I do believe you love him, my dear," Lord Delaware said, his spade stilling in his hand. "Is it possible after such a bad beginning?" He regarded her gravely.

Serafina lowered her gaze. "I do," she said softly. "I love him with all my heart. You won't tell him though, will you?" she asked nervously. "I don't think he'd like to hear it."

"Not like to hear it?" Lord Delaware said, incredulity coloring his voice. "Why ever not? What man doesn't want to know that his wife loves him?"

Serafina pressed her palm against her forehead, wishing she hadn't spoken so freely. "I shouldn't have said anything. It's just that Aiden doesn't love me, and I don't want to make him uncomfortable with unwelcome emotions."

Lord Delaware snorted. "That's the biggest load of poppycock I ever heard. Aiden could use some love in his life. He's never had it, not where it mattered, and that's my fault for shutting myself away and not tending to his needs." He sighed heavily, digging the point of his spade into the earth. "I didn't deal well with Isabel's death, you see. I let Aiden fend for himself, and Charlotte too when it comes down to it, and I have only myself to blame for their misery."

"You were in pain, Papa. You couldn't help grieving," Serafina said, trying to be fair.

"Nonsense," he said bluntly. "I could have tended to the needs of my children instead of indulging myself. I could have given Aiden support and encouragement instead of blaming him for my wife's death. If I could take the last twenty-eight years back I would, but I can't, and I know it. But if there's any hope for Aiden it lies with you, my dear, so you love him as he deserves, and don't you worry about sparing his feelings just because he doesn't think he has any."

Serafina reached her hand out to his, tears blurring her eyes. "You're a good man, Papa, and I can understand why my father held you in such high regard. I feel as if in some way my own father has been given back to me through you, and I am so grateful, so very, very grateful for that."

"Good heavens, child. You might make me believe you even love me a little," he said, his own eyes tearing up.

"But I do," she said, squeezing his dirt-encrusted fingers. "I really do. Is that really so hard for you to believe?"

"I've been a fool," Lord Delaware said roughly, rubbing his eyes with one hand, leaving a streak of mud behind. "I've done so many things I regret. But the one thing I'll never regret is arranging your marriage to my son, as self-serving as it was at the time." He pulled out his handkerchief and blew his nose hard. "The first kind thing God has done since taking my Isabel away was sending you to us, and for that I will be eternally grateful." He mopped at his eyes. "I'm sorry. Forgive an old man his sentimentality."

Deeply moved, Serafina wrapped her arms around his neck. "Dear Papa," she whispered against his rough cheek, "I forgive you everything, for you brought me to Aiden, and for that I will be eternally grateful. Maybe we both had to wait until the time was right. But as a result, not only do I have a papa to love, but a sister and a husband to love as well."

Lord Delaware disentangled himself. "Good heavens, girl," he said gruffly. "Are you forgetting yourself? We have a choir practice to attend. Tomorrow is our debut, and it won't do to forget it."

"Certainly not," Serafina said, laughing and loving him all the more. "We'd better hurry."

They walked back to the house, both wrapped in their separate thoughts, Serafina's focused on counting her blessings.

17

"Aiden?" Serafina knocked on the study door, hoping Aiden wasn't too busy to see her. She'd had a wonderful idea when she was dressing for dinner, and she wanted to present it to him privately. But the real truth of the matter was she didn't want to be away from him for another minute. Her idea was really just an excuse to be in his company.

"Come in," he called and put his pen down as she entered. "Hello, sweetheart. To what do I owe the honor of this visit?"

"Am I disturbing you?" she asked, her heart skipping a beat as he smiled warmly at her. He was so beautiful, so incredibly beautiful and so very masculine, and yet he was capable of such gentleness. But best of all, he was hers, hers to love and honor, just as she had vowed.

"Not at all. I was just finishing up some paperwork before dinner. We have a ship sailing to Nice next week and I have to approve the cargo invoices. But you haven't told me why you're here." He came around his desk and gave her a kiss, his mouth lingering on hers. "Or did you simply miss me?"

Serafina ran her hands down his chest, savoring the smooth hard planes under her palms, remembering exactly how they looked beneath his jacket and shirt. "I suppose I missed you a little," she said, slipping her arms around his lean waist, wishing she could tell him the truth—that she'd missed him terribly, even though she'd seen him only two hours before at choir practice. And then she'd found it very hard to concentrate on her job, her gaze straying to him the entire time as if she were a besotted schoolgirl.

"Good," he said. "I'd hate to think you'd forgotten all about me. So. Are you ready for our big day tomorrow?"

"Oh, yes. I think we'll do brilliantly. Everyone seems so excited, and won't Charlotte be surprised?"

"I think I can safely say that Lottie will be overcome, but I can't swear it will be with joy. I have no idea what she'll make of seeing the household staff standing in church singing their hearts out, side by side with her father, brother, and sister-in-law."

"Will she think us undignified?" Serafina asked with a worried frown. "I know how strongly she feels about observing the proprieties."

"I wouldn't give it another thought. My sister is a touch top-lofty, I'm afraid, but I suppose she has little else in life other than position and God to think about. Maybe being in London will do her some good."

"That's why I wanted to speak to you," Serafina said. "If she's going to come to London with us, then she'll need some nice dresses, and there won't be time to have anything made. Would you mind terribly if Janie alters some of my clothes? She's clever with a needle, and you bought me far more dresses than I can use."

"I hadn't thought of that . . . hmm." He scratched his cheek. "I suppose Lottie's dresses are a bit subdued, but that's the way she likes them."

"I know, Aiden, but she's such an attractive woman. She ought to look her best, now that she's finally come around to the idea of going out in society."

"But you heard her last night, sweetheart. She said that was only for the sake of appearances, that she felt she had to do her duty. I'm not sure she'll think that her duty extends to wearing pastels and lace and ribbons."

"Well, as far as I'm concerned, it's hard to feel gay when one is dressed as if in mourning. I can try to persuade her, at least."

"As you wish," Aiden said, dropping a kiss on her hair. "You are thoughtful as always toward Charlotte. Now why don't you sit down in that armchair and provide a glorious distraction for me while I finish up my work? I won't feel so put-upon if I have your beautiful face to look at."

Serafina blushed. "Aiden, you don't have to flatter me. I honestly don't mind being plain as long as my looks don't worry you."

"Plain?" He stared at her. "Serafina, I swear to you, I've never been inclined to flatter you—I don't have to."

"You don't?" she said uncertainly, not sure of what he meant. "Why not?"

"Why not?" He cupped her face in his hands and released a long breath. "Because, my sweet girl, you happen to be the most beautiful woman I've ever laid eyes on."

Serafina's mouth dropped open in sheer astonishment. "No," she said flatly. "I don't believe it."

"Believe it," he replied quietly. "I've thought so from the first moment I saw you. You took my breath away. This isn't the first time I've told you what I think of your looks, you know."

"But I—but I always thought you told me I was pretty because you wanted to make me feel better about myself, or because you were trying to have your way with me," she whispered, taken aback.

Aiden burst into laughter. "Do you really think I'm that much of a hypocrite?"

"No—no it's not that," she said quickly. "It's just that I know I'm odd looking. I always have been, you see."

"Odd looking is an interesting way to describe you," he said, running his thumbs over her cheeks. "I'd say you were enchanting. Unique. You make other women look boring." His thumb rubbed over her mouth. "You have the widest, most extraordinary eyes I've ever seen, and your mouth is the most delectably kissable mouth I've ever encountered. So soft and full, and so very responsive."

"And my front tooth is crooked," she pointed out, about to melt into a puddle at his touch. She still couldn't believe he actually thought her beautiful but the way he looked at her made her feel it.

"That front tooth of yours is not what I'd call crooked.

It's—it's as unique as the rest of you, and absolutely perfect as far as I'm concerned." He covered her mouth with his and ran his tongue over it, sending little shocks through her body. "Mmm. You see?" he said, lifting his head, his breath coming faster. "Dear God, Serafina, but you're dangerous. I can't come near you without wanting to do all sorts of deliciously erotic things."

"I think that must just be your nature," she said, wishing he would do deliciously erotic things to her. She loved the way he touched her, the way he made her blood sing in her veins.

"I really did made a bad impression on you the day we met, didn't I?" He sighed, stroking her back. "I wish I could say I was sorry, but I'm afraid that I was smitten by you on the spot. I swear to you, I really don't go around behaving like a depraved rogue, assaulting innocent women. I couldn't help myself."

"You may have behaved like a depraved rogue, but I have to admit, I did think you were the most handsome man I'd ever seen. I'm certain you've had women fluttering around you since you were old enough to notice."

Aiden kissed her again, his lips soft and warm on hers. "Jealous?" he asked softly. "You have no reason to be. I'm all yours, sweetheart. But I'm happy to know my face pleases you."

"Everything about you pleases me," she said, resting her cheek on his chest, drinking in his scent, that faint mixture of sandalwood and lime and pure Aiden. She longed to tell him how she really felt, but at the same time she couldn't bear to have him laugh at her, all because he thought she was living in a fairy tale, still expecting him to be a prince. He didn't believe in love to begin with, so he was bound to think her the biggest sapscull.

"And you please me greatly, every last inch of you," he said, his fingers straying to her nape. "I should have remembered to dress your aunt down on that subject as well this morning. She had no business making you think you were plain or undesirable."

"She never actually said I was plain or undesirable," Serafina said in her aunt's defense. "She just told me I wasn't pretty, but then it's not Auntie's way to praise." Serafina paused. He had spoken with her aunt? The thought made her nervous in the extreme. Aunt Elspeth could be depended on to go off half cocked on any number of subjects and Serafina only hoped the subject hadn't been her. "Aiden . . . what did you dress my aunt down about this morning?"

"Oh, a number of things," he said, idly playing with a lock of her hair. "But what really sent me into a temper was discovering that your dear, misguided aunt has been doctoring the dinner wine."

"*What?*" Serafina took an appalled step backward. "What on earth are you talking about?"

Aiden shook his head. "As I said. She's been putting some kind of brew into the dinner wine thinking it would boost my sexual potency, as if it needed boosting."

"Oh, no . . ." Serafina pressed her hands against her mouth, horrified that Elspeth would have done something so awful. No wonder poor Aiden had been suffering so severely. "Oh, Aiden, I'm so sorry—I had no idea."

"Neither did I until Janie waltzed in with the decanter so your aunt could dispense another dose and accidentally spilled the story, not realizing I was there. Dear God, but I was tempted to strangle Elspeth."

Serafina wanted to drop through the floor. She couldn't believe Elspeth had resorted to such a low ploy. On the other hand, it was just the sort of mischief her aunt couldn't seem to stay out of. Strangling Elspeth did have its appeal. "She—she means well, truly she does."

Aiden grinned. "I'm sure she means well, but I'd rather she didn't take out her good intentions on me. I only hope my father and Plum recover from the effects or we'll lose all the female staff."

"*That's* what's been making Plum and your father behave so badly?" Serafina couldn't help the gurgle of laughter that escaped. "I did wonder . . . oh, dear." She covered her mouth with her hands, trying to sober. "I—I'm sorry. I shouldn't find this so amusing. Auntie shouldn't have interfered."

"Your aunt is a meddlesome nuisance, although I must confess I'm fond of her." He tilted his head and regarded her curiously. "Serafina, there's something I've been meaning to ask you about your Aunt Elspeth. I suppose I should first tell you that I walked into an extraordinary scene this morning."

Serafina winced. The mental image of what Aiden might have witnessed was not reassuring. "You probably just saw Auntie honoring the Sabbat," she said, trying to gloss over her aunt's more peculiar habits.

"I believe that what you really mean is that your aunt practices witchcraft," he said dryly.

"Well, it's not witchcraft exactly. She, um . . . she just prefers the old ways."

Aiden raised one eyebrow in cynical question.

"Oh, all right," Serafina said, heaving a resigned sigh. Aiden was far too astute to be put off by prevarication, and the situation was already too far gone, if he'd seen Elspeth in full ritual preparation. "She's a Wiccan. Some people call them witches, and they are really, but not in the way you might think. They only practice magic for good, and even though Auntie doesn't always get it right, she only has the best of intentions. She's really most devout."

The corner of Aiden's mouth twitched. "I suppose she only rides her broomstick on All Hallows' Eve?"

"Oh, no," Serafina said earnestly. "Broomsticks aren't for riding—that's an old tale invented by witch persecutors. Brooms are ritual tools used for purification. And All Hallows' Eve—Samain is the proper name, actually—is a sacred night in which to honor friends and relatives who have died."

"Wonderful. I can just see your aunt now, calling up the souls of the dead. The house will be littered with them."

"Don't be silly. She wouldn't think of doing such a thing. Anyway, even if you wanted to, you can't call up souls who have gone on to other incarnations," Serafina replied logically.

"I see." Aiden rubbed a finger over his eyebrow, then dropped his hand with exasperation. "Are you telling me that your aunt's filled your head with claptrap about reincarnation on top of everything else?"

"It's not claptrap," Serafina said hotly, wondering why everyone but herself and Elspeth had such a problem with the idea. "It makes perfect sense, and I think you should try not to be so close minded. What is far more illogical is to believe your soul was created just to have one life and then go play in the clouds with harps for the rest of eternity. Where's the sense in that, may I ask?"

Aiden threw his head back and roared with laughter. "Ah, sweetheart," he said, wiping his eyes. "You'll never bore me, I'll give you that. But do me a favor and keep your opinions to yourself, would you? I'd hate for the vicar to get wind of your theology—we'd all be excommunicated and Charlotte would never forgive me." He grinned broadly.

Stung by his attitude, Serafina planted her hands on her hips. "There's nothing unchristian about the doctrine of reincarnation, and furthermore, I don't think God is nearly so narrow-minded as you, Aiden Delaware. He put plants on this earth, didn't He, and they die and are reborn every year. Why shouldn't people be reborn after they die?"

"It sounds exhausting to me." Aiden took her firmly by the shoulders and sat her down in the armchair. "Now enough of this nonsense. I need to finish my work." He picked up a book from the floor and put it in her lap. "Here, why don't you read this? It's a history of shipbuilding over the ages. I think I can safely guarantee that none of the people between the pages have popped back to life, for if they had, we'd be in serious trouble. Scoundrels, the lot of them."

He went back to his desk and sat down, instantly losing himself in thought.

Serafina gave him one last hard look, then opened the book and started turning the well-worn pages. Aiden had clearly read the book time and time again, and she soon could see why, for the subject matter was fascinating. The pages were adorned with beautiful copperplate illustrations, the history beginning with the Bronze Age vessels that had traveled the Mediterranean three thousand years before in the time of Odysseus. It described the ancient coastal cities they visited, the trade routes they followed, the cargo they carried.

She carefully flipped through the pages, interested not so much in the shipping aspects of the history, but by the carefully outlined details of the development of various civilizations—Greek, Roman, Italian, Arabic, they were all covered. She'd never realized how intertwined they were, how often countries had changed hands. By the time she'd reached the section on the Byzantine Empire she was enthralled.

And then her hand froze as she turned another page, and she stared, not believing her eyes. She looked again, harder, sure she had to be seeing things. For there on the page was an illustration of a city she had seen time and time again, but only in her dreams.

Kyrenia, the caption read. One of the more important Greek city-states during the Byzantine Empire, owing to its rights to the huge timber forests so necessary for shipbuilding.

A city climbed up a hill, crowned by a castle, the sea glittering behind it.

Serafina's fingers tightened painfully on the edges of the book as her heart started to pound furiously. She could hardly focus through her shock, but she forced herself to read the text.

The island of Cyprus, one of the earliest centers of Christianity, was particularly important to the Byzantine Empire at this time as a direct result of its strategic location to Syria, Palestine, Egypt, and Anatolia. During the 7th and 8th centuries it was often used as a springboard for attacks launched by both Islam and Constantinople against each other, the island suffering constant Arab invasions as a result. However, the kings of Cyprus continued to maintain their own hierarchy throughout this period of turmoil, which ended only in 965 when the emperor Nicephorus II Phorus finally delivered the island from Arab attacks. However, the port of Famagusta, located on the south side of the island, held exclusive harbor rights owing to its fortuitous positioning, a source of continuous conflict between the kings of Kyrenia and Famagusta. This was to be the cause of great tragedy for the island.

Serafina passed a hand over her eyes, fighting waves of dizziness. A conversation echoed in her head, dimly recalled through the pounding in her head. . . . *I thank God that this city-state is located in an inconvenient position for raiding—look at what Famagusta has had to endure, being a direct target on the southern side. . . .*

It had been Adam speaking, the night of their wedding feast, she remembered now. *Do you mean my mother's resentment of the killing harbor fees that the king imposes on every ship going out and coming in? If I had the principal port on the island I would probably do the same. . . . Famagusta has a stranglehold over us and we'd be unwise to object to their policy. We learned that lesson twenty years ago.*

Kyrenia. She remembered the name, Adam speaking that too. *All of Kyrenia has turned out for our wedding party. . . .* Something to do with Adam's mother—and Michael. A man called Michael Angelus, Adam's dearest friend. Something. . . . And then she remembered. A premonition of disaster.

Serafina covered her face with her hands and gave a low moan. The book slid to the floor with a dull thump.

"Sweetheart? Serafina? What is it?" Aiden's hands on her shoulders, his voice alarmed. "You're pale as a ghost."

She looked up at him, his face swimming before her eyes. "Aiden," she gasped, drawing in air, trying to retain a grip on reality. Aiden. It was Aiden. There was no Adam. There couldn't be; she'd only dreamed him. He was a figment of her imagination—this was all a figment of her imagination. Kyrenia, Famagusta, Arab raids, all the stuff of dreams. And yet images swam before her eyes, images of chaos and people crying out, fleeing from a city in flames. "I—I can't breathe," she choked, feeling suffocated. Smoke. Smoke filling her lungs. "I can't breathe."

He quickly scooped her up in his arms, holding her as easily as if she were a child. "It will be all right, sweetheart," he murmured, but his voice held deep concern. "You must be exhausted—I kept you up most of the night. I'll take you upstairs."

She pressed her face hard against his shoulder, her body trembling uncontrollably as she tried desperately to shut out the terrible images of people dying, being slaughtered in the streets, blood flowing, deep red rivers of blood. "Your father. Tell your father—"

"Don't worry about him. He won't mind if you miss dinner. You need to rest. . . ." The words came faintly through a mist. She struggled to say something else, to give a warning.

And then blackness mercifully engulfed her and she saw no more.

Serafina woke to moonlight streaming through the window. She didn't know how much time had gone by. Aiden was nowhere in sight, although a chair had been pulled up next to the bed. She sat up, one hand pressed against her temple, trying to orient herself. She knew she'd fainted again, but this time she hadn't had any wine, so she couldn't blame it on that. The last thing she remembered was being in Aiden's study, reading a history book. And—and then something had happened, something alarming.

She drew in a sharp breath as memory returned in a rush. She'd seen the illustration—that was it, the illustration of a city-state called Kyrenia. And text had filled the page, text that mentioned places, names, and events she'd been sure she'd invented.

A chill of fear ran down her spine and she buried her face in her hands, so confused she could hardly think. Was it *possible*, remotely possible that she hadn't made these things up? But how could she have known of them? She'd never heard of an island called Cyprus—had she?

She frowned in concentration, trying to remember if perhaps her father had spoken of it during one of his history lessons. And yet she couldn't recall his ever touching on that part of the world. Maybe she'd read about it somewhere else and simply forgotten, the information seeping back in a dream state. That was the only explanation she could think of.

But something else tugged at the back of her mind, something insistent, like a whisper she couldn't quite hear. *Time will run back . . . time will run back. . . .*

She slipped out of bed, desperately needing to be outside where she could think, breathe, be close to the goddess. Maybe she could help Serafina, offer her comfort, for Serafina's deepest fear, one that appeared more possible by the moment, was that she might not be in her right mind.

Throwing a shawl over her nightdress, she crept out of the house by the back way, careful to avoid being seen. She didn't want to be caught and forced back to bed as if she were sick, for that was surely the conclusion Aiden must have reached. He certainly couldn't have divined the truth, that once again she had lost her grip on reality. That was all Aiden needed—an insane wife. She wrapped her arms around her midriff, telling herself that she couldn't be crazy, she just couldn't be.

Her heart pounded rapidly in her chest like a frightened, caged bird and she started to run, as if she could escape the terror that tore at her.

The grass felt cool and damp under her bare feet as she raced toward the bridge and the hill that would take her up to the huge old oak tree, the place of sanctity and shelter that she sought out whenever she was troubled.

The oak tree stood proud and tall, fully leafed out now, moonlight catching in its massive branches, casting deep shadows on the ground. Serafina took a deep breath and released it, then threw off her shawl and knelt at the foot of the oak, her body trembling all over as she reached her hands out and touched the trunk with her fingertips.

"Gracious goddess," she whispered. "You who are the queen of the gods, the lamp of night, the creator of all that is wild and free; mother of woman and man; lover of the horned god and protectress of all the Wicca: descend, I pray, with your lunar ray of power upon my circle here!"

She bowed her head. "Oh, mother, help me? Please—I'm so lost, so confused. I don't know what is real anymore." Her voice caught on a sob. "I thought I understood, I truly did. I gave up the false dream to accept my true destiny, to love Aiden, for in your wisdom you gave me to him. But now I know nothing but that I do love Aiden. And I'm so afraid of what is happening to me." Her shoulders began to shake, and her tears flowed hot down her cheeks as she poured out all her fear and confusion. "Am I mad?" she cried. "Why else is this happening to me? Oh, blessed mother, nothing makes sense anymore! I feel so alone. . . ."

She wept until she had no tears left, until she was no more than an empty vessel, not even Serafina anymore, but a soul lost and adrift with no safe harbor to anchor in.

It was then that she heard the voice, clear and high, coming all around her, as real as any voice she had ever heard.

"Be still, beloved, and be of good heart, for you walk the path of truth."

Serafina lifted her head in wonder. "Mother?" she whispered. "Is it you?"

"It is I who speaks to you through the ages, who guides and nurtures you always," the voice intoned. "I give you no burden that you cannot bear, I offer you no knowledge you cannot endure. Seek the truth, my child. Seek the truth and know that it is I who brings it. Follow your heart. Always follow your heart and the truth will reveal itself. . . ."

The voice faded, becoming nothing more than the sound of the wind blowing gently around her.

Serafina shakily wiped her eyes, then stood, her heart suffused with joy. She had not been deserted after all. She knew all would be well. She had been blessed.

The goddess had answered her prayers.

18

"What in the name of God?" Aiden took in the empty bed, the empty room, a thrill of alarm running through him. He'd only gone downstairs for fifteen minutes to have a quick bite to eat, and Serafina had vanished. He was worried enough about her—this was the second time she'd fainted since he'd been married to her.

The highly unpleasant thought occurred to him that maybe Elspeth had been dosing her as well, but with something other than wine. It was the only explanation he could think of.

He looked next door, then tore downstairs, but she was nowhere to be found, and none of the servants had seen her.

"Excuse me, Father, Lottie. A word alone with you, Miss Beaton," he demanded, striding into the drawing room where Elspeth was playing her nightly chess game.

"Don't you cheat and move my bishop," Elspeth said, looking over her shoulder at Lord Delaware as Aiden took her by the arm and practically dragged her out of the drawing room. "What's your rush, boy?" she snapped, shaking his hand off as they reached the hall.

"What have you been giving Serafina?" he hissed.

"What are you talking about?" she said, glaring at him with annoyance.

"I know I said Serafina didn't come down for dinner because she was tired, but she fainted tonight, Miss Beaton, and it's not the first time."

"Nonsense," Elspeth said. "Like myself, Serafina's health

has always been perfect. You probably wore her out." She sniggered. "Told you the potion worked."

"Enough!" he roared. "Have you or have you not been feeding my wife some of your poison?"

"Certainly not," Elspeth said indignantly. "The dear girl has no need of it, unlike *some* I know. I told you, she's more than likely exhausted and that's nobody's fault but your own."

"If she's so exhausted, then I'd like to know why she's left her bed and why I can't find her anywhere in the house."

"How am I supposed to know?" Elspeth said with a shrug. "She's free to come and go as she pleases, isn't she? What do you think, you can chain her to your bed now that you've finally managed to consummate your marriage?"

Aiden wanted to throttle her. "Never mind," he said. "Never mind. You answered my question."

"Good, then I can return to my game. I'm about to beat your father for the fourth time straight. If your wife's disappeared, that's your business, and you'd better busy yourself with finding her." She turned and marched back into the drawing room.

Aiden muttered a string of curses under his breath, then stalked back upstairs to their bedroom, concern growing by the minute. He tore off his jacket and neckcloth and went to the window, looking out into the warm, moon-washed night.

Tinkerby came in behind him. "No sign of her, my lord," he said. "I looked in Miss Elspeth's quarters just to be sure. Can't think what got into her ladyship to disappear like this. She's usually a reliable girl." He crossed his arms over his barrel chest and bent his head in thought. "Mayhaps she went out to sing one of her songs," he said after a moment. "It is Midsummer, after all."

Aiden's head shot up. "What are you talking about?" he demanded, looking over his shoulder.

"I told you, it's Midsummer," Tinkerby said, as if that explained everything. "It's one of them pagan high days or something."

"I don't see what that has to do with anything," Aiden said in frustration, then frowned as a perfectly dreadful idea seized hold. "Oh, God—*please* don't tell me she's a bloody witch like her blasted aunt." He scrubbed his hands through his hair. "Tinkerby? The truth, please, and I'd like it now."

"She's not exactly a witch, my lord," Tinkerby said, shifting his weight to his other foot, looking extremely uncomfortable. "She's just picked up a bit here and there from her aunt, but she doesn't practice magic or anything—or at least I don't think she does."

"Oh, this is bloody marvelous," he spat out, picturing his wife flapping around on a broomstick next to her aunt. "She's not *exactly* a witch? What the hell is that supposed to mean?"

"Just that she's a little paganish, if you know what I mean," Tinkerby said, rubbing one large ear. "She likes to go on about gods and goddesses, that sort of thing. And she goes out and sings to them."

"She sings to them. I see. Of course she does," he said, covering his eyes with one hand. "And where does she do this singing, exactly? Obviously not in the kitchen with the rest of us, since the only songs I've ever heard come out of her mouth have been perfectly respectable hymns."

"I've often seen her go up to that big oak tree on the other side of the river. Of course at Clwydd it was the cliffs, but you don't have any of those here, so I suppose a tree has to do."

"This is just splendid," Aiden muttered. "My wife is singing songs to a tree. All right, I'd better go and fetch her back before she catches her death."

He set off across the lawns at a quick pace and crossed the river, thinking he really had married a wood nymph after all. He ought to have realized after their absurd conversation in his study that she had some peculiar notions, but it had never crossed his mind that Elspeth had managed to stuff her brain full of nonsense so successfully.

He took the hill easily in long strides, the half-moon lighting his way, not that he needed it. The path was as familiar to him as the back of his hand, trod daily in childhood, although other than his wedding day he hadn't been up here in a long time.

He understood why Serafina had chosen this spot—it was a place for dreaming, for spinning fantasies. He knew. He'd done enough of that in his own time, although thank God he'd outgrown the habit. Serafina, apparently, hadn't. But then that came as no real surprise, given her penchant for weaving fairy tales about princes and true love.

He supposed he should be grateful that she'd managed to come around to the idea of a real-life husband, even if he couldn't make her dream come true. She certainly seemed receptive to what he could give her, given her enthusiastic response to lovemaking, and that had gratified him enormously. He couldn't remember a finer night of passion, and he wasn't about to miss another, especially if Serafina was restored enough to go flying off to practice pagan rituals by the light of the moon.

He reached the crest of the hill where the land flattened out to form a meadow. And stopped dead in his tracks, drawing in a sharp breath of wonder at the sight before him.

Serafina stood at the edge of the pond, bathed in moonlight, her long dark hair streaming down her back, the white cambric of her nightgown blowing about her slender ankles. The ancient oak framed her with its branches, a fitting backdrop for a wood nymph. She'd raised her arms above her head, the palms outstretched, her face lifted toward the starry heavens as she sang, her pure high voice soaring in a slow, haunting melody he'd never heard but which stirred his very soul with its ethereal beauty.

> "O gracious goddess, O gracious god,
> on this night of Midsummer magic
> I pray that you charge my life with
> wonder and joy. Help me in attuning with
> the energies adrift on the enchanted night air.
> I give thanks."

He watched spellbound as she began to dance, her voice still soaring in the plaintive notes, but now without words.

She moved effortlessly in circles, her bare feet skimming the grass as her lithe body gracefully undulated to the eerie music, a true queen of the fairies.

He felt as if he was caught in the spell of the sirens, listening to the Pythagorean music of the heavenly spheres, a moment outside of time in which loneliness was forever banished, where nothing existed but Serafina and himself, the heavens above and the earth below. He felt as if they had always been here in this place, as if a shower of starlight had cascaded down over them, obscuring everything else. *Time will run back and fetch the age of gold. . . .*

Aiden shook his head, passing a hand over his eyes as if he could bring himself back to his senses, but they had slipped from his grasp. It was this that was real, his other life no more than a vague shadow, nearly forgotten. Serafina and her song, they were the only reality in this unearthly place.

He walked toward her slowly as if in a dream, his feet moving of their own accord, one hand outstretched. Serafina slowed, then stilled, her song dying in her throat as she sensed his presence and turned.

She did nothing, said nothing, just gazed at him with her wide dreamy eyes, eyes that seemed to reflect the moon itself, her arms loosely held by her side. And then she smiled.

It nearly undid him, that smile, so full of mystery and promise. She might have been the goddess herself, calling to him through the ageless past as her hands stretched out toward him, inviting.

Two swans, one white, one black, floated soundlessly and unconcerned on the still surface of the pond as he skirted its edge. Serafina stood equally soundless, the silence of the night broken only by the sighing of the wind and the distant call of a nightingale. Waiting. Waiting for him.

He reached her, could hear the soft sound of her breathing. His hands moved into her hair, twining in its thick silky depths. His mouth came down on hers, tasting, seeking more as his tongue delved into its sweet warm recess.

Dewdrops, he thought through the thick haze in his head, and yet he'd never felt so clearheaded in his life. *Dewdrops and flowers*. He greedily drank more like a bee seeking sweet nectar, and she gave it to him readily, her breath coming hard and fast in her throat, her pulse fluttering rapidly under his fingertips as she answered his kiss fully, her tongue tangling with his in passionate response.

His arms moved around her, drawing her fragile body close, his hands exploring her curves, running over her finely made bones. He reveled in her heady, musky fragrance that smelled of the earth itself, his heart pounding painfully in need. He couldn't think, could barely breathe, could only revel in the feel of her soft, sweet body pressed against his, could only sweep the thin layer of cloth up over her hips, his hands seeking her bare flesh, so soft, so smooth. He cupped her buttocks and pulled her hard against his erection, wanting her to feel the intensity of his desire for her, the force of his need.

She shuddered in response, her fingers tugging at his clothes, and he impatiently pulled at his shirt, unbuttoning it with no care. Her hands slipped inside the open material, smoothing over his burning flesh, pushing the linen off his shoulders and arms, raising her face for his kiss as sweet whimpers came from her throat, driving him into a frenzy of excitement.

He took her mouth hard, driving his tongue into its warm cavity, wanting to claim every part of her for his own, his hands wandering restlessly over her back, bunching her nightdress in his fingers. Impatiently he raised his head long enough to pull the shift over her head and tossed it to one side, lowering her to the grass, coming over her with his body, pressing her back into the cool earth.

So beautiful . . . so perfect, he thought as he bent his head to one high, round breast, the nipple such a delicate pink, already erect for him. He drew it into his mouth, tasting, pulling, reveling in her little cries, in the way she twisted under him, her hips pressing against his, one leg twining over the back of his thighs, then the other.

He groaned at the contact, wanting her so badly he felt he might come apart with need. Quickly sitting up, he jerked off his boots, then stripped his trousers away, never taking his eyes from her as she lay in the grass with her arms over her head, watching him steadily with her luminescent eyes, her lips slightly parted, the rapid rise and fall of her breasts the only movement she made.

Aiden had never seen anything so breathtaking in his life. He was humbled beyond measure by her beauty, intoxicated by her primal femininity. He felt like a god coming to his goddess, a goddess who lay fertile, filled with abundance, waiting only for him to sow his seed in her. He felt like the wind, like lightning and thunder and lashing rain, all the elements unleashed in the glorious storm of passion that swirled in him.

He came back down to her, stroking her soft hair, running his mouth over her forehead, her cheeks, gently biting her chin, moving up to her generous mouth and covering it in a long, deep kiss as one hand sought and found the downy curls at the apex of her thighs. She gasped under his mouth, parting her legs to give him fuller access, and he slid his fingers between her wet silky folds, so ripe, so ready for him. She arched beneath his touch, moaned as he circled her hard little nub, cried out as he dipped his fingers into her soft woman's flesh, so mysterious, so tantalizing. She was full of dewdrops there, too, was overflowing with them.

He couldn't help himself—he had to know how she tasted. He shifted his weight, sliding down until his head was at a level with her hips, then shaped her thighs with his hands, lifting her knees and lowering his head, running his tongue over her plump lips, sliding between and stroking, teasing, until her soft cries filled the night. She tasted of sunshine and earth, of flowers and rainfall, had an effect on him like the headiest of wine.

He gritted his teeth, not knowing how much longer he could hold off. He wanted to pleasure her, but touching her like this made him mad with lust, desperate to be inside her, buried in her heat. Just as that dire thought crossed his addled brain, she tugged at his shoulders with a moan, pulled him up toward her, spreading her legs wide in invitation, her small hand taking his engorged shaft and guiding it to her entrance, her breath hot and fast on his cheek.

With a stifled sob of relief he rose over her and thrust into her searing flesh in one long smooth stroke, and she took his full length with welcome, little gasps whispered against his ear as he moved deep in her, his rhythm fast and even, spiraling them both toward a shattering climax, his muscles straining as he reached a peak of unbearable sensation.

He slid his hands under her buttocks and lifted her even closer, his head arching back, a harsh cry breaking from his throat as his ejaculation burst from him, pouring into her in scorching waves. It shattered him, tore him into a million pieces, reconfigured him into something entirely different.

He dimly heard her answering cries as her muscles contracted fiercely around him, sending him back over the edge again, until he felt as if he might well die from an excess of pleasure. He had never, *never* experienced anything so incredible in his life.

Her sharp cries finally faded into little sobs, and her hands gradually loosened their grip on his back, then fell away altogether, her breath coming in shallow pants at the base of his throat.

Aiden felt sanity return as his heartbeat slowed. He looked down at her, this extraordinary woman who was capable of shaking him out of all semblance of control, who was so damned responsive that she sent him reeling even now. Tears slid from the corners of her closed eyes, trickling down her cheeks, and he pushed himself up on one elbow in sudden concern, wondering if he'd been too hard with her.

"What, sweetheart? What makes you cry? I didn't hurt you, did I?" he whispered, kissing the salty trails.

"Anything but," she said with a shuddering breath. "Oh, Aiden . . ." She pressed her soft lips against his shoulder. "I—I can't explain."

"You don't have to explain," he said, stroking damp tendrils of hair off her face. "I was right there with you. Dear God, sweetheart, that was extraordinary." He shook his head in perplexity. "I don't know what happened. One minute I was watching you dance, and the next . . . I don't know. I honestly don't know." He fell onto his side, pulling her leg over his hip, reluctant to move out of her. "Everything seemed to disappear. I feel like a damned fool for saying so, but I swear to God I thought I'd gone into another dimension."

"It must be Midsummer magic," she said with a shaky laugh, kissing his throat. "Fairy time."

"I don't know the first thing about Midsummer magic, but I'll take your word for it. Shakespeare had the right of it, I think." He wrapped her up in his arms. "You put the fear of God into me when you disappeared like that," he said, his voice muffled against the cascade of her hair, hair that smelled faintly of lilacs. "Why did you vanish? Was it just to sing your song? It was beautiful, by the way, one of the most beautiful things I've ever heard."

She turned in his embrace and looked into his eyes. "You don't mind? I wanted to honor the god and goddess on this night, and I needed to do it out here, next to the oak tree."

"Mmm," he murmured. "I can understand that well enough. Old Jehovah always has had a certain majestic presence."

"Jehovah?" she said, running her fingers through his hair. "Is that what you call it?"

"I've always thought of it like that, I suppose because it's so old," he said, reaching for one of her hands and kissing each finger.

She smiled. "You're a great deal more fanciful than you like to have people believe."

"It's a good thing, now that I've discovered I have a pagan wife," he replied dryly. "You might have told me, sweetheart. Here I was thinking that you were forming a choir because you had a deep and abiding love for the Church."

"Music," she said absently, entwining her fingers with his. "I love music. It doesn't matter what kind, as long as it's beautiful. And I'm *not* a pagan, not really." She thought for a moment. "I just believe that there are all sorts of ways to honor deity. Church is nice, but so are the ancient rituals. They make me feel closer to heaven *and* earth. In church all they talk about is leaving earth as quickly as possible to get to heaven, which I find baffling since so much trouble went into putting us here."

Aiden chuckled. "I wasn't far off in calling you Titania, was I? You make a very respectable queen of the fairies. You certainly cast an enchantment over me."

"Do you think that's what I've done, Aiden?" she asked, her expression deadly serious. "I—that is, I don't want you to think that I cast charms and spells like Aunt Elspeth. I wouldn't ever do such a thing."

Aiden burst into laughter, finding her utterly adorable. "I don't think for a moment that you were trying to capture my image in a mirror to weave some sort of love spell over me, if that's what you're worried about. I'm sure I'd be immune, being the hardheaded man I am."

"You're certainly hardheaded," she agreed with a little smile, but her eyes held sadness. "Then again, you've lived a hard life, so it's not surprising. I understand much better now why you think the way you do."

"Oh, do you?" he said, certain that Serafina had no clue at all as to how he thought. If she had, she wouldn't be lying next to him regarding him with such supreme trust. He slipped out of her and rolled onto his back, gazing up at the starry sky. Serafina was a complete innocent with no experience in dealing with men other than himself. And he was no shining example of the male species, although a fairly typical model.

She deserved a great deal more than what he had to offer, and he couldn't help feeling like a cad in the face of her unwavering devotion. She had no real idea what kind of life he'd lived, how many women there had been, how cavalierly he'd treated them until she'd come along. And now here he was, taking advantage of her innocence, behaving like a lust-crazed fool, all because his wife had captivated him with her sea-green eyes, her sweet, unaffected nature. He wished to hell he was capable of the sort of romantic love she wanted, but he wasn't, and there was nothing he could do to change that.

If he had an honest bone in his body he would enlighten

her then and there as to just what sort of a man he really was and shatter every illusion she'd ever had all over again.

The problem was that he obviously wasn't an honest man, for he had no inclination to do so. He found that he liked having her regard him as some sort of hero, as misguided as the impression was.

"Aiden?" she asked, her voice filled with hesitant question.

"Hmm?" he replied, dragging his gaze back to her. He propped himself up on his elbow. "What is it?"

"I was just wondering what you were thinking."

"Nothing you want to know about," he replied dryly. "My inner workings don't bear close examination, especially not the kind of scrutiny you like to bring to them."

"I'm sorry—I didn't mean to scrutinize you. I only meant that you can't have found it easy growing up here without any mother at all, never mind the rest of your troubles with your father and sister. You must have had a very difficult time all on your own."

Aiden, taken off guard by her statement, sat up abruptly, a hard, uncomfortable lump forming in his throat. He wasn't accustomed to sympathy. He didn't really know what to do with such an unfamiliar sensation. Vulnerability wasn't his strong suit, and Serafina made him feel more vulnerable than he ever had, damn her anyway. He hadn't ever anticipated that she'd crawl under his skin to such a degree, make him feel so exposed, and he didn't like the feeling in the least.

He wasn't a hero, as much as he liked the notion. It was one thing to be seen as one, another to live up to the image. There was no way he could meet her impossibly high expectations, and perhaps it was best if he did shatter her illusions, now, before things went any farther.

He also wasn't accustomed to lying stark naked in the moonlight with a woman he'd just made passionate love to, talking about the innermost places in his heart. Making love to Serafina was one thing; speaking of things he'd kept buried for most of his life was another.

"Aiden? What's wrong? Did I say something I ought not to have?"

"Not at all," he said, suddenly wanting nothing more than to be alone, away from her searching questions, back in a place of privacy. He found her nightdress in the tangle of clothes around him. "Here, put this on," he said brusquely, handing it to her. "I'd better get you back to bed. You're suffering from exhaustion as it is, and exposure won't help matters. I shouldn't have kept you out here at all."

He shrugged himself into his clothes, ignoring the sudden hurt that clouded her face.

He was too busy trying to ignore his own pain.

19

$\mathcal{S}$erafina opened her eyes to the morning light, her heart heavy. She wasn't sure what had caused Aiden's abrupt emotional withdrawal, but it had left her shaken and miserable, especially after they'd shared such an incredible experience, a moment of grace that she knew with certainty had been given by the god and goddess.

Aiden had been there with her in that other place, as lost to time as she was, she was sure of it. He had given himself completely to her and just as completely taken himself away again as soon as his ardor had cooled. He walked her back to the house, saw her to bed, and disappeared downstairs again, saying only that he needed to finish his paperwork.

His arms had come around her in the small hours before dawn, holding her loosely against him, but he disappeared just as abruptly only three hours later. She kept her eyes closed, not wanting him to know she was awake, but aware of every move he made as he dressed and softly shut the door behind him, leaving her alone again.

The goddess may have been right about Serafina following her heart, but she hadn't taken Aiden's heart into consideration.

Aiden didn't even have a heart, not really, not if he could make love to her like that in one minute and coldly shut her out in the next as if she had no more use to him. The only conclusion she'd been able to draw was that now he'd taken what he'd wanted, conquered her so completely, boredom had set in. Boredom, probably tinged with disgust that his wife danced and sang half-naked in the moonlight like the pagan he thought her. Of course he'd taken advantage. Not because he loved her, but because she'd made it so convenient for him.

All the solace the goddess had given her the night before, all the joy she'd experienced in Aiden's impassioned embrace was gone as if it had never been, leaving her with a heaviness that dulled her heart and senses. *Seek the truth and know it is I who brings it . . . I offer you no knowledge you cannot endure. . . .*

She had sought the truth last night, and it had indeed been given to her. She wished she'd never asked.

It was Sunday, the day for the choir to sing at the church, but she'd lost her enthusiasm for their debut. She listlessly picked at the breakfast Janie brought on a tray, listening with half an ear to Janie's chatter, wondering where Aiden was, why he'd left their bed before she woke.

"Isn't it exciting, my lady?" Janie said, pulling a peach-colored silk walking dress over her head. "The day is finally here, after all our work."

"Yes, it is exciting," she said numbly as Janie did up the last buttons on the dress Serafina had been saving for the occasion.

"Oh, but my lady, you have no idea—my mum and my brothers and sisters are all in a flutter, waiting to hear us. Even my Uncle George is coming to church, and he hasn't attended a service in years! And Plum looks about to burst— he's wearing his finest suit of clothes."

"I think that's wonderful," Serafina replied as Janie adjusted her bonnet. "Janie . . . where's Lord Aubrey?"

"Right here," Aiden said, coming into the bedroom. "Why, Serafina, you look very nice. That's a fetching bonnet you're wearing."

She forced herself to smile. Aiden regarded her pleasantly enough, but she was no fool. The warmth, the real warmth that had shone from his eyes the last few days was gone, replaced by an expression of polite civility.

"Thank you," she said, feeling even sicker. This was love,

this horrible feeling of emptiness, of loss? This was love, this distance he'd created between them that she had no idea of how to span?

I give you no burden that you cannot bear . . . the goddess had said, clear as could be. Serafina hoped that was true, for she felt like dying.

"Serafina?" Aiden said, gesturing Janie out of the room. "You're pale. Are you still feeling ill?" he asked.

"I'm perfectly well. I must be nervous about this morning, that's all." She ducked her head and looked in the mirror, pretending to tidy her hair, desperate to avoid his gaze.

"Are you sure that's all?" he asked, casting a glance at her tray. "You've hardly eaten a thing, and you had no dinner last night. Furthermore, you fainted yesterday evening."

"Of course I'm sure," she replied, lying through her teeth for the first time in her life. "My appetite always disappears when I'm nervous, and I'm sure that nerves are what induced my silly faint in the first place."

He was only pretending concern, she told herself. Aiden Delaware was an earl to the marrow, always the correct gentleman, in bed and out. He probably behaved the same to every woman he bedded, having his roguish way and then politely seeing them out the door. His wife was a slightly more troublesome matter since he was stuck with her, but she was sure he'd find a way to deal with that problem.

Still, if nothing else, she had her pride. She wasn't going to let him know for an instant that he'd broken her heart. She would play the dutiful wife to the hilt and never trouble him again with unwelcome love, never show him that she yearned for him with every fiber of her being and probably always would. She'd never again allow herself to give into her innermost feelings.

Adam and his fantastical Cypriot kingdom could go hang, and Aiden Delaware could hang along with them. The Aiden she thought she loved was as much a figment as Adam had ever been, and she was through with both of them. She didn't care if there was a grain of truth to her memories of a life lived nearly a thousand years before on a remote Byzantine island. She had a current life to get on with, and Aiden was going to be as minimal a part of it as possible. He had to be. She didn't think she'd survive otherwise.

"Perhaps you should stay home today," Aiden said with a frown. "I don't like your pallor. A church choir is one thing, but your health is another."

"Please do not concern yourself with my health," she said, forcing lightness into her tone. "I assure you, I am merely a trifle tired."

"Tired? Ah well, I can't be surprised." He came up behind her and lightly rested his hands on her shoulders. "I did keep you out rather late and you were already exhausted."

Serafina inclined her head, wanting to scream. He'd kept her out late? That was all he had to say about what had transpired between them? "It is only my fault if I choose to indulge myself in the night air," she replied, turning and fixing him with a falsely bright smile. "We mustn't keep your father and sister waiting. I'm sure they're anxious to be on time for the service."

Aiden looked at her with puzzlement, but he dropped his hands. "As you say. The staff has already gone ahead."

"Then we must be quick to follow." She picked up her gloves and pulled them on. "Come along, Aiden. We have a job to do, and we shouldn't dawdle."

She took a neat step away from him before he could say any more and swiftly walked out of the room, wishing she could disappear altogether.

Charlotte allowed Raphael to deposit her in the pew in the first row of the Dundle church, her usual position from which to oversee services. She reluctantly removed her arms from around his neck, savoring the touch of his crisp neck-cloth, the soft curl of hair just above it, even though she knew she shouldn't. She had come to church to repent, not to think lascivious thoughts.

"Thank you," she murmured, her eyes lowered as she adjusted her skirts about her legs, legs that were becoming surprisingly strong and vital, as responsive as the rest of her body.

She smiled to herself, her secret huge inside her.

"Are you comfortable?" Raphael asked, leaning his head close to her ear. "Would you like another cushion?"

Charlotte took his hand, squeezing it softly. "You are always so kind, but no, I am as comfortable as can be expected."

"Let me just pull the stool under your feet." Charlotte could just imagine what must be going through his mind as his strong hands slid over her ankles, making sure her feet were properly placed.

He sat up again, no betrayal of amorous feeling on his handsome face, but then Raphael always held his emotions in perfect check. She shivered, aware now how it would feel to have his fingers slide higher, reach up under her skirts, touch her in the way she knew he'd always longed to do.

She shot him another sidelong glance. The day would come soon enough when she felt his hands there, his face twisted up in longing the way Frederick's did when he fondled her most private place. Just as he had again early this morning, bringing her to another peak of ecstasy, unable to resist her. She was so ashamed to be thinking about their encounter at all, but she couldn't help herself.

She wanted to squirm, remembering how Frederick had come into her room, his face frozen, but his eyes hungry with desire as he'd started to rub her, trying to pretend that nothing had passed between them.

She had gone along at first with the pretense, but before long she hadn't been able to resist opening her legs again, inviting him to dip his fingers between her quivering lower lips. And it had taken even less time to persuade him out of his livery, to show her his naked body, his huge organ ready again to tease her, its distended purple head stroking and sliding helplessly against her wet, aching opening, gaining no entrance, for she would be a virgin when Raphael married her.

She briefly came out of her trance as the vicar started to read the first lesson from John. It was one she could have recited from memory herself. She often thought that if she'd been born a man, she would have made an excellent minister. But then, if she'd been born a man, she would have been in line for the marquessate instead of her brother.

... *That which was from the beginning, which we have heard, which we have seen with our eyes, which we have looked at and our hands have touched* ...

Our hands have touched. The words caused her to slip back into wicked memory, powerless to resist the dark thoughts, even with the knowledge that such things were sinful to contemplate in church, to contemplate at all, let alone act upon.

But oh, what excitement, what power she felt when Frederick panted and groaned and begged to be let into her sacred recesses. She'd had no choice but to let him take her with his mouth instead, using his tongue instead of his engorged shaft to penetrate her, poor boy. She could hardly deny him that pleasure when she'd denied him everything else, and he'd stabbed at her hungrily like a dog slathering at a meaty bone.

And his helpless groans as he ejaculated between her breasts had only made her feel more powerful. ...

A little moan slipped from her lips unbidden, and Raphael glanced over at her with a frown of concern, then took her hand in his. "All right?" he whispered.

She nodded, her eyes lowered, and let him keep her hand, knowing exactly where she'd like it to wander. Her gaze flickered to his groin. She couldn't help flushing, thinking of their wedding night, of how he would look when he came to her bed, revealed in all his male glory. She knew how powerfully he would possess her, so masterful, nothing like pathetic Frederick, a lowly footman.

No, she'd be taken by a duke or not at all. ...

Her head shot up as her brother, her father, and Serafina suddenly rose and left the pew, followed by the staff of Townsend, who filed up the nave from their position in the back of the church. They gathered to one side of the altar, and Charlotte stared at them, unable to imagine what they thought they were doing by breaking the ordered routine of the service.

And then to Charlotte's disbelief they opened their

mouths and started to sing, the two-part harmony soaring through the church.

"Teach me, my God and King, in all things thee to see;
And what I do in anything, to do as for thee.
All may of thee partake; nothing can be so mean,
Which with this tincture for thy sake,
Will not grow bright and clean.
A servant with this clause, makes drudgery divine,
Who sweeps a room, as for thy laws,
makes that and the action fine.
This is the famous stone that turneth all to gold;
For that which God doth touch and own
Cannot for less be told."

A horrified gasp finally slipped from Charlotte's paralyzed throat as they brought the hymn to a close. She turned abruptly to Raphael, expecting to find him looking as distraught as she felt. But instead he smiled down at her, his eyes alight with pleasure.

"A fine surprise, is it not?" he said, squeezing her hand. "They're very talented."

Her mouth worked, but nothing came out. She couldn't believe they had all gone behind her back like this, disturbed the sanctity of the service with song. And a mocking song at that, the servants singing about their place in the world as if they thought themselves equal to their betters—and her family, her own family encouraging them in this sacrilege, standing up with them in this mutiny against her.

Her face burned with mortification, but she forced herself to return Raphael's smile, her frozen lips trembling with the effort. "Very—very nice," she stammered in an undertone, trying to maintain her composure, for the last thing she wanted Raphael to see was the fury that raged in her breast. He couldn't possibly have realized that they all conspired against her authority, or he would have immediately put a stop to the travesty.

"They've practiced for over a week now," he murmured as they burst into another song, the vicar beaming at them and then at Charlotte from his place behind the pulpit. Her idiotic father couldn't be expected to understand what a fool he appeared, but Aiden—Aiden, the future marquess, should have known better. It only went to show how thoroughly his wife had taken him in, for the old Aiden would have been sensitive to his sister's delicate feelings and never stood for such a mockery, let alone participated in it.

Charlotte had never felt so betrayed in all her life. She wanted to scream with fury. Serafina was behind this—she'd been biding her time, waiting to find a way to humiliate her sister-in-law, pretending affection, all the while plotting to usurp Charlotte's authority in the face of the entire congregation where Charlotte could do nothing, say nothing, without appearing uncharitable.

Oh, Serafina may indeed have thought she'd found the perfect knife to bury in Charlotte's breast. But Charlotte would do her one better. Charlotte would marry a duke, rule over a household far grander than any Serafina could ever aspire to. Serafina and the servants she was no better than could rot in hell for all Charlotte cared.

She couldn't wait to see the expression on Serafina's face when Serafina realized that her oils had worked far better than she could ever have anticipated, that they had unlocked the door to Charlotte's future greatness.

She would have power. She would have control. She would be a duchess ruling over one of the finest estates in Great Britain, and all Serafina would have was a second-rate estate, a doddering father-in-law whom no one respected, and a husband who was no better than a lap dog. Society would laugh in Serafina's face. Charlotte would see to that, make sure that the true story of Serafina's sham marriage came out, once Charlotte had secured her own future.

Two more days and she would be in London, ready to put the final stage of her plan into effect. And then they'd all be sorry for the way they'd treated her.

But she wasn't about to tip her hand yet. She had too much at stake to risk having Raphael guess at her true feelings.

She covered Raphael's warm hand with her gloved fingers. "Isn't it marvelous?" she said enthusiastically. "We have our very own church choir at last. God has indeed been gracious in bringing Serafina to us, for I am sure it was she who so thoughtfully arranged this?"

"She did indeed," Raphael said, squeezing her fingers in loving approval, and she was at least pleased with that, even if he did smile a little too broadly when Serafina's name came up.

Charlotte became acutely aware of a pair of eyes boring into her, and she quickly turned her head, only to find that detestable biddy Elspeth gazing at her from her seat farther down the pew, a self-satisfied smile playing around the corners of her little pursed mouth.

Charlotte jerked her gaze away abruptly, a chill running down her spine as if someone had just walked over her grave. She'd always despised Elspeth Beaton, finding her an unnerving woman with a gaze that was far too keen, as if she could look beneath one's skin and see all one's darkest secrets. But Charlotte knew that was ridiculous. Elspeth was probably just shortsighted.

Charlotte would see that she got her just desserts too.

Oh, yes, one way or another Charlotte would see they all burned in hell.

London was by far the biggest city Serafina had ever seen, and the sights and sounds overwhelmed her. But Raphael's townhouse overwhelmed her most of all. She hesitantly alighted from the carriage, craning her neck up.

The white granite structure graced nearly one half of Hanover Square and Serafina felt not only dwarfed by it, but thoroughly inadequate to handle what lay inside. She didn't have the first idea of what to say to Raphael's mother, who would surely find her lacking in every regard other than her clothing, no matter what Raphael had said about her kind intentions.

She glanced nervously over at Aiden, but he seemed oblivious to her fear, attending instead to his sister. That didn't surprise her. The distance between them had only increased in the last two days, Aiden continuing to be polite and considerate toward her, but providing precious little else in the way of communication.

He had banished her as effectively as if he'd slammed a door in her face, leaving her alone and outcast on the other side. Despite her determination not to let his coolness trouble her, she couldn't help feeling deeply hurt. For whatever she tried to tell herself to the contrary, she loved him from the depths of her soul, and that wasn't something she could unmake.

He slept in their bed, but barely touched her except inadvertently in his sleep. He came to the table for dinner, but only offered a word or two, his thoughts obviously elsewhere. Even on the long ride to London, he'd been preoccupied, letting his father and Charlotte carry the conversation. Since Lord Delaware hadn't had much to say, that left Charlotte to hold Bible class, which only grated on Serafina's already raw nerves.

"Shall we go in, my dear?" Lord Delaware said, tucking her hand into the crook of his arm. "You've been staring at Raphael's house as if it were going to jump out and bite you. A bit jittery, are you?"

Serafina shook herself out of her troubled thoughts. "I do feel a little daunted," she admitted. "This is all very new."

"And sudden too," he said with a reassuring squeeze of her fingers. "You haven't had much time to adjust to the idea of your presentation to society. But you'll do well, my dear, I'm sure of it. Heavens, if you could bring so much sunshine to Townsend in such short order, just think what you can do to the stuffy people of London."

"That's what worries me," she said with a crooked smile. "I'm not very good with stuffiness. I think your friends are going to find me the veriest greenhorn."

"Nonsense," he said, guiding her up the steps, "and they're not my friends in any case. I haven't had any of those since my dear Isabel died, and it's no one's fault but my own. So let us both look at this town excursion as a new beginning. I reckon my knees are shaking every bit as much as yours."

Serafina couldn't help laughing. Lord Delaware was an

endearing man, and his kind words reassured her. She drew herself up and lifted her chin, determined not to be cowed. After all, she'd managed well enough in Raphael's grandiose country house.

As soon as Charlotte was comfortably settled in her chair, the butler led them through the cavernous entrance way into an ornate drawing room, paneled throughout in oak, decorated in fine tapestry chairs and marquetry furniture.

"Your grace, your guests have arrived," the man intoned to Raphael, who was engaged in writing something at a spectacular French ormolu desk.

He immediately rose and came forward, wearing a smile of warm welcome that immediately reassured Serafina. "Excellent," he said, pressing a kiss on Charlotte's hand. "Charlotte, you are looking even prettier than the last time I saw you and that was what, only three days ago?"

Charlotte smiled softly up at him. "Thank you, Raphael. I am in excellent spirits, even lighter now that I am here with you."

"Well, I'm glad I lighten someone's spirits—I generally feel as if I have the opposite effect on people. But that's what comes with being a duke. All that pomp and circumstance is so depressing."

"Nonsense," Charlotte said. "You are an example to the people."

"I certainly hope not," Raphael retorted. "Hello, Serafina." He lifted her hand and dropped a light kiss on its back. "Buck up, there's a good girl," he murmured in a low voice. "You haven't entered the lion's den." He straightened. "My mother's been anxiously waiting to meet you," he said in a normal tone. "I don't think she's been so excited in years."

Serafina was sure that was true—the duchess had probably been at the smelling salts if not the brandy in an agony of anticipation over what she'd let herself in for. "Is the duchess here?" she asked in a small voice. Despite how happy she was to see Raphael's familiar smiling face her legs felt like jelly.

"She'll be down momentarily." He turned to Aiden and clapped him on the back. "Well met, cousin. You made good time. I've ordered tea for the ladies, but I thought you and your father might be in need of stronger fortification."

"I'll join the ladies with tea," Lord Delaware said to Serafina's infinite relief, for it appeared as if he really was determined to stay sober despite his nerves. "But I'm sure Aiden would be happy for some of your fine sherry."

"Thank you," Aiden said, shooting Serafina an odd, searching look she couldn't decipher.

She chose to ignore him and moved over to Charlotte, seeking to distract herself. "This is a beautiful house, is it not?" she remarked, for lack of anything better to say.

"This house is representative of a remarkable piece of history, my dear Serafina," Charlotte said in a superior tone that only added to Serafina's discomforture. "Although I have not visited it since the time I was a small child, I can tell you that it contains some of the finest treasures to be found in England. For example . . ." Charlotte proceeded to reel off a long list of antiquities and paintings, her second favorite subject next to God.

Serafina listened patiently, tuning out most of Charlotte's drone. She was far more interested in observing Aiden and Raphael, for other than their encounter in the meadow after her fall, this was the first opportunity since her marriage that she'd had to watch them together.

They appeared at complete ease in each other's company. All the stories Raphael had recounted to her about his friendship with Aiden came flooding back and she could see how close they really were. She couldn't help the twinge of guilt that tugged at her. She knew so much more about Aiden than he realized.

He had no idea that she and Raphael had also become friends, good friends, that he had been a constant topic of conversation during those three weeks Raphael had patiently tutored her. He had no way of knowing how far Raphael had brought her along on the path to accepting her marriage, how much he had prepared the ground for her being able to fall in love with her husband.

For all Aiden knew, she and Raphael were little more than strangers. And that thought made her uneasy for the first time, for despite her recent alienation from Aiden, the last thing she ever wanted was for him to feel betrayed, to think they'd deliberately withheld a secret from him.

Something dark and frightening tugged at the back of her mind, a hazy thought she couldn't grasp hold of, but she shivered with a sense of foreboding.

Time will run back. . . .

Serafina passed a hand over her face, forcibly jerking her attention back to Charlotte, but her skin felt clammy, a cold sweat covering her from head to toe, leaving her weak and shaken. And she had no idea why.

Aiden kept a discreet but watchful eye on Serafina as he conversed with his father and cousin. He was fully aware of how apprehensive Serafina had been about this trip, so apprehensive that she'd been pale and withdrawn, had hardly spoken a word in the last two days. Not that he'd been feeling particularly talkative himself. He honestly hadn't known how to behave toward her after what had passed between them the other night.

He still reeled from the shock of having his soul stripped naked and he had no intention of repeating the experience, no matter how fond he might be of Serafina. There were some things that didn't bear exposure to the light of day, and his heart was one of them.

The trouble was that Serafina had an uncanny ability to go marching all over his inner recesses with no effort at all, and he was powerless to resist her, a highly dangerous state of affairs.

He'd deliberately avoided any further physical contact with her that night, terrified that making love to her again would send him back to that other place where he lost all sense of order, even identity, his defensive shield torn away, leaving him exposed and shaken.

And he hadn't made love to her since, mainly because he'd been concerned about her health. She'd been looking so pale and he certainly didn't want to induce another faint. But he didn't know how much longer he could stay away. Serafina was more irresistible than ever.

"Well, here you all are," the duchess said, coming swiftly into the room with a rustle of silk, a warm smile of welcome on her beautiful face, so like her son's. "Delaware, I'm so glad you decided to accept my invitation—and Aiden, dearest, how nice to see you after all this time!"

"It's good to be home," he said, meaning it. "You haven't aged a day since I last saw you."

"Flatterer. And Charlotte—what a wonderful treat. You look exceeding well, my dear," she said, bending down and kissing Charlotte's cheek.

"Thank you, Duchess," Charlotte said, accepting the kiss with a light flush on her cheeks. "You are so kind to have us."

"Nonsense, child. It is about time that you paid me a visit." She turned and held her hands out to Serafina. "And you, of course, are Aiden's new wife. This is a happy occasion indeed."

"How—how do you do, your grace," Serafina stammered, dropping a wobbly curtsy, panic written all over her face. Aiden wished there was something he could do to reassure her, but she was on her own now, as she would be for much of the week.

"My dear child, what a pretty thing you are," the dowager duchess said, catching Serafina's hands up and regarding her with pleasure. "Raphael had told me so, of course, but I'm delighted to see for myself at last. You're a true beauty, just like your mother."

So, Aiden thought. Rafe had been going on about Serafina's beauty, had he? He couldn't say he liked the idea. Actually, he didn't like it at all.

But Serafina was oblivious of the black direction of his thoughts. "You knew my mother?" she asked with real pleasure.

"I did indeed, and although I didn't know her very well, I remember her most affectionately. We were all saddened by her untimely death."

Aiden had always been exceedingly fond of the duchess, but he liked her more than ever for making an effort to put Serafina at ease. He couldn't help feeling a stab of guilt that he'd never even bothered to ask about Serafina's mother.

He realized that there were a great many things he hadn't asked Serafina about her life, taking her years with Elspeth for granted, as if there had been nothing before them, even though he was aware that her father had died when she was only nine.

It occurred to him that maybe he hadn't wanted to know about her early life, that because he had never cared to look back on his own childhood, he had ignored Serafina's. And yet she had suffered too, losing a mother and then her father only a few years later. He felt ashamed of himself for assuming he was the only one who had experienced a crushing loss, and he hadn't even known his mother, who had died only minutes after he'd drawn his first breath. His loss seemed insignificant in the face of the grief Serafina must have experienced.

"Thank you," Serafina said. "It's very kind of you to say so."

"Not at all," the duchess replied. "It's the absolute truth. You must have been very young when your mother died, so perhaps you don't remember her well."

"I was five," Serafina said, smiling shyly. "But I do remember her. She used to sing me to sleep. She had a beautiful voice."

"She did, my dear, I remember that now! She used to sing at the pianoforte after dinner. A voice like an angel, everyone said."

"And Serafina has inherited it," Aiden said, thinking back to the night he'd heard her sing up in the meadow, the unearthly beauty of her voice, rising to the heavens and taking his heart with it. He pushed the image away, for it brought back far too many disturbing memories.

"Serafina formed a choir for the Dundle church as it happens. You must come and hear us the next time you're at Southwell."

"A choir? What a marvelous idea—I've always found the Dundle services dull, and some music will improve them greatly. Aiden, you have brought Townsend a fine bride."

"I'm delighted that you approve," he said, ridiculously pleased.

"Naturally I approve, dear boy. Now, if I could only find someone as charming and clever for my eldest son, I'd be the happiest of women."

"I thank you for your concern, Mama, but I think I'll choose my own wife," Raphael said dryly.

"Then I wish you'd get on with it, darling, for I'm out of patience," the duchess replied just as dryly, fixing Raphael with a stern eye. "You should take a page from your cousin's book, for I'll be long in my grave at the rate you're going about the matter."

Aiden grinned. This was a conversation that had been going on for years and wouldn't end until the day that Raphael found himself at the altar, not a day Aiden anticipated any time in the near future. Raphael was as dead set against marriage as Aiden had always been and was determined to avoid its clutches for as long as possible. He doubted the duchess would have satisfaction for a good long time to come.

"I feel sure Raphael will marry as soon as he finds the right woman," Charlotte said quietly, her gaze cast down at her hands. "It takes time to find a woman properly suited to be a duchess. There is breeding to be considered, the correct upbringing, and of course Raphael will need a wife with a level head who knows how to manage his households."

Aiden's heart broke for his sister, who'd been so cruelly cheated by fate. She would have made some man a fine wife and yet she never complained, always thinking first of the happiness of the people she loved.

Her presence here today was the perfect example of her devotion, for he knew how difficult she found facing the outside world in her condition. And yet she was willing to do so because he'd asked, just as she'd gone out of her way to befriend Serafina for the same reason. And now here she was, selflessly promoting Rafe's marriage, even though Aiden suspected she would have a hard time seeing her dear friend take a wife and fill his house with children she could never have.

"I'm sure Rafe will get around to doing his duty eventually," he said tactfully. "But being Rafe, I suspect he'll tell us nothing until the very last moment, so I suggest we change the topic of conversation."

"I couldn't agree more—let's leave the dreary subject of my marriage alone," Raphael said firmly. "In any case, we have more important business to get on with. Why don't you tell everyone what you've planned for the week?" He led his mother to a chair and planted her in it.

Successfully distracted, the duchess began to outline the round of activities she'd organized. "I thought it was best to start by paying calls, for in that manner I can introduce Serafina and Charlotte with a minimum of fuss and speculation. The week will culminate with the ball I've organized here to formally present Aiden's sister and wife. Word is already racing about town and naturally the invitations are coveted, so we will have a large turnout, but before the ball we will attend Lady Dudley's rout, Sir George and Lady Hopley's musical evening . . ."

Aiden listened to the tediously long list with one ear, but he couldn't help watching Serafina out of the corner of his eye.

She sat on the sofa, her hands in her lap, her expression faraway. But instead of the faraway appearance she usually assumed when she was daydreaming, her eyes looked clouded, troubled, and he could only imagine that she was still in a state of dread over the coming week.

Something tugged painfully at his heart, and he had to stifle a strong impulse to go to her and take her in his arms, kiss away her fears, tell her she would enchant society exactly as she'd enchanted him.

He glanced over at Raphael, only to find that his cousin

wasn't listening either—instead, he too watched Serafina, a slight frown creasing his forehead. But it wasn't a frown of disapproval. Aiden knew all of his cousin's facial expressions, as subtle as they were. There was concern on his face, and what Aiden might almost misconstrue as real affection in his eyes.

He shook himself out of that thought, since he knew perfectly well that Rafe and Serafina were only barely acquainted. And yet . . . and yet there had been his behavior after her fall, his real alarm for Serafina that Aiden had attributed to the same reason for his own terrified reaction—a long-ago accident that had ended in disaster.

But that same sense of unease pricked at him now as it had then, that there was more to their relationship than either had told him about, and he didn't like the idea that they were keeping something from him. He didn't like it at all, any more than he liked the idea that Rafe admired Serafina's beauty.

Aiden's mouth tightened into a hard line, a dark suspicion forming in the back of his mind, too ridiculous to entertain, and yet it wouldn't go away.

Don't, Raphael, she'd said. When he, Aiden, had been kissing her. Her confusion immediately afterward. The look on Rafe's face now. Serafina's recent unhappiness. Her sudden change of heart to allow him to make love to her. And it had been surprisingly easy to take her virginity after all her protestations about fearing the act. Then there had been her fainting spell the next day.

He passed a hand over his face. It wasn't possible. It just wasn't possible. He refused to entertain the notion that the two of them had betrayed him during the time that he'd been away. Rafe would never do such a thing. Nor would Serafina, sweet, open, honest Serafina. Serafina who said that vows meant more to her than anything.

And yet there was her recent distance toward him, her dread of their London stay in Raphael's house, a dread she'd never actually voiced but which was as clear as day to him.

He squeezed his eyes shut, remembering what Plum

had said about Serafina disappearing every afternoon on her horse, a horse Rafe had given to her. And Serafina's evasiveness when he'd asked her about how she'd spent that time.

Had Serafina given herself to her husband only to be sure he wouldn't question the paternity of a child she produced in eight or nine months' time? Maybe the fall she'd taken hadn't been an accident after all, but a deliberate attempt to rid herself of a child fathered by her lover. No. He wouldn't believe it. Not of his wife. Not of his closest friend on earth.

Aiden's hands clenched into fists at his sides. Coincidence. That was all it was. That was what it *had* to be.

But he resolved to keep a very close eye on them both.

20

Serafina clenched her teeth against a renewed attack of nerves as Janie dressed her for the ball. She might have found going about in society a marginally less grueling experience than she'd originally anticipated, but tonight was another matter entirely.

Janie adjusted the slip of pale green satin, then arranged the white lace robe over it, lovingly fingering the edging of pearls and bouquets of silk wildflowers. "Oh, my lady," she breathed, standing back and gazing at Serafina in admiration. "You look like a princess, you do."

"I don't know about that," Serafina said, as Janie fetched the wreath of roses and placed it on her coiled hair. "I'm sure princesses look a great deal more poised. I honestly haven't minded the social calls and I actually enjoyed the musical evening, but I feel like a lamb going to the slaughter tonight. Oh, Janie, what happens if I make a complete fool of myself in front of four hundred people?"

"I don't know why you'd think that," Janie replied. "You just wait till his lordship sees you. He probably won't leave your side all evening, he'll be so besotted."

Serafina very much doubted that optimistic statement. She was sure that Aiden would be too busy with their guests to give her much thought. Maybe that was just as well, for it was important that she continue giving the impression of being gay and carefree, happy in her marriage, and it was a hard facade to keep up when she was in Aiden's presence, misery constantly gnawing at her. The distance between them had only increased, the air fraught with tension whenever they were alone.

Oh, Aiden was attentive enough in public, but he kept well away from her in private, even going so far as to sleep in the bedroom next door, his excuse being that she needed her sleep owing to the late nights and constant activities.

But she knew the truth of the matter. And so did Aiden, as much as he pretended that there was nothing amiss between them. He was in his world now and had no more use for her. Aiden, who was always surrounded by women—old women, young women, beautiful women, sophisticated women, all competing for one of his dazzling smiles, a few minutes of conversation.

Aiden took the attention in his stride as if he hardly noticed. He made introductions, squired Serafina around by the arm, behaving like the perfect husband, making small talk to her. All a sham, a horrible sham. They never laughed together anymore. Aiden never once cast her that intimate glance of amusement that she so loved, as if they shared a private joke.

Instead he watched her constantly, his gaze cool and assessing, as if he expected her to trip up at any moment and embarrass him. She tried to pretend she didn't notice, but she could hardly help feeling his eyes on her back as she moved about a room. Once those eyes had been kind. Once they had held affection. Even passion. And now they held nothing at all.

She'd had two days of true happiness with him. Two days that would have to do for the rest of her life. He had brought her joy. And he had taken it away again.

Serafina sank onto the chair in front of the dressing table, resting her cheek on her fist. She was constantly surrounded by people all the time, but she'd never felt so alone.

A light tap came at the door and Janie opened it, slipping out as Aiden came in, a square box in his hand.

Serafina's head shot up and she stood, grasping the edge of the table for support. "Aiden . . . what are you doing here?" He looked unbearably handsome in his black silk coat, black knee breeches and white stockings, the brilliant blue of his eyes made only more startling by the absence of color in his dress. She had an irrational hope that he would take her in his arms, hold her close and reassure her, tell her he did still care about her, if only a little.

But instead he stopped in the middle of the room. "You look—you look particularly beautiful this evening," he said, clearing his throat.

She glanced away. "Thank you," she murmured, wishing he wouldn't bother to prevaricate. She knew exactly what he thought of her. "I imagine it must be the ball dress. But then you chose it, so I can't be surprised you're pleased."

He didn't reply to that. "I have something for you. These belonged to my mother," he said, his tone cool. "I managed to buy them back from the jeweler my father had sold them to. I wanted to thank you for everything you've done this week for my family. It can't have been an easy time for you, but you held your own."

"I tried my best," she said through the tightness in her throat. Didn't he know she would do anything for him, anything at all, even now? "It is my family too."

"Yes, of course," he said. "Well, I think that all in all the week has been a big success. My father has been on perfect behavior, and he's gone a long way toward changing people's minds about him. But I'm most pleased about Charlotte, for she is a different woman altogether, full of animation and conversation and confidence." He actually smiled.

"Yes," Serafina said, knowing the smile wasn't meant for her. "Your sister has blossomed under the attention she's received. Everyone has been most generous to her, and I think tonight will be her crowning moment, or so she's said to me. You owe a great debt to Raphael and his mother for offering their hospitality and support."

Aiden's face froze. "I'm sure I do. You and Rafe certainly seem to have become fast friends."

"I like your cousin. He is kind." *Unlike you*, she thought bleakly. "And he is amusing."

"Amusing?" Aiden said, raising an eyebrow. "I don't know how many people would describe Raphael as amusing. Most would say that he strikes the fear of God into them. But then you and he are on another footing altogether from everything I've observed. Positively cozy, I'd say."

Serafina blushed hotly, feeling ashamed all over again for having kept the truth from Aiden. But now was not the time to begin explaining. He already looked angry, and he'd probably only become even angrier if he knew her secret. Maybe she'd wait until they returned to Townsend and tell him about her lessons with Raphael then.

"I see that you don't wish to discuss this particular topic," he said, his eyes flashing not fire, but blue ice, and a chill of alarm ran down her spine.

"I—I think we're expected downstairs," she stammered, wondering if he already knew, if that was why he was regarding her so frostily.

"Very well, Serafina. But rest assured that I will take the matter up with you when we return to Townsend. You are rather transparent, my dear, no matter how clever you think you've been in keeping the truth from me."

He tossed the box on the dressing table. "Here. You might as well wear these, since we're keeping up pretenses so nicely." He turned on his heel and strode across the room, jerking the door open.

"Aiden, wait—" But she was too late. The door slammed behind him. She reached for the velvet-covered box with shaking fingers and opened it. Inside lay a stunningly beautiful diamond and emerald necklace, matching earrings, and a square-cut emerald ring.

"Oh, Aiden," she whispered on a shuddering breath, wishing he'd given them to her in kindness instead of as an empty, contemptuous gesture. But that was her fault too, for it was clear now that Aiden knew everything, and he was furious.

Serafina put her head on her arms and cried as if her heart really might break.

Aiden kept one eye on Serafina as she dealt with the endless stream of introductions as people came swarming through the door. She kept a smile pinned on her face, murmuring all the right things, and he could find nothing to fault her for. Other than her treachery with Raphael, which she'd as good as admitted.

And for that he wanted to murder them both.

He was jolted out of his thoughts by the next set of names being announced.

"Lord Segrave, Mrs. Robert Segrave . . ."

Aiden glanced down the receiving line, only to see the unwelcome person of Alice Segrave bearing down on them, followed by Edmund, who had the narrow face of a weasel and the same beady eyes. He stood behind his mother and regarded Serafina as if he'd come across something that smelled foul.

Aiden wanted to punch him.

"Why, dearest Serafina," Alice cooed in saccharine tones, taking her hand. "What an age it has been. I simply must felicitate you on your marriage. What a lucky man Aubrey is, to be sure." She fixed Serafina with a glacial smile, her eyes like twin daggers. "Luckier than my Edmund, who was the rightful heir to that fortune," she spit out in a swift, vicious undertone, obviously meant for Serafina's ears alone. "I hope you both choke on it, you hideous girl."

Serafina's mouth dropped open and shut again and she took a tiny step backward.

"Ah, Segrave and his charming mother, I see, always with something pleasant to say," Aiden snapped in cold fury. No one would speak to his wife in such a manner, most certainly not those two, who had already done enough damage to her. "Would you like me to have them removed, my dear? I'm sure the duchess didn't realize she'd mistakenly included vermin on the guest list."

Edmund and his mother both turned bright red. "I—I beg your p-pardon?" Edmund spluttered. "How dare you, sir!"

"Oh, easily. I don't take kindly to lies, slander, or defamation of character, an area in which you both seem to have considerable expertise. Nor will I stand by and listen to my wife insulted. Serafina?"

She shook her head. "There's no point in making a scene,"

she said in a strangled voice as heads began to turn. "Let them pass."

"Very well," Aiden said. "I bow to my wife's generosity. But be warned, both of you. Keep out of her way and out of mine, for I do not have such a generous nature as my wife, nor do I have an aversion toward creating a scene if the situation calls for one."

Alice Segrave shot Serafina one last hateful look and swept away, her son following like a dog at her heel.

"Thank you," Serafina said softly, her eyes filling with tears. "I never thought to see them again. How did you know?"

"Oh, I heard the first load of venom directly from Edmund's mouth some time back before we were married. Tinkerby filled me in on the rest of their story, or what he knew of it. I'm sorry, Serafina, I had no idea they were on the guest list—I imagine the duchess thought she was doing the correct thing by inviting your relatives."

"It doesn't matter," she said, looking down at the floor.

"It does matter, but it's better not to dwell on their presence," he replied. "It's time to open the dancing, and as Rafe is the host and the ball is in honor of you, you're going to have to lead off with him. I doubt that will be a hardship, though," he added, the thought of Raphael touching his wife in any fashion infuriating him.

She caught her lip between her teeth. "Aiden—"

"Later," he snapped. "I haven't the patience now. Get on with it, Serafina, and it will behoove you to remember that not only are the eyes of society on you, but mine are as well."

Serafina lowered her gaze. "I will not let you down," she mumbled.

Aiden snorted. "It's a little late for that, isn't it?"

All the color drained from her face and she stared up at him. She looked as if he'd just struck her. And in a way he had.

"As you say, my lord," she murmured. "But you cannot lay all the blame entirely on me, can you?"

Aiden just shook his head. "You do have an interesting

way of looking at things," he said, a bite in his words. He offered her his arm. "Allow your husband to lead you into the ballroom. At least it's one service I can offer you that you're not likely to refuse."

She had no choice but to rest her hand in the crook of his elbow and walk by his side through the throng of guests who parted to let them pass. Raphael stood next to Charlotte on the edge of the dance floor, and Aiden strode directly to him.

"My wife," he said curtly, handing Serafina over to Raphael. He abruptly turned on his heel and walked away, wanting nothing more to do with either of them.

Serafina wanted to drop through the floor, she was so humiliated and upset by Aiden's behavior. How could he be kind and protective of her one minute, saving her from the Segraves, and turn back into an icicle the next?

"Oh, dear." Raphael glanced down at her, then looked after Aiden with a frown. "Did the two of you have a spat? Aiden appears a little unstrung."

Serafina drew him to one side. "Raphael—we need to talk privately."

"This does sound serious. Well, we can't talk now—the quadrille's about to start. Why don't you meet me later outside in the garden when we both have a moment? I'll try to catch your eye."

Serafina nodded in relief. Raphael would know how to put things right. He always did.

She danced the quadrille with Raphael, relieved she remembered the steps he'd taught her. Next she waltzed with Aiden, but she took no pleasure in her very first dance with him, for he spoke not a word to her, his hand clamped on her back like a vise as he moved her in quick abrupt circles. She could feel the anger emanating from him and his controlled violence frightened her.

He bowed and released her at the end of the dance as if she were a perfect stranger and Serafina wanted to die in mortification, for she knew what people must be thinking.

She danced a polka and another two waltzes and the quadrille again with gentlemen whose names she barely remembered, all the while keeping an eye out for Raphael's signal, but hardly missing all the charming women that Aiden found to dance with.

And finally, when she was nearly ready to drop from exhaustion, Raphael quietly disappeared through one of the side doors onto the terrace with an almost indiscernible nod of his head in her direction, and Serafina followed as soon as she could disengage herself.

Charlotte saw Raphael slip out alone onto the terrace, and chose that moment to make her move. She'd been waiting in an agony of anticipation for the last three hours. Tonight was her big night, the biggest of her life, and she'd planned it so carefully. She would find a private moment, a magic moment, and she couldn't have asked for a more perfect one.

She positioned herself near the door, then wheeled her chair outside when no one was watching. But to her disappointment, Raphael was nowhere to be seen. She wheeled herself over to the balcony and looked down.

He was there, for she saw his silhouette below, standing quietly in the shadows.

Her heart pounding with excitement, she decided the best approach was to call his name. He would naturally come up one side of the double stairs in response, and when he did, she would stand and walk into his arms.

She was just about to open her mouth when his voice floated up to her through the dark and for one bewildered moment she thought he was speaking to her. But she immediately realized her mistake. Now that her eyes had adjusted she could make out the figure of someone else who had joined him. A woman. She wanted to scream with frustration.

"All right, what is all this about?" he said. "You and Aiden are glaring at each other like cats and dogs, and this isn't the first time."

With a jolt of alarm, Charlotte realized he addressed Serafina.

"Oh, Rafe," Serafina said, using his familiar name. "It's

awful! I think that Aiden's somehow discovered about the three weeks I spent with you, and he's very, very angry. You didn't say anything, did you?"

"Me? Good God, no—I swore to you I wouldn't. What makes you think he knows anything?"

Charlotte's hands gripped the arms of her chair as a cold sweat broke out over her body.

"It's just something he said about our being good friends," Serafina said. "And—and I can't explain why, but he knows, I'm sure of it, and I think he feels we've kept a secret from him. He says I let him down." She covered her face with her hands. "I don't know what to do."

"Serafina . . . you might be making more of this than is necessary. I'll speak to Aiden if you like, but—"

"No. No, don't say anything to him. He's upset enough as it is and I don't want him to be angry with you as well, especially when it was all my idea."

"Not entirely," he said, rubbing the bridge of his nose. "If you remember correctly, I approached you first."

Charlotte thought she might be sick. She pressed her hands so hard against her mouth that she tasted blood. It was all she could do not to cry out. *No, Raphael!* she screamed silently. *Not you. You would never do such a thing, never. You are chaste, a Christian man who loves me. Not her, me!*

"Yes, yes, that's true," Serafina said, dabbing at her eyes with her handkerchief. "But that shouldn't matter. I'm the one who betrayed him."

To Charlotte's horror, Raphael straightened and took Serafina in his arms. "Shh," he said against her hair. "I think betrayal is too strong a word. You only wanted to learn how to be a good wife."

"I did," she said with a hiccup. "I really and truly did."

"Then that's what is important. It will all blow over soon enough, you'll see. Aiden's temper never lasts for long." He released her. "I have to admit I felt guilty as hell about going behind Aiden's back, but Aiden will come around to understanding, I'm sure of it. The way I look at it, I did him a favor."

Charlotte's eyes bulged. A favor? Raphael had cuckolded her brother and he thought he'd done him a *favor*? It was the most disgusting thing she'd ever heard, but she should have expected no less from Serafina. Raphael was another matter entirely. How could he be so dissolute as to give Aiden's wife lessons in lovemaking? Oh, it was beyond conscience.

"You did do him a favor. Until recently he was pleased enough with everything you taught me."

Raphael laughed. "That's a relief, thank God. I would hate to think I'd misled you in such an important responsibility."

"You were everything that was kind. You really should find yourself a wife, Rafe. You'll make some lucky woman a good husband."

"Pray God matters never come to that. I don't think I'm cut out for marriage, Serafina." He sighed. "To tell you the truth, I'm hoping Hugo will work his wildness out of his system and settle down. He can provide my mother with the grandchildren she wants and take care of heirs for the dukedom at the same time."

"You don't want to marry?" Serafina said, her astonishment carrying clearly to Charlotte. "But why not?"

Charlotte could have told the silly strumpet exactly why not, but she held her silence with an effort. It wouldn't do for Raphael to know she'd overheard them.

"Because I don't want to marry for less than love, and I've never found a woman who inspired that emotion in me. I doubt I will at this late date."

"Oh, Raphael . . . that's so sad. I hate to think of you going through life all alone. Maybe if poor Charlotte hadn't been crippled you could have married her."

"*Charlotte?* Are you mad?" he said, staring at her. "I wouldn't marry Charlotte if she were the last able-bodied woman on earth. I don't mean to sound uncharitable, but the woman's a harridan. She'd make my life a living hell, Serafina, with her constant blather about position and duty, never mind her religious drivel."

Charlotte's hands dropped from the arms of her chair, her entire world disintegrating around her. It couldn't be true. Raphael loved her. He'd always loved her, forsaken other women because of that love. He'd never given her any other indication. But to hear he thought her a harridan . . . that she blathered, spoke religious drivel?

Charlotte felt as if he'd driven a stake through her heart.

"Oh," Serafina said. "I suppose that's true. But I thought you were fond of her."

"I am fond of her, in the way one is fond of an irritating sister. You can't tell me you find her an easy companion."

"No, but she does try to be kind."

"Yes, she does, but do me a favor and forget about trying to marry me off. I hear enough of it from my mother. I'm perfectly content as I am." He smiled down at her. "The closest I've ever come to domestic tranquility was the three weeks we had at Southwell, and when that ended I was happy to go back to behaving like a bachelor. Come, we should go back inside. Our guests will wonder what's become of us."

"Thank you for listening," Serafina said, tucking her handkerchief away. "I might not have solved anything, but I do feel a little better."

"That's good. You can always come to me with anything, Serafina. That's what friends are for."

Charlotte hastily wheeled her chair away from the balcony and deep into the shadows as they came up the stairs and disappeared into the ballroom.

A black fury took hold of her, a hatred unlike any she had ever felt before, coiling in her gut like a poisonous snake, constricting her until she could hardly breathe.

How dare they? How dare they take away everything she had ever wanted, how dare they talk about her as if she were a troublesome nuisance only to be tolerated? They were nothing more than Godless adulterers who had deceived everyone around them with their innocent behavior, all the while wickedly fornicating right under Charlotte's nose.

Her entire body shook with rage. Betrayed. Betrayed by the man she loved, had always loved so selflessly. Betrayed by her sister-in-law, who wanted nothing more than to humiliate Charlotte, make her inconsequential in her own home. Betrayed by her brother who had brought the witch into their lives and hadn't even been able to keep her faithful to him for more than one night.

Betrayed. Betrayed. Betrayed.

The words echoed over and over in her head, pounding like a hammer pounding nails into a coffin. And that was where her future lay now, as good as buried. Her moment of glory had been snatched away, her bright dream of being a duchess with power and money and influence forever crushed.

But she would find a way to make them suffer as they'd made her suffer. She would not rest until they paid for their sins, she swore it on her soul.

She would keep her secret to herself, use it to her own advantage when the time was right. No one needed to know she could walk as well as she once had. She would give them no reason to think anything was different, not until she'd found a way to exact her revenge.

It took her another ten minutes, but she managed to school her face into a calm smile and wheel herself back through the door, thinking all the while of how to make the best use of her newfound information.

"Charlotte, I am so sorry for ignoring you all this time," Serafina said, taking a chair next to Charlotte, longing to kick off her slippers and rub her aching feet. "But I think I have done my duty for the time being and no one will fault me for sitting by your side for a few minutes."

"Do not trouble yourself in the slightest, dear sister," Charlotte said, patting her hand affectionately. "I have been entertained nearly all of the evening—and the things I have learned. La! You would be amazed by how informative an evening like this can be."

"Really? I'm afraid I've learned nothing at all except a lot of names I will shortly forget again. I'm not very good at this sort of thing," she said ruefully. "You are much more adept at social conversation than I."

"Ah well, I was brought up to it, wasn't I?"

Serafina didn't know what to say to that, since Charlotte

had been a recluse from the age of twelve with a father who scarcely conversed at all and a brother who was largely away. But it was true that Charlotte had shone all week, dazzling people with her witty repartee.

Serafina on the other hand had felt a complete dullard, her tongue twisting into knots when it came to making clever conversation. "I'm so happy it will all be over after tonight and we can finally return home to some peace and quiet."

"I imagine Raphael feels the same way," Charlotte said, looking at her sideways from under lowered lids.

"He's been very generous, hasn't he? I'm sure he thought the week perfectly tedious. Although his mother seemed to enjoy herself enormously."

"The duchess has always been a social creature. She never did like rusticating, unlike Raphael. But he seems to find all sorts of amusing things to do in the country, doesn't he?"

"If you call farming amusing, I suppose so." Serafina didn't really want to talk about Raphael. The subject reminded her of her troubles with Aiden, which she was doing her best to forget. Aiden had been studiously ignoring her since their one and only dance together, behaving as if he didn't have a care in the world, which only upset Serafina more.

Aiden was the most unfeeling man she'd ever had the misfortune to meet, a man with an icicle for a heart. The more she thought about it, the angrier she became that he would take such exception to a few lessons to improve herself for his sake, even if she hadn't told him about them. She'd hardly committed a crime, after all, only an error of omission.

"Lady Aubrey, Lady Charlotte?"

Serafina looked up to see one of the most beautiful women she'd ever laid eyes on addressing them. Her hair, arranged in the height of fashion, was the color of autumn leaves, her complexion a perfect peach, her eyes a sultry brown. She was dressed in an exquisite gown of pale blue silver lamé over a blue satin slip. She took Serafina's breath away.

"Forgive me for introducing myself, but since I am an old

acquaintance of Aubrey's I hoped you wouldn't mind. I am Lady Harriet Munro."

"How do you do," Serafina said, rising, wondering why Charlotte's eyes had sharpened with such acute interest.

"Lady Munro," Charlotte said, her face breaking into a welcoming smile. "Of course. I have often heard my brother speak of you."

"Has he? How gratifying. I had to see for myself the bride Aubrey took." She looked Serafina up and down, amusement lighting her face. "What a charming dress, Lady Aubrey, and how well it suits you. I believe it is one of Mme. Bernard's? And yours as well, Lady Charlotte."

"My brother has always patronized Mme. Bernard," Charlotte said. "But how clever of you to recognize her work."

"Not really," Lady Munro said with a shrug of one bared shoulder. "I was at the salon when your brother ordered his wife's trousseau. Actually, I should say when he tried to order it." She laughed, a light, tinkling sound. "The poor man hadn't the first idea of what he was doing and begged me to take over for him. I'm so pleased to see that Mme. Bernard followed my suggestions to the letter as evidenced by both your gowns."

Serafina drew in a sharp breath. *This* woman had been responsible for the beautiful wardrobe Aiden had given to her? And he'd never said a word, taking all the credit himself. She flushed a deep pink, humiliated to the bone. "My husband was very generous," she said, trying to collect herself. "And you were most kind to be of assistance to him."

"Oh, well as for that, Aubrey never did know what he was doing when it came to attiring a woman. I see that Lady Aubrey had one of her ball dresses altered for you, Lady Charlotte. How well it looks on you."

"Thank you," Charlotte said, although she looked severely annoyed that Lady Munro knew the dress hadn't been made for her. "I had nothing suitable. Our plans were made at the last minute."

"So I understand," Harriet Munro said, toying with her fan. "Perhaps next season you will be better prepared."

She turned her attention back to Serafina, who was beginning to feel uncomfortably like a mouse stalked by a cat. "Your cousin Segrave is a friend of mine. Imagine my surprise when he told me you had come out of hiding in Wales after all these years. Who would have imagined Aubrey would marry you so quickly—although I believe he had his financial difficulties to consider?"

Serafina had no idea what was behind this woman's vindictiveness, but there was no doubt in her mind that Lady Munro had not come over to be pleasant. She couldn't catch her breath to speak, overcome with the horrible sensation that she'd just traveled back eleven years to her last day at Bowhill, no more than the same ugly piece of riffraff who didn't belong and never would.

"Please excuse me," she stammered. "I see someone beckoning to me."

She started across the room as quickly as she could manage without actually running, her cheeks flaming. Whomever Lady Harriet Munro was and whatever her relationship with Aiden, Serafina had no desire to ever tangle with her again.

Trust Aiden to have a serpent for a friend.

Aiden was just escorting the duchess back into the ballroom from the supper room when his gaze caught the appalling sight of Harriet Munro engaged in conversation with Serafina and his sister. His heart nearly stopped in his chest. Harriet was capable of the worst sort of venom, and he didn't doubt she was unleashing some of it on Serafina as he watched.

He hadn't even realized Harriet was in attendance. She hadn't come through the receiving line and he hadn't heard her announced, so he could only think she'd come in late. "Oh, God no," he muttered as Serafina turned away abruptly and fled.

"What is it, my boy?" the duchess asked, ever alert.

"Nothing—just an unexpected and unwelcome guest who is more than capable of doing mischief," he said. "Will you excuse me, Duchess?"

"Certainly," she said graciously, releasing his arm.

Aiden stormed toward Harriet, determined to find out what she'd said to make Serfina flee as she had. He might be furious with his wife at the moment, but he couldn't help feeling protective of her, no matter what she'd done. No one deserved the wrath of Harriet. He knew.

"Why, Harriet," he said, attempting to look calm, when inside he was raging. "What a surprise to find you here. I see you've made the acquaintance of my sister."

"And your wife," she said with a catlike smile. "What a *rural* creature she is."

"Will you excuse us, Lottie?" He took Harriet by the elbow as his sister looked on in surprise, but he didn't have time for explanations, not that he would have had anything suitable to offer.

"Aiden," Harriet protested as he steered her toward the door, "what do you think you're doing?"

"I'd like to ask you the very same question. Don't you think your appearance here is in extremely questionable taste?"

Harriet shot him a sly, sidelong look. "You can't expect to protect your wife from all your past mistresses, Aiden. Half of London would be eliminated from your guest list."

Aiden wanted to shake her till her teeth rattled in her beautiful head. "Don't be absurd," he hissed, forcing a smile as he passed curious onlookers. "Tonight is my wife's debut. Couldn't you have left her alone to enjoy it? What did you do, come straight out and tell her that you and I were lovers at one time?"

"I didn't have to. She divined that all by herself, I believe."

"With considerable help from you, no doubt." Aiden marched her to the entrance hall. "Lady Munro's cloak, and quickly if you please. Her ladyship is feeling unwell."

"But Aiden, I've only just arrived," she said in a furious undertone. "What will people think?"

"I don't give a damn. Most of them probably already know exactly what to think, given this cursed city and its gossip. You're leaving now, and I'm going to see you to your carriage," he spat out, throwing her cloak over her shoulders. "And you can do your best to look faint for anyone watching." He practically pushed her out the door and down the steps of the town house, pulling her along the sidewalk.

"Darling, I do think you're being unreasonable. Really, your behavior is scandalous."

"Begging your pardon, madam, but it is your behavior I find scandalous. How *dare* you approach my wife like that?"

Harriet assumed a sulky look. "It's not as if you care. You didn't even want her, everyone knows that—word is all over town that you only married her for her money. Even you admitted that to me."

"I may have married her for her money, and I may not have wanted her at the time, but I want her now, and by God I'll fight for what's mine!"

Harriet's eyes widened. "Don't tell me you've gone and fallen in love with the silly country mouse," she said incredulously. "You, the infamous Earl of Aubrey, man without a heart? Please. It's laughable, Aiden."

Aiden took her by the shoulders in a punishing grip, and this time he did shake her, hard. "What lies between me and my wife is none of your business, nor is it anyone else's. I warn you, Harriet, stay away from Serafina, or I swear I'll make you sorry." He released her abruptly, his body shaking with rage.

Harriet brushed off her shoulders. "For a man whom Edmund Segrave says danced with his wife only once this evening you're in remarkably high dudgeon over a harmless little conversation."

"Nothing about you is harmless, my dear. Now take yourself off," he said, angrily depositing her in front of her carriage.

"I'm not inclined to stay where I'm not wanted," she said, drawing herself up. "But this absurd attachment you've taken to the girl won't last, Aiden. I of all people should know."

"But I never loved you, did I?" he retorted coldly, turning on his heel and storming back toward the house.

He stopped abruptly halfway up the street, hearing his own words echoing in his head.

But then I never loved you, did I?

"Oh, dear God," he groaned, rubbing his hands over his

face. "Oh, dear God, Aiden Delaware, you have truly lost your mind."

He straightened his shoulders and went back to the ball, more confused than he'd ever been in his life.

21

Hot coals wouldn't describe what Aiden felt he was standing on as they saw the last of their guests out. He was acutely aware of Serafina's near presence, her musical voice saying her farewells, her hand reaching out to touch various other hands. But not his. Never his.

He'd danced with her twice more, just to put Edmund Segrave and his vicious tongue to rest. He had smiled at her, brought her lemonade, just to be sure no one else had reason to question his feelings. He didn't even know what they were anymore. He knew nothing, understood nothing.

He was still angry, but his anger had been tempered by doubt that he might have been wrong about her, that he might have misconstrued an innocent friendship. His loins ached for her—they hadn't stopped aching even when he'd been sure she'd betrayed him. And although he might not have any control over his loins—he hadn't had since the day he'd met her—he fully expected to have control over his heart. But even that had deserted him, leaving him in a place of chaos.

As soon as the last guest had gone, Serafina turned to him. "Good night, Aiden. Thank you for a lovely evening." But there was no sincerity in her voice, and the absence of it stung him. She said good night to the others with a great deal more warmth, kissing first his father's cheek, then Charlotte's and the duchess's. And finally Rafe's, which only made his blood boil.

But she didn't kiss his cheek. Never his.

He watched her climb the stairs after the others, his heart aching as much as his loins, cursing himself for a fool. He was about to follow her, determined to finish the conversation he'd started earlier and dig out the truth of her relationship with Raphael, when Charlotte stopped him at the foot of the stairs.

"Aiden, a word with you?" she asked, her expression urgent.

"Lottie, not now. We're all tired," he said, sure she wanted to interrogate him about his abrupt departure with Harriet. The last thing in the world he needed was a lecture now from his sister about his behavior. "Let me carry you up to bed."

"This won't wait, Aiden. Please?" she said, in the pleading tone he could never refuse. "I'm sure I cannot sleep tonight as exhausted as I am, not unless I speak to you first."

"Very well," he said impatiently. "But make it fast, Lottie. I'm in no mood for nonsense."

He wheeled her into the drawing room and leaned one shoulder against the mantelpiece, crossing his arms over his chest. "Well?"

Charlotte ran the tip of her tongue over her lower lip. "This is awkward, Aiden. Deeply painful, in fact. But I feel you must know."

"Know what?" he said, staring down at the toe of his pump and heaving a resigned sigh.

"It's—it's about Serafina and Raphael," she said. "I heard them tonight when they were talking alone in the garden."

Aiden's head snapped up, his eyes narrowed in sudden attention. "What are you talking about?" he demanded.

"I—I know I shouldn't have been listening, but I went out for a breath of air—it was so stuffy in the ballroom. And I overheard them. Oh, Aiden," she cried, tears starting to her eyes. "How can I tell you?" She dug out her handkerchief from her bodice.

"Just tell me, damn you," he said, his heart turning to stone.

"Aiden, they have sinned most grievously against you," she said, her eyes streaming now. "For three of the weeks you were in London after your marriage they—they carried on at Southwell!"

Aiden slowly straightened. "What are you implying?" he whispered, the words barely coming out.

"Must you force me to say it? They were—they were f-fornicating together," she sobbed, burying her face in her hands.

"You *heard* them say this?" Aiden wrapped his hands into tight fists, trying to hold on to control as his world crashed down around him.

"Yes," she wailed. "Serafina thinks you know about it, and she was afraid of what you might do. And . . . and Raphael— oh, poor Raphael, led into evil by that strumpet—he said that he thought you would understand. He must have believed you wouldn't care, but I knew you would, that you would feel dishonored." She dissolved into a fit of weeping.

Aiden very carefully walked over to the window. His legs felt as if they wouldn't hold him. He leaned his hands against the cold pane and looked out over the quiet street into the dark night, broken only by the hollow yellow mist of the street lamps. "Thank you for bringing the matter to my attention," he said very softly. "Leave me now, Lottie."

"But Aiden—what are you going to do?" she sniffed. "You must do something. Oh, I *knew* that girl was trouble the minute she showed her face. I tried to warn you. . . ."

Aiden spun around. "I said leave me, Lottie," he roared. "Have one of the footmen take you up to bed. I have to think."

His sister gazed at him, her eyes wide with fright. "Very well, Aiden. Whatever you wish." She wheeled herself out of the room and quietly shut the door behind her.

Aiden felt as if he were drowning. He couldn't catch his breath. This was his worst nightmare come to life. It was Arthur, Guinevere, Lancelot all over again. He had been betrayed by his wife and his best friend.

True. It was true after all.

Charlotte in all her innocence could never have made such a thing up, would never make such a thing up. She cared too much about Raphael to falsely accuse him. And she couldn't possibly have known about the suspicions Aiden had entertained, since he'd never breathed a word of them to another soul.

Truth. Cold, hard, ugly truth.

And he felt like dying.

"Serafina, dearest? May I come in?"

Serafina turned from her dressing table. Charlotte sat in her chair in the open doorway, her face pale and anxious.

"What is it Charlotte?" she asked, wishing everyone would leave her alone. She'd already had to face Janie this morning and her endless questions about the ball. A conversation with Charlotte was more than she could stand.

Aiden hadn't come home last night. She knew. She'd knocked on his door in the night, wanting to speak to him, to set things straight, for she couldn't bear any more of the tension between them, no matter the consequences.

But he hadn't come to bed, and according to Tinkerby, he'd never come upstairs. One final inquiry had established that Aiden had gone out and hadn't returned.

"Oh, Serafina, I must ask the most enormous favor of you," Charlotte said, wheeling herself over to the dressing table. "My dear sister, I don't think I can tolerate another moment of London. I am exhausted and overwrought, and I want nothing more but to return to Townsend. Will you accompany me?"

Serafina rubbed her aching forehead. She hadn't slept a wink in the night. "But we're all scheduled to go home tomorrow. Can you not wait until then?"

"I don't think I can. My back hurts most dreadfully, and I long for my oils and my own bed. I realize I'm being demanding, but I thought you might understand."

Serafina sighed. It was true that Charlotte did look drawn, and if she was in pain, then the best place for her was in her own home. Charlotte had had a trying week, and it was no wonder she was overwrought. Serafina's own nerves were frayed beyond endurance.

"Very well," she said, trying to be charitable, even though the last thing in the world she wanted to undertake was a long carriage journey. "When would you like to leave?"

"Bless you!" Charlotte said, relief written all over her face. "You are the kindest sister that ever was. I knew you would help me, so I already ordered the carriage. Our clothes can be packed later and follow tomorrow."

"Do you mean you want to leave now? Right now?" Serafina said, unprepared.

"Yes. You see, if we leave now, then we will arrive by nightfall. Otherwise, we might have to stop at a coaching inn, and I don't know if I could bear another night in a strange bed."

"But Aiden's not even home yet. We can't leave without telling him."

"Don't concern yourself with Aiden. I will write him a note explaining all. My dear brother would far rather I look after my health than worry about him, I assure you."

"Yes, I suppose that's true," Serafina said. "All right, Charlotte. Let me just finish dressing and I'll join you downstairs and explain to the duchess."

"The duchess will be abed for hours yet, but Aiden can tell her everything. I'd inform Raphael, but he has already gone out."

"Whatever you wish." Serafina was happy to hand the task of writing to Aiden over to Charlotte. She really didn't have anything to say to him, not anymore.

They arrived at Townsend at nine that night. Serafina had slept on and off during the journey, and Charlotte had been unusually quiet throughout, no doubt due to her own exhaustion and the pain she suffered.

"I'll call for Frederick to come and get you," Serafina said to Charlotte, alighting from the carriage, her bones stiff from twelve hours of travel.

Plum appeared at the door, surprise written all over his face. "Your ladyship! We weren't expecting you until tomorrow." He peered over his shoulder. "Are their lordships with you?"

"No, Plum. Lady Charlotte decided she needed to return home immediately, so we came ahead by ourselves."

"Never mind, she's probably worn down. May I welcome you back, my lady? We missed you sorely, if it's not presumptuous to say so."

"Not at all—I'm happy to hear it," Serafina said with a weary attempt at a smile. "I missed all of you too. Has my aunt retired for the evening?"

"Oh, no, my lady. Your aunt went off last week, saying she was going to pay a visit to some friends. She didn't leave her direction, but she gave me a letter to deliver to you on your return. I'll just collect it."

"Thank you, Plum," Serafina said, curiously wondering what friends her aunt had suddenly acquired. Elspeth didn't have friends to keep her company, she had earth deities. "And please summon Frederick. Her ladyship will want to go straight to her room."

"Very good, my lady." He scurried off and Serafina walked into the hall, pulling off her gloves. It was good to be home. She'd missed Plum's cheerful face, all the servants with their easygoing attitudes and friendly bantering.

Plum delivered a folded, sealed piece of paper on a silver salver and Serafina tore it open, perusing Elspeth's spidery, nearly indecipherable writing.

> *My dear Serafina,*
> *I've had the most wonderful surprise. A coven exists quite close to this area in a small town near Grantham. One of my sister Wiccans in Wales wrote to their high priestess, giving my current direction, and as a result I have been asked to pay their coven a visit.*

Serafina glanced up as she heard footsteps coming across the marble floor. "Freddie!" she said with pleasure. "How are you . . . oh, dear. You're looking a trifle peaked." That was an understatement. Frederick looked as if he'd just eaten a bad apple.

"Just a touch of indisposition. Welcome home, my lady."

"Thank you. Her ladyship needs to be carried from the carriage."

"Yes, my lady, Plum told me," he said morosely, dragging his feet toward the door.

Serafina turned her attention back to Elspeth's letter, reminding herself to see to a tonic for Freddie in the morning.

Naturally this is an invaluable opportunity to further my research, so I am taking advantage of the invitation. I shall be away no more than a fortnight, dearie. I do hope your adventures in London were satisfactory, although I can't think you took any enjoyment from them.

Fondly,

Auntie Elspeth

Postscript: I have taken Basil with me, so you needn't worry about feeding him. And be sure that none of those nosy maids goes poking about in my chambers. I have left everything exactly as I want it. A. E.

Serafina folded the letter up with an exasperated shake of her head. Aunt Elspeth could be depended on to set the Grantham coven on its ear. She might well be back sooner than she expected.

Frederick carried Charlotte into the hall and placed her in her chair. "To your room, my lady?" he asked, looking a shade paler than he had when he went out the door.

"I do not wish to go to my room just yet," Charlotte said, to Serafina's considerable surprise. "Lady Aubrey and I have not eaten since breakfast. We will take a light supper in the dining room. Inform Cook, if you please."

The last thing Serafina wanted was to share a light supper in the dining room with Charlotte after twelve full hours in her company, but Serafina couldn't refuse without sounding churlish.

They sat silently at the table as platters of cold meats and cheeses were brought, Serafina about to fall asleep over her plate. They ate just as silently, Serafina picking at her food. She had no appetite. Just as she thought the interminable meal was over, Charlotte wiped her mouth with her napkin and folded her hands primly together the table.

"So, Serafina. It is time you and I had a talk."

"A talk?" Serafina said, her heart sinking. "Do you think it might wait until morning, Charlotte? I am dreadfully tired."

"It will not keep until morning. This is an issue that must be addressed now and the real reason I wanted to come back to Townsend with you alone, for I did not want to put Aiden through the pain of having to speak to you himself. He is distraught enough as it is."

Serafina couldn't think for the life of her what Charlotte was talking about, but she didn't like the ominous tone of her voice, nor the piety of her expression, always a bad sign. "I'm afraid I don't understand," she said, twisting her napkin between her fingers.

"I think you understand well enough, as does Aiden. He and I had a long talk last night, a disturbing talk. I felt it was my Christian duty to inform my brother of the conversation I overheard between you and Raphael."

"The—the conversation? What conversation?" she said, perplexed.

"The one you wished no one else to hear, the talk you and he had in the garden during the ball. I was sickened, Serafina. Sickened."

Serafina sat bolt upright, her blood running cold. "You *eavesdropped* on us?" she said, appalled that Charlotte would lurk in the dark, listening to a private conversation without informing them of her presence. "How could you?"

"How could I? It is not I who am on trial here. It is you, you and your whorish ways," Charlotte said, the bones of her knuckles showing white as she squeezed her hands together, her mouth pursing. "Did you think you could get away with your foul behavior, that no one would ever know of your sin?"

"What sin? What sin have you conjured up for me now?" she asked, her eyes flashing with sudden anger. "I have done nothing wrong, other than keeping a small secret from Aiden, and you know that if you heard us talking."

"You call it a small secret? Oh, you are a vile woman indeed! When you first came to Townsend I had my doubts about you, severe doubts, and I tried to warn my brother." Her face twisted into an ugly sneer of hatred. "But he wouldn't listen to me. He was taken in by your pretty face, by what you might offer him in bed—oh, I know all about it, about how you cast your lures out to him, all so you could have your way. And it worked, didn't it? You blinded my brother with lust so that he could no longer think straight!"

Serafina stared at her, wondering if she was listening to the ravings of a madwoman. "It's late and we're both tired," she said, doing her best to sound reasonable. "I'm sure that in the morning you will feel more yourself."

"Don't you patronize me, you whore of Babylon! You thought you could take over, didn't you? You thought you could have it all—Townsend, Aiden, even Raphael. Well, my pretty, you've been caught out, and Aiden knows all about how you sinned with his cousin while he was away."

"Oh dear Lord in Heaven . . . what did you tell Aiden?" Serafina whispered. "*What did you tell him?*"

"I told him the truth. I told him about your secret trysts at Southwell. Every afternoon, Serafina, for three full weeks. Can you imagine what he had to say about that?" Charlotte smiled at her triumphantly, her eyes glazed.

All the blood drained from Serafina's face. She thought she might be sick right there at the table. "You—you told Aiden that Raphael and I were lovers?" she managed to say, forcing back her nausea. "And he believed you?"

"Of course he believed me. He knows I wouldn't lie to him. He never wants to lay eyes on you again, Serafina, and I can't say I blame him."

"Oh, you despicable woman!" Serafina cried, her heart twisting in her chest. She could see Aiden's face now as Charlotte spun her half-truths into lies, weaving them into a story that Aiden would find impossible to dismiss. Charlotte had twisted the innocent words that she and Raphael had exchanged into a sordid story of lust and treachery. "How could you do such a terrible thing to your brother?"

"I did nothing to my brother," Charlotte said furiously.

"It was you—all you and my whore-mongering cousin. All I did was open Aiden's eyes. And now he knows what sort of woman he really married." She placed her palms flat on the table and leaned over them. "I do believe the only course of action left to you is to return to Clwydd first thing in the morning and never darken our door again. This is what Aiden wishes, and I suggest you are long gone before he returns, for if you are still here, Aiden will be sure to make you very sorry."

Something in Serafina snapped. For weeks she had bent over backward trying to be kind to Charlotte, to make her life as happy and comfortable as possible, had put up with Charlotte's diatribes and religious ravings, and this was how Charlotte repaid her? By trying to destroy Serafina's marriage with unfounded accusations, accusations designed to dishonor Aiden? She wouldn't let it happen. She couldn't. She loved Aiden too much to allow Charlotte to hurt him like this.

"No," she said.

"No? What do you mean by that?" Charlotte said, her jaw dropping open.

"I mean no, I won't go," Serafina said, sudden fury surging through her veins, giving her the strength to face down Charlotte. "If Aiden wishes me to leave, he can tell me so himself. I won't be tossed out of Townsend by you, Charlotte. I certainly won't be forced away by charges that have no basis in truth."

Charlotte stared at her. "And you think Aiden will believe you, that he even wants you anymore? Think again, you stupid girl. Where do you think he was all night?" She smirked. "Shall I tell you? He went to his mistress. That's right, Lady Harriet Munro. From the expression on your face, I see you guessed about her."

"No, I—I don't believe it," Serafina stammered, feeling as if Charlotte had just driven a knife into her heart and twisted it.

"Then you're even more stupid than I thought. The two of them were lovers four years ago before Aiden left the country, and they picked up right where they left off. Apparently the only person who didn't know of their relationship is you, his wife." She threw her head back and laughed, a harsh, cruel sound. "He even walked her to her carriage last night, where no doubt they planned their assignation for later."

Serafina shook her head back and forth in denial. And yet images of Harriet Munro taunting her came back all too clearly. Harriet, who had bought Serafina's trousseau at Aiden's request. Beautiful Harriet, who had looked at her with mocking disdain as if she were a pitiable creature.

She pushed her chair away from the table and stood, her eyes blinded by tears. "That may well be true," she choked. "But I still will not leave. I will wait for Aiden."

"Have you no pride?" Charlotte said, toying lazily with her knife.

"Perhaps I have too much. I don't know. All I do know is that this is between Aiden and myself."

"Oh, you cuckold your husband with his best friend and you still expect him to take you back, even knowing that he has someone far more desirable than you to indulge his carnal appetites with?"

"I won't listen to any more of your slander, Charlotte," Serafina said, her legs shaking so badly that she could hardly stand. "I'm going to bed."

"Very well. Go to your bed. It will be the last night you sleep in it."

Serafina stumbled toward the door, unable to bear another second of Charlotte's viciousness. She thought she had reached the depths of unhappiness last night, but she realized that she had only scratched the surface.

Now she was looking into the true face of hell.

"Where the devil have you been?" Aiden roared as Raphael finally appeared in the library. Aiden had been pacing all day and half the evening, waiting for his black-hearted cousin to appear and his mood, already foul, had only grown worse. He'd had no sleep, and walking the streets of London until ten in the morning had only given him a raging headache.

To return to the news that Charlotte had taken Serafina back to Townsend at Serafina's request hadn't helped. He'd never been so angry in his life. Charlotte's note had only enraged him more.

"My, my. You seem to be in a righteous temper," Raphael said mildly. "The footman gave me fair warning, but he didn't use the full descriptive power necessary. What's gotten into you?"

"You damned well know what's gotten into me. Or perhaps you don't, given that you've been gone since morning." Aiden clenched his teeth together, trying desperately to control his rage.

"I went to Reading on business," Rafe said, pouring two glasses of cognac and handing one to Aiden. "Did something happen while I was away?"

"Oh, let's see," Aiden said, slamming his glass down on the side table. "Serafina left. She felt she couldn't face either of us. I can't imagine why."

Raphael took a sip of his cognac. "Then I gather the cat's out of the bag."

"You filthy devil!" Aiden spat out. "How can you stand there and look at me as if you're some innocent in all of this—as if I wouldn't give a damn what you and my wife got up to while I wasn't around to notice?" He wanted to choke Raphael. "I should call you out for what you've done, and if I didn't respect your mother so much, I probably would!"

"Duels are more Hugo's sort of thing, but I do think you're overreacting to a few tutorials I gave Serafina, Aiden."

"*Tutorials?* Is that what you call it? By God, Cousin, if you got her with your by-blow during one of your 'tutorials,' I swear I'll kill you!"

Raphael's hand froze, and he slowly put his glass down. "What did you say?" he asked, his voice very low.

"You heard me, damn you. My God, I always held you in the highest respect, Rafe. I believed you to be a man of honor, but that's a joke, isn't it?" He glowered at his cousin, so bitter and hurt he could hardly speak.

Raphael picked up a quill from the desk and turned it

around in his fingers, then threw it back down. "Do you know," he said slowly, "if I weren't a man of honor, I'd probably tear your head off for that remark." He rubbed a hand over his face, then looked up, his gray eyes dark with anger. "Where the *hell* did you get the cork-brained idea that I seduced your wife?"

Aiden shoved his hands on his hips. "Are you trying to deny it? Don't bother—Charlotte heard everything you and Serafina said last night and she passed it straight along. She told me all about your assignations at Southwell while I was away."

"Aiden . . . I don't know what Charlotte told you, but believe me when I tell you that she got hold of the wrong end of the stick. It's true that Serafina spent three weeks visiting Southwell, but I never laid a hand on her, I swear it, not unless it was to teach her how to dance, or curtsy, or climb in and out of a carriage without her skirts flying up."

He rested his hands on the desk and regarded Aiden intently, as if willing Aiden to believe him. "She wanted to learn how to behave like a countess, and I took it upon myself to teach her as a favor to you. It was her idea to keep it a secret—something to do with her pride, and also her concern that you might mistake her motives again."

Aiden's eyes narrowed. He wanted to believe Raphael more than life itself, but he wasn't about to accept such a facile explanation, not when Charlotte had damned Raphael so completely. "Do you think I'm a complete fool?" he said.

"I'm beginning to think you might be, yes," Rafe agreed, a glimmer of a smile showing around his mouth. "Aiden, I *know* how you feel about your wife. I've known since the day before your marriage."

Aiden stared at him. "What kind of miserable excuse is that supposed to be? I may have thought Serafina was a conniving harridan, but that's no reason to—"

"No, you clod pole," Raphael said, cutting him off. "I mean that I realized almost immediately that Serafina was your wood nymph."

Aiden's mouth opened in shock, and he quickly snapped it shut again. "You—you did?"

"Yes, of course I did," Rafe said with exasperation. "Do you see now? I wasn't going to say anything to you, since you obviously didn't want me to know, but I'm not quite as stupid as you apparently think me." He rubbed his cheek with one finger. "What truly galls is that you also think me capable of such an underhanded act. Aiden, I would never betray you. Never, no matter the circumstances."

Aiden slumped into a chair. "And Lottie would never lie," he said. "So explain that."

"I can only think that Charlotte badly misunderstood what she heard. What other explanation is there?"

Aiden dug in his coat pocket and pulled out Charlotte's note. He'd reread it countless times in the course of the day, each word confirming his darkest suspicions. He abruptly held it out to Raphael. "I think you'd better read this before you protest your innocence too loudly. Serafina's admitted to everything."

Raphael took it and scrutinized Charlotte's neat penmanship. He read it twice, a deep frown marking his brow, then looked up. "Aiden, this is deeply troublesome. I don't want to speak against your sister, but does this sound like something Serafina would say? Listen."

Aiden had memorized the entire contents, but he nodded anyway, too tired and disillusioned to protest.

"My dear Aiden," Raphael read, "your wife came to me this morning in a state of terrible distress. She confessed her sins against God to me and begged me to take her back to Townsend. She wishes you to know that she regrets her adultery deeply, but realizes that you will never take her back. She plans to return to Clwydd where she will spend the remainder of her life making penance to God." Raphael rubbed the back of his neck and glanced up at Aiden. "And so on in that vein. Has it occurred to you that Serafina would never—but never—think in those terms, even if there was any truth to this adultery nonsense?"

"What are you getting at?" Aiden said impatiently. He didn't even know why he was listening to Raphael at all. "It's all there as clear as day."

"What I'm getting at, you bloody idiot, is that Serafina is a little pagan. Surely you've realized that by now?"

Aiden sat bolt upright, his fingers grasping the arms of the chair, thinking of Serafina singing in the Midsummer moonlight, of Serafina spouting off about reincarnation, explaining the tenants of the Wiccan religion to him. If she made penance to anyone it would be to her precious goddess, not the God of the Christian church. "Dear Lord . . ." he said slowly as Raphael's point hammered home. "She is a pagan, isn't she?"

"Yes, and given that, the last thing Serafina would do is confess her supposed sins against God to Charlotte, whose views of religion she finds oppressive in the extreme. *Think,* Aiden. Who does this letter sound like to you?"

Aiden squeezed the bridge of his nose with his fingertips, trying to absorb all the unsavory implications. "It sounds like Charlotte," he said, as painful as the admission was. "But maybe she was just putting what Serafina told her into her own words," he said in defense of his sister.

"Nonsense," Raphael said succinctly. "Charlotte must have written this claptrap without Serafina's knowledge or consent, because Serafina and I never committed adultery in the first place. Serafina wouldn't admit to something that never happened."

Aiden's head swam with confusion. It had to be one thing or the other. Either Charlotte had lied, or Raphael was lying now, and it was beginning to look more and more to him like Charlotte was guilty of an enormous deception. The more he thought about it, the more Raphael's explanation of befriending Serafina on Aiden's behalf made sense. It certainly explained their easy affection for each other. And if Charlotte had lied, that meant that Serafina and Raphael were innocent, and that thought gave him back hope. It gave him back Serafina.

"But—but why would Lottie write something so patently untrue?" he said, still unsure, hoping against hope that there was a reasonable explanation for Charlotte's actions.

"I don't know," Raphael said, shaking his head, looking as confused as Aiden felt. "I honestly don't know. But she did, and she must have thought she could get away with it, that you would believe this tripe. She wouldn't have the first idea that Serafina would never use this kind of language, for I know Serafina has always guarded her tongue carefully around your sister when it comes to her religious beliefs."

He threw the note down on the desk in disgust. "I don't know what this is all about, but I don't like it. I don't like it at all. It sounds to me as if Charlotte is not only trying to run Serafina away, but she's also trying to destroy our friendship."

"But for what reason?" Aiden cried desperately, knowing in his heart that Raphael spoke the truth. He could see it in Rafe's face, hear it in his voice. And if he really searched his soul, he also knew that Serafina wasn't capable of the behavior Charlotte had accused her of. He probably wouldn't even have listened to her if he hadn't had his own nagging doubts, the doubts of a jealous fool.

Serafina had honored her vows after all, and that mattered more to him than he ever would have imagined. Right now it meant everything.

His lifelong loyalty to his sister tore at him, but so did his devotion to his cousin and his wife. He could find no defense for Charlotte, no excuse. And that broke his heart.

"I have no earthly idea," Rafe said. "Charlotte obviously has some nefarious plan in mind. She thinks that not only can she banish Serafina to Wales, but she must also be convinced that you're too proud to go after her. I don't know why she thought I'd sit back and do nothing, unless she really does believe that I'm guilty of seducing your wife."

"This is insane," Aiden said, covering his eyes with one hand, trying to make sense out of the entire mess. "How the hell did we ever come to this place?"

"You've never had reason to doubt Charlotte's word before this. But you have even less reason to doubt mine. I bear no ill will toward you, Aiden, even though you can be a blind idiot at times."

Aiden raised his head. "God, I'm sorry, Rafe. I should never have accused you."

"I can marginally understand why you might have leapt

to the wrong conclusion—and I'm partially to blame. I should never have agreed to keep the lessons a secret. But never mind that now. We had better get to the bottom of this before Serafina is hurt."

The thought of Serafina being hurt in any way was enough to propel Aiden to his feet. "Let's go."

"Oh, no, my friend," Raphael said, staying him with a hand on his shoulder. "Not until you get a few hours' sleep. You look dead on your feet. We can leave in the morning."

The last thing Aiden wanted was to sleep, but he saw the sense in Raphael's insistence. He wouldn't be any good to anyone in his state of exhaustion. He could hardly think straight.

"Very well," he said reluctantly. "But we leave for Townsend at first light."

"We leave at first light," Raphael agreed. "And don't worry overmuch, Aiden. Serafina loves you, of that I'm sure. She won't run away, especially not over a pack of lies."

"I don't know," Aiden said, rubbing his hands hard over his face. "I've behaved like the biggest fool, Rafe. She has every reason to leave me, given the things I've said and done. If anyone's hurt her, I have—my God, I practically accused her of adultery to her face, even before Charlotte got her claws into me."

Rafe gave him a hard look. "Do you mean to say you came up with this piece of idiocy all on your own?"

Aiden grimaced. "I'm afraid so, and if you'd like to take a swing at me, you have my full permission. But I sensed there was something you were both keeping from me, and that was the only conclusion I could draw. I did have my reasons, but I can see I put the facts together back to front."

To his surprise, Raphael laughed. "Remind me never to fall in love. That lofty emotion seems to make jealous fools out of the most reasonable of men."

Aiden chose not to answer Rafe's pointed remark. If torment, desperation, and helplessness were love in disguise, then he wanted nothing to do with it. "I owe Serafina an enormous apology," he said instead. "I can only hope she'll understand." She had to understand. He didn't know what he'd do if she turned away from him now.

"I'm sure she will, but you can deal with that tomorrow. Go to bed; we'll tackle this again in the morning. I think the bigger problem is Charlotte, and I for one want to set her straight before she does any more damage."

Aiden nodded, thinking it would be a miracle if he didn't put his hands around his sister's throat and strangle her.

22

The late afternoon skies opened and began to pour with rain, which suited Charlotte's dark mood perfectly. She couldn't believe that Serafina was still at Townsend, that she'd had the nerve to defy Charlotte. She'd been so sure that the whore would leave by morning, once she had the night to contemplate the wrath awaiting her when Aiden returned. But instead she had defiantly gone out to work in the garden, peasant that she was, studiously ignoring Charlotte, as if that would make a difference.

Aiden would take care of Serafina soon enough, that was certain. The look on his face when Charlotte told him of his wife's unpardonable sin had spoken worlds. In some ways, she could hardly wait. As for Raphael, Aiden would never speak to him again. Raphael might even choose to leave the country in disgrace, which would suit Charlotte beautifully. She didn't ever want to look at his face again. He had deceived her in the worst possible way, and she held nothing but hatred in her heart for him.

Charlotte opened her Bible, finding her favorite psalm, the very first one, and recited it aloud, taking comfort from it.

"Blessed is the man who does not walk in the counsel of the wicked or stand in the way of sinners or sit in the seat of mockers. But his delight is in the law of the Lord, and on His law he meditates day and night. He is like a tree planted by streams of water, which yields its fruit in season and whose leaf does not wither. Whatever he does prospers."

God always looked after the righteous, Charlotte thought with satisfaction. She moved on to the second verse, relishing the words and their message.

"Not so the wicked!" she read. "They are like chaff that the wind blows away. Therefore the wicked will not stand in the judgment, nor sinners in the assembly of the righteous. For the Lord watches over the way of the righteous, but the path of the wicked will perish."

She closed her Bible again, resting her hands on it. "Just so," she murmured. "Just so."

She stretched her arms over her head, her body sated and relaxed from Frederick's amorous administrations that morning. Unfortunately he was going to have to be disciplined, for his enthusiasm for his task had distinctly waned, and that wouldn't do at all. Imagine his asking to be assigned to another position in the household—the nerve of the man! He ought to be honored to serve her. She wasn't about to let him go now, not when she'd finally found someone who could meet her needs.

She wheeled herself over to the door, listening to be sure there was no one moving about on the other side, then wheeled her chair back to the middle of the room, just in case she needed to return to it in a hurry. She had no intention of having anyone discover that she could walk—far better they thought her a helpless cripple.

She stood and strolled over to the window, looking to see if Serafina still labored on her knees, a fitting position for her. But Serafina was no longer in the garden, chased away by the sudden downpour of rain. A pity. She would like to have seen Serafina covered in mud, her hair streaming around her face, looking like the harlot she was.

A sudden disturbance in the hallway shook Charlotte out of her thoughts and she scurried back to her chair, quickly arranging herself in it, and just in time, for the doors flew open and Aiden stormed in, his face as dark as the thunderclouds outside. Perfect. He was as angry as when she'd last seen him, which bode only ill for the trollop he'd married.

"Aiden," she said, reaching one hand out to him, intending to feed his mood. "My poor brother. I'm so glad you've come, for your wife—"

"Be still, Lottie," he roared, halting directly in front of her chair. He glared down at her, his eyes snapping cold fury.

Her eyes widened and one hand went to her throat. She had never seen Aiden like this, and a tremor of fear ran through her. "What—what is it? What's happened?" she stammered, recoiling as Raphael appeared behind him in the doorway, looking every bit as furious as Aiden. He closed the doors behind him, shutting out the faces of the curious servants who had gathered in the hall.

"Perhaps you can tell me," Aiden said, leaning over her, his hands braced on the arms of her chair. "Just what the *hell* have you been up to?"

Her startled gaze flew to Raphael, who had pulled a piece of paper out of his coat and held it up in the air between two fingers, one eyebrow arched. It was the note she'd left Aiden; she recognized the writing paper. She looked back at Aiden in confusion. "I—I don't understand. I explained everything. Are you angry I left without speaking to you first?"

"What I am angry about, Charlotte," he said, biting out every word, "is that for reasons known only to you, you decided to slander my wife and our cousin. Would you like to explain yourself?"

"But I—I didn't slander anyone," she said, her heart starting to race in alarm. "I only told you the truth." She pointed an accusatory finger at Raphael. "Ask him," she said, putting as much disdain into her voice as she could.

"Do you think I didn't?" Aiden said, straightening, two pale lines of strain running from his nose to his mouth. "Do you think I brought Rafe along simply because I wanted the company of the man you said defiled my wife?"

Charlotte swallowed, bile burning bitterly in the back of her throat, as bitter as the hatred that burned in her heart. "I suppose he denied it. But he would, wouldn't he?"

"How *dare* you," Raphael said, striding forward. "How dare you turn a blameless conversation into a vile pack of lies? You had nothing—nothing—on which to base your accusations, Charlotte. And yet you went straight to Aiden and poured out a whole sordid story that existed nowhere but in your imagination."

"So *you* say. You forget that I heard you. And I saw you too, saw you take that whore into your arms in an embrace. Explain that, why don't you?"

"You little fool," Raphael said, regarding her with icy disdain, "I was offering Serafina some comfort and reassurance. She was upset. It's no more than I'd do for any friend."

Charlotte narrowed her eyes. "And shall I tell Aiden why she was upset, Raphael? Shall I tell him that she felt guilty and terrified that her husband would discover the truth about the two of you?" She smiled nastily. "Did you tell Aiden that you did him a favor in teaching his wife how to make love to a man?"

"Enough!" Aiden shouted. "I've heard enough from you. My God, you have a filthy mind for a woman who quotes the Bible morning, noon, and night. You even manage to take the Good Book out of context, tormenting everyone around you with your misplaced piety and constant judgment as if you were God Himself."

Charlotte gasped in shock that Aiden would be so cruel. "I—I do no such thing," she protested. "I only honor the word of God and speak it to remind others of His way." She fumbled for her handkerchief, tears of injury stinging her eyes. "Aiden . . . Aiden how could you turn against me like this? How could you doubt my good intentions? I've always had your best interests at heart."

"So you've always said. I begin to wonder. Why would you write me a note supposedly voicing Serafina's remorse, her intentions of leaving me when it is more than obvious that Serafina said nothing of the kind? She had nothing to be remorseful for!"

Charlotte's mouth tightened. Serafina. It always came back to Serafina. Oh, how she'd like to see her gone for once and for all. "Serafina was in no state to write herself. She asked me to relay the message to you."

"The truth, Charlotte. You see, you don't know my wife at all. That's where you stumbled." He folded his arms across his chest. "Not only is Serafina innocent of any wrongdoing, but she also doesn't subscribe to your brand of hellfire and damnation. Serafina would never have said the things you put in her mouth for any reason."

Charlotte paled. She felt cornered, trapped. Aiden somehow knew that she had fabricated the letter's content, and panic seized at her chest. "I only did it for you, to make your life easier," she stammered, terrified of what he might do. "Oh, Aiden, don't hate me—please. I thought it was best if I took her away. She had hurt you so much already, and I didn't want you to have to—"

"To what?" he interrupted coldly. "To speak to my wife myself? To divine the truth straight from her? Did you really think I'd leave it there, Charlotte, allow you to poison my mind so completely against her?"

Charlotte sobbed into her handkerchief, more from outrage than any remorse. She had done the right thing, she knew it. But the only way to recoup the situation was to pretend to be contrite, for Aiden would never forgive her otherwise.

"I'm sorry," she said, wiping her eyes again. "I meant no harm."

"I find that hard to believe," Aiden said. "I can't help but wonder what you said to Serafina after you took her away. I suppose you heaped your venomous accusations on her too?"

"I—I told her that I couldn't approve of what she had done," Charlotte said, avoiding the real essence of their conversation.

"And when you finished telling her that, you oh-so-gently suggested that she leave Townsend, is that right?"

"Yes!" she cried. "And why not? She betrayed you. Why should she be allowed to stay here in my house after what she did? But she wouldn't go."

"Good for her," Raphael said. "I'm glad there's someone around here who stands up to your bullying."

She hated Raphael twice as much in that moment. "I most certainly did not bully her. I only tried to point out the error of her ways and she refused to listen to me. But she denied nothing, Aiden. Nothing!"

"If I know anything about it, you probably never gave her a chance," Aiden said with disgust. "Dear God, but you can be vicious, Charlotte. You've probably had Serafina in a state of panic, thinking I believed your lies, damn you. Where is she?"

"How should I know?" she said, dabbing delicately at her nose. "I'm not my brother's keeper."

Aiden snorted. "That's a new one. And from now on you can keep your damned quotations to yourself. I won't hear you use the Bible to further your own twisted purposes."

Charlotte drew herself up indignantly. "I have never twisted the Bible nor used it to further my own purposes. I follow the path of the Lord."

"Oh?" Aiden said sarcastically. "Then you tread an interesting path in His name. I doubt it's one He had in mind."

"You would hardly know," she spat. "You have lived a godless life for years, Aiden Delaware. I know all about your fancy women, your libertine ways. How dare you accuse me, I who have lived a blameless life?"

"I'm beginning to wonder just how blameless your life has been, Charlotte. You have used your position here for years to make a number of lives miserable." He shook his head. "I think I understand far better now why Father took to drink—it wasn't just losing our mother, although that's when his problems started. But having to live under your harsh yoke was enough to drive him to permanent inebriation, and I can't say I blame him for wanting to drown you out. I thank God Serafina came along when she did and brought some happiness back to this place."

"Your wife has done nothing but interfere," Charlotte said furiously. "She has turned my carefully ordered household on its ear, made a mockery of discipline. Only a fortnight ago she announced that she thought the servants should have a full day off every other week! How am I supposed to run Townsend with a spoiled staff, I ask you?"

"I think it's best if you don't run Townsend at all," Aiden

said curtly. "I will hire a housekeeper to take over your duties. From now on the staff will report to my wife, which is how it should have been from the beginning. But that was my mistake."

Charlotte shrank back in her chair. "You—you can't mean it," she said, her blood running cold. "Aiden—no," she pleaded. "Townsend is my life. It's all I have."

"And if you wish it to stay that way, then you will never speak ill of Serafina again. Because if you do, I swear to you I will send you to live somewhere where your vicious tongue can't be heard for miles around. Furthermore, you won't have a staff to bully."

Charlotte cheeks flamed hot with anger and humiliation. She quickly bowed her head before he could see the loathing in her eyes. "As you say, Aiden," she said, her voice shaking with an effort to control it. He wouldn't take control of Townsend from her. She wouldn't let him. She would just have to think of something to make him change his mind.

Aiden nodded. "I'm glad that's understood." He turned to Raphael. "I am deeply sorry for all of this. I'm going to find Serafina."

Charlotte heard the doors open and close. She looked up, only to find Raphael still there, gazing down at her with an unfathomable expression.

"You believe me, don't you?" she said, desperately needing an ally. As much as she despised him, he was all she had left. "I truly meant no harm."

Raphael stroked the corner of his mouth with one finger, then dropped his hand to his side. "Aiden's gone after his wife. I'm going home. Good day, Charlotte."

He turned on his heel and strode out.

Charlotte plaited her trembling fingers together and stared down at them, her head spinning with shock. First Raphael had shattered her dreams of glory, and now Aiden had taken away the only thing left that she cared about, her control over Townsend.

This was all Serafina's fault. All of it. There was only one thing left to be done.

*　*　*

As soon as the rain started pelting down Serafina took cover under the protective canopy of the oak tree. She'd gone up to feed the swans, who had learned to float over as soon as they saw her appear on the crest of the hill. She took comfort in their serene presence, their easy trust. Trust. There was little enough of that to be had in her life.

She huddled under the oak, her back pressed against its massive trunk, waiting for the storm to pass. Thunder rolled and cracked, lightning flashed across the distant sky. She might be utterly alone, but she took comfort from the primal raging of the elements, so pure, so powerful. Here there was no sin, no evil. Here was safety, all the safety she had left in the world.

"Hestia," she prayed, looking up through the thick branches. "Goddess of hearth and home, protect me now, I beg you. Keep me safe from false accusations, from ill intent. Let Aiden know the truth, for I cannot bear him to think I betrayed him with another, even if he himself did the same."

A drop of rain fell on her cheek and then another and another, and as she reached her hand up to wipe them away she realized they were warm, her own tears. She lowered her forehead onto her raised knees, letting the tears come as they would, pouring down her cheeks like a river of heartbreak.

Follow your heart and the truth will reveal itself . . .

The words floated like a whisper through the howling of the wind, just as she had heard them once before in a time of despair. But she had followed her heart, she thought miserably. That was the trouble. She had followed it and it had only led her to disaster. Was that the truth the goddess had meant? That Aiden, whom she loved desperately despite herself, had taken another woman to his bed? *Know that I don't intend to break my marriage vows,* he'd sworn under this very tree on their wedding day. But he had.

He had lied to her. He had betrayed her. He had believed his sister's allegations against her. And yet she still loved him. To try to excise Aiden would be like trying to cut her heart out, an impossible task. He had made her his, and she couldn't change that one unassailable fact. She just wasn't sure how to go on loving him and survive.

"Serafina . . ."

This voice was real, its deep pitch achingly familiar. Her head jerked up. Aiden stood only feet away, his face streaming with rain, his jacket plastered against his hard muscular form.

She jumped to her feet, staring at him as if he might be a specter. But he was all too solid, and the last person in the world she wanted to see. Her first impulse was to flee, but the only path before her would take her directly to him.

Instinct took over. She spun around and reached for the first low branches of the oak, using them to pull herself up. She climbed furiously, not even bothering to test her weight in a headlong rush to escape him.

"Serafina, you idiot, what are you doing?" he cried, running toward the tree in long strides. "Are you mad? There's lightning striking all around. Get down from there!"

"No," she called over her shoulder. "Go away. I don't want to talk to you." She couldn't reach the next set of branches, so she settled herself in the crook of a limb and pressed her cheek against the trunk, breathing hard.

"You may not want to talk to me, which I can well understand," he said, peering up at her through the leaves. "But I want to talk to you, and I'm damned if I'm going to do it like this. Please, sweetheart, come down. It's dangerous up there, it really is." He sounded truly frightened.

"I won't come down, and don't call me sweetheart," she said, anger replacing panic. "You don't mean it, and I won't be lied to."

"I'm not lying to you," he said, raking his hands through his wet hair, sending sprays of water flying. "I have nothing to lie to you about, for God's sake! If anyone's been lied to, it's me—and not by you, by Charlotte."

Serafina's eyes widened. She shifted on the limb so that she could see him better. "You *know* she lied?" she asked, not sure she could possibly have heard correctly. "But she said—she said you believed her—that you never wanted to see me again."

"I know what she said, or at least I assume I know, and right now I don't give a damn about any of it. Please, come down out of this tree before I'm forced to come up after you?"

"But—but I don't understand . . ." Serafina said, her head spinning. Charlotte had been so clear. Aiden hated her. Aiden thought she'd been unfaithful to him. He wanted her gone. But the way he was looking at her right now, his eyes filled with real concern, made a lie out of that too. And he'd just said that he hadn't believed a word of what his sister had told him.

"I know you don't understand," Aiden said, his voice rough. "If you'll just remove yourself from your perch, I'll explain everything." He flinched as a bolt of lightning struck on the other side of the pond. "Now!" he roared.

She swallowed hard. It was all well and fine that he'd dismissed Charlotte's horrible charges against her, but he still had some equally horrible charges of his own to answer to. "What about Harriet Munro?" she demanded.

"What about the bloody woman?" he said, his eyes flashing with frustration. "She's a silly, vain peahen and nothing but a thorn in my side. Is that what you want to know?"

Serafina glared at him. "If she's such a silly, vain peahen, then why did you sleep with her?"

Aiden threw his hands up in the air in exasperation. "What the hell difference does it make? She was conveniently there. I was stupid. I don't know! It's water under the bridge, for the love of God."

"She was 'conveniently there'?" Serafina said furiously, appalled that he could be so callous, so dismissive of his wedding vows. "And just because you were angry with me for doing something I hadn't, you decided it was well within your rights to go and do the same thing?"

Aiden stared up at her. "What? Oh, dear God . . ." He bent his head, his shoulders taut. And then he looked up again. "Is that what Charlotte told you? That I spent the night with Harriet when I didn't come home?"

Serafina didn't bother gracing his question with a reply. If there had been an acorn in easy reach she would have thrown it straight down onto his handsome face.

"I swear to you, sweetheart, all I did the other night was

walk. I pounded the stinking streets of London, trying to escape from Charlotte's accusations against you. I haven't been with Harriet in four years."

"You took Harriet to her carriage," Serafina said accusingly.

"Yes, and practically threw her headfirst into it. I was furious with her. I saw her talking to you and Charlotte, and I saw you remove yourself, obviously upset. So I decided to remove her from the premises altogether."

"She chose my trousseau." Serafina said flatly, only slightly mollified by this husbandly gesture of protection.

"She told you that, did she? Well, it's true in part," he said, rubbing the back of his neck. "Tinkerby and I were floundering about. I'd already told Mme. Bernard what sort of styles and colors I thought would suit you best, but the details were beyond me, so Harriet, who happened to appear out of the blue, stepped in. Serafina, will you *please* return to earth before I find myself picking up a pile of cinders?"

"You didn't make love to her?" she demanded, still not entirely sure he was telling her the truth.

"No!" he cried, slamming his palms against the trunk of the tree. "Damn, that hurt," he said, shaking his hands furiously.

"Serves you right," she muttered with satisfaction. "Why should I believe you?" she called down to him. "You're a self-styled rogue and—and you've been behaving as if you don't even care whether I live or die."

"You think I don't *care*?" he said incredulously. "Sweetheart, my problem is that I care too much—do you really think I've ever let anyone get under my skin the way you have? I'm driven to distraction with how much I care. Why the hell else do you think I'd come chasing after you at breakneck speed—not mention risking my life by standing under a tree in the middle of a lightning storm? And I wish you'd come down."

"You honestly didn't make love to Harriet?" she asked, chewing on her lip.

"Serafina, why would I make love to anyone else when you're the only woman I want and ever will? I love you!"

Serafina stared down at him. "What?" she whispered. "What did you say?"

"I love you," he roared. "Now come down!"

Serafina couldn't move fast enough. She felt like singing a song of joy as she put her hands behind her and shimmied forward, her feet reaching for the branch below. But in her haste her feet slipped and went out from under her. With a sharp yelp of alarm she found herself tumbling through thin air with nothing to give her purchase.

"Sarah! Oh God, Sarah!" The heart-wrenching cry tore from Aiden's throat as she fell, only dimly heard in her short plunge to earth.

His arms caught her fast, breaking her fall, and they both landed on the ground in a heap, a whoosh of air exploding from Aiden's lungs.

He raised himself onto his elbows, breathing hard, gazing down into her face. "Are you all right?"

She nodded faintly, her eyes huge with wonder.

"Thank God," he said with a sigh of relief. "You scared the life out of me." His expression suddenly changed from tenderness to one of unmitigated fury. "Don't you ever, *ever*, do that to me again," he said ferociously, abruptly standing, "or I'll—I'll horsewhip you. And get out from under this damned tree," he added, hauling her to her feet. "You have no more sense than a child in leading strings."

He stalked off to the edge of the spread of branches, his back turned to her, his hands shoved on his hips, his head bowed as his shoulders rose and fell rapidly.

"Aiden?" she said, the song in her heart rising to a blissful crescendo. *Thank you, goddess. Thank you,* it caroled.

He looked over his shoulder. "What?" he asked curtly, still looking shaken.

"What did you call me?" she asked, her face wreathed in an enormous smile. Blessed. She was truly blessed.

"A damned fool?" he replied dryly.

"No. When I was falling," she said, her heart about to burst with happiness.

He frowned. "I called your name."

Serafina crowed with laughter and ran toward him like a

bullet exploding from a gun. She threw her arms around him, and the force of her body hitting his before he had a chance to brace himself knocked him to the ground again. Serafina fell on top of him, laughing like a maniac.

"You did!" she crowed, covering his face with frantic little kisses. "I knew I heard it right—oh, *Aiden*," she said, throwing her head back in exaltation, "I knew it!"

Aiden lifted his head slightly, pinned down by her weight. "What did you know?" he said, looking baffled by her delight.

"That you really were destined to be my husband," she said, knowing there was no way to explain. It didn't matter. She rested her forehead against the base of his warm throat where his pulse beat steadily. Life. Aiden's soul—Adam's soul. One and the same. Here. Now. It all made sense, it all finally made sense. She hadn't been fantasizing or even descending into madness for a single moment. The goddess had tried to tell her, and she simply hadn't understood. Or believed hard enough. But she believed now. Oh, how she believed. All her dreams had come true.

Aiden was Adam and he loved her.

"I love you too," she breathed, moving up to kiss his mouth, affirming the truth of her declaration.

Aiden's arms came around her hard, holding her fast, returning her kiss in full measure, opening his mouth, possessing her fully as his tongue met hers, sending her into whirling spirals of desire. He deftly turned her onto her back, his thigh pressing between her legs as he pushed her back against the wet grass, his hands loosening the ribbon that restrained her hair.

He lifted his head, his fingers combing through her heavy locks as he gazed down at her, his sapphire eyes filled with longing. "Serafina—oh, Lord, my sweet, you're so beautiful. How could you have thought for a moment that I would ever want another woman after being with you?"

She smiled up at him, her hands stroking his cheeks. "I was being foolish. I listened to Charlotte's lies against you, and I should have known better." She sighed with simple happiness. "All I want is you. Always."

A great honking came from behind them and they both turned their heads toward the source.

The swans lifted their wings in unison, one pair white, one pair black, their necks craned back, their beaks raised as they called their song to the sky. The clouds had parted and a brilliant shaft of sunlight fell onto the glassy surface of the water just where the swans floated, illuminating them in the gray light.

Aiden grinned. "I want to make love to you here and now, but I'm damned if I'll do it in the full view of a pair of birds who have nothing better to do than honk at us. I want a warm, dry bed, and a great deal of privacy for what I have in mind."

Serafina burst into laughter. "You've suddenly become shy, have you? I don't remember your minding the swans too terribly the last time we were out here."

"I hardly registered the bloody swans the last time we were out here, but I'm not about to give them a repeat performance." He stood and scooped her up into his arms. "We're both wet, muddy, and bedraggled, thanks to you." He kissed her nose. "And you look utterly adorable, by the way."

"I think I like you muddy, wet, and bedraggled," she said, wrapping her arms tightly around his neck. "Are you planning on carrying me all the way back to Townsend?"

"I am. What sort of gentleman would I be if I allowed you to get your feet wet?"

Serafina nuzzled the soft lobe of his ear. "My feet couldn't get any wetter, and you're no gentleman in any case," she said softly.

"You're right about that. And I'm about to prove it to you."

23

"*H*ome, my sweet, and not a moment too soon for what I have in mind," Aiden said, carrying Serafina up the steps, her arms wrapped in a most satisfying fashion around his neck, her cheek resting against his. It felt so damned good to have her back in his arms, and it was going to feel even better once he'd gotten her safely upstairs to their bedroom, where he planned to show her exactly how he felt about her.

The last thing he'd expected was to make an impassioned declaration of love to her while she was sitting ten feet above him, wrapped around a tree limb, but the words had come out unbidden and they were the truest he'd ever spoken. And now they were out, he had no intention of retracting them. Rafe was right. He was head over heels in love with his wife, and he felt like the luckiest man on earth.

With his usual efficiency, Plum opened the door just as Aiden reached it.

"Oh—my lord . . . her ladyship? Is she injured?" he cried, his usually composed face badly out of place. "Oh, heavens above! Shall I call the doctor?"

"Her ladyship is perfectly well, if a little wet," Aiden said with a laugh, although he was touched by Plum's fervent devotion to Serafina. "We've both had a soaking, thanks to my wife's penchant for running about in thunderstorms."

"So I see, my lord," Plum said uncertainly. "It will be a miracle if you don't both catch your deaths. I should call for the doctor right now."

Serafina lifted her head. "Don't worry, Plum. A little rain never hurt anyone, despite what your mother may have told you."

The idea of Plum having a mother struck Aiden as being singularly amusing, although he supposed Plum must have one somewhere. He couldn't help imagining an older, female version of the balding butler, sitting in a cottage somewhere knitting socks for her dignified son.

"From the looks of it, my lady, the rain has only done you good," Plum said. "The color's back in your cheeks, and that's a blessing to be sure." He turned his gaze to Aiden. "Lord Delaware returned from London in your absence, my lord, bringing Janie and Tinkerby with him. And your sister wishes a word with you."

"You can tell my sister to go hang," Aiden said succinctly. He had no intention of getting into another sparring match with Charlotte, especially with what he had in mind for Serafina.

"Aiden?" Charlotte's pleading voice came from the open doors of the drawing room. "Please? I need to speak with you and your wife."

"I think we should at least give her a minute," Serafina murmured quietly against his ear. "She deserves that much, Aiden. She probably feels terrible."

Aiden swore softly under his breath, then gently set Serafina on her feet. "One minute, Charlotte, and one minute only," he said. "We both need to get out of our wet clothes."

He put his arm around Serafina's waist and led her in, both of them leaving wet trails in their wake. He hoped Charlotte was having heart palpitations at the sight of them dripping water and mud all over the immaculate marble floor, not to mention the priceless Aubusson carpet.

"Well?" he demanded as soon as he'd shut the doors behind him. "What do you have to say?"

"Only that I'm deeply sorry," she said, gazing down at her lap. "I was—I was wrong to have accused your wife and Raphael of misconduct. I should have looked farther into my heart and known it could not be true."

"Tell that to Serafina," Aiden said bitterly. "You've caused unnecessary anguish, Charlotte, and all because you leapt to a ridiculous conclusion."

"Yes. Yes, that's true," she said, raising her tearful blue gaze to his. "It is I who needs to repent, I see that now. Please accept my apologies."

"I think it's best if we put the incident behind us," Serafina said quietly. "There's no need to dwell on what is past. I'm sure we can go on perfectly comfortably, just as before."

"Thank you," Charlotte whispered, her handkerchief clasped to her mouth. "You are generous in your forgiveness, dear sister. I am sure I do not deserve it, but I find you most Christian in your kindness."

"I agree with Serafina," Aiden said, surprised that his wife was prepared to excuse his sister so readily, but relieved that she didn't intend to make a scene. There had been enough of those to last a lifetime in the last two days. "Let's all try to pretend this never happened," he said, although something tugged uneasily at the back of his mind, a feeling that Charlotte's contrition was too easy. "But everything I said to you earlier stands," he added, to be sure he'd made his point perfectly clear. "Now if you'll excuse us, we need to change into dry clothes."

"Of course," Charlotte said, twisting her handkerchief into a tight knot. "Please, do not let me keep you a minute longer."

Aiden took Serafina's hand and practically pulled her out of the room, other, more important things on his mind than his sister's lukewarm apologies.

Aiden closed the bedroom door behind them and cocked one eyebrow at Serafina. "Well, wife," he said, looking her up and down. "What do you suggest I do with you?"

Serafina touched a finger to her chin. "Ravish me, my lord?" she said hopefully. She could think of nothing she'd rather have him do.

Aiden burst into laughter. "You've never been one to mince words, and ravish you I will. But first let's get you out of your wet dress."

He turned her and undid the buttons on the back,

smoothing the material down her arms and dropping a lingering kiss on one bare shoulder as her dress fell in a heap on the floor. "Mmm," he murmured as he slid his warm hands up her waist, lifting her chemise over her head.

The cool air caressed Serafina's skin as he bared her breasts, running his palms over them, cupping her in his hands, shaping her to his touch. "Oh, God you feel good," he said hoarsely, pulling her into his arms and raking her mouth with a deep, demanding kiss.

She trembled furiously under his touch. So long. So very long since he had held her like this, caused her body to sing with hot excitement. She pushed the jacket off his broad shoulders, her fingers seeking the hard planes of his chest beneath the damp linen of his shirt. His nipples sprang up under her touch and he groaned, releasing her for a moment as he tore his jacket and shirt off, then reached down and yanked off his boots, tossing them to one side.

"Aiden," she whispered as he pulled her into his arms again. "Oh, how I love you. I don't think I knew how much until I thought I'd lost you. But are you sure you feel the same way?" she asked uncertainly. "I know you wanted me to come down from the tree and you might have said anything to accomplish your objective."

He lifted her easily in his arms and deposited her on the bed, coming down next to her, his eyes flashing blue fire. "I do love you," he said, his voice rough. "I think I must have done from the moment we first met, but I was too damned stubborn to admit it to myself, and for that I could kick myself."

"It doesn't matter," she said softly, running her fingers through his thick, silky hair, hugely relieved. "You know it now, and that's the important thing."

He kissed her chin. "I might know it, but I have to admit that I'm scared to death, and the last week taught me why I should be. Jesus, Serafina, I've never been so plagued by furious emotion, and none of it was fun. I never thought in a thousand years that I'd be a jealous husband, but loving you has turned me into a mindless, raving lunatic." He sighed. "I'm sorry, sweetheart. I'm sorry I ever doubted you, and I'm even more sorry that I behaved like such a bastard in London when that was the last thing you deserved."

"Don't, Aiden," she said, blinking back tears. "I'm just as responsible. I could have told you I loved you, since it was the truth. I should certainly have told you from the beginning about Raphael. But now that you know the truth—you do know the real truth?" she asked, not sure on that point.

"Yes, I know the truth. Rafe told me all about your lessons. And I ought to have figured them out for myself, for only Rafe is capable of turning a wood nymph into a perfect countess in three short weeks." He grinned. "But thank God he had the good sense to leave the wood nymph in place. I'd have strangled him if he'd spoiled you. There's a reason I fell in love with you, you know."

Serafina laughed through the blur of her tears, thinking that Aiden had very little idea of why he'd fallen in love with her. He wasn't to know she was his destiny, had always been his destiny, and she doubted he would believe her if she was silly enough to tell him. Which she had no intention of doing. A slip of his tongue in a moment of panic was one thing. To be told he really had once been a prince was another. "Raphael said he could make anything pretty," she said instead. "You should have seen him try, though. His patience must have been sorely tested."

"I doubt it—Rafe has always liked a good challenge, and he doesn't take defeat easily. However, my cousin is the last person I want to think about right now." He pressed a kiss on her forehead.

"Aiden—what about Charlotte?" Serafina asked, wanting to have everything clear between them before they went any farther.

"What about bloody Charlotte?" he said impatiently, tracing the curve of her throat with one finger.

"You won't stay angry with her, will you? She may have made a bad mistake, but we all make mistakes, and Charlotte did seem sorry. I don't want her to suffer unduly."

Aiden lazily cupped one breast, flicking her nipple with his thumb, sending pulsing waves of desire through her. "I don't think she'll suffer unduly. By tomorrow morning she'll be back to her old managing self. And I don't want to think about Charlotte either, or my father, just in case you plan to bring him up next."

Serafina hadn't thought about Lord Delaware at all, but since Aiden had introduced the subject, she thought she might as well dispose of it. "Have you forgiven him?" she asked, trying to ignore the treacherous calling of her body. "He did behave himself beautifully in London. In fact, I think he managed to charm a large number of people."

Aiden released a long breath. "Yes, he did. And yes, I've forgiven him, although it will take some time for me to feel fully in accord with him—there's a lot of healing still to be done. And no, I don't wish to discuss the subject any further at this moment." He dropped his head to her breast, drawing it into his mouth, his warm tongue flicking over her hard, sensitive nub, driving her into a frenzy as his hands reached for her buttocks and cupped them.

She shivered, reveling in his touch. "I love you so much it hurts," she murmured, running her hands over his strong back, his shoulders. "I think I must have loved you forever."

Aiden took her face between his hands and looked into her eyes, his gaze dark and intent, his fingers lightly tracing the lines of her cheekbones. "I don't know about forever, but I do know that you're my life, Serafina, everything that's important to me. I never thought I'd be lucky enough to find love, but against all reason I have, and I have no intention of ever letting you go for any reason."

A fresh rush of tears flooded Serafina's eyes. He really did love her. She knew it by the tenderness in his voice, the way he touched her, so gently, with such reverence. *Swear you'll love me forever* . . . Aiden. He had been brought to her through time, given back to her. Her memories had sustained her through years of waiting, but the reality of his love was the true gift she'd been given.

She lifted her head and kissed him, her arms twining around his neck. "Make love to me," she whispered. "Seal our vow, Aiden."

He didn't answer her with words, instead moving over her, his hands and mouth answer enough as he caressed her naked flesh, playing over her willing, hungry body until she gasped and writhed beneath his heated touch. His fingers slipped low, tangling in her damp curls, seeking her core, and she drew in a shivering breath as he caressed her there too, driving her to a fury of excitement.

He made a low sound in his throat as she cried out, pushing her hips up against his hand, her body reaching toward the peak of ecstasy, straining toward release. He gave it to her, his fingers stilling as she shuddered violently, her sharp cries of pleasure stifled by his mouth as he kissed her hard, his tongue thrusting deep. Heat. Fire. So much love.

His shaft throbbed against her belly through the doeskin of his trousers and with an impatient oath he sat up and stripped them off, repositioning himself between her thighs.

"Serafina . . ." he moaned, sliding into her, so hard, so vital, filling her completely with his length as he thrust. "Oh, God. Oh, God Almighty, that's so nice."

She gave herself over to him completely, her body moving frenetically to meet his as he possessed her, pressing deep, withdrawing, plunging back into her, and she sobbed with pleasure at each renewed thrust. Her world spun away from her until there was nothing left but Aiden's body in hers, on hers, his harsh pants against her cheek, his salty sweat on her tongue as she swept it over his flaming skin, her hands stroking and caressing, urging him faster and harder.

"Aiden! Now!" she cried, her body shattering into a thousand pieces of unbearable sensation, the vortex of the universe sweeping her into its middle, creation itself, dark and light joining together in an elemental explosion that threatened to unmake her.

Aiden stiffened, his body wracked with shudders as he threw his head back and cried out savagely, his hips jerking as the heat of his seed washed into her in life-affirming waves.

"Swear you'll love me forever," he gasped against her mouth.

"I swear it. Forever and beyond."

A vow kept. A promise fulfilled. And a new beginning,

for they had love between them now, strong and sure and unquestionable.

Serafina's hands loosened on his back as her tremors subsided. She'd never felt so weak, her limbs like water. He moaned and rolled half off her, burying his face in her hair.

"I think I'm dead," he managed to croak. "And if this is heaven, I think I'll stay."

Serafina gasped with laughter. "If this is heaven, your sister will not be pleased."

"Oh, God," he groaned, nuzzling the curve of her throat. "Don't you dare bring my sister up at a time like this. If I know anything about it, Lottie is sitting downstairs, her head filled with dark thoughts about the sinful things we've been doing."

Serafina lifted her neck for his caress. "Don't be awful, Aiden. Charlotte is more likely immersed in her Bible, finding an appropriate passage to explain away her behavior."

Aiden raised his head. "I can think of any number of more appropriate passages. For example, 'thy two breasts are like young roes that are twins, which feed among the lilies.' The Song of Solomon."

And so saying, he bent his head to her breasts again and fed on them until Serafina forgot that anyone existed in the world but the two of them.

They missed dinner altogether, Aiden turning the last of the afternoon and all of the evening into a feast of passion. Serafina woke as the full moon rose, her stomach churning with hunger. Aiden lay in a tangled heap of bedclothes, one arm flung over his head, his breathing deep and heavy with sleep.

She smiled, not surprised that he was exhausted. He'd held nothing of himself back, showing her just how fully love could be enacted, how many satisfying paths it could take.

She slipped into a night robe and dressing gown and stole quietly out of their room, creeping down the stairs. Nothing stirred, and she was grateful, for she didn't want to disturb any of the servants who had gone to a well-deserved rest a good two hours before.

But as she reached the hall she heard a low moan as if someone might be in pain. She stopped and listened carefully. The moan came again from the direction of Charlotte's apartment, adjacent to the library.

She knew Charlotte suffered deeply on occasion, so she walked softly over to her door and lightly knocked, hoping she might be able to help. There was no answer. Serafina carefully turned the handle and entered the dark sitting room. A beam of light came from the bedroom door, half opened. The noise came again, this time a long, low whimper.

She made her way across the room, trying to adjust her eyes to the dark. And froze in shock as the candlelight flickering in the bedroom illuminated the scene on the bed.

Charlotte lay with her nightdress thrown up above her breasts, her body bared. And Frederick the footman lay stretched between her legs, his head buried between Charlotte's thighs.

"More!" Charlotte spit out, the crop in her hand descending on Freddie's bare back and buttocks. "Deeper, harder, you fool!"

"I can't, my lady. Please—I can't anymore," Frederick moaned, twisting his head up to gaze at Charlotte imploringly. "I don't want to. I beg you!"

The crop whipped down in a stinging lash, leaving yet another red welt on Frederick's back. "Don't you tell me what you cannot do, what you want and don't want. You work for me and you will not slack! Harder, I tell you. Give me satisfaction, you mindless servant!"

Serafina stumbled back against the wall, her hands covering her mouth against a wave of sickness that reached bone deep. She had just witnessed something horribly ugly, an act that made a travesty of lovemaking. For what she'd seen had nothing to do with love. Charlotte, God-fearing Charlotte, was forcing a helpless footman to pleasure her, beating him to a pulp in the process.

Charlotte had told her that she had never lost the feeling

in her legs when Serafina had been trying to convince her to use the oil. She had only spoken of her constant pain, and it had never occurred to Serafina that the oil might work too well, awakening sexual feelings in Charlotte, although nothing excused her lecherous behavior. No wonder Frederick had looked so ill when they returned. Charlotte must have been tormenting him for some time.

She had half a mind to go in and drag Frederick away, but she knew she couldn't do that—not without creating terrible embarrassment for all three of them. The thought crossed her mind to go and wake up Aiden, make him stop Charlotte's vicious attack. But Aiden would be horrified, even if he did rescue Frederick. He would never be able to erase the picture from his mind of his sister lying naked, legs flung open, whipping a footman into submission, and Aiden didn't deserve that. No, Serafina would never tell a soul about what she'd seen.

She would simply have to find a way of handling the situation on her own. In the morning she would have a private word with Frederick—find him another position without letting on that she knew what Charlotte had driven him to do. Maybe Raphael would be willing to hire Frederick at Southwell. She would send him a note in the morning.

Serafina staggered out of the room, managing to reach the safety of the outdoors before she was violently ill.

Charlotte's chest churned with panic as she wheeled herself down the upstairs back corridor of the house, a route Serafina took every morning on her way down to collect her gardening equipment as soon as she'd breakfasted in her room.

She was sure—absolutely certain—that she'd seen Serafina the night before, skulking about in Charlotte's sitting room. She had only caught a brief flash of a white dressing gown and long dark hair from the corner of her eye, gone immediately, but there was no one else in the household who matched that description.

And if she knew anything, it was that Serafina would go directly to Aiden with her foul gossip. She hadn't yet, for

Aiden had appeared downstairs for an early breakfast and he had said nothing to her, nor given her any indication that he knew what Frederick had been doing to Charlotte only hours before in her bed. Aiden would never keep silent over something like that.

She had to do something now to keep Serafina from spilling the truth, for once Aiden heard, Charlotte was as good as gone. He'd never believe her protestations, not if his wife did the accusing. Aiden had shown his true colors the day before when it came to his whore, believing her word over anyone's, the fool.

There was no time to waste. Serafina needed to be dispatched, and quickly. It was the only solution to all of Charlotte's problems. Once Serafina was out of the way, life would return to normal.

She waited in the open doorway of the linen closet next to the stairs, her hands clutching the heavy crystal paperweight in her lap, its sharp facets digging into her fingers. What happened if Serafina changed her routine? Suppose she decided to seek out Aiden instead and unburden her secret?

And then Charlotte heard a rustle of skirts coming down the hallway, the tap of shoes on wood. Her heart leapt with anticipation as Serafina rounded the corner. She held her breath as Serafina came closer, her face all innocence, so unsuspecting.

Charlotte chose her moment carefully. She wheeled out of the doorway, feigning surprise just as Serafina reached the top of the stairs.

"Oh!" she cried, one hand going to her throat. "It's you, dear sister—you startled me. I was just counting the sheets and pillowcases. As usual we've come up a few short."

Serafina's step slowed, then stopped. "Have we?" she said, her face neutral, betraying nothing of what Charlotte knew she must be thinking. "I'm sure you'll track them down in no time."

"Naturally I will. Are you on your way out to the gardens?"

"Yes," Serafina said. "Your father will be waiting. If you'll excuse me?" She turned.

In that moment Charlotte lunged out of her chair, her hand raised. She brought the paperweight down on the side of Serafina's unsuspecting head with a loud crack, putting all of her weight into the blow.

Serafina cried out sharply, then slowly crumpled to the ground, her temple spreading with bright blood. Charlotte prodded her with her foot, but Serafina didn't move.

With a smile of triumph, Charlotte bent down. Serafina's face had turned white, her lips blue.

It took almost no effort to roll Serafina to the top step, and with one hefty push, she sent her tumbling down the steep stairs.

She watched with satisfaction as Serafina's body bumped and twisted until it landed at the bottom in an inert heap like a limp, broken doll.

She took a moment to wipe the paperweight clean of blood and hair and scrubbed at her fingers to remove all traces of her crime, shoving the stained handkerchief into her sleeve. And then she returned to her chair and quickly wheeled away, disappearing into the bowels of the house.

24

"*M*y lord! My lord, come quickly—there's been a terrible accident!"

Aiden dropped his pen as Plum appeared in the doorway, out of breath, his face as pale as a ghost's. "What is it?" Aiden demanded, slowly rising, his heart pounding in dread. Plum's expression of severe distress bode only ill.

"Her ladyship—she fell down the back stairs, my lord. She's hardly breathing . . . we don't know if she's broken her neck or what else is wrong with her, but she's bleeding badly from her head." He wrung his hands together.

"My sister?" Aiden said, swallowing hard.

"No, my lord—your wife. Frederick found her. Lord Delaware's gone for the doctor."

Aiden tore across the room, thrusting past Plum and out into the hall. Not Serafina. It couldn't be. Not his sweet Serafina, his very life.

Plum chased after him, pointing up the stairs, and Aiden took them two at a time.

She lay on their bed, half her face covered in a mask of blood, the rest of it ashen. He might have thought she was dead but for the uneven, shallow rise and fall of her chest.

He dropped to his knees, taking her hand in his, trying to still the panic in his heart. "Sweetheart?" he whispered, smoothing her hair back off the uninjured side of her brow. "Serafina? Please, my love, open your eyes. Look at me, sweetheart. I'm here. I'm here."

Janie rushed in with a bowl of water and linens draped

over her arm, her face streaming with soundless tears. "My lord. Oh, my poor lord," she said, putting the basin down next to the bed. "How could such a thing happen to our angel? I only spoke with her half an hour ago, and she was hail and hearty. God couldn't be so cruel as to take her from us, he just couldn't."

Aiden didn't reply. He couldn't. If he tried to speak, he knew he'd start to rage against God Himself, and Serafina needed all the help she could get.

Janie wrung out one of the cloths and gently began to pat at Serafina's face, wiping away the blood. "There, my pet. We'll look after you, we'll see you right," she crooned. "You just hold on, for everyone's counting on you."

Aiden watched every move Janie made, but he flinched as her administrations revealed a deep gash on Serafina's temple. It was all he could do not to fling the woman away and take the cloth from her, but his hands were shaking too badly to do Serafina any good.

A deep reddish-purple bruising ran from the edges of the open wound, spreading all the way down her cheek to the fragile skin behind her ear. Looking at it, Aiden didn't know how she'd survive. And he didn't even know what other injuries she might have.

In that moment Aiden wasn't sure he wanted to survive either.

The doctor came and went. He stitched Serafina's head up and pronounced her neck in one piece, no other bones broken. But his news was nevertheless grim. "I'm sorry, my lord," he said, just before departing. "Your wife has suffered a severe concussion, the result of a serious blow to the head. There is no telling what might happen."

"Will she live?" Aiden asked from between gritted teeth, his effort at control nearly killing him.

"I cannot say. I would not hold out great hope, for her breathing is erratic at best. Only time will tell, but I would prepare myself for the worst." He didn't meet Aiden's eyes, gazing instead at a point over Aiden's shoulder, not a good sign, Aiden knew. "Please call me should there be any change. The best you can do is keep a vigil."

Aiden nodded curtly, not trusting himself to speak. He went back up to the bedroom and took up a chair next to Serafina's bed, vowing not to leave it until she decided to either live or die.

Three days passed. Raphael, his father, his sister, Tinkerby, Janie all took turns staying at Serafina's side. But Aiden refused to leave for a moment. He allowed their presence, only because he knew they cared about her and would be even more distressed if he turned them away. But nothing changed. Serafina lay deep in a coma, the fragile skin of her eyelids bruised and blue over her closed eyes. He ate only because he had to eat, but only managed a bite here and there. He slept fitfully in his chair, waking at the slightest sound.

He'd never felt more helpless or more frightened. Death hovered close by, a constant companion. He could feel it pulling at her, Serafina's tenuous grip on life slipping farther away. She began to babble, a stream of delirium, calling names he'd never heard, with the exception of one.

Adam.

She spoke it repeatedly, her hands clutching at the bed-clothes, her head tossing back and forth. Adam. Aiden's heart twisted every time he heard it, the name she'd called him twice before, once the first time he'd put her to bed, the second—he could hardly bear to think about the second, in the peak of climax.

Adam.

He hated the man. He hated whomever he was, who stole Serafina's confused dreams from him even now. He hated all the names she cried out: Clio, Michael, Leo. But he hated Adam most of all. And the one name she never murmured was his own.

If Elspeth had been around, he would have interrogated her until she was forced to tell him everything about Serafina's previous life. Tinkerby had been no help, roundly insisting that he'd never heard of any of the people Serafina asked for now. Aiden didn't even know where Elspeth was, the one person who should have been there for Serafina. And he hated Elspeth too for deserting Serafina in a time of need.

When the truth came down to it, he hated everyone, God included. But he hated himself most of all. For as illogical as it was, he and only he was responsible for Serafina's welfare. And therefore he was responsible for her predicament now. If Serafina died he would have only himself to blame.

On the fourth day, Elspeth appeared out of the blue.

Aiden lifted his weary head as she came careening into the bedroom, her face drawn into tight lines of concern.

"What's this I hear about my dear girl?" she demanded, marching over to the bed and looking into Serafina's face. "Plum said she fell down the stairs. I don't believe a word of it. Serafina may have her faults, but she's always been graceful." Elspeth lifted one of Serafina's eyelids and peered into her unseeing eye. "Four days of this, Plum said? Hmm."

"Leave her alone," Aiden snapped, too tired to go into a full-fledged roar. "The last thing your niece needs is to be mauled. Or doctored by you. She's delirious, Miss Beaton, and your poking at her isn't going to accomplish a thing."

"And what would you know of it, my boy?" Elspeth said, tapping her finger against her cheek. "What's she been saying that makes you think her delirious?"

Aiden raked his hands through his hair, longing to throw the old woman out of the room. "She's been calling out all sorts of names, and maybe you can explain that. They're people she's never before mentioned, but the way she's been going on you'd think they were her dearest friends on earth."

"Serafina didn't have any friends to speak of before she came here, other than the people she sang with in the church choir and a few villagers," Elspeth said, frowning. "Who is she asking for?"

Aiden told her, out of his mind with worry. "Day and night she tosses, crying and moaning, making no sense."

Elspeth just nodded. "I see," she said, gazing down at Serafina. "I should have expected something like this."

"What in God's name are you talking about, woman?" Aiden, already pushed beyond his endurance, really didn't think he could bear any of Elspeth's foolish babble.

She gave him a sharp, assessing look, and once again he saw a keen intelligence in her eyes that belied the vapid old woman he was accustomed to. "I don't expect you to understand, but I can tell you that Serafina is not suffering from the effects of a concussion," she said. "She is suffering from an injury of the mind, and it's one that took place a good long time ago. If you want your wife back, then you're going to have to help me—you, your father, your sister, and the duke."

Aiden stared at her in disbelief. "My dear Miss Beaton, the doctor has made a diagnosis, based on his considerable medical knowledge. I hardly think you have the experience to contradict him. And you still haven't explained a damned thing about these people Serafina is calling for."

Elspeth regarded him impatiently. "That's because the people she's calling for are no longer known by those names, not in this lifetime. And I haven't time to go into it, not if Serafina is to recover. If you have an iota of sense in your head, you'll do as I ask and gather your family and the duke. The rest will become clear."

Aiden rubbed his hands over his face. "Miss Beaton. I know all about your witchcraft and your lunatic ideas about reincarnation, and I don't want to hear another word on the subject. Furthermore, if you think I'm going to subject my wife to one of your nonsensical rituals in her condition, you had better reconsider."

Elspeth drew her tiny body up, her eyes flashing. "You think you know all about it, do you? And I suppose you know better than I who Adam is and why Serafina calls for him? I suppose you also know why Serafina loved you long before she ever laid eyes on you, why she waited for you so patiently?"

"Now what are you going on about?" Aiden cried, thoroughly sick of Elspeth and her convoluted ideas.

"*You* are Adam, you idiotic man. And Serafina has dreamed of you since her childhood—not as you are now, but as you were then, and just as blind, I might add. It wasn't Serafina's fault that you all came to a bad end, anymore than it's her fault that the same thing is happening all over again, with Charlotte at the heart of it, just as before."

Aiden sank into the chair, trying to make sense out of what Elspeth was saying, but he couldn't find anything to grab hold of, other than Elspeth was suffering from dementia. *He* was supposed to be this mysterious Adam? That in itself was laughable.

"See here," Elspeth said, bending over and stroking Serafina's brow. "The child needs to journey to find the truth, and I'm the only one who can help her, but I can't do it by myself. If you love your wife, Aiden, then support her now. Trust that I won't hurt her."

Aiden looked up at her, torn by confusion. Nothing had helped Serafina so far, and she showed no signs of improvement. Something had to change or he would lose her. He couldn't really see the harm in what Elspeth was proposing, even though he thought it was a bunch of poppycock. "What are you going to do?" he asked listlessly.

"As I said, I'm going to take her on a journey. It will be a long and difficult one, but she has to travel back eight hundred and . . ." Elspeth thought for a moment. "Eight hundred and fifty-three years. To a place called Cyprus."

Aiden sat up very straight, suddenly alert. "Cyprus?" he said. He'd been to Cyprus . . . even though it was under Ottoman rule it was an island he'd been strongly drawn to, a place that felt incredibly familiar. In fact he had been alarmed by just how familiar it was, how he seemed to know beforehand how the cities were laid out, Kyrenia in particular.

A cold sweat sprang to his brow. He'd never been able to explain the experience to himself—or why he had read whatever he could find on the place. "Why Cyprus?" he asked warily.

"Because that is where you and Serafina lived. And although she was called Sarah then, she was your wife and you loved each other truly. The problem was that your father and sister and Raphael lived there also, all of you making a muck of things," Elspeth answered tartly.

"How—how do you know this?" he said, thoroughly bewildered.

"Because I was there too, and maybe I have a better memory than the rest of you fools. It all ended in disaster, and Serafina's the only one who has the good sense to know it, which is why she's in such a terrible state now, worrying that you will all come to another bad end." She planted her hands on her hips. "I doubt you know the first thing about karmic debt, but it's time for it to be cleared, and apparently your wife is the only person who can do it. But she has to be surrounded by the people who created it in the first place."

Aiden passed a hand over his eyes. Sarah. Elspeth had said Serafina's name was Sarah. And he had called her that when she'd fallen from the tree, he remembered now. *I knew I heard it right,* she'd said joyfully. And later. *I think I must have loved you forever. . . .* As he must have loved her. As he had loved her from the first moment in the woods.

He knew it was insane even to consider the idea, but if Elspeth was right, everything made sense—why Serafina had insisted she loved him long before they met. Why she had called him Adam. Even why she had behaved in such an odd fashion the night she'd been reading his history of ship building, the book falling to the floor, open to the pages of Cypriot history. Over eight hundred years ago. She had gone into a blind panic, unable to breathe, insisting he tell his father something. And he had mistaken her terrified ramblings for exhaustion, a simple faint. Not the first time. Not the first time.

And if Elspeth was right, then Serafina was somehow in danger.

He stood, the decision made. "I'll gather everyone. And I hope to God you know what you're doing, for if any harm comes to my wife, I'll hold you fully responsible."

Elspeth arranged the room to her satisfaction, placing Aiden on Serafina's left, Raphael on her right, Lord Delaware at her head and a strongly protesting Charlotte at her feet, exactly where she belonged.

Elspeth had a strong suspicion that Serafina had not fallen down the stairs by herself, but she declined to say anything. For the moment. She hoped that the truth would come out for Serafina's sake, but she had more important work to do right now.

"I have no idea what this is all about, but I don't like it," Charlotte said, steely faced as Elspeth lit the candles and the censer. "I'm only here because Aiden asked me, not that he explained a thing. This looks disgustingly heathen to me."

Elspeth glared at her. "It is heathen, and you don't have to like it. All you have to do is keep your mouth shut until I'm finished. I wouldn't have you in here at all if I didn't need you."

Charlotte gripped the arms of her chair. "How dare you!" she cried. "I won't be a part of this unchristian charade. Aiden, I cannot think what's come over you to subject us all to this—this witch's sorcery!"

"Be silent," he snapped. "I don't want to hear a word out of you, whatever happens. Consider yourself warned, Charlotte."

Elspeth wanted to applaud. It was about time Aiden saw his sister's true colors. He was going to see a lot more than that by the time she was finished.

"Keep your trap shut, there's a good girl," Lord Delaware said mildly. "Nothing else has worked for dear Serafina and Aiden seems to think Miss Beaton knows what she's about. I reckon we'll soon see."

Raphael said nothing, but he watched Elspeth like a hawk.

"It is time," Elspeth said. "And whatever happens, no one must speak." She raised her arms and uttered the protective chant.

"I am protected by your might, O gracious goddess, day and night. Thrice around the circle's bound, evil sink into the ground." She recited the invocation of the goddess and the god. And then she began the task she'd been preparing herself for over countless years.

"Here is the boundary of the circle of stones.
Naught but love shall enter in,
Naught but love shall emerge from within.
Charge this by your powers, old ones!

Time will run back and fetch the age of gold . . ."

Serafina fought through the swirling mist from which she could find no escape, images forming and vanishing, fragments of vision she couldn't grab hold of. She only knew that there was danger, terrible danger. Time . . . time was all confused, running into itself, the past and present merged. And all she wanted was to find a way to escape, to go home to Aiden.

And then she felt him there with her in the mist, saw his beloved face, felt the pressure of his fingers on hers, steadying her. She pulled him toward her, taking strength from his presence. The mist began to clear, and images began to form in earnest, of herself and Adam, Clio, Michael, Leo, Bishop Margolis. But it was no dream. She and Aiden were the observers and the performers both, merged into one.

Serafina finally understood. They were to journey together, back to the place where everything had begun. Danger . . . there was danger, and unless she discovered what terrible thing had happened in that long ago time and place and laid it to rest, the tragedy would be repeated.

She pulled on Aiden's hand, urging him to come with her.

Elspeth's chant sent chills down Aiden's spine and set his teeth to chattering. He clutched Serafina's hand and it grew warmer. She seemed to be tugging on it as if she were trying to draw him near. Yet he felt as if more than his hand were being pulled. It was as if his soul were being drawn out of him, bearing him toward something, something that filled him with the unbearable pain of betrayal, yet he was compelled to follow.

Elspeth's voice came only faintly now, and Charlotte's face swam before Aiden's eyes, her expression twisted into one of loathing. *Mad*, he thought. *She's mad.* And then he thought maybe it was he who was mad as her image shivered, wavered, transforming into someone else. Charlotte. But not Charlotte. A woman. Wearing a circle of gold on her head.

His confused gaze swept the room, but he was no longer in his bedroom at Townsend. He stood in a great hall before two thrones on a dais. And he was no longer Aiden, but a man called Adam. Adam of Kyrenia, prince of the city-state.

Raphael was there too, his dearest friend then as he was now. Michael. Michael Angelus. He remembered. *Oh, God. He remembered.* And Elspeth stood silently off to one side, only she wasn't Elspeth at all, but Bishop Margolis, who had married him and Serafina the year before. No. That was right, his wife's name was Sarah. And she stood next to him, her golden hair tumbling in a braid down her back. But there was something wrong. Something terribly wrong.

He realized that it was his father who sat in one of the thrones. His father, then called King Leo. And Charlotte sat in the other, only she was his mother, Clio of Curium, and she was hurling intolerable accusations at his wife and his most trusted friend.

"*I tell you, she fornicates with your captain of the guard, Michael Angelus,*" Clio spat.

"*No,*" he cried, each of her words biting viciously, painfully into his heart. "*I do not believe it—I will not believe it. What proof, I ask?*"

"*I saw them together. I saw them with my own eyes.*"

"*She speaks falsely, Adam,*" Sarah said, turning to him, her eyes huge and hollow in her white face. "*You must listen to me and to Michael. This is all a fabrication.*"

Adam looked over at his wife, his beloved wife, the only woman he had ever loved, ever would love. And he didn't know what to think, what to believe anymore. His mother would never lie, not over something so important as this.

Sarah and Michael. They had grown close over the last year. And he had never had reason to suspect them, not until this afternoon when his mother had called them all together and pointed her finger, sworn to their adultery.

"Why would she fabricate such a thing, Sarah? What possible reason?" he demanded, his voice low and angry.

"She plots to invade Famagusta and she knew Michael was going to come to you and expose her scheming, so now she discredits him. Michael will tell you it is the truth, if you will only listen!"

"Nonsense," Clio cried. "This is a feeble attempt to mislead you, my son, to divert your attention from their wicked deed."

"What do you know of this, Father?" Adam asked, praying his father would shed some light, offer up an answer. But his father only shook his head, ineffective as ever.

"I know of no plot and no adultery either," he mumbled. "But I feel sure dear Sarah would never be unfaithful. Isn't that right, Father Margolis?"

"You fool!" Clio said furiously, not giving the bishop a chance to answer. "You would contradict me, when I have told you what I saw? You wait anxiously for your son's wife to produce his heir, and now for all we know it will be Captain Angelus's brat she will drop—if she's not barren altogether."

"What say you, Angelus?" Adam asked coldly, the image of Michael and Sarah in bed together too terrible to contemplate.

"I say again that your mother accuses me falsely. I tell you that she plots for the Kyrenia army to overthrow Famagusta, that I heard of her plan and told her it was madness, that it would only lead to disaster." He stood before Adam unflinching. "And it is not I who pursued your wife with lustful intent, but your mother who came after me in that manner. When I spurned her advances, she went into a rage and threatened retribution."

"No!" Adam roared. "No more—no more of your lies, do you hear? You cannot think I would give credence to such a twisted story? How dare you first defile my wife and now accuse my mother of not only scheming, but of entertaining corrupt thoughts?"

"I only speak the truth, Adam."

"You know nothing of the truth," Adam said, rage half blinding him. "I should order you killed for your treachery. But instead I strip you of your rank, Michael Angelus. And I banish you from Kyrenia for all time."

He held out his hands for Michael's sword of office, the gesture nearly bringing him to his knees. Betrayed. By his wife. By his friend. Betrayed.

Michael placed the sword in his open palms. "You are a fool," he said flatly. "I can only hope to God you realize it before it's too late. Too late for your wife, who loves you and only you. And too late for Kyrenia, for you can be sure the king of Famagusta will take swift and brutal vengeance if he even hears word of your mother's plot."

Adam couldn't bear to listen to another word. He turned on his heel. The bishop laid a restraining hand on his shoulder as he pushed past.

"Adam. Reconsider. You are not in possession of all of the facts," he said quietly.

"I've heard everything I need to," Adam snapped. "Do not think to interfere!" He stormed from the hall, his heart, his faith, his very soul torn to shreds.

"Adam—Adam!" Sarah had looked everywhere for him. She finally tore over the high meadow hoping to find him there. She had to make him see sense. She had to, although she didn't know how. Adam loved his mother. He trusted her. Apparently he trusted her so much that he believed Clio's word over his wife's. And his friend's.

That hurt her terribly all by itself, that he doubted her love for him, her fidelity. But what was even more terrifying was that Adam refused to hear of his mother's plotting. For Sarah had a terrible sense of foreboding that it would bring Kyrenia to ruin.

Her heart leapt with relief when she finally spotted him.

He stood on the flat top of the hill, his back to her, his face turned to the glittering sea. He didn't hear her approach, but the minute she placed her hands on his arms he spun around.

She wanted to cry. His face was ravaged with grief, his dark eyes filled with anger.

"You," he said, jerking away from her touch. "What do you want? Have you not hurt me enough for one day?"

"Adam, Adam—you must listen. I have done nothing, I swear it on my very soul, on every vow I have ever made you. I love you!"

"You love me," he said harshly. "You love me so much that

you could not resist Michael's embraces. Does he please you more than I do in bed, Sarah? Or perhaps you were just growing bored with the same man, so betraying me didn't weigh heavily on your conscience."

"No!" she cried. "No—I have never betrayed you. Never . . . I couldn't, Adam. And Michael wouldn't. He loves you far too much."

"How fortunate I am to have two people who love me so deeply," Adam said, his eyes snapping with sarcasm. "I'd hate to think of what depths the two of you would have stooped to if you merely liked me. Although I can't think of much lower acts than adultery. Murder, perhaps?"

Sarah slammed her fists against his hard chest. "Oh, you can be a stubborn fool!" she cried in frustration. "I've told you the truth. Michael tried to tell you the truth. And all he got for his trouble was banishment."

"Would you rather I'd had him beheaded?" he said, catching her wrists up. "I thought you'd prefer I leave your lover in one piece."

"He was never my lover," she said, shaking her head furiously. "And I never thought you would be so stupid as to believe the lies your mother handed you. I've seen her, Adam, stalking Michael over the last year like a hungry lion after a tasty deer. I believe Michael when he says she wanted retribution for his rejecting her—and I also believe she wants you to know nothing of her other scheme."

Adam's eyes narrowed dangerously. "Do not compound your sins by slandering my mother. She is a God-fearing woman, and although she may be disappointed by my father's weaknesses, she would never break her marriage vows. Unlike you."

Sarah sank to her knees, her head bowed, her shoulders shaking with the sobs that wracked her. He wouldn't listen. No matter what she said, he refused to hear. "If that's what you believe, then why don't you banish me as well?"

"Because I love you too much," he said, his voice breaking. "God help me, I still love you."

She raised a tear-streaked face to him. "Then believe me, for I love you more than life, Adam. Do you think I could have lain in your arms last night, been with you in the way I was if that were not the truth? How could I even think of being with another man when we have such happiness together?"

Painful uncertainty chased over his features. "I don't know," he whispered. "I don't know. God in heaven, I've prayed I'm wrong. I've prayed for that harder than I've prayed for anything in my life."

She reached up and took his hands. "Then your prayer has been answered. For I swear to you on everything I hold holy that I have not been unfaithful. May God strike me dead if I'm lying."

He dropped to his knees and took her face between his hands, searching her eyes. "I want to believe you. Oh, God, how I want to believe you. But why would my mother lie?"

"Because she has never liked me," she said simply. "And because she was frightened that Michael would tell you the truth and you would believe him. So she struck first."

Adam looked at her long and hard, and she returned his gaze evenly, praying he would hear her.

And then he squeezed his eyes shut for a long moment. When he opened them again they were filled with tears. "Sarah—my love. You really are telling me the truth, aren't you."

"I have never lied to you. Not about anything," she said, her own tears falling freely.

"No, you haven't. Dear God, you haven't. I don't think you could." He rested his forehead against hers. "I'm sorry. I should never have doubted you, never have taken my mother's word over yours, not for any reason. Can you forgive me?"

"Anything," she whispered. "But it is Michael's forgiveness you should worry about."

"Lord above, but I've made a mess of things," he said, rubbing his hands over his face. He sighed. "I'll go find him, apologize. Try to explain that I'm the fool he called me."

"It is too late. He has left, Adam, and I don't know if you can ever bring him back. I don't even know where he was going."

"I'll think of something," he said, standing and holding his hand out to her. "I'm bound to hear of his direction sooner or later. But Sarah—about this other business, my mother's plan to invade Famagusta. I know that she has been annoyed with the king and his policies for years, but our army will not act unless it is on my father's orders."

"*Then you had better pray that she does not try to talk him into giving that order,*" Sarah said, taking his hand and rising. "*For if he does, we will all pay and pay dearly.*"

"*I will have a word with him. And with her. And I will let her know what I think of her, of her filthy lies about you and Michael.*"

Sarah nodded. She knew Adam was good to his word. But she couldn't shake off the feeling that it might all be for naught.

The scene faded and Serafina could see nothing at all but the thick fog that reengulfed her. And yet a hand held hers, Aiden's hand, for she knew the touch of his fingers. No. It was Adam's hand, clutching at hers, pulling her through the castle.

"*Run, Sarah, run! They're storming the south walls!*"

Shouts of confusion. Screams. And the smell of smoke. Smoke everywhere. The crackle of fire.

Adam dragged her out through the lower passage into the open air. Her eyes burned and her lungs sucked at the air. But there was no escape. The invading soldiers were everywhere, their swords flashing high, sweeping down in brutal strikes, shields clanging as they cut their way through Kyrenia's army, an army taken badly off guard. And Michael was there, fighting in the front lines.

He saw them, shouted even as he fought. "*Betrayed—a spy in the court! I came back to give warning. Get to Paphos—seek sanctuary—we are lost here!*"

Michael's sword clashed again and again, but he was no match for the two soldiers who attacked him. His armor was pierced by a single well-aimed thrust to his chest, and he fell before Sarah's horrified gaze, blood trickling from the corner of his mouth. And lay still, the wound to his heart a mortal one.

Adam cried out in anguished fury. He raced to Michael's side, taking up his sword, viciously slicing at Michael's attackers, bringing them both down. Another soldier came at him and he fought him off, his face a mask of rage.

Sarah grabbed up a sword from a fallen man, holding its weight in both hands. She skirted the edge of the battle, making her way to Adam.

"*Sarah! For God's sake, escape,*" he cried frantically, looking *over at her, blood trickling down his forehead.* "This is no place for you!"

"I will not leave your side," *she said.* "We will die as we have lived—together."

He opened his mouth, but his protest was cut off by a woman's scream that came from high above.

Clio stood at the edge of a castle window, her dress aflame. And then she jumped, her body tumbling through the air to land with a heavy thud in the courtyard, her broken limbs twisted up underneath her.

Adam had seen. The expression of shock on his face told Sarah everything. And that one moment of inattentiveness cost Adam his life. Sarah screamed out a warning as a soldier rushed up behind Adam, his sword descending in a blinding flash on Adam's shoulder, biting into his neck.

Adam dropped to his knees with a strangled cry, then collapsed onto his side.

Sarah threw herself on top of him, her arms pulling him close, her sobs wracking her body. "Adam—no . . . Adam!"

He shivered, then whispered against her ear with his last breath. "I love you, Sarah. I'll always love you. . . ."

And Sarah heard no more, a cold stab of steel piercing her back, surprisingly painless. Her last thought before darkness took her was that it wasn't an end. There would never be an end. Only another beginning.

Light floated over Serafina, lifting her, carrying her high out of the mist to a place so bright it was blinding in its clarity. So joyful, peaceful, so full of love. All the darkness was washed away, the terror, the helplessness. She was safe, safe at last.

Time was . . . time is . . . she heard, the whisper faint, like the gentlest of breezes. *The circle is complete. . . .*

The whisper grew closer, a voice in her ear, the most beautiful voice she'd ever heard, singing a song composed of starlight and moonbeams, a heavenly chorus. And in the song were words, and in the words were knowledge and reason, a message of hope, a litany of love.

And then she was home. Hands lifted her, drew her close. Tears fell on her face, hot, human, the very essence of life.

Aiden's tears, Aiden's voice, huskily murmuring to her. "Thank God . . . thank God."

Serafina opened her eyes and smiled.

"My love. Oh, my love," Aiden said, cradling her head against his chest. "You've come back to me. You've come back."

He kissed her hair, her forehead, so full of relief and love that he didn't know how to contain it all. The journey he'd taken with her, the heart-wrenching story that had unfolded had humbled him beyond belief, taken him beyond doubt to understanding, memory flooding back as if they had experienced it all over again.

Sarah. Adam. A life lived long ago and far away, a love untouched by time. She had always known. It was he who had been blind.

She stirred in his arms and gazed up at him, her eyes hazy, dreamlike, a smile lingering on her lips.

The silence hung unbroken, Raphael's face streaked with tears, his eyes fixed on a point in the distance. Aiden glanced over at his father, one of his hands resting on Serafina's head, his own head bowed. Aiden shifted his gaze to Elspeth.

The light that had enveloped her during the ritual had faded now, and she had assumed her normal proportions. Everyone had gone back to normal, as if the last half hour had never been.

But he was prepared to believe anything now, anything at all. *There are more things in heaven and earth, Horatio, than are dreamt of in your philosophy. . . .*

And then he looked at Charlotte. Her face was wooden, her gaze fixed on Serafina, fear sharp in her eyes. Charlotte. Clio of Curium. And not the first time she had leveled a false charge of adultery.

"My dear sister," she said, wringing her hands together, "thank God you have come back to us! All your strange babbling had me fearing for your sanity."

Serafina's smile faded. "There is nothing wrong with my mind, Charlotte—it is perfectly rational, although I did go on a strange journey. And I was given a message to deliver to you." She released a heavy breath. "Deity cannot be used for personal gain or to further a hunger for power. As one sows, so will one reap. Evil begets evil and the chains that bind you can only be broken by true faith and love for your fellow man."

Charlotte's fists slammed down on her chair. "Blasphemy, I say! All of you have been taken in by this witch's ramblings, and yes, I condemn her as a witch and her evil aunt with her. I know what you think, that I was this Clio, that I brought disaster down on your heads."

"And ended that life, your body broken, as it was once again broken in this lifetime," Elspeth said. "A just payment of a debt, Charlotte."

"You're wrong," Charlotte cried. "I am blameless, and I can prove it, curse you!"

Aiden watched in frozen shock as his sister heaved herself to her feet, taking three steps toward the bed, her eyes blazing with fury.

"You see? No chains bind me. I am sound in body, sound I tell you!"

Raphael moved so quickly that Aiden hardly had a chance to register. He grabbed Charlotte in a viselike grip. "You damned little liar," he shouted. "How long? How *long* have you been deceiving us?"

Charlotte twisted frantically in his arms. "I—I haven't been deceiving you. I wanted it to be a surprise. I was going to tell you the night of the ball, but then I heard what you said about me." She clawed at his face. "I hate you, I hate you for leading me to believe you cared about me, that you would marry me if I could walk."

"Marry you? Are you out of your mind?" Raphael said incredulously, tightly restraining her. "What in hell ever gave you that idea?"

"You gave every indication. Every indication," she sobbed. "And then you took it all away from me because of her." She pointed an accusing finger at Serafina. "Not one of you sees what she really is. Evil—corrupt!"

"Is that why you tried to kill her?" Elspeth asked abruptly. "Did you think that removing Serafina would put an end to your problems?"

Aiden drew in a sharp breath. Charlotte? His sister was responsible for pushing Serafina down the stairs? He opened his mouth, but the words wouldn't come, fury robbing him of speech.

Charlotte's head snapped around and she glared at Elspeth. "I don't know what you're talking about," she snarled. "You're nothing but a spiteful old witch. You'd say anything to malign me. You've always despised me."

"Sweetheart?" Aiden asked, praying Elspeth was wrong. He had seen for himself how vicious Charlotte could be, but he couldn't believe she would go so far as to attempt murder. "Do you remember what happened?"

Serafina's fingers tightened around Aiden's hand. "My aunt speaks the truth," she said quietly, turning her level gaze to Charlotte. "You were there that morning. You stood up from your chair and you hit me over the head. And I think you and I both know why."

Charlotte's face turned white as chalk. "You're lying. You're lying." She looked around frantically. "Don't believe a word the whore says. None of it's true!"

Aiden snapped. "Damn you," he cried. "Damn you for your petty jealousies, for your bitterness toward Serafina, all because she is everything you're not. It must have killed you to hear the servants crying their eyes out the last few days, singing hymns outside the door while they kept a vigil for a mistress they love when all you've ever inspired in them is fear."

He ran trembling fingers through his hair. "My God, I don't know what happened to you to turn you into such a monster—you have been given nothing but love and kindness, sympathy that you didn't even deserve. Damn you for trying to poison me against my own wife. But that wasn't enough for you, was it, Charlotte? When that plot failed, you tried to murder her, didn't you?"

Charlotte stared at him, hatred burning in her eyes. "All right," she shrieked. "But it's your own fault—everything is your fault. You brought her here, you let her displace me in my own home. You even threatened to send me away—me, your sister, your own flesh and blood."

"You're no sister of mine," he roared. "Not any longer. And there's only one place I can think of that's fit for you, for I'm damned if you stay here for another day."

Charlotte shrank back. "What—what do you mean to do with me?" she asked, her voice suddenly very small and frightened.

"You're such a religious fanatic that I think that Anglican convent in Yorkshire you've spoken of so fondly will suit you best. You can spend the rest of your days repenting your sins, Charlotte, and I hope each one of those days brings you as much misery as you've given to the people around you. And not just for the first time."

"No . . ." she moaned. "Oh, no—Aiden please. I'm sorry, I swear I am. I'll make amends, I'll even go to live on one of our lesser estates."

"I think not," he snapped. "Raphael, call for a footman to take her to her quarters. And you, Charlotte, pack your clothes. You won't need much where you're going."

"Please—won't you reconsider, Aiden?" she sobbed as Raphael forcibly pushed her back into her chair and wheeled her toward the door.

"I will not. You have worked the last of your evil here."

"If I were you, Charlotte," Raphael said tightly, "I would thank my lucky stars that Aiden isn't bringing you up on charges of attempted murder." He shut the door behind them, leaving a heavy silence behind. Aiden had nothing to say. He took Serafina's hand in his, drawing strength from her gentle clasp.

"Aiden." His father, looking as shaken as Aiden felt, laid a gentle hand on Aiden's shoulder. "If it helps at all, my boy, I think you've made the right decision. As much as it pains me to say it, Charlotte deserves nothing less for what she's done. What she tried once she might well try again, for I don't think the girl is entirely balanced in her mind."

Aiden soundlessly shook his head.

"I agree with your father," Raphael said, returning to the

room alone. "I don't believe you had any other choice. A convent is the perfect place for Charlotte. Maybe she'll learn some genuine piety."

"I doubt that, but at least she's going to be safely put away, and it's about time," Elspeth said tartly. "But never mind Charlotte. Serafina will make a full recovery, and that's all that's important."

"I told the staff as much," Raphael said. "You should have seen their faces—they looked as if they were going to burst into cheers."

"As it should be." Elspeth blew out the candles one by one. "So. The debt is released and the tragedies of the past cleared. You are all free to live your lives without fear of repeating the same mistakes. And you, Aiden, and you, Serafina are finally free to experience the fullness of your love for each other, as it was meant to be in the beginning."

Serafina sighed, a soft little sound. "I've been charged with bringing you each a gift," she said. She turned her head and looked at Raphael, who picked up her hand and squeezed it.

"For you the gift is the knowledge that never again will you fail to make your voice heard. And know that the devotion that sustained you then sustains you always."

Rafe cleared his throat, then dropped a kiss on her hand. "Thank you," he said quietly.

Serafina looked up at Lord Delaware. "You have won your battle. Never again will you desert those who love you. You have been given the gift of strength and the courage to follow your own path."

She looked up at Elspeth and smiled. "And you, my dear aunt, already know what your gift is. You have finally learned to use it wisely."

Elspeth's face broke into a broad grin. "And you're still a Miss Bossy-Boots. I don't know why I bother with you at all."

"Oh, yes you do," Serafina retorted, her grin matching Elspeth's. "You can't keep from wanting to help people. Bishop, Wiccan, you have always followed the path of truth."

"Naturally," Elspeth said with satisfaction. "But I have always known that. And now I will leave you alone." She picked up her censer, delivered one last beaming smile on them and pranced out.

Lord Delaware bent down and gently kissed Serafina's forehead. "I'll leave the two of you as well. An extraordinary day. Never heard anything like it, but all's well that ends well."

Raphael shook his head. "That's putting it mildly. I think a large snifter of cognac would be in order." He put his arm around Lord Delaware's shoulder and led him out.

Aiden waited until the door had closed behind them, then sank down on the bed, drawing Serafina into his arms. "Sweetheart. I honestly don't know what to say. As my father said, it's been an extraordinary day."

Serafina gazed up at him. "Do you believe me now? That we really were destined to be together?"

"Oh, yes, I believe you," he said fervently. "But, dear God, I feel as if we've just been through a hurricane." He sighed and rested his cheek on her hair. He was weak with relief that it was all over, that Serafina was safe and sound and back in his arms. And he intended to keep her there until the day he died. Only this time he planned to die from old age.

Serafina snuggled close against him. "A hurricane indeed," she said. "But like a hurricane, the wake of the wind brings peace with it."

"Peace," he repeated, sensing a change deep in his soul. "For the first time in memory, I truly do feel peaceful as if something dangerous and unsettling has been blown away."

Serafina turned to Aiden, her eyes filled with such tenderness that it was all he could do not to kiss her senseless.

"It is your gift, my beloved," she said, her hand lightly stroking his face, "to have been given clear sight. Never again will you confuse misplaced loyalty for love, for love will always guide you. And that is the greatest gift of all."

His arms tightened around her, his heart squeezing just as hard. "Serafina," he murmured against her hair. "I only know I love you. And you are a greater gift than I ever hoped for. That is more than enough for me."

* * *

"So, Basil," Elspeth crooned happily, having explained everything to the bird in satisfying detail. "There is only one thing left to be done before my work is complete and I can finally go home."

She pulled out her book of magic, looking up the chant for invoking forgetfulness. "No need for any of them to carry the dark burden of memory any longer, now that it's all been settled. The lessons will remain with them, deep in their hearts, but by morning they'll have forgotten everything else, and that's as it should be. The present will stay just that."

She made her circle and cast her last spell, then put her book away for good.

Love would do the rest.

The Four of Hearts Checklist

Books by Marsha Canham:
_ STRAIGHT FOR THE HEART
_ IN THE SHADOW OF MIDNIGHT
_ UNDER THE DESERT MOON
_ THROUGH A DARK MIST

Books by Jill Gregory:
_ WHEN THE HEART BECKONS
_ DAISIES IN THE WIND
_ FOREVER AFTER
_ CHERISHED

Books by Joan Johnston:
_ MAVERICK HEART
_ THE INHERITANCE
_ OUTLAW'S BRIDE
_ KID CALHOUN
_ THE BAREFOOT BRIDE
_ SWEETWATER SEDUCTION

Dell